Alison Roberts is a New Zealander, currently lucky enough to be living in the South of France. She is also lucky enough to write for the Mills & Boon Medical Romance line. A primary school teacher in a former life, she is now a qualified paramedic. She loves to travel and dance, drink champagne, and spend time with her daughter and her friends.

Award-winning author **Louisa George** has been an avid reader her whole life. In between chapters she's managed to train as a nurse, marry her doctor hero and have two sons. Now she writes chapters of her own in the medical romance, contemporary romance and women's fiction genres. Louisa's books have variously been nominated for the coveted RITA® Award and the New Zealand Koru Award, and have been translated into twelve languages. She lives in Auckland, New Zealand.

SINGLE DAD
IN HER STOCKING

ALISON ROBERTS

A PUPPY AND
A CHRISTMAS
PROPOSAL

LOUISA GEORGE

MILLS & BOON

First Published in Great Britain 2019
by Mills & Boon, an imprint of HarperCollins*Publishers*
1 London Bridge Street, London, SE1 9GF

Single Dad in Her Stocking © 2019 by Alison Roberts

A Puppy and a Christmas Proposal © 2019 by Louisa George

ISBN: 978-0-263-26997-0

Printed and bound in Spain
by CPI, Barcelona

SINGLE DAD IN HER STOCKING

ALISON ROBERTS

MILLS & BOON

CHAPTER ONE

'OH, NO...YOU can't be serious.'

'I'm so sorry, Dr Cunningham, but there it is. I'm sure
you understand that acute appendicitis isn't something
we can plan for. We're doing our very best to find someone else to fill the position but, realistically, that's not
going to happen until after New Year. People want to be
with their families over the festive season and...it's such
late notice. It's the twentieth of December, for heaven's
sake. Christmas is only a few days away, you know.'

Of course he knew. There was tinsel in all sorts of odd
places in his emergency department here at the Cheltenham Royal Hospital and there was a small Christmas tree
in the waiting room. Some staff members had taken to
wearing earrings that had flashing lights or headbands
with reindeer antlers or little red hats with pompoms attached and he kept hearing people humming Christmas
carols. They'd even had a man in a Santa suit come in by
ambulance earlier today after suffering a suspected heart
attack as he coped with all those small people wanting
to sit on his knee and have their photographs taken in
the town's largest department store.

And, of course, he knew that people wanted to be
with their families. Or felt obliged to be. It was precisely

the reason why Max Cunningham always worked right through the holiday season to make sure as many people as possible in his department could have time at home with their loved ones. He'd done it for so many years now he was quite comfortable ignoring the commercial hype that tried to make it compulsory for happy families to gather and have an over-the-top celebration as they enjoyed each other's company. It was as much of a myth as Santa Claus as far as he was concerned—or it was for the Cunningham family, at any rate.

Everybody knew that. He could just imagine how much of a field day any gossips of Upper Barnsley would have when the news of a third December tragedy to hit the Cunningham family filtered out. Talk about history repeating itself.

It's struck again, they'd probably say. *The Christmas Curse of the Cunninghams...*

He'd been too young to do anything but cope the first time when his mother had died. Last time had been gutting when he'd lost his only brother but he'd got through it. Somehow. Life had gone back to normal. But this year was different. This year, his entire world was being tipped upside down and the phone call he'd just taken meant that Max could expect even more disruption. So much more, he wasn't at all sure he knew what to do about it and feeling less than confident was as new and uncomfortable a sensation as any of the changes that were about to happen in his life. Nothing was ever going to go back to normal now, was it?

'Hey...it can't be that bad.' The Royal's senior nurse in the emergency department, Miriam, came into Max's office. 'Here, have a chocolate. I thought I'd bring you one before they all got scoffed by those gannets in the staffroom. Look, how cute are these? Like little plum puddings.'

Max shook his head. 'No, thanks. I'm not really in the mood for chocolate. I've got a bit of a problem, to be honest.'

Miriam's face creased in sympathy. 'I did hear that something was going on. To do with your brother? And his children…?'

'My brother Andy died just over a year ago. A car accident.' It was a testament to how Max managed to keep his private life private that nobody here was aware of the full story but Miriam was trustworthy—the kind of motherly type that inspired confidence from both her patients and her colleagues. A great listener, too, with enough life experience to offer sage advice in almost any situation. Max could do with some advice.

'It was his wife, this time,' he added. 'Or, I should say, his ex-wife. I haven't seen his children since his funeral. I didn't even know that there was a third one.'

'Oh?' Miriam's eyebrows rose as she sank into the chair in front of Max's desk. 'Why ever not?'

Max sighed. 'His marriage had broken down and he was dealing with difficult custody issues. He didn't know that his wife was pregnant when she left and she obviously wasn't too keen to keep in touch with the rest of his family after he died. She moved all the way up to somewhere north of Glasgow.'

'And she's the one who's just died?'

'Yes. She was taking the oldest one to school. Ben. He's six. Icy road and an elderly driver must have panicked when he went into a skid and put his foot down on the accelerator. She managed to shove the baby's pushchair out of the way but got killed instantly herself. There was an elderly aunt or someone who made funeral arrangements but she couldn't take care of the children. They were all put into foster care while they tried to track down any other family.'

'And you're the children's guardian?'

'So it would seem. Maybe it was a legal document that got overlooked in the separation and then Andy died so a formal divorce never happened. It's a good thing. It would have been appalling if Andy's kids had been left in foster care when they've got an uncle and grandfather who are quite willing and able to take care of them.'

Well…being willing was one thing. Being able could prove to be a lot harder.

'Your dad's the GP in Upper Barnsley, isn't he?'

'Yes. And he lives in a house that's ridiculously big for one person, but the house has been in the family for generations and he says the only way he's leaving it is feet first when they carry out his dead body.' Max found a smile. 'That's also a good thing because there's plenty of room for the children. His housekeeper is happy to help out a bit more than doing her usual weekly shop and clean and I'd made arrangements for a live-in nanny who was going to get here tomorrow, in time for when the children arrive.'

'Sounds like you've got things well under control.'

Max rubbed at his jaw. 'I thought I had. But I've just had a call from the agency and the nanny got rushed into hospital a couple of hours ago with acute appendicitis. She's probably on an operating table as we speak…and they have no one else available until after New Year.'

'Oh…no…' Miriam's despairing tone was an exact

echo of the one he'd used on receiving that news. 'I wish I could offer to help but I've got family coming from all over the country this year. Christmas dinner for fourteen people and I've only got one day off to do the rest of the grocery shopping. It's going to be a bit of a nightmare.' But the older woman's smile suggested that she was rather looking forward to the chaos.

'I do have an idea, though,' she added a moment later.

Max was open to any ideas because he had none of his own. He could even feel an edge of panic hovering—as if he was about to go into a skid that he wouldn't be able to control—like the unfortunate one that had killed his ex-sister-in-law a few weeks ago. Who was going to get injured by this one? Himself or his father? His nieces or nephew? He was about to become the father figure to children who had suffered unimaginable loss of both their parents and their home. Their whole world. Was he about to stumble at the first hurdle of this new journey? No…he couldn't allow that to happen.

'What's your idea?' he asked.

'There's an agency we've used before. London Locums. They're a specialist medical recruitment agency and they might be worth a try even with such short notice and at such a difficult time of the year. I could ring them if you like?'

'But I need a nanny, not a locum doctor.'

Miriam's smile was gentle. 'Don't you think it would be better for those poor children to have family looking after them instead of strangers? Why not get a locum to cover *you*? That way, you could be with the children to help them settle in. They must be so scared by all the changes happening around them.'

Max swallowed hard. He was a bit scared himself,

to be honest. It wasn't that he didn't like children. He had enjoyed being an uncle and welcoming his brother's first two children into the world and he got on very well with the small people who came through the doors of his emergency department. He just hadn't ever planned to have any of his own.

Ever.

The disintegration of his own happiness when he was a child, after losing his mother—the sun of their family universe—had left an indelible stain. He had watched his father grapple with a sadness that meant he had no resources to provide for the emotional needs of two young boys and it had been Max who had tried to help his younger brother. That the sadness had morphed into a lasting depression that his father would never admit to or seek help for had cemented the deeply absorbed knowledge that the fallout of a family breaking apart for whatever reason was simply not worth the risk.

Max Cunningham had finally discovered the delicious balance of his passion for working hard and as brilliantly as possible with playing just as hard outside of work hours and that time almost always included a beautiful woman as a playmate. Max was confident that he had honed his skills in making a woman feel very, very special but only for a limited amount of time, of course. He wasn't ever going to get caught in the trap of having his happiness depend on a family, only to have his world destroyed. If his own childhood memories hadn't been enough, his brother's death last year had more than reinforced his belief that the risk was far too great. He hadn't ever intended to be responsible for the happiness of others either, by trying to create and protect the safety of a family unit or to patch up the fragments of a world that had been irreparably broken.

But, here he was, about to attempt exactly that and the responsibilities about to land on his doorstep were more than daunting. Who knew how traumatised these children already were? The girls might be too young to remember losing their father last year but little Ben was six and maybe he was already trying to wear the mantle of the oldest child and look after his siblings and Max knew how hard that could be. And Miriam was right. The children had been in the care of total strangers since they'd lost their mother and that wasn't acceptable. Max might think his world was being upended but for his nephew and nieces the only world they knew had just vanished for ever.

'And it's *Christmas*,' Miriam added softly, as she got to her feet—as if that settled the matter. 'They're family. And they need you.'

'Emma?'

'Hi, Julie.' Emma Moretti paused beneath the bare branches of trees in London's Hyde Park as she answered her phone, watching a squirrel race up the trunk of the nearest tree. 'I hope you've got some good news for me?'

Julie was the manager of London Locums, the specialist medical recruitment agency that Emma had been employed by for the last few years.

'You're not going to believe it. After telling you there was absolutely nothing on the books for the Christmas period, I just got a call from someone at the Royal in Cheltenham. They're desperate for someone to take over from their emergency department HOD. Seems he's got some family crisis happening until some time in early January.'

'ED? My favourite.' Emma's outward breath was almost a sigh of relief. She was desperate to get out of London for a few days. At least until Christmas was over. There were too many memories here and it felt harder this year, for some reason. Maybe she hadn't got past things as well as she thought she had. Or maybe it was because, at thirty-six, her last birthday had reminded her that the window of opportunity for having the family she'd always dreamt of was beginning to close. Worse, she still wasn't sure she was ready to do something proactive about that. Even after nearly five years, she hadn't ever given serious thought to changing her single status.

'Are you sure, Em? I don't think the Royal really expects us to be able to provide someone at such short notice and you know how crazy emergency departments can get over Christmas. People drink far too much and there's all those weird accidents you hear about, like people falling off the roof because they're trying to change the bulb on Rudolph's nose or something. You could just go on holiday if you wanted to escape. Somewhere nice and warm like the Maldives. Or Australia? Goodness knows you've earned a break and they're talking snow here. Possibly a white Christmas for once.'

Going on holiday alone would be the worst thing to do. It would give her far too much time to think. To remember things that were better left in the past.

'You know me,' she reminded Julie. 'I kind of like crazy.'

'What about Italy, then?' Julie was a good friend as well as her employer. 'When did you last have Christmas with *your* family?'

A long time ago. But not quite long enough, it would seem, because she still wasn't ready for a full-on Italian-style family gathering. Or perhaps it had just become a habit because locums were always in such demand over holiday periods.

'Are you kidding?' Emma tried to keep her tone light. 'My cousin has just had twins. My mother will be crying in the corner because her only child is thirty-six and still single and maybe she'll never get any grandchildren of her own. They'll probably drag in every eligible male in the village and try and arrange a marriage on the spot. You have no idea the kind of pressure that will entail.' She managed a laugh. 'Give me medical chaos any time. Please, I need to be in Cheltenham. My family won't mind. They know I always work over Christmas.'

'Well…if you're sure. It does have accommodation on offer as well. A modern apartment near the hospital. Let me see…a suburb called Montpellier.'

'Sounds French. *Trés chic.*' Emma drew in a deep breath. 'It's perfect, Julie. When do I need to be there?'

'Early tomorrow afternoon by the latest. Someone called Miriam will give you an orientation tour and supply the keys to the apartment. I'll text you the details.'

It was no more than a brisk walk to the compact basement apartment where Emma lived alone. It wouldn't take her long to pack. She'd been with London Locums long enough to know exactly what she needed to take and to be ready to leave the city at a moment's notice if necessary. It had been a huge lifestyle change to leave her secure position as a junior consultant in a paediatric ward, but it had been the perfect choice at the time. There was an adrenaline rush to be found, never knowing what kind of job would be around the next corner. She could be taking over a general practice in a remote area to give a sole GP a proper holiday, doing aeromedical retrievals from some exotic location with a seriously ill or injured person who needed to come home or plugging a gap in a hospital roster like this time. And an emergency department really was her favourite place to work—maybe because it was a bit like her lifestyle. You got to do all sorts of exciting, satisfying things but only for a brief time. Patients got moved on to other departments. She got to move on to other positions and that was the way she liked it.

If you never put down roots or formed deep attachments, there was no danger of having the pain of them getting ripped out, was there? Life was so much easier this way.

A busker, just outside the park gates, was—predictably—singing a Christmas carol. Emma increased her pace as she tried to escape the lyrics of 'Mary's Boy Child' because it never failed to bring tears to her eyes every time. Just those four words—*born on Christmas Day*—could still potentially rip a hole in her heart.

It was five years ago now, though. She would have expected it to be getting easier year by year and it was... except for Christmas. Sometimes it felt as if the whole world was conspiring to remind her in agonising detail of how hard it had been to have coped as well as she had. Especially being here, because the hospital where it had happened—and where she'd worked at the time—was just on the other side of the park.

Thank goodness she could head out of town first thing tomorrow.

Emma couldn't wait. She made a mental note to make sure she had some chains in the back of her SUV. Just in case. A town as big as Cheltenham was highly unlikely to get snowed in but it was surrounded by winding country roads and isolated villages. A white Christmas with all the extra chaos that could bring to an emergency department?

Bring it on…

'She's here, Max. With an apology for being a bit late but she said the traffic on the M40 was diabolical. There'd been a crash.'

'No problem. At least she's here now. Thanks, Miriam. Can you give her a really quick tour of the department to get her up to speed to start her first shift tomorrow morning and then bring her in here? I've got a couple of things I must finish but then I'll be heading off to Upper Barnsley. I'll need to be there when the children arrive.'

'Of course. You'll be wanting to give her the keys and any instructions for your apartment?'

'I think it would be polite to actually show her the apartment myself. It's only a few minutes' walk away, after all. It's not going to hold me up. Oh…' Max lifted an eyebrow. 'What's her name?'

'Emma…something. Sounded Italian but I can't remember. She looks competent, though.' Miriam's mouth twitched. 'I'm sure you'll approve.'

Max cringed just a little at the inference he couldn't miss. Yes, he appreciated good-looking women and there never seemed to be a shortage of contenders to fill the inevitably changing position as his out-of-work-hours companion but there was something in his senior nurse's expression that made him think his reputation might not be something to be proud of. Well, it was irrelevant now, anyway. Even if he had any opportunities to meet someone new in the foreseeable future, he wouldn't be able to take advantage of them. He had other, far more pressing, responsibilities that were due to land on his doorstep in—he swallowed hard as he glanced at his watch—only a hour or two from now.

He turned his attention back to the computer screen in front of him. There were a few last-minute adjustments to make to the rosters to ensure that this department ran as smoothly as possible while he couldn't be here. He needed to give this Emma his personal mobile number as well so he could be on call to give her any advice if she needed it.

An Emma with an Italian-sounding surname was ringing a vague bell in the back of his mind as he pulled up a spreadsheet. It came with an image of a laughing young woman surrounded by children, holding a baby that had his hands tangled in her long ponytail. A quintessential 'earth mother' type, which, of course, had made her an absolute 'no-go' type for Max—no matter how gorgeous those generous curves and dark eyes and that smile had been.

Good grief…that had been ten years ago but the memory was astonishingly clear, now that he had dredged it up. They'd both been junior doctors on a paediatric ward at the same time. And her name was Emma…dammit… what had her surname been?

'Moretti.'

Max's gaze flicked up to the figure standing in the doorway of his office. He'd been totally lost in thought and the fact that the answer to his internal query was being answered in person had just thrown him completely.

'I'm Emma Moretti,' she said, coming further into the small space. 'Miriam said to pop in and see you?'

Was it really the same woman? This Emma Moretti was nothing like the one Max had just been remembering. She was slim and smartly dressed and had short, spiky dark hair like a brunette pixie. She wasn't smiling but her eyes were certainly dark enough. Almost as black as her hair. And she was staring at him with just the same astonished intensity that he knew he was subjecting her to.

'*Max?* No way...' Her lips were curving into a smile now and, suddenly, Max could see the woman he remembered. The life and soul of any party, especially if there were children involved. And that thought led straight to another party he couldn't help but remember. The Christmas function for the staff of that paediatric ward. That sprig of mistletoe he'd held over Emma's head. That kiss... The way they'd both laughed and blamed it on the prosecco because they couldn't have been more wrong for each other.

Emma was still smiling. 'I knew the HOD was a Dr Cunningham, but I never for a moment thought it might be you. I would have imagined you to be living in a place like New York by now. Or Sydney, maybe.'

A large, vibrant city that would be a perfect social playground for someone with a reputation like himself? That cringeworthy moment he'd had earlier came back to bite a little harder. Ten years on and he hadn't changed much, had he?

Unlike Emma.

'And I would never have imagined you working as a locum. I would have imagined you to be completely settled in one place by now. With a husband and half a dozen kids.'

He was genuinely curious about what had happened

in her life but he knew he'd just stepped over a boundary of some kind. He saw the instant the shutters went up.

'Nobody has half a dozen kids these days, Max. How irresponsible would that be, given global resources?'

Max cleared his throat. 'Precisely why I haven't contributed to the population statistics myself.' He shuffled some papers on his desk to cover the slightly awkward atmosphere. 'Did Miriam give you enough of a tour? Are you happy to start your first shift at seven a.m. tomorrow?'

'I'm happy.' Emma's nod was brisk. 'I've had a lot of experience working in unfamiliar surroundings and I can quickly get a feel for how helpful the staff are going to be. You've obviously got a great crowd here and I don't anticipate any problems at all in covering for you. I assume you have a trauma team on call as well? With specialists from other departments?'

'Yes. I can't guarantee there'll be a consultant from every department available on the bank holidays but there should be someone from orthopaedics, general surgery and neurology who'll get here as fast as possible if the alert is activated. We only do that if we know there's major trauma coming in. Otherwise, we assess and call in consults as needed. Same goes for medical or obstetric emergencies.' Max closed down his computer and got to his feet. 'I'll be available by phone at any time. Don't hesitate to call. I can probably come in if there's a real crisis. I'll be just outside of a village that's halfway between Cheltenham and Cirencester, which is only twenty minutes away—unless this forecast for snow is accurate.'

'I'm rather hoping for a white Christmas,' Emma

said. 'Especially seeing as I've got accommodation that's within easy walking distance.'

'Speaking of which…let's go.' Max headed towards Emma to reach for his coat that was hanging behind the door. He caught a faint scent of something clean and crisp as he got closer. Lemons, maybe? Or mandarins…?

'Sorry?' Emma was blinking at him. 'Where are we going?'

'To the apartment.' Max held open the door of his office. 'I thought I'd show you around, seeing as it's mine.'

The HOD of the Royal's emergency department was making his own apartment available for his locum?

And the HOD was Max Cunningham?

Emma was still getting her head around both of these startling pieces of information as she followed him out of the emergency department via the automatic doors that led to the ambulance bay.

It would probably be a swanky penthouse apartment, she decided. Very modern and luxurious and not at all to her taste but perfect for a brief stay. Unless…oh, help… could there be something really tacky like mirrors on the bedroom ceiling?

Everybody had known what Max Cunningham was like back in the day of their junior rotations. Not that that stopped women from joining the queue. And why not? Max was drop-dead gorgeous, totally charming and knew how to make any woman feel special. He'd had a catchphrase, hadn't he?

Oh, yeah… Emma bit back a smile as they turned out from the hospital grounds and waited for a set of traffic lights to change so that they could cross the busy main road. She remembered it now.

We're here for a good time, not a long time...

Playboys had never been remotely Emma's type but she had understood the attraction. Felt it herself, in fact, even though she wouldn't have touched him with a bargepole as far as a relationship went. The man had actually kissed *her* once, at that Christmas party and... and...good grief... How was it possible to remember a moment like that with such astonishing detail after so many years? She could feel her toes trying to curl themselves up inside her shoes so it was a relief to start walking swiftly across the road. She certainly wasn't going to start wondering if the toe-curling was due to embarrassment or the intense desire that kiss had generated. There were decorations overhead, she noticed, trying to distract herself further by looking up. Long strings of icicle lights that would look very pretty at night.

'Five minutes' walk, that's all,' Max was saying. 'And the place should be perfectly clean. My housekeeper went in a few days ago and gave it a thorough going-over and changed the linen and so on. I'll make sure you have her number as well, in case you need anything else.'

'That's great. Thank you very much. I usually end up in a hotel or something when I'm doing a short locum like this.'

'We did think of that, but a quick check told us that there was nothing available. For some reason, Cheltenham seems like a very popular destination for the festive season.'

'No room at the inns, then?' Emma caught Max's sideways glance. 'Quite appropriate, really.'

His smile hadn't changed at all. Or the way the corners of his eyes crinkled to make his appreciation appear completely genuine. Ten years had given him a few grey hairs and deepened those lines a bit but, if anything, they had just made Max even more attractive.

'Here we are...' Max keyed a code into the front door of a very modern building and led the way to an elevator. He pushed a button that wasn't the top floor.

'Not the penthouse?' Emma murmured. 'You surprise me, Max.'

He shook his head. 'Was I really that much of a plonker in those days?'

'Not at all. From what I remember you were a brilliant doctor. You just had a reputation for playing as hard as you worked, I guess.'

'Those days are over.' He didn't sound too happy about that, Emma thought, but he wasn't about to tell her why. 'The penthouse here is very nice, I believe,' he added. 'But it's empty most of the time. The guy who owns it is something high up in a bank and has to travel a lot.'

Emma followed him out of the elevator. She watched as he unlocked the door but then her gaze dropped.

'What's that?'

'What?'

'All that water.'

The carpet outside the door was soaked. As Max lifted his foot, his shoe was dripping. 'Oh, *no*...' He pushed the door open and stepped in. The tiled entrance-way to his apartment shimmered like a small lake. 'Stay there,' he warned Emma. 'This doesn't look good.'

But she followed him in, looking over his shoulder as he checked a bathroom to see whether taps had been left on. There was a bedroom that had water dripping from the bulb in the ceiling light.

'It's coming from upstairs,' Max muttered. 'A burst

pipe, perhaps…' He sighed. 'I've been staying with my father for the last few days or I might have noticed this happening soon enough to prevent this much damage.'

So that was the family crisis? His father being ill? He certainly didn't need this complication on top of other worries. Emma felt very sorry for Max but it was very clear that she wasn't going to be able to stay here. It was the main living room that was the real disaster. Enough water had seeped into the ceiling to make the plaster-work too heavy. Large sections had fallen to cover the couches and a glass-topped coffee table.

To give him credit, Max was very calm as he took control of the situation. 'I'll have to call the building manager,' he said. 'Give me a minute.'

As soon as he'd made the call, he turned back to Emma. 'You can't stay here, obviously,' he said. 'We'll find a hotel nearby—there'll probably be somewhere we overlooked before. I'll pay for it.' He was focused on his phone again. 'Let's just see what's available on one of those comparison sites.'

Emma had taken out her own phone. A minute or two of silence and then they both looked up.

'Not looking good, is it?' Emma said. 'As soon as I put the dates in there's no availability at all.'

'There'll be something.' Max was obviously trying to sound reassuring. 'We might have to look a bit further afield, that's all.' He hesitated, glancing at his watch. 'That could take a bit of time but don't worry, I'm not going to leave you in the lurch. You can come with me for the moment. As I said, the place I'm staying is only twenty minutes away so, even if we can't find you a suitable hotel room tonight, it won't be a difficult com-mute tomorrow morning unless the weather turns nasty.'

'I've got chains,' she told him. 'But…this is your father's house you're talking about, yes?' A hotel room would be preferable. Perhaps Emma should just stay in town and keep trying to find something.

'He'll be just as concerned as I am that my locum is well looked after,' Max said. 'It's a big house and there's more than enough room for visitors. It was probably built to cater for a Victorian couple who had twelve children.' He gestured for Emma to lead the way out of the apartment. 'They weren't so worried about global resources in those days.'

He might be making a joke but a glance at his face suggested to Emma that the hypothetical camel's back might have just been loaded with the last straw.

'I should keep trying to find a hotel,' she said. 'I wouldn't want to intrude. Not if your father is so unwell.'

'Unwell?' Max's eyebrows rose. 'He's as fit as a fiddle.' He looked at his watch again and stifled a groan. 'Come on, you'll have to follow me to Upper Barnsley in your car. We don't have that much time before the children arrive.'

Children?

But hadn't Max said that he hadn't personally contributed to the population statistics? Emma was curious but the look of fierce concentration on Max's face was enough to stop her asking any more questions as they hurried back to the hospital car park. Besides, the mention of children had reminded her of that assumption he'd voiced—that she would have a husband and a tribe of children by now—and there was a sting in that assumption that needed to be dealt with. Back in those days, she had assumed exactly the same thing so it was no wonder he was surprised. She had been more than surprised herself, of course. Having her life derailed like that had been devastating but at least she was well past the toughest time of her life, when working only with children and babies as a specialist paediatrician had proved hard enough to have dimmed the joy and she'd been tempted to change the direction she had chosen for her career. She could cope with children.

As long as she didn't get too close to them…

Life had a habit of upending plans sometimes and it appeared that it was happening again, Emma decided, as she followed Max out of town and into the pretty countryside of the Cotswolds with its narrow roads and tiny villages full of trees and stone-built cottages. Her most recent plans had already gone more than a little awry, with her accommodation proving uninhabitable. The person she was replacing was unexpectedly someone she had once been more than a little attracted to, even though she would never have gone there, and she was now being whisked away to some unknown but large house by this still very attractive man and there were children involved, which didn't make any sense at all. Unless Max had acquired an instant family by marrying someone who already had children? Or this house with far too many bedrooms was being run as some kind of foster home or orphanage?

She hadn't even started her new locum position and they still had several days before Christmas arrived but it seemed like the chaos had already begun. As a few fat flakes of snow drifted gently onto her windscreen, Emma found she was smiling wryly.

Almost grinning a few moments later, in fact.

She had needed a distraction and it would appear that the universe was providing one.

CHAPTER TWO

UPPER BARNSLEY WAS bigger than other villages they had driven through, with its high street full of shops, a village green and a market square with a tall Christmas tree as a centrepiece. Moments later, Emma was following Max's vehicle down a long, tree-lined driveway to stop in front of a house that took her breath away. She was still blinking up at the huge, three-storeyed gabled mansion with imposing chimneys and ivy creeping up its stone walls as Max opened the heavy wooden front door and waited for her to go inside.

'You grew up here?' Somehow it didn't fit with the image of the contemporary 'man about town' she'd met in that London paediatric ward a decade ago. She gazed from one side of the entranceway to the other. There was probably a library in here. And a drawing room like they had in those period dramas on television with dogs lying in front of an open fire big enough to roast an ox. 'This is amazing.'

Max simply nodded. 'It's been in the family for more than a hundred years. Known locally as Cunningham Manor.' He raised his voice. 'Dad? You here?'

A woman who looked to be in her late fifties appeared from a doorway at the far end of the entrance foyer. 'He's in the west wing,' she told Max. 'Oh…who's this?' She was wiping her hands on her apron and beaming as she came towards Emma. 'I'm Maggie—Dr Cunningham's housekeeper. Dr Cunningham senior, that is,' she added.

Max took pity on her. 'The west wing is a private joke. Dad's the GP for Upper Barnsley and the lower level of that side of the house used to be the stables, I believe. It was converted to be a clinic years before I was born.' He turned to the housekeeper. 'This is Emma Moretti,' he told her. 'She's the locum who's taking over from me at the hospital until we get the nanny situation sorted. She also happens to be an old friend of mine. We worked together in a paediatric ward a very long time ago.'

Emma wasn't about to contradict him publicly but calling her a friend was stretching things a little. They had been colleagues and she'd totally respected his abilities as a doctor but she'd never trusted him enough to think of him as a friend. Or maybe she hadn't trusted herself? If they'd got close, she might have given in to that major attraction she'd felt for Max and how embarrassing could that have been? It had only taken one kiss for him to laugh about how she was 'so not his type'. She'd agreed, of course, and laughed along with him. How else would one save face at a time like that? Besides, he'd been right. He was 'so not her type' as well, but it had been a bit of a put-down to find out that the attraction hadn't actually been mutual.

'Oh…wonderful.' Maggie was still smiling. 'You'll need all the expert help you can get with these babies.'

Babies? A chill ran down Emma's spine. Max had said children, not babies.

Children were so much easier to be around than babies.

Especially newborn babies. She could work with them, of course, but preferably in a clinical setting rather than, say, an accident scene. And never in a private home. Even in a medical situation, being present at a birth or close to a tiny baby made the scars on her own heart ache. She might have built barriers to protect herself enough to live with the pain of only ever having a few hours with her own precious baby but she had no desire to deliberately test how strong those protective walls might be.

'I didn't bring Emma here to stand in for the nanny,' Max told Maggie. 'She's supposed to be using my apartment but there's been a small catastrophe with an upstairs flood and she needs to stay here until we can sort that out.'

'It's okay.' Emma found her voice. 'I'm sure I can find somewhere in town. It sounds like you're going to be very busy if…if you're expecting…babies?'

What on earth was going on? she wondered. Was Max sharing custody for stepchildren of a failed marriage? Had he married someone who had already been pregnant with twins, perhaps? Or triplets? The thought of multiple newborn babies made Emma want to head straight out of the door and keep on going. She even looked in that direction, only to find a broad-shouldered older man coming in through the front door, with a small, scruffy white dog at his heels. It was a vision of what Max would look like in about thirty years' time, she realised. Except that this man didn't have the same charming smile. If anything, he was glowering at Emma.

'What's going on? Who's this? A new nanny?' He shut the door, turned and made an irritated sound. 'Pirate, come here.'

But the small, scruffy dog had made a beeline for

Emma, was sitting at her feet and staring up at her with black button eyes. She guessed that he was mostly a West Highland White terrier but it was easy to see where his name had come from because he had a black patch covering one eye and ear. He was very cute. And he was wagging his tail. It was impossible not to bend down and offer him her hand. The small black nose felt cold and damp as it touched her skin.

'Look at that,' Max said. 'That doesn't happen very often. Pirate likes you. And no,' he told his father. 'This is Emma, who's going to be my locum at the Royal. I told you about that plan.'

'I thought she was staying at your place.'

'My place is wrecked. I'll explain later. The kids are due to arrive any minute. Maggie, could I ask you to make up another bedroom for Emma for tonight, at least? It seems that there aren't any hotel rooms to be easily found.'

'No, really… I should go.' Emma actually took a step towards the door. 'If I can't find a hotel room in Cheltenham, I could try Gloucester…?'

'Nonsense.' Maggie's hand was on Emma's elbow. 'We've got ten bedrooms here and I got an extra one ready in case the children wanted their own rooms later but I'm sure they'll want to be together at least for now. Come with me.'

So they were children now? Emma was becoming increasingly confused.

'It's snowing out there,' Max's father said, coming towards her. 'You don't want to be going anywhere if you don't have to. You might get stuck until they come to clear the lanes. I'm James, by the way. James Cunningham. Max seems to have forgotten his manners.'

Max shrugged and offered Emma a crooked smile but there were frown lines on his forehead. And some kind of plea in those dark eyes? The tension in the air here was palpable and Emma suddenly felt trapped but she couldn't run away if someone needed help, could she?

'And you're most welcome to stay,' James continued. Yes, there was a hint of the same kind of smile that Emma remembered his son using to devastating effect. Even a short-lived twinkle in his eyes. 'Pirate is a very good judge of character.' He snapped his fingers at the dog, who instantly went back to his master. 'I'm going to make sure the fire's going properly in the drawing room. Central heating is one thing, but you need to see some flames to feel properly warm when it's snowing.'

Maggie was pulling gently at Emma's arm. 'Come upstairs,' she invited. 'You'll love this room. So much better than a hotel, I promise.'

Perhaps it was best if she stayed for one night, Emma thought. It might only be mid-afternoon but it was already looking a lot darker outside and what if she went hunting for a hotel room and couldn't find one? She would hardly want to start her first shift in an unfamiliar emergency department having slept in her vehicle overnight. Besides, she had to admit she was curious. She wanted to see more of this impressive house. She also couldn't deny that part of her wanted to know what was going on in Max Cunningham's life. It almost felt like they had something in common here, in that their lives weren't turning out how they might have anticipated—or wanted—when they'd last been in each other's company.

The sweep of the wide staircase was dramatic enough to conjure up images of women making a grand entrance in exquisite ball gowns. The first part of the hallway it led to looked down over the entrance foyer. Emma could see Dr Cunningham senior disappearing through a door with his dog by his heels. She could also see Max, who was simply standing still as if he was taking a breath in order to size up an accident scene, perhaps. Or what looked like it might be a complicated resuscitation.

The way he cradled his forehead in his hand a heartbeat later, rubbing both his temples with his thumb and middle finger, added to the impression of a man out of his depth, and it was enough to touch Emma's heart. She knew, better than most, how life had a habit of side-swiping you sometimes and it never hurt to offer kindness.

Sometimes, it could save a life.

'Here you are.' Maggie stopped at one of several doors further down the hallway. 'This one's got its own bathroom so it will be perfect for you, I think.'

Emma followed her into the room. She could actually feel her jaw dropping. A four-poster bed? A massive wardrobe and dressing table that looked like museum pieces, an ornate fireplace with leather armchairs positioned in front of it and a cushioned window seat set into the mullioned window. The floorboards were polished wood but there was a large rug with a Persian design.

'I hope it doesn't smell musty,' Maggie said. 'I've only had a day or two to change linen and try and air things out. Some of these rooms haven't been used since Max and Andy left home and that's a very long time ago, now.'

'Who's Andy?' Emma was still gazing around the room. Her earliest years had been in a small Italian village. Her recent years had been in a cramped one-bedroom flat in central London. She'd only ever been in houses like this when she'd paid an entry fee and stood behind the braided red ropes.

'Max's younger brother.' Maggie had been leading the way to an interior door that must lead to the en-suite bathroom but now she paused. 'He hasn't told you what's going on, has he?'

Curiosity battled with an odd sense of…what was it? A desire to protect Max—or at least his privacy—perhaps?

'It's probably none of my business,' she said quickly.

'Nonsense.' Maggie flapped her hand. 'You're part of it for the time being, anyway, so you may as well know. The children that are arriving here any minute are Andy's children. They're orphans now and Max is their legal guardian.'

Wow… No wonder Max was looking like he was about to face a daunting situation. Everybody had known that he was a diehard bachelor even a decade ago. And while he'd been great with the children on that paediatric ward, he'd confessed more than once that that was because he could hand them back to their parents. Or get a nurse to change a nappy or deal with any tears and tantrums. That he'd never want to have any of his own.

And he'd just lost his brother?

'I'm so sorry,' Emma said. 'I really shouldn't be intruding. Not when the Cunninghams have just lost such a close family member.'

Maggie shook her head. 'Andy died just over a year ago. And his marriage had fallen apart a year or more before that. They did try and work things out, and that must have been when Alice was conceived, but then it turned nasty and lawyers got involved. Simone moved away, broke a court order and took the kids with her and broke Andy's heart at the same time. He died in a car accident not long after that. He'd been drinking and drove straight into a tree.'

'That's tragic…'

'Mmm.' Maggie hesitated for a moment and Emma wondered if there was more to that accident than simply drink-driving but if the housekeeper had been about to voice her own opinion, she obviously changed her mind. 'Even worse, Simone wouldn't let the family have anything more to do with the children after Andy was gone. She was living up in Scotland and Dr Cunningham didn't even hear about her death until after her funeral. Until someone in Social Services had tracked down legal documents that gave Max guardianship.' Maggie was moving again. 'Come and see your bathroom. There should be everything you might need.'

Emma took in the clawfoot iron bath with its brass tapware, separate shower and shelves piled with fluffy towels. 'It's beautiful.'

'It is.' Maggie smiled. 'This was the master suite in the early days when the boys were little ones. Dr Cunningham senior couldn't bear to stay in it after his wife died and then he decided he'd just stay in the Green Room. Oh…is that a car I can hear?' She walked swiftly to the window and peered down. 'It is. I'd better go and help. There was supposed to have been a nanny here already to be with the children but she got sick and that's why you're here. To cover Max at work so that he can stay home to look after them all.'

Unsure of what she should do, Emma followed the housekeeper. Her head was spinning slightly with the tales of tragedy this family had experienced. What had happened to Max's mother? she wondered. And how old had Max and his brother been when she died? She was also trying to do a bit of maths in her head. If Andy had died over a year ago and his ex-wife had already been pregnant, then this baby Alice had to be at least several months old now. Not a newborn.

She could cope with that. For one night, it shouldn't be any problem at all, even if this wasn't exactly the kind of clinical situation that was part of her protective walls. As for Max—she had no idea how he was about to cope. He had years and years ahead of him as a guardian. Remembering the way he'd been cradling his head in his hands when he thought he was not being observed, Emma couldn't believe that he'd magically changed his attitude to children in the last ten years and would be quite happy to be sharing his life with them from now on.

'Where are they?' Maggie opened the front door but there was no sign of a car. 'Oh, no…they must have gone through to the clinic parking.'

'There's another car.' Max was standing beside her.

James Cunningham had come into the entrance foyer to see what was going on but Emma hung back, near the staircase, wondering if she should, in fact, go back upstairs for a while. How terrifying would it be for small children to arrive and be faced with so many strangers? Even if they'd met these members of their extended family it had apparently been more than a year ago and they would still be traumatised by the loss of their mother.

Through the wide gap of the open front door, she could see a large people-carrier type van that had parked a little way away from the entrance to the house and someone was getting out of the driver's seat. Max walked out into the snow that was still falling to greet the newcomer. But someone else was running towards the front door of the house from the opposite direction. A middle-aged woman who was looking very anxious.

'Dr Cunningham? Is the clinic closed already?'

'Surgery finished an hour ago, Jenny.' But James was frowning. 'What's wrong?'

'It's Terry. He's got terrible chest pain and his spray isn't helping. He wouldn't let me call an ambulance. It was all I could do to persuade him to come and see you and he only did that because you're right next door.'

Behind Jenny, Emma could see that children were being helped out of the van. A boy who might be about six or seven. A smaller girl. The driver was opening the back hatch which looked to be full of luggage and items like a pram and cot. Max was unclipping a baby seat. Emma's mouth went a little dry. Maybe this was going to be harder to cope with than she'd thought.

James looked towards where his grandchildren were being ushered towards him. He turned his head to look in the other direction, presumably to the 'west wing' that housed his general practice clinic. His duty lay in both directions, with the professional one clearly more urgent than the personal.

And, suddenly, Emma knew exactly how she could help everyone here, including herself. Years of honing her skills to be able to work to the best of her ability in unfamiliar places made it automatic to take charge but, as a bonus, it felt as if her protective walls were suddenly strengthening themselves around her and keeping her in her safe space. She walked towards the anxious woman.

'I'm Dr Moretti,' she told her. 'I can help you.'

* * *

Only a couple of minutes later, Emma was opening the door to the clinic with one of the keys on the ring James had given her.

'There's a twelve-lead ECG machine in the treatment room,' he'd told her. 'If it looks like an infarct, call an ambulance and then let me know.'

'I can handle it,' Emma had promised.

Jenny and her husband, Terry, followed her into what was clearly a waiting room.

'How's the pain level, Terry? On a scale of zero to ten, with zero being no pain at all and ten being the worst you could imagine?'

'Seven,' Terry told her. 'It's like a knife in my chest. It's hard to breathe, even.'

'Let's get you lying down so I can have a good look at you.' Emma walked ahead, opening one door and then another. There was a small kitchen, a storeroom, a consulting room and…yes…what looked like a treatment room, well set up for minor procedures or more extensive assessments. She recognised the machine for taking a twelve-lead ECG, spotted an oxygen cylinder in the corner of the room and was relieved to see a defibrillator on another trolley. If Terry was having a heart attack and in any danger of an imminent cardiac arrest she had the means to deal with it. She also knew that one of the keys on the ring she was holding was to open a drug cabinet that James had told her was well stocked.

On first impressions, Terry didn't look like a man who was in the middle of having a heart attack. His colour was good, he wasn't sweating and he seemed to be clutching the side of his chest rather than a more classic sign of pressing his hand to the centre. He'd also told her that he wasn't feeling sick in any way but Emma wasn't about to make assumptions. She helped her patient climb onto the bed and lifted the back so he wasn't lying completely flat.

'Let's get that coat and jumper off and unbutton your shirt, Terry.' Emma opened the drawer on the ECG trolley and took out electrodes. 'So you've been getting angina for a while?'

'Just a bit. And only when I'm doing too much.'

'He's taken up jogging,' his wife told Emma. 'I told him he's going to kill himself but he's determined to lose the weight.'

'And you were jogging when the chest pain came on?'

'No…' Terry lifted his arm out of the way as Emma stuck the final electrodes on the left side of his chest. 'I was getting the damned turkey out of the freezer in the barn.'

'It was far too big to go in the freezer in the house.' Jenny nodded. 'And it takes days and days to thaw.'

'It was like carrying a giant, slippery rock,' Terry complained. 'And then I started to drop it and almost tripped over something at the same time and it went flying.' He gave a huff of something like laughter that turned into a groan. 'So to speak… Anyway, it was when I bent down and picked the turkey up that the pain came on. By the time I got it into the laundry tub, I could hardly stand up.'

'Does anything make it worse?' Emma asked, still smiling at Terry's attempt at humour. 'Like taking a deep breath?'

Terry tried to breathe in and groaned. 'Yep…that really hurts.'

'And you used your angina spray?'

'Didn't do a thing.'

'Okay.' Emma was becoming more confident that she wasn't dealing with a critical cardiac event. 'Keep really still for me for a few seconds, Terry. I'm going to do the ECG.'

With the sheet of graph paper in her hand a short time later, Emma smiled at the anxious couple in front of her.

'Good news,' she told them. 'This all looks absolutely normal. There's no sign of your pain being due to angina and certainly no indication that you're having a heart attack.'

'Oh…' Jenny started to cry. 'I was *so* worried.'

'What is it, then?' Terry asked.

Emma handed Jenny the box of tissues. 'I suspect you pulled a muscle between your ribs while you were wrestling with that frozen turkey,' she told him. She put her hand on the left side of his chest. 'Tell me if this hurts…'

Jenny stayed by the head of the bed, watched the thorough examination her husband was receiving and listened to the advice about cold and heat packs and using anti-inflammatory medication.

'Are you sure it's not a heart attack?' she asked.

'Quite sure.' Emma smiled. 'But you did the right thing in getting it checked out. I'm going to take your blood pressure while you're here too, Terry.'

'Imagine if it *had* been a heart attack.' Jenny reached for another tissue. 'Right before Christmas. I know it's terrible at any time of year but there's something about Christmas, isn't there?'

'Mmm…' Emma stuck the earpieces of a stethoscope into place as a hint for Jenny to stop talking. She didn't need a reminder of how much worse it was to have a tragedy at Christmas time. She placed the disc of the stethoscope over the artery in Terry's elbow as she pumped up the blood pressure cuff.

Jenny hadn't taken the hint. 'It's like the poor Cunninghams. Ruined Christmas forever for those poor boys. They used to call it "the Cunninghams' Christmas Curse" in these parts.'

Emma knew she shouldn't encourage gossip but it wasn't as if she'd asked a question aloud. Her startled glance had been enough to prompt Jenny to continue.

'Their poor mother,' she said sadly. 'Fought off the cancer for such a long time and all she wanted was one last Christmas with her little boys but they didn't even get the decorations up.' She lowered her voice. 'And they've never been put up again, from what I heard. Not in that house…'

Emma let the pressure out of the cuff slowly. Concentrating on the figures as she heard a pulse begin and then disappear again didn't stop part of her brain absorbing the information she'd just been given. What a sad house this must have been for Max—especially that first Christmas without his mother.

'Your blood pressure is on the high end of normal,' she told Terry. 'Are you on any medication for that?'

'Yes. Dr Cunningham looks after me well, don't you worry about that. Can I get dressed again now?'

'And then there was last year.' Jenny handed her husband his jumper as he finished buttoning up his shirt. 'Losing poor Andy like that. It shouldn't have happened at all, but to have it happen in December. Another Christmas funeral…' She clicked her tongue. 'And now…those children… What sort of Christmas is this going to be for those poor wee mites?'

Terry's head popped out of the jumper's neck. 'That's enough, Jen,' he said quietly. 'I'm sure Dr Moretti isn't interested in hearing all this gossip.'

'It's not gossip,' Jenny said defensively. 'We care about each other in Upper Barnsley, that's all. Especially our closest neighbours.' She smiled at Emma. 'Are you here to help Dr Cunningham, then? It's about time he had another doctor to help him in this clinic. Young Max is brilliant but he's always been one for an exciting life. He doesn't want to leave that big emergency department at the hospital.'

'I'm actually here to help at the hospital,' Emma told them. 'But, right now, I'm going to go and show Dr Cunningham your ECG, Terry, and let him know that you're okay.' She held the door open for the couple. 'Have you got plenty of anti-inflammatories at home?'

'Oh, yes.' Jenny nodded. 'And don't go bothering Dr Cunningham with my Terry's problems right now. I suspect he's got enough of his own...'

'You need to follow the directions on the tin for how many scoops. Level scoops, like this...' Maggie scooped the formula and showed Max how to level it off with the back of a knife. 'Put it into the bottle of warm water. Attach the nipple and ring and cap like this...and then shake it.'

Maybe baby Alice could smell the milk being prepared and she was sick of waiting. Or maybe she didn't like the unfamiliar male arms that were holding her right now. Whatever the reason, her unhappy whimpers were steadily increasing into shrieks that were pulling the tense knots in Max's gut tighter by the second.

'Are you sure you can't stay, Maggie?'

'I'm sorry, Max, but it's impossible. I've got my daughter, Ruth, arriving and she's nearly eight months pregnant and on her own. She'll be exhausted after that long drive up from Cornwall and I haven't had proper time with her since that bastard of a boyfriend walked out on her a few weeks ago. We've got a lot of talking to do about how she's going to cope.' Maggie took the cap off the bottle and upended it. 'Shake a few drops onto your wrist, like this. If it's the right temperature it won't feel either hot or cold. There…that's perfect.' She held the bottle out to Max. 'Try that. She's probably eating solids now as well and there's plenty of baby food in with all that other shopping that's in the pantry but she'll be wanting her milk for comfort right now, I expect.'

He took the bottle and offered the teat to the baby. Alice turned her head away and arched into his arm as if she was trying to escape.

'Take her into the drawing room with the others,' Maggie suggested. 'This is all new and strange for her too, and it might help if you're sitting in a comfy chair with her brother and sister nearby.'

Max walked out of the kitchen and into an entrance-way that looked like it had exploded into a collection point for a children's charity over the last thirty minutes or so. A portable cot had a few stuffed toys and books in it. There were car seats and a pram and even a high chair, along with boxes of baby supplies like nappies and formula and suitcases that he'd been told were full of clothing. The social worker who had delivered the children and their belongings had been apologetic but in a hurry to get away before the snow started settling on the country roads and Maggie, who'd done far more than anything her part-time position with the Cunninghams had ever expected of her, was obviously worried about leaving the men to cope but also anxious to get back to her own family.

'You go, Maggie,' Max told her. 'I've got this.'

The older woman gave him a searching look. 'Are you sure?' she asked quietly. 'I don't want to leave you in the lurch. Ruth would understand if...'

Max shook his head. 'These children are my responsibility,' he said. 'Between us, Dad and I will figure it out.' He joggled the baby in his arms and, for a merciful few seconds, the howling seemed to lessen.

'You've got that lovely Emma to help, for tonight at least.' Maggie was heading for the coat rack. 'If you're sure, then... I'll come back as soon as I can in the morning if the roads are clear enough.'

As she opened the door, Max could see a car disappearing down the driveway. Emma had spent a good deal of time assessing that unexpected patient who had turned up but she hadn't summoned an ambulance or come to find his father so he had assumed things were under control. Some things, anyway. Baby Alice was crying again as he went into the drawing room.

His father was sitting in his usual chair by the fire but Pirate had disappeared beneath the chair, which was highly unusual. On the sofa next to the chair were the two older children, Ben and Matilda. They were both sitting silently, side by side, holding hands. Six-year-old Ben was clutching a very small artificial Christmas tree in his other hand that was devoid of any decorations. Four-year-old Matilda had a toy rabbit with long legs and rather chewed-looking ears clamped under her arm. They both looked accusingly at their uncle when he came in carrying their miserable baby sister.

Max sat in the matching leather wing chair on the other side of the sofa, settled Alice into the crook of his elbow and tried to get her to accept her bottle again. Her renewed cries were so loud he didn't hear the door opening. He didn't notice that every other head in the room had turned to see who was coming in or that Pirate had wriggled forward enough to peer out from under the chair.

What he did become aware of was that fresh lemony scent he'd noticed when Emma had come into his office in what was beginning to feel like a previous lifetime. And when he looked up, it felt like the depth of understanding in Emma's eyes told him that she knew exactly how far out of his depth he currently was. That, no matter how determined he was to do the right thing for his nieces and nephew, it felt like he was drowning. But there was something else in her eyes that looked as though she was tapping into something much deeper. Darker.

Fear...

But why would Emma Moretti, of all people, feel afraid when faced with a miserable, hungry infant? She'd been the first to offer cuddles or bottles to their small patients in that paediatric ward, the first in line to be present at a birth or do the newborn checks on those slippery, squiggly little bundles that Max had found quite alarming at the time. If anything, he would have expected her to scoop Alice out of his arms and rescue the situation like some sort of Christmas angel, albeit with dark eyes and hair and olive skin instead of peaches and cream and blue eyes and golden hair.

But she was just staring at him and...yes...he was sure he could see fear in those astonishingly dark eyes.

What on earth had happened, he wondered, to have changed her like this?

The curiosity was fleeting, however, because despite Alice's cries still increasing in volume, he could hear the landline of the house ringing from the hallway. His father seemed oblivious, slumped in his chair as if he had no idea quite how to deal with what was going on around him. Emma had clearly heard the sound of the telephone and the way she raised her eyebrows was an offer to go and answer the call but Max acted without really thinking. He could handle a phone call far better than what he was trying to cope with right now.

He walked towards Emma and shoved Alice at her, knowing that she would instinctively hold out her arms to take the baby. Then he passed her the bottle of milk, turned away and walked out of the room.

CHAPTER THREE

EMMA WATCHED IN horror as Max walked out of the room and left her—literally—holding the baby.

And maybe Alice was significantly older and heavier than a newborn but, for a heartbeat, Emma simply froze because this baby wasn't sick and she wasn't standing here in the capacity of a doctor. This baby needed feeding and she had just been forced into the position of being a surrogate mother—something she wouldn't have volunteered for in a million years.

Turning away from watching Max leave, Emma found herself looking at the two small children who were sitting on the couch and staring at her. They both looked scared. That something terrible was happening with their baby sister, perhaps?

'It's okay,' Emma heard herself saying calmly. 'I think she's just hungry.'

She could do something about that, she realised, and that was the only thing she needed to think about right now. Anything else, including how this was making her feel, would simply have to wait but, as she moved to sit down, it seemed that the shock of having the baby shoved into her arms was receding enough to make it bearable. She would certainly not have volunteered to take the baby and feed it but, now that it was happening, Emma found that it hadn't smashed through her walls the way she might have feared that it would. This was someone else's baby, not her own. A healthy baby that just needed to be fed. Surely she could cope with this?

She chose to sit on the couch beside the other children, not wanting to take over the chair Max had been using. Or maybe she thought it might comfort the infant in her arms to be near her brother and sister. She settled Alice into the crook of her arm and offered her the nipple of the bottle, sliding it into her mouth that was opening for a new wail. Surprised eyes stared up at her and then, mercifully, that little mouth closed over the teat and Alice began sucking vigorously.

In the sudden silence that fell, Emma was aware that the older children were still watching. Max's father had turned to peer at her from behind the wing of his chair and even the dog had wriggled forwards far enough to see what was happening beyond the safety of being beneath his master's chair. She could hear the fire behind its screen, crackling softly in this new silence, and then she could hear Max coming back into the room. Or maybe she could feel the change in the atmosphere as he entered—that kind of electricity that charismatic people radiated.

'That was the builder,' he said. 'They've fixed the leak in the apartment above mine but it's going to be a big job to get things fixed and cleaned up. It certainly won't be happening before Christmas.'

James Cunningham grunted. 'Can't say I'm surprised. It's hard enough to get tradesmen in a hurry at the best of times.'

Max sat down in the other wing chair, his gaze fixed

on Alice. 'You always did make it look easy,' he murmured. 'You're just a natural, aren't you, Emma?'

Emma said nothing. She couldn't say anything. Not with that damned lump that had just formed in her throat. Breathe, she told herself. You only need to breathe.

The silence returned and then Max sounded like he was making an effort to break it.

'Is that your special Christmas tree, Ben?'

Emma glanced sideways to see Ben nod solemnly. 'You've got to have a Christmas tree,' he told his uncle. 'It's a rule.'

'Oh?'

Emma could understand the note in Max's voice—as if he was wondering what other 'rules' Ben might be holding as sacrosanct.

Ben nodded again. 'That's how Father Christmas knows where to leave the presents. It should go near the chimney.'

Emma lifted her gaze to look around the huge room they were in. She wondered what this little boy might think of those paintings in their ornate frames, the ornaments on sideboards and the baby grand piano in the corner. Was he used to this kind of house or was it making this an even more frightening experience for him?

But Ben was sounding worried rather than frightened when he spoke again.

'Where's *your* Christmas tree, Grandpa?'

This time, the silence in the room was filled with a tension that made a knot start to form in Emma's stomach. There was level upon level of misery here that she could feel as if it was her own. Some of it *was* her own but she had learned long ago how to shut that away and it was actually quite empowering to find she could hold and feed baby Alice without falling apart in any visible manner. Looking down, she met the fixed gaze of those dark baby eyes on her own and could be confident that all was well in this tiny human's life for the moment, at least, as she sucked down the rest of her milk. It wasn't the case for anyone else in this room, was it?

Emma looked at the children beside her on the couch. The little boy was still staring at his grandfather, waiting for an answer to his question about the missing Christmas tree. The little girl seemed to sense Emma's gaze and returned it with such a solemn one of her own that, if her arms weren't full of baby Alice and her bottle, she would have instinctively wanted to gather this child to her as closely as she could to give her a big hug. James was stroking an imaginary beard as if it might help him find an answer and Max…

Well, Max was looking at *her*.

As if he knew that she knew why Christmas hadn't been celebrated in this house for probably decades and why a simple child's question was creating such tension. As if he had no idea how to defuse it and as if he was trusting her to help in the same way that she had managed to conquer the difficulty he had faced in getting the baby fed.

Just for a heartbeat, Emma could see something she was quite sure she'd never seen before in Max Cunningham's eyes. Bewilderment, almost. The look of someone who'd lost something very important and had absolutely no idea where to start looking for it. There was something sad in that gaze as well and that made her realise he must know exactly how his nephew must be feeling right now and that could be what was making it so hard for him to find the right thing to say. A tragic history had repeated itself and a small boy had lost his mum just before Christmas.

The squeeze on Emma's heart was so tight it was painful. Painful enough to set off alarm bells that suggested a potential breach in any protective walls that needed maintaining but she had to ignore that for the moment. She was an adult and she had had plenty of time to develop coping mechanisms she could tap into a bit later. Doing something to try and make these children look and sound a little less sad was far more urgent.

'Sometimes,' she told Ben, quietly, 'things happen that can get in the way of remembering rules. I'm sure your Uncle Max or your Grandpa will know where to find a Christmas tree.'

James leaned forward to pick up a poker and prod the fire, making a grumbling sound that could have been disapproving but Max was nodding as if this was, indeed, the solution.

'A real one,' he said. 'We can go and look in the woods tomorrow, Ben. You can choose a branch and I'll cut it off. Or, if we can't find one, we can drive into town and buy one.'

'How old are you, Ben?' Emma asked.

'Six.'

'That's old enough to make decorations for the tree, then. Like silver stars. I can show you how to do that.' She offered a smile. 'My name's Emma.'

The little girl was wriggling closer. 'I'm four,' she whispered, 'and I like stars...'

'You can help too, sweetheart,' Emma promised. She just had to hope there would be a supply of cardboard and silver foil somewhere in the house.

'That's Matilda,' Max said. 'But she likes to be called Tilly.' He was smiling at Emma.

And it was such a genuine smile... Nothing like the charm-loaded curl of his lips with that mischievous edge that had always won him so much attention from women. This time, that automatic hint of flirting that Emma had remembered so clearly was completely absent and it changed his face. It made him look a little older. Softer—as if he was perfectly capable of providing the care and commitment these children were going to need so badly even if he used to say it was the last thing he ever wanted to do.

Alice had finished her bottle and felt sleepy and relaxed. Emma shifted her to an upright position and began to rub her back. Seconds later, the loud burp broke both the new silence and quite a lot of the tension in the room.

'I'm hungry,' Ben said.

Emma caught the slightly panicked glance that was exchanged between the two Cunningham men.

'Maggie's left a pie in the oven,' Max told his father. 'And chips.'

'I like chips.' Ben slid off the couch. He stood there, waiting for one of the grown-ups to move as well.

But, for a long moment, nobody did and Emma could understand why. This was it, wasn't it? The first step into a life that was never going to be the same again for either of these men and it was huge and daunting and they'd been thrown into the deep end. None of it was Emma's responsibility, of course, but the people who were going to suffer if it turned into a disaster were only children and these children had suffered enough, hadn't they?

It seemed that Max was thinking the same thing because they both got to their feet in the same moment.

He stepped towards Emma and took the sleeping baby from her arms.

'It's okay,' he said. 'I can manage.'

'I'm here,' Emma reminded him gently. 'I may as well help you manage for tonight, yes?'

There was always something about a man holding a baby that tugged at the heartstrings. But there was something else about this particular man holding a baby that actually brought a lump to Emma's throat. This had to be his worst nightmare, inheriting a ready-made family including a baby, but he was stepping up to the challenge and determined to do his best and that was courageous and kind and…it tugged at her heart so hard she couldn't look away from his eyes.

She hadn't remembered them being quite such a dark blue.

Or quite so…intense.

It almost felt as if he was seeing her…*really* seeing her…for the first time ever.

Man…

Those eyes… So dark they looked bottomless. You could fall into eyes like that and get totally lost. And, just for a heartbeat, that was exactly what Max wanted to do. The rollercoaster of emotions he was currently riding was proving even more overwhelming than he'd feared it would be.

His heart had gone out to his nephew and nieces the moment he'd seen them but he was little more than a stranger to them and, oddly, that hurt. There was so much stuff that had come with the children and he wouldn't have even known how to make up a bottle if Maggie hadn't helped. He might have failed in feeding

Alice if he hadn't forced Emma to help so he could add a sense of failure into the mix. He was worried about how his father was coping, especially after that question about the Christmas tree. They hadn't put a tree up in this house since his mother had died, leaving a huge pine tree undecorated and a shattered family that barely noticed the showers of dead needles that came weeks later.

On top of that, there were feelings of heartbreak for these children. Part of him just wanted to gather them all into his arms and somehow let them know that he was going to protect them for ever, but he could sense their shyness and knew he would make things worse if he tried to force closeness. He felt gratitude to Maggie for all her extra work and, currently, he was just so, so glad that Emma was here in the house. Trying to convince her that he was up to this task was giving him a lot more courage than he might have otherwise found in the face of such a daunting challenge.

There was also the way she'd been looking at him after Ben had asked about where the Christmas tree was. It had made him think that she knew the answer to that innocent question, which was not unlikely given that she'd spent time with Terry and Jenny. Jenny wasn't a gossip by any means but she was one of the villagers who all knew the Cunninghams' history and she was a woman who loved to chat. Max didn't mind if Emma did know because there was also something in that look that gave him the impression that she understood how much it might hurt and, in turn, that was giving him the oddest feeling of connection. Something that was disconcerting because he'd never associated a feeling like that with any woman. It had to be just another side effect of this strange situation. It was also something that was irrelevant because the children were the only people that mattered right now.

'What's first?' he asked. 'Shall I feed the children?'

'How 'bout you and your dad sort some of their things out? Find things like pyjamas and toothbrushes? You could put Alice in her pram for the moment while she's asleep. Show me where the kitchen is and I'll sort out the pie.'

'And chips.' The small voice came from right beside Max's leg and he looked down to find Ben standing close by. 'And sauce. Red sauce.'

'Is that a rule?' Max asked. 'Red sauce for chips?'

Ben nodded. He was holding out his hand towards Matilda. 'Come on, Tilly,' he said. 'It's time for tea.'

'It is,' Emma said, as Matilda slid off the couch. 'And after that it will be bath time and…what happens after bath time?'

'Storytime,' Ben said. 'And…and then…'

His small mouth wobbled as it turned down at the corners. It was painfully obvious that the prospect of bedtime in this new, scary house was too much even for a very brave child who was doing his best to look after his younger sister himself. The squeeze in Max's chest was so sharp it made the back of his eyes prickle. He bent down so that he could say something quietly, just for Ben.

'It's going to be okay,' he whispered. 'I promise.'

Ben's eyes were a dark blue. Like his father's had been. Like all the Cunningham men, for that matter. They were also far too serious for a six-year-old boy.

'It's a new rule,' Max added gravely. 'And I try very hard to never break rules.'

* * *

Having so much to do to start getting the children settled into what was going to be their new home was helpful for the next few hours. Having Emma there to answer the questions James and Max kept coming up with was also very helpful.

'Should we put Alice's cot in the same room as Tilly and Ben?'

'It might be better to put it in your room to start with. That way, if she wakes up, she won't wake up the others.'

'But…what will I do with her if she does wake up?'

Emma's smile was kind enough not to make Max feel inadequate in any way. 'Give her a bottle of milk. Change her nappy. Cuddle her.'

Ben and Matilda ate enough of their dinner for Emma to be looking pleased when Max went to tell her that he had unpacked the suitcases to find pyjamas.

'Shall we go up those big stairs?' She made it sound like an adventure. 'I know where there's a bath that's got feet.'

Ben shook his head. 'A bath doesn't have feet,' he told Emma. 'It can't walk.'

'No. This one just stands there but it really does have feet. Like a lion's paws. Do you want to see?'

Max watched her go up the stairs with a child on each side of her, holding her hands. Ben still had the little Christmas tree in his other hand, he noticed. And Tilly was holding her rabbit by one foot so that its head, with those chewed ears, was bumping on every tread. James was coming down as they reached the halfway curve.

'Have you got hot-water bottles?' Emma asked him. 'It would be good to put them in Ben's and Tilly's beds.

And put some of their toys there too, so it'll feel more like home.'

The men didn't get the distribution of stuffed toys quite right but it was easy enough to fix as the children climbed into the twin beds that were side by side in one of the smallest bedrooms. It was James who agreed to read a bedtime story to his grandchildren while Pirate lay outside the bedroom door. Max was learning how to bath Alice and get her ready for bed. At six months old she was nothing like as fragile as a newborn, of course, but she still felt very small in Max's hands and it was fiddly enough to get her into her nappy and her stretchy sleepsuit to make him break out in a bit of a sweat.

'So you've put her cot in your room?' Emma asked.

'Well…the room I use when I'm staying, yes. It might be a good one for the nanny to use when she gets here.'

'Have you plugged in the baby monitor?'

'Yes. And, if I leave the door open, I should be able to hear if Ben or Tilly wakes up too. You don't think they'll sleepwalk or anything, do you? What would I do if they did?'

'If they do get up, they'll just be looking for comfort,' Emma told him. 'Cuddles. You could stay with them until they go back to sleep. Or let them share your bed.'

There was a hint of mischief in Emma's eyes as she made that suggestion. As if she knew perfectly well that sharing a bed in order to comfort small children was a totally alien concept for Max. As if she was trying to lighten the atmosphere a little too, to defuse some of the tension of the evening. The idea that Emma might be at all concerned for his own wellbeing did make him feel rather a lot better, in fact.

'Are you hungry?' she asked. 'There's plenty of pie and chips left.'

'And red sauce?'

The smile he received from Emma felt like a reward for what seemed like a major achievement in caring for the children for the first time. Glancing at his watch, Max was astonished at how much time had gone by. 'It's late,' he said. 'No wonder I'm starving.'

'Let's see if we can get Alice settled properly. Your dad should be back from taking Pirate for a walk by then and we can all have something to eat.'

James came back with the news that, while the snow had settled in places, it seemed to have stopped and the roads were still clear enough to be safe for Emma to drive back into Cheltenham in the morning.

'And they're very good about getting the snow ploughs out on our road first,' he told her as they ate dinner together at the old table in the huge kitchen. 'One of the perks of being the only local doctor.'

'Do you do nights as well?' Emma asked.

It was Max who shook his head. 'Theoretically, that's covered by an afterhours service from town,' he told her. 'In reality, though, Dad often gets called.'

'I don't mind,' James said. 'I've known these families for a long time. They trust me. Thanks for taking care of Terry today, Emma. Jenny's still overanxious about his angina.'

'It was a pleasure.' Emma sounded as though she meant it.

James stood up to take his plate to the sink. 'Might turn in,' he said. 'It's been a big day.' He snapped his fingers and Pirate jumped out of his basket near the Aga. 'Can you look after the fire, Max?'

'Of course. Sleep well, Dad.'

The huff of sound was doubtful and the words were an under-the-breath mutter as James left the room. 'Let's hope we all get some sleep.'

Emma stacked the dishes into the dishwasher but Max wouldn't let her do anything else in the kitchen.

'Maggie will be back in the morning. Being used as a housekeeper or a nanny is not part of your locum contract, you know.'

Emma shrugged. 'They say that variety is the spice of life. To tell you the truth, I've never been in a house like this before and it's amazing.' Which it was. Every room she had seen in this old house was beautiful but her favourite so far had to be the kitchen, with its old range and the dresser with the antique china and an ancient scrubbed table that reminded her of outside terraces in Italy because it made her think of generations of extended family gathering to eat together. The time had flown, as well. They'd been so busy with dinner and baths and getting everybody settled into bed that Emma hadn't had time to worry about how it could potentially be messing with her head and, in fact, now that she did have the time to think about it, she was confident that she could deal with it.

'The children really haven't been much trouble, have they?' she said aloud. 'And the way Ben tries so hard to help look after Tilly is just gorgeous.'

'Mmm…'

The tone in that sound gave Emma's heart a squeeze as she pushed the door of the dishwasher closed. It was a note of trepidation. Fear, almost.

She caught his gaze. 'It's going to be okay, Max,' she

said softly. 'You'll work things out. I know it feels huge and scary at the moment but just take it a day at a time. An hour at a time, if you need to.'

'Is that your strategy for when you find yourself in totally unfamiliar surroundings in your locum work?'

Emma smiled. 'Sometimes I'm taking it a second at a time. Oh…did you want some dessert? Ice cream, like the kids had, maybe?'

Max made another huff of sound. 'I think I need something a bit stronger than ice cream. Do you fancy a small whisky?'

Emma wrinkled her nose. 'I don't do whisky. A glass of wine would be nice, though. White, if you have any.'

'There's usually something in the fridge. Or there's rather a large wine cellar downstairs and it's cold enough at this time of year to be perfectly drinkable.'

The thought of being in a house that had a large wine cellar was as surreal as every other surprise this day had thrown at her. 'Just a small glass,' she warned. 'I've got a very early start tomorrow. I'll need to leave at least an hour to get into Cheltenham in case there's more snow in the night. More, if I need to put the chains on my tyres. And my shift starts at seven a.m., yes?'

'You're onto it.' Max was heading towards a large fridge. 'You sound like you could cope with anything, in fact.'

'It's part of what I like about locum work. You never quite know what's round the next corner. I've been out to remote islands off Scotland in a boat. I did a stint with an air rescue service in Canada once too, and our agency specialises in insurance company work when an injured or ill traveller needs to get brought back home. I went out to an oil rig in a helicopter once.'

'Sounds exciting.'

'I love it. But it can be daunting as well. That's how I know that sometimes you need to focus on just the next step in front of you and block out the big picture.'

'I think I'd rather be on the way out to an oil rig than wondering what I'm going to do with unhappy children in the middle of the night.'

Emma took the glass of wine Max had poured for her. Her smile was one of both appreciation and, hopefully, some reassurance. The softening of his features and that hint of a smile told her that it seemed to have helped.

'Come in by the fire for a minute. I need to make that safe for the night and the whisky's in there too.'

And maybe he needed a bit more reassurance? Emma could provide that. For the sake of Max and his father. And those beautiful children. She'd been perfectly genuine when she'd told Max that the children hadn't been any trouble to look after and she was quite hopeful that she wasn't going to be kept awake tonight by ghosts from the past. Even when she had been helping Max bathe and dress the baby she had been able to keep that door in her own heart firmly closed. These children were like patients. Helping them was just an unexpected—and temporary—twist in her professional life.

It was no great hardship to take a few minutes to sit and sip an excellent wine in front of the fireplace, either. Despite the size of this impressive room, the flames created a flickering light and warmth that made the area directly in front of it seem homely. Almost intimate.

'So how long have you been working as a locum?' Max asked when they had chosen to sit at either end of the big couch rather than use the wing chairs.

'A bit over four years, now.' She had been offered bereavement leave but Emma had found she needed to get back to the job she loved so much, even though she'd been conscious of how hard it was going to be to work amongst young children and babies for a while. She'd learned to cope faster than she'd expected, however. She'd built those walls and kept going but some of the joy had gone and, as the months wore on, she'd known that if she wanted to move forward with her life and re-claim that joy, she needed to make some big changes. Hearing about someone's exciting career as a locum had happened at just the right time.

'If I'd ever thought about it, I would have said you'd be a consultant paediatrician by now.'

Emma tilted her head but didn't say anything. She could have agreed with him and said that was exactly what she'd been planning on being but, if she told him that, she'd have to tell him why it hadn't happened and she didn't want to go there. It was easier to focus on what else he'd just said that implied he'd never given her another thought after the time they'd worked together.

It was inevitable that that took her mind back to their kiss. The one *she'd* never forgotten…

Max broke the silence. 'I guess none of us know what twists and turns life has in store for us. We just know that they're going to happen—usually at what seems to be the worst possible time.'

'Mmm.' Emma could certainly agree with that. For a long moment, they both sipped their drinks and the si-lence was companionable. She knew she might be tak-ing a risk that could destroy this pleasant ambience but Emma was curious. There was so much about Max that she'd never known. Would never have guessed.

'How old were you when your mum died, Max?' she asked gently.

His glance was swift. Intense. 'So Jenny did tell you? Or was it Maggie?'

'They both told me a little. Not much. Maggie told me about your brother. Jenny said something about your mother.'

'Something about the "Curse of the Cunninghams", perhaps?'

Embarrassed, Emma dropped her gaze. She'd hate Max to think she'd been gossiping about his family.

'It's okay,' he said with a sigh. 'I know people like to talk and it's no wonder it's all resurfacing now. Here it is, Christmas again, and tragedy number three strikes the Cunningham family.'

'That should be it, then.'

'Sorry?'

'Bad things are supposed to come in threes.' Emma bit her lip. The tragedies that had befallen this family were nothing to make light of but all she wanted to do was offer…something. Comfort wasn't possible but perhaps some hope? 'Christmas will be different this year.' She offered a smile this time. 'I'm sure the tree will just be the first of all the rules that Ben knows about.'

Max snorted. 'Christmas rules are just part of the commercial hype that's all this season is all about. Reasons to make you spend more and more money.'

'You think?'

'I don't imagine this is the first Christmas you've worked so you know about the effects of the kind of stress it creates. People drink too much. Domestic violence goes through the roof. It's marketed as a promise for peace and love for everyone who bothers to follow all those "rules" but anyone who stands back far enough can see it for what it is.'

There was a defensiveness in his tone that made Emma think he was protesting too much. Because he'd had to—to protect himself? Because it was so much harder if you let yourself sink into what was missing from a celebration of family? She, of all people, could understand that.

'I don't believe that,' she said quietly. 'I'm not saying it's not a particularly difficult time for a lot of people but, if you're lucky, it's an opportunity to hit pause for a day. To celebrate the things that are really important— like family and friends. And, yes, we do that by buying stuff and eating special food but that's okay too, because it's all part of what makes it special. And they're not "rules". They're traditions and every family makes their own. I expect Ben is holding onto the ones he knows about as tightly as he can because he's lost just about everything else.'

Emma had to stop talking then, so that she could swallow the lump in her throat. She could feel Max's gaze resting on her.

'So...why aren't you with *your* family, then? You do have one, don't you?'

Emma nodded. 'In Italy. We have quite different traditions there. Like the feast of the seven fishes on Christmas Eve—the *Festa dei Sette Pesci*. And there's always a nativity scene in the house and someone gets chosen to put the baby Jesus in the crib on Christmas Eve.' She let her breath out in a sigh. 'I haven't been back home for a few years, though.'

'Why not?'

'As a locum, it can be one of the busiest times of the year because so many people want time off to be with their families.' Emma closed her eyes for a heartbeat, ignoring the faint alarm bell in her head. She had, albeit unintentionally, stepped into a private part of Max Cunningham's life. It was only fair if he knew a little more about her, wasn't it? 'Plus, I had a pretty rough Christmas a few years back and I needed some time out. Especially from my family, who would have insisted on talking about it endlessly.'

'What happened?'

'Um…well, it started a bit before Christmas, I guess, when the guy I thought I was going to marry walked out on me. But then…someone special died…'

'At Christmas time?'

'On Christmas Day.' Emma gulped in some air. 'I knew it was coming but that doesn't necessarily make it any easier at the time, you know?'

'Oh, yeah…' Max's tone was heartfelt. 'I know.' It was his turn to take a deeper breath. 'I didn't answer your question before. I was eleven when my mum died. My brother Andy was only eight. Not much older than Ben.'

'Oh, Max… I'm so sorry. That must have been so hard for you all.'

'I think we were too shocked to think about Christmas that year. It was the next one that was the hardest. Andy wanted it to be like it had been, but it was too hard on Dad. I found him crying and that shocked me so much. I had no idea what to do.'

'Of course you didn't. You were a child.'

'I'm not proud of what I did do.'

Emma watched the way Max's face creased into lines of regret. 'I'm sure it wasn't that bad.'

'I told Andy that Father Christmas wasn't real. That it had been Mum who'd put all the decorations up and all those presents under the tree and in our stockings and that, now she wasn't here, it couldn't happen any more because it would make Dad too sad.'

Oh… Emma could just imagine the serious conversation between two small boys. A fragmented family trying to find a way to be together without it causing too much pain for anyone. It was heartbreaking.

'So it didn't happen that year. Or the next. And then we just got used to it. We'd give each other a gift but we never put up a Christmas tree again or did any of the other decorations that Mum used to love—like winding long ropes of artificial leafy stuff like ivy and holly with its red berries between the bannisters on the staircase and hanging little bunches of golden bells on every door so that they jingled whenever they were opened and closed. Andy started doing it all again once he had children of his own, mind you.' Max drained his glass. 'Me, I just got more cynical about it all but then, it only really matters for the kids, doesn't it?'

'I'm not sure about that,' Emma said slowly. 'But it's certainly a very special time of the year for children. Exciting…and magical, until you know the truth about Father Christmas.'

Max grimaced. 'Don't worry. I'm not about to burst the bubble for Ben or Tilly. They've got more than enough of real life to get their heads around at the moment.'

'But…' Again, Emma bit her lip. This really wasn't any of her business.

'But, what?'

'It's just that…well…putting up a Christmas tree is only a part of it. And it's only a decoration if you don't really believe…'

'In Father Christmas?'

Emma shook her head. 'No. In family. In celebrating the bond. Or, in your case this year, perhaps it's about creating a bond. The new one that's going to be the foundation for Ben and Tilly and Alice to feel like they belong.'

Max was staring at her. 'I can't do that.'

'You can. You and your dad. All you have to do is love these children and I'm sure you do already.'

'Yes, but...we don't know how to do Christmas. It's been more than twenty years since we even had a piece of tinsel in the house. Dad wouldn't want it.'

'Are you sure? It's been a long time, Max. Sometimes it takes a gentle push to get people past something that's holding them back. This new family of yours is a gift. It could turn out to be the best thing that could have happened.'

'The breaking of the curse?'

'If you like. The start of something new, anyway. Something very special.'

Emma's tone had softened as she thought about these two bachelor men of different generations sharing their lives with three small children. About the amount of love that would be available within the thick stone walls of this ancient house. She was smiling at Max as she finished speaking. He was holding her gaze with that kind of intensity she had felt before—when it had seemed like he was really seeing her for the first time.

'You're right,' he said softly. 'This could be the most important Christmas these kids will ever have. It *has* to be special.' He still hadn't broken the eye contact and Emma was starting to feel an odd tingle spreading through her body.

'You have to help me, Emma. Please...' The plea in

Max's tone was so heartfelt. 'I don't know how to do this by myself. I… I need you…'

The tingle had just reached Emma's toes.

'We *all* need you,' Max added, as if summoning every power of persuasion he could find. 'Me and Dad. Ben and Tilly and Alice. Probably Pirate too. Just to be here when you're not at the hospital. Just to be…well…just to be *you*… And…and you did promise to show Ben and Tilly how to make stars and we didn't get time to do that tonight, did we?'

Emma nodded. 'I did say I'd show them how to make stars.'

But to stay here in this house?

To spend Christmas with a family?

It was terrifying and compelling at the same time. Emma knew she should run a mile but there was something in her way.

Maybe it was a small boy with solemn eyes. A little girl with a bunny that had chewed ears or a baby that had been watching her as if she was the most important person on earth as she'd sucked her bottle. Perhaps it was a man of her father's generation who loved his little dog but had lost the joy of this season so long ago. Or… maybe it was this man who was looking lost but was so determined to do his best for the entire little family that had just turned up on his doorstep. A man who wanted her to be here. Who *needed* her…

Christmas… With children. And a baby. How could she possibly cope with saying yes?

But Max needed her. Perhaps everybody needed her because she was outside the tragedy that had brought them together so maybe she could see what needed to happen more clearly. How could she possibly say no?

CHAPTER FOUR

WHO WOULD HAVE THOUGHT?

Max had certainly never expected to be here, in the Christmas grotto of Cheltenham's largest department store. Or to be in sole charge of three small children, for that matter, but it seemed that things were going well on this outing. They had been going surprisingly well for the whole day, so far, in fact. He had wrangled the three different sizes of safety seats into his vehicle, figured out how to operate the three-wheeled mountain buggy for Alice and had taken the children on a drive to find a service station that hadn't run out of Christmas trees yet, after deciding that taking the children into the patch of forest on their property and trying to saw off large branches probably wasn't the most sensible idea. It was only after he had tied the tree securely to the roof rack of his Jeep and was planning to head back home to Upper Barnsley that Ben had informed him of the next Christmas 'rule', which was a visit to tell Father Christmas what they hoped would be their special gift this year.

So, here they were. Father Christmas, resplendent in red suit with white faux fur edging to match his luxuriant beard and the trimmings on his hat, was sitting on a large red velvet-covered chair with a golden edging.

Christmas carols were playing softly in the background and the store staff were wearing red hats or headbands with glowing yellow stars. There were Christmas trees with twinkling lights and fake snow on either side of the chair, giant teddy bears, burlap sacks with the corners of pretend gifts peeping out and a life-sized reindeer that had a round red nose and a mouth curved into a rather unlikely smile. It was everything that Max had dismissed about Christmas for as long as he could remember.

Commercial hype. Children begged their parents to bring them here and there would be plenty of other shopping that needed to be done at the same time. Max could see the stoic expressions on some of the parents' faces already as they kept their places in the queue of over-excited children who were waiting their turn to whisper their secret Christmas wishes into the ear of the man who could make it happen. The children standing close to Max weren't over-excited, however. Ben and Tilly were standing very quietly, holding hands, beside the buggy in which Alice was soundly asleep for the moment. Too quietly, Max decided, looking around at the shining faces of other children and the way they were bouncing on their toes, barely able to contain themselves, when it was nearly their turn.

'What are you going to ask Father Christmas for?' he asked Ben.

Ben gave him a patient look. 'It's secret,' he said. 'It's—'

'—a rule,' Max said at the same time. He smiled at Ben. 'I get it.' He wondered if there was any way he could manage to stand close enough to overhear the request, however. Because how else was he going to know what he could get as Christmas gifts for his nephew and nieces?

They moved up the queue a little and Max let his gaze roam away from the grotto towards the strategically placed aisles of every kind of decoration you might want for your house or tree. During a breakfast that was still chaotic even though Maggie had arrived not long after Emma had left for the hospital, he'd told James about his decision to buy a Christmas tree and he'd been on the point of suggesting that they already had all the decorations they could possibly need, boxed up and stored in the attic. It was instantly obvious that his dad knew exactly what he was thinking about and it was just as clear that he wanted to avoid that discussion at all costs. The haunted look in his eyes was swiftly followed by excusing himself to go into the clinic rooms to get ready for a morning surgery followed by house calls.

'You know what?' Max said to Ben.

'What?'

'I think we're going to have a new Christmas rule this year. One that's just for us.'

The deep crease that appeared on Ben's forehead made his glance even more suspicious.

'Only if you think it's a good one,' Max added gravely. 'I reckon you know more about the rules than me.'

Ben considered this and then nodded his agreement. 'What is it?' he asked.

'Well…we've bought a new Christmas tree, haven't we?'

'Yes.'

'And we need to put things on it to look pretty, yes?'

'Stars…' Tilly was listening to the conversation. 'Emma said we can make stars and I can help.'

'I know.' Max had the sudden thought that maybe he might have a word in the ear of Father Christmas himself when they got close enough. So that he could put in a request that Emma would stay in the house for the next week at least. She hadn't exactly said yes when he'd asked her last night. But she hadn't said no either, so he hadn't given up hope. 'I'm sure she will,' he reassured Tilly. 'Emma is not the kind of person who would break a promise. But I was thinking that we might need something else to go with the stars. Something special that you guys can choose all by yourselves. After you've had your photo with Father Christmas.'

Ben was still frowning. 'But why is that a new rule?'

'Because we'll do it every Christmas,' Max told him quietly. 'And that means we'll always have special decorations to go on the tree that you know are yours because you chose them.'

Would the message beneath his words that Max only recognised himself as he was saying them be understood on some level by the children? That he was trying to make a promise that they were safe now and that he would do everything in his power to ensure that there weren't going to be any more huge and traumatic changes in their lives? It seemed to have helped a little, because Tilly's face was starting to look like the other little girls in this line. Her eyes were almost shining.

'Fairies,' she whispered. 'I like fairies.'

'I'll help you find a fairy,' Max said. 'Maybe one that can go right on the tippy top of the tree?'

They were getting closer to the front of the queue now and they were all watching as a small girl was lifted onto Father Christmas's knee. He tilted his head and she cupped her hands around her mouth to keep her wish secret and then beamed at her mother, who was standing beside the photographer. Noticing that the mother's purse was already open so that she could purchase the image should have scored another point for the commercialism that Max detested but, oddly, it didn't. What he could see was the love in this mother's face, her pleasure in having brought her daughter to the Christmas grotto and the sheer joy in the little girl's face.

And he remembered something else then. From the time before he had learned to dismiss everything about Christmas. He remembered being taken to see Father Christmas when he wouldn't have been much older than Ben. With Andy, who would have been about Tilly's age. And their mother had been watching them with love written all over *her* face and…and…

And he could remember the magic. The belief that the man in the red suit could make something special happen. He could also remember that belief becoming something even bigger when he'd come downstairs on Christmas morning to find the gift he'd set his heart on underneath the tree—his first two-wheeler bike with red tinsel wrapped all over it. His wish had come true and it was the best thing *ever*.

Look at that… His mother had the biggest smile on her face as she stood there wrapped in his father's arms. *I wonder how Father Christmas got that down the chimney?*

Max had known. By magic. And even though he knew perfectly well now that it had been his parents who'd put the bike there, he also knew that there had been magic involved. The kind of magic that Emma had been talking about in the bonds within a family. About the sharing and celebration and joy. And she had been right about something else too. These particular children needed to find new bonds that they could trust enough to feel safe and they needed a particularly special Christmas this year.

But he needed help to make that happen. From someone who knew far more about children than he did. Someone who knew more about families than he did and who was warm and caring enough to be able to encourage the connections that would lead to bonds that could form and then get stronger and stronger.

'Do you want to go and visit Emma after we're finished here?' he asked Ben and Tilly. 'It's not far away to where she's working in my hospital. If we find out what she needs to help you make stars, we could pick that up on the way home.'

Emma's first thought when she came out of a curtained cubicle and saw Max Cunningham coming into the emergency department of the Royal with the three children in tow was that something was wrong. Her heart skipped a beat as she imagined one of the children was ill or injured and that must have shown in her face as she walked towards them because Max was smiling reassuringly.

More than reassuringly, actually. He was smiling at Emma as if she was the person he most wanted to see in the world and her body was responding with that glow of warmth and funny tingling thing that went down to her toes. It was impossible not to smile back. Or to hold the gaze of those amazingly blue eyes. He'd always been a very good-looking man but ageing ten years had added a maturity that was even more appealing. It wasn't hard to stamp on her body's response, though, and tell herself how stupid it would be to entertain any ideas of Max being aware of any physical reactions to *her* proximity. She only had to remember how he'd laughed after that kiss. How quick he'd been to reassure her.

'Don't worry, Emma, you're completely safe. We both know you're so not my type and I'm certainly not yours…'

She'd laughed along with him, albeit a heartbeat later. He was right. What woman in her right mind would willingly go near someone who was guaranteed to break their heart if they were silly enough to fall for him?

Her smile was fading as the memory flashed through the back of her mind but Max was still beaming at her.

'We just came in to say hullo,' he said. 'I wondered how things were going?'

'Everything's great,' Emma assured him. 'It was quiet enough first thing for me to get to know my way around and meet most of the staff. Miriam's been amazingly helpful.'

The senior nurse was making a beeline for the group as she was speaking.

'Emma's a complete pro,' she told Max. 'I doubt there's anything she couldn't cope with.' But Miriam's attention was on the children and she automatically reached into the buggy to unclip and pick up the baby as Alice began to whimper. 'May I?'

'Please do,' Max said. 'But she's due for a nappy change and a bottle. We've been busy visiting Father Christmas in Derby's department store.'

'Just the sort of thing a grandma is expert in,' Miriam responded, as she gathered Alice into her arms. 'Is everything in that bag there?'

'She's hungry,' Ben told Miriam.

'I think you're right, lovey. And what about you? We've got some lovely Christmas cookies in our staff-room that look like snowmen. Would you like to come and have some?'

Ben nodded solemnly and Emma had to smile as she saw Tilly's hand slide into his. If her big brother was going to get cookies, she wanted to go too.

Max was still smiling as he watched Miriam take Ben's hand to lead both the older children towards the staffroom.

'You look like you're having a good day,' she said.

'So far, so good.' Max nodded. 'I did want to get close enough to hear what Ben and Tilly were asking Father Christmas for but it didn't work.' He raised an eyebrow at Emma. 'Maybe you could find out? I'd really like to put something special under the tree for them both.'

Was he expecting her to be heading back to the Cunningham house after work? It was only then that Emma realised she hadn't made any effort to look for alternative accommodation yet. She'd been far too focused on her work in this new emergency department. She could find out, she thought. She could help the children write a letter to Father Christmas, maybe, to put into the fire so it went up the chimney. If she promised to keep their secrets, they might tell her exactly what to write.

'Oh, we got a tree too,' Max continued. 'And they both chose some decorations to go on it. Ben got a box of tin soldiers and Tilly chose an angel to go on top of the tree—although she thinks it's a fairy.' His gaze was roaming around his department over Emma's shoulder. 'So…have you had any excitement?'

'Not really. We've only used a resuscitation room once, for a serious stroke that came in early this morning. Apart from that, it's been the usual range of problems like chest pain and asthma and some diabetes complications. There was an interesting tib/fib fracture, though…it—'

But Max obviously wasn't listening. His gaze was fixed behind Emma. About where the first set of automatic doors to the ambulance bay were.

'Something's happening,' he interrupted her.

Emma turned swiftly to see someone standing outside the outer doors that needed a code to open. It was a man who had a child in his arms and, even from this distance, Emma could see that the child was bleeding heavily. One of the two paramedics who were using the space between the sets of doors to finish some paperwork and clean a stretcher moved to press the button that would open the doors at the same time as both Emma and Max had moved close enough for the inner doors to slide open.

'There's more.' The man carrying the injured child was out of breath and sounded panicked. 'Out on the main road. A truck just smashed into about three parked cars. They need help…'

Another ED consultant was right behind Max and Emma.

'I'll take him,' she said. 'Do you want me to activate the trauma team as well?'

'Yes.'

Both Emma and Max spoke at the same time and she had the immediate thought that perhaps she should let Max take charge of this emergency, even though, technically, she was here to do his job. He must have felt her swift glance because he caught her gaze and he clearly wasn't thinking about whether or not he was even supposed to be there.

'We'd better get out there,' he said. 'We're needed.'

Emma hadn't been waiting for his direction. She was already heading for the outer doors despite being in her scrubs, with nothing more than a long-sleeved tee shirt underneath the tunic.

'I'll get our kit,' one of the paramedics said. He turned to his partner. 'You bring the truck so we can transport more quickly.'

Glancing back into the department as the child was carried inside for assessment and treatment, Emma saw Max hesitating for a brief moment before he followed her and he too was looking back into the department. Towards the staffroom where Miriam had taken the children to give them cookies? Emma could sense that he was struggling with something different this time. Not who should take charge of this incident but with his new responsibilities as a father figure clashing with what he was programmed to respond to as an emergency physician. Was this another reminder of just how much his life was changing? His next words confirmed her line of thought.

'Tell Miriam where I am,' he called after his colleague. 'Ask her to keep an eye on the children for me?'

And then they were outside and running towards the scene that lay just out of the hospital grounds, in the direction that Emma had taken only yesterday when she'd walked with Max to see his apartment. The same intersection where they'd waited for the traffic lights to change and she'd noticed the impressive overhead decorations of icicle lights. Any thought of pretty things to do with Christmas was totally incongruous at this moment, however. It looked as though a large truck had failed to notice the line of stationary cars waiting at a red light and had smashed into the end of the line, in a nose-to-tail concertina of at least three vehicles that suggested a great deal of speed had been involved. The truck had tipped sideways with the impact and there was another vehicle almost hidden beneath the body of the truck.

Emma had seen plenty of road traffic accidents over the years but nothing quite like this. There was a crowd gathering, with people trying to get into vehicles where doors had been crushed and couldn't open. They must have come from the lines of traffic now building up in a traffic jam on all sides of the intersection because many of them looked deserted, with doors hanging open. There were flashing lights and sirens coming from all directions as emergency service vehicles rushed to the scene but, even over all that noise, Emma could hear the cries of frightened people. Her steps slowed as she got closer to the carnage and—although Max had been a step or two ahead of her the whole time they'd been running—he seemed to sense the distance between them increasing and he also slowed, turning back to catch her gaze.

'You okay, Em?'

She nodded, sucking in a deep, deep breath. She knew she had the skills to tackle a scene like this but, for this moment, it was overwhelming. The temptation to hang back and allow Max to take the lead was strong but there was something equally strong and that was a hard-won determination to face up to the most difficult things life could throw at her and Emma wasn't about to throw away any part of her confidence in being able to do that successfully.

Max was still holding her gaze and it felt as if he

could sense that momentary doubt. As if he was having a similar one of his own, even, and wondering if he should take the lead.

'We're right beside the hospital,' she said, turning her head now to survey the scene and assess the dangers and where they might be needed as a priority. 'All we need to do at this point is to make sure they're stable enough to get them inside. Basics. Airway, breathing, circulation. Look after the cervical spine. We've got lots of help. The firies will cut into the vehicles for us if it's needed. The paramedics can direct the extrication and transfer.'

'Here...' A paramedic was coming towards them. 'Put these on.'

'These' were fluorescent vests with the word 'Doctor' on the back on a reflective strip.

'No...hang on...' A female paramedic was pulling off her jacket, which she handed to Emma. 'You're going to freeze in scrubs. Put this on first.'

'But what about you?'

'I've got something else I can wear.'

'Has anybody started triage?' Max asked.

'We've only just got here. That's our MCI command vehicle arriving now, behind the fire truck.'

Emma knew that MCI stood for Mass Casualty Incident. She looked at the line of crushed vehicles. Should they start at the front and work back? One of the cars was sandwiched between one in front and one behind and it looked as though the damage in that case was worse than the others. But what about the vehicle beneath the overturned truck?

Max clearly wanted to start the work that urgently needed to be done here. Emma shoved her arms into the warm jacket.

'Have you got triage labels?'

The paramedic who'd opened the ambulance bay doors of the Royal to let in the man with the injured child was beside Emma now. 'I've got them,' he said. 'Can you come with me? We'll do a first sweep and if you're both with me, I can leave you to start treating any red labels and move on. We still don't know what we're dealing with in terms of numbers or severity of injuries.'

Emma had worked with the triage labelling system as well. A red label meant that the victim could only survive with immediate treatment. They might have an obstructed airway or rate of respiration that was far too slow or fast, a very rapid heart rate or an absent radial pulse indicating low blood pressure, potentially from severe blood loss.

The first car in the line had been shunted well into the intersection. There were bystanders clustered around the driver's side of the car. The window was broken and Emma could see the deflated airbag hanging from the steering wheel.

'She's awake,' someone told them. 'She says her neck hurts and she doesn't want to try moving.'

She was conscious, breathing and talking so this driver wasn't going to get a red label indicating the need for urgent intervention to save a life. A potential neck injury could still be serious but it could wait.

'Tell her to keep as still as possible,' the paramedic instructed. 'Someone will be with her very soon.'

They moved swiftly to the next vehicle. The paramedic was using his radio to relay information to the person who was taking charge of the scene and would use the available resources of people and equipment according to information coming in and any changes during the operation. Police officers were on scene now, as well, moving bystanders out of the way and trying to clear the blocked traffic.

There were two people inside the second vehicle, both conscious.

'It's my leg,' the front seat passenger groaned. 'I think it's broken.'

The driver was only semi-conscious. 'Where am I?' she mumbled. 'What's happened?'

More paramedics had arrived on scene and were immediately dispatched to manage these patients.

It was the third car in the line that was the most seriously damaged, apart from the one beneath the truck, and it was rapidly, sadly clear that there was nothing they could do for this woman. Her black triage label was a sombre confirmation that the rescue teams were not needed.

'Maybe if we'd got here a bit faster?' Emma said.

But Max shook his head. 'Unsurvivable injuries. I suspect the force from behind and the weight of obstruction in front was enough to just snap her neck.'

A fire crew was close and had a tarpaulin to put over the car containing the fatality.

'Truck driver seems uninjured,' they told Emma and Max. 'Got himself out of the cab. The cops are having a word with him.'

'I'll go and check him out.' The paramedic's tone was carefully neutral. It was obvious that the truck driver was responsible for this horrific crash that had killed at least one person but they couldn't make judgements about the driver involved. It was possible that it was a medical event or mechanical failure that had caused him to hit a line of stationary vehicles at high speed.

The fire crew was also making decisions about how to get to the car trapped beneath the truck and Emma heard someone talking about stabilising the truck until they could get the machinery they needed to lift it clear. Looking at how crushed the car was, with its roof almost down past the level of the steering wheel, she fully expected that the driver would be another fatality. She bent to try and look through the front window on the passenger's side.

'Careful, there, Doc,' one of the fire officers shouted. 'We're not sure how stable it is.'

The call was enough to have Max by her side instantly and it felt as though he was there to try and protect her. He was certainly ready to assist. Or did he want to take over?

'What can you see?'

'Facial injuries. I can't see any chest wall movement...' Emma had her bottom lip caught between her teeth as she scanned the driver's body as best she could. The seat had been flattened by the roof being crushed so he was lying almost flat, still wearing his seat belt. She couldn't see any major bleeding other than the injury to his face but... 'Oh...' Emma felt her heart skip a beat. 'I *can* see chest wall movement. He's breathing. Or trying to...'

Max had his head right beside hers now, as he tried to get a visual assessment of the crash victim. He was so close she could feel the warmth of his skin and, like the way he'd looked at her when they'd first arrived on this scene, it seemed that just being close to him was empowering Emma with more confidence than she'd ever known she had.

She turned to the fire crew. 'I have to get in here,' she said. 'It's urgent.'

'We're still assessing how stable this truck is. We can't start cutting the car up for access until we've got jacks in place or lifted the chassis clear.'

'There's no time for that.' Emma shook her head. 'Can you break this back window? I reckon I could get in there.'

'There's hardly any space in there.' The paramedic had come back. 'There's no way we could get a spinal board in and get him out.'

Both the paramedic and Max were tall, broad-shouldered men. They wouldn't even be able to get through a window space. But Emma could—if she was brave enough. Again, as she had when first arriving on this scene, she had a moment of wondering if she might be about to tackle something that might defeat her. And, again, she found herself catching Max's gaze. This time, it felt different. He wasn't considering taking over because he couldn't do what Emma could attempt, thanks to her size. This time, it felt as if he was offering her encouragement. Bolstering her confidence by letting her know that he believed she could do this. And it felt…great. It was exactly what she needed to vanquish any beat of fear.

'I can get in,' she told them. 'I need to secure his airway. I can work in a tight space. You could pass me in the gear I need.' She had to try and save this man. He'd been simply sitting in his car, stopped at a red traffic light, and his world had just been overturned in a split second and it just…well, it wasn't fair…

The chief fire officer looked undecided but Emma held his gaze to give him the silent message if he wasn't going to help her, she was going to try by herself.

He finally nodded. 'Okay. Stand back and I'll get the window out.'

* * *

He should go back to his emergency department, Max thought. It wasn't just that he'd left all the children in the care of a staff member. He was automatically focusing on how the department was going to cope with a sudden influx of trauma patients. He knew that his staff would be managing the first of these patients from the crash scene perfectly well, but the more seriously injured, like the semi-conscious driver of the second vehicle, might be stretching immediate resources and they needed to plan for someone who could need major resuscitation—if they could get him into the department alive. Or maybe it should be Emma who went back to manage the department, seeing as she was officially doing his job today.

But right now she was wriggling herself through an empty window space of a crashed car and somehow contorting her body so that she could touch and assess the unconscious driver. She was inside a partially crushed car and there was a heavy truck still lying across the vehicle. It looked difficult and bloody dangerous and…and there was no way Max was going to leave until he knew that Emma was okay. He couldn't believe the courage she'd shown even crawling into that vehicle. The fact that she now sounded calm and in control of the situation was, well…it was seriously impressive.

'He's got multiple fractures in his face and his airway's obstructed.' Emma put down the bag mask she had been trying to use to assist the man's breathing. 'There's no way I'm going to be able to do an orotracheal or nasotracheal intubation. How far away are we from being able to get him out?'

Max signalled one of the fire officers and repeated Emma's query.

'We're getting some jacks in place. It should be safe enough to cut the side out of the car in about ten minutes.'

Emma had heard the response. 'Too long,' she said. She was almost lying down beside her patient in the narrow space left in the crushed car but she twisted her head to look directly at Max.

'Surgical cricothyroidotomy?' she suggested.

'It's what I'd do in ED.' He nodded. 'But have you got enough space in there?'

'It'll have to be enough,' Emma said. 'His pulse is dropping. We're going to lose him if I don't do something right now. I need some fresh gloves, a number ten or eleven scalpel, a bougie and a size six endotracheal tube, please.'

It was Max who handed everything that Emma required in through the empty window space, reaching in so that he could place things in her hands without her having to try and move. With her new gloves on, he watched her find her landmarks on the man's neck, stabilising the larynx with one hand and then locating the space between the thyroid and cricoid cartilages. He was ready to hand her the scalpel as soon as she was ready to make her first incision.

'I'm through the cricoid membrane,' she said, seconds later. 'I'm going to make the horizontal incisions now.'

Max knew this was where things could get messy and enough blood could not only obscure the field but undermine the confidence of anyone who might not be very familiar with this emergency procedure. He knew that Emma was going to be working purely by feel from now on and when there was movement of the crushed vehicle from what the firies were doing to stabilise the truck above them, he held his breath to see whether that might give Emma enough of a fright to interfere with what was the critical moment of her attempt to save this man's life.

It didn't seem to rattle her at all. She slid the bougie guide into the hole she'd made in his neck, slipped the endotracheal tube over the top of the bougie and managed to make it look easy to secure the tube, despite the awkwardness of the space she was working in and gloved hands that were slippery with blood.

'Can you see where the bag mask is?' she asked Max.

'It's right behind you.'

'I can't reach…'

'I've got it.' Max leaned further into the car and picked it up. He pulled off the plastic face mask and the paramedic beside him had the attachment needed so that Emma could clip it to the endotracheal tube.

'Equal chest movement,' she said a moment later. 'Can we get some oxygen on? I'd like to get an IV in, as well.'

Max could see the firies setting up their hydraulic cutting gear right beside him. As he looked at the officer in charge he received a nod in response.

'They're ready to start cutting,' he told Emma. 'Is he breathing well enough to wait a couple of minutes until we can get him out? The sooner we can get him into the department the better, yes?'

'Of course.' Emma had one hand on the man's abdomen, feeling for his efforts at respiration. She had her other hand on his wrist, feeling for his pulse. 'Okay… yes…let's get him out of here.'

She stayed with her patient for as long as possible as the firies cut through twisted metal and lifted a door and the central pillar out of the way. Then she had to move and the paramedics took over, being the experts in getting the victim onto a spinal board and then out of the vehicle and onto the waiting stretcher. It took only a few minutes but, for that period of time, Max had Emma standing right beside him and he could sense her focus on what was happening for her patient and a tension that suggested that a successful outcome to this case was very, very important to her.

He was looking at her face as the badly injured man was finally lifted from the car and, as if sensing his gaze, she looked up at him and he could see what he had suspected in her eyes. Emma was determined to win this fight for life. She not only had a bucket of courage, this woman, but she loved her job as much as Max loved his and she truly cared about doing the absolute best she could for anyone under her care. It was a moment of connection that was as powerful as it was brief.

Their patient had been freed but needed more intervention and then a high level of monitoring even for the few minutes it would take to get him inside the hospital walls. The other victims of this incident had already been transported into the Royal's emergency department and that was where Emma and Max both headed back to now. There was still a lot of work to be done and Max wanted to be working alongside Emma to make sure the department could handle everything that needed to be done for everybody involved.

It was then he realised that, during the tense minutes of assisting Emma in the amazing job she'd just done in saving a man's life, he'd actually forgotten that he had other responsibilities as well. That there were three small children waiting for him, probably in the staffroom of his emergency department. He felt completely torn in that moment—in two very different directions—and it was overwhelming.

Had Emma sensed that it was almost too much? Was that why she chose to look up from her patient for a heartbeat and catch his gaze? There was a softness to her mouth that hinted at a smile and there was a confidence in her eyes that told him she thought they were winning. That they had a very good chance of winning this challenge they had just tackled together.

Max chose to take something more from that look as well. That he might well be facing the biggest challenge of his own life but he had a very good chance of winning that too. Especially if he could persuade Emma to hang around, even if was only for a short time. And then he remembered that was why he had dropped by the hospital in the first place—to try and persuade her not to find alternative accommodation.

He'd have to wait before he could find an appropriate moment to do that so he hoped the children were happy to stay for a bit longer. That would also give him time to think up an approach that Emma couldn't refuse.

He could remind her of her promise to help Ben and Tilly make stars.

Or he could remind her of what she believed about Christmas. About the magic that could happen when a family came together to celebrate the bonds they had. The love. He could tell her what he believed—that they all needed Emma to make that happen.

CHAPTER FIVE

THIS FELT AS if it could be a mistake.

As if Emma was doing something that meant she was stepping over a line and it might be impossible to step back again even if she really needed to. But here she was, doing it. Driving back to Upper Barnsley. And it was Max Cunningham's fault.

He had made it impossible for her not to return to the manor house after her shift had ended. He had stayed on at the Royal, allowing staff members to take care of his nieces and nephew, until they had stabilised all the victims of the major accident and their patients had been transferred either to Theatre under the care of surgical teams or admitted to various wards for further treatment.

And then he'd brought the children in from the staff-room or the relatives' room or wherever someone had been caring for them and Ben had pinned Emma with that gaze that was far too serious for a six-year-old boy to have mastered.

'Is it time for you to go home now, Emma?' he'd asked.

'I guess it is,' she'd admitted, checking her watch. But just where it was that she would be heading as her temporary home was totally unknown. She hadn't found a single moment today to go online and check for the availability of hotel rooms within a manageable distance.

'Are we going to make stars?' Tilly's gaze was almost as sombre as her brother's—as if she was still processing her new knowledge that life didn't always deliver what it was supposed to. 'I like stars and…and you said I could help.'

Ben still had her pinned. 'You promised…'

Technically, Emma had offered rather than promised to show the children how to make stars but the semantics were irrelevant because she couldn't let Ben and Tilly down.

Or Max…

If he'd brought these children in to see her as a form of emotional blackmail to get another night of her assistance with their care, he had certainly achieved his goal but that wasn't what Emma was thinking about as her gaze touched, and then held, his.

To be honest, she wasn't thinking of anything very coherent at all. It was more of a feeling. A warmth. They had worked together this afternoon. They had saved a life and the connection that gave them was more than simply professional. They had shared a goal and they'd needed each other in order to achieve it and they had succeeded and…trust between them had been born. It was that trust that was creating a warmth that started in Emma's chest and unfurled and grew to reach right to the tips of her fingers and toes.

Or maybe the connection had already been there from years ago and had been rediscovered.

And maybe a new depth to that connection had been established between them yesterday when Emma had been present while Max was struggling to get his head around the enormous changes that had just overturned his world. She had helped because she was there and she couldn't *not* help but then he'd asked her to stay. He'd said that he *needed* her…

Whatever it was, it was powerful. And it was touching something very deep in Emma's heart. Not in the space that was still locked away because she didn't quite recognise this new part of her heart. It felt like no-man's land, halfway between caring so much that something could tear your heart apart when you lost it and caring only because you knew that it was temporary so the loss was already built in—the now very familiar space that her locum work had given her in her professional life and the avoidance of any long-term relationships had provided in her private life.

For a moment, Emma had to shake off a longing that came completely from left field—that she was over being in this space and ready to put roots down and create a life that wasn't going to keep changing. As always, the best way to deal with a doubt like that was to think of a positive point to balance it and there was one that sprang to mind instantly. It almost felt as if she could allow herself to enjoy the sensations that came from unwrapping an old attraction that didn't seem to have faded at all because this was as temporary as her new position being the stand-in HOD of the Royal's emergency department. She knew that when this locum position ended she would walk out of the job and away from Max Cunningham and his now very complicated life would be none of her business. Perhaps she could even allow herself to enjoy the company of young children—away from her professional environment—

which was something she knew she had instinctively kept herself away from.

It was all temporary. Keeping her word to show Ben and Tilly how to make stars committed her to no more than spending one more night at the manor house. She could find the time to search for a hotel room tomorrow.

Pulling her car to a halt beside Max's, outside his family home, Emma sat still for a moment, watching Max get out of the driver's seat and move to open the back door to lift his small passengers from their car seats. He paused for a heartbeat, however, and looked over the Christmas tree strapped to the roof of the vehicle to catch Emma's gaze, his lips curling into a smile.

Emma's breath came out in a sigh that held the edge of an unexpected sound.

Oh, yeah…that attraction hadn't faded at all. It seemed to have matured into something that had rather a lot more bite to it and she recognised the tiny sound that had escaped with her breath for what it was—an expression of physical desire.

Lust, even…

It had been a weird thing to think about as he unclipped Tilly's safety belt and lifted her from her car seat but there was no way that Max could have stopped the memory filling his head.

That time he'd kissed Emma Moretti under the mistletoe at the paediatric ward's staff Christmas party. He hadn't given it any more thought after it had happened because, no matter how soft her lips had been and how delicious the curves of her body were and how astonishingly powerful the urge to do a lot more than kiss Emma had been, it was never going to happen.

Emma was the earth mother type. The type who was destined to marry and have a family as soon as possible. A huge family, probably, seeing as she had adored children and babies so much and, because that was something Max wanted to avoid at all costs, it had been easy to dismiss the attraction that had both led to and been inflamed by that kiss.

Dismissing it hadn't made it go away, though, had it? Judging by the kick in his gut that Max recognised all too easily as a reaction to a very healthy physical attraction, it was actually stronger than it had ever been.

Was that because there were things about Emma that were familiar but other things that were so very different? She was just as gorgeous as she'd been ten years ago, even though she was less curvy and she had cut off those glorious long waves of her hair and she seemed... what was it, exactly? More contained, perhaps? Less ready to laugh or even smile. Yes, she was definitely different but that gave the attraction an edge of mystery that added surprisingly to its power.

Emma wasn't the only one who was different, either. Who could have predicted that he'd be the one who'd end up with what seemed a huge family and the earth mother would still be alone?

He set Tilly down on her feet beside Ben, who immediately took hold of his sister's hand, and then he unclipped the bucket seat that Alice was strapped into.

'Okay, guys. Let's go inside and say hullo to Grandpa and then I'll bring the Christmas tree inside.'

But James Cunningham was nowhere to be seen. Neither was their housekeeper, Maggie, though she'd left a note in the kitchen with a list of food she had prepared for both the children and adults.

'Dad's probably in the clinic. Or on a house call. Or he might have taken Pirate for a walk.'

Or he might be avoiding spending time with his grandchildren because, like Max, he was still grappling with how to cope with his new responsibilities.

Alice had begun to cry as they'd come inside. Max had a brief but fierce yearning for the old days in the paediatric ward when he'd been working with Emma and how he had been able to hand a baby back to its mother or a nurse when it needed changing or feeding, but he wasn't about to repeat his actions of the previous evening of shoving Alice into Emma's arms.

Not when he had been quite aware of that flash of something like panic he'd seen in her eyes, even as her arms had gathered the baby close. Besides, he had to learn how to cope and this was as good a time as any. He pulled wipes and a clean nappy from the bag of supplies he had taken into town earlier and set about making Alice comfortable. It was a mission to deal with all those fiddly little fasteners on her stretchy suit and clean that tiny bottom when she was kicking her legs so energetically and by the time he carried the baby into the kitchen to get on with his next task of preparing a bottle of formula he found Emma sitting at the long table with an array of materials in front of her that included all the cardboard boxes she had gathered at the hospital before coming home.

She was cutting a shape from the cardboard as Max held Alice with one arm and used his free hand to measure scoops of formula into a bottle the way Maggie had shown him yesterday.

'So this will be a big star,' Emma told Ben and Tilly. 'And I'll make a shape for a small star, as well. You can trace around them on other pieces of cardboard and then I can help you cut them out.'

'I can cut things out all by myself,' Ben said.

'Me too,' said Tilly.

Emma's nod was apologetic. 'Of course you can,' she said. 'But I can help if you want me to. And when we've cut some out, I'll show you how to cover them with the silver foil. And then we need to make a hole in one of the pointy bits.'

'Why?'

'So we can tie the stars to the tree. I'm sure we can find some string somewhere.'

Ben looked up at Max as he shook the bottle to dissolve the formula in the cooled boiled water. 'Did you bring the tree inside, Uncle Max?'

'Not yet, Ben. But I will, just as soon as I give Alice her dinner.' He tested the temperature of the milk against his wrist and hoped that how confident he'd just sounded was justified. He still hadn't managed to get Alice to accept a bottle from him yet. Last night he'd needed Emma to rescue him. Maggie had been on hand this morning and Miriam, along with other staff members, had been only too happy to take over when he'd taken the children into work.

Max was holding his breath as he took a seat at the far end of the kitchen table, tipped Alice back into the crook of his elbow and offered her the teat of the bottle as her hungry whimpers became more frantic. He saw the startled expression on her face as she looked up at this new person trying to feed her but she had already tasted the milk and hunger seemed to win the battle with any lack of trust. Her lips closed around the teat and her tiny hands came up to help Max hold the bottle as she began to suck.

He knew he was smiling as he looked up to see if Emma had witnessed this triumph. Max felt absurdly proud of himself. So much so, he actually had a bit of a lump in his throat. He could do this. He *was* doing it.

Emma had a rather oddly shaped cardboard star in her hands and she was showing the children how to wrap it in silver foil but she must have been watching Max's efforts with Alice from the corner of her eye because she caught his gaze as the contented silence of the baby continued and her smile only made him feel even prouder.

Emma was impressed.

And then something weird happened.

It was like one of those photographs where the image had been captured from multiple cameras surrounding the group or one that had been created during that mannequin challenge that had gone viral where everybody froze in the middle of doing something. The effect was that Max was suddenly and acutely aware of so many tiny things, all at once.

There was the weight and warmth of the baby in his arms and the feather-light touch of those miniature fingers against his own hands. He could smell the combination of the milk she was drinking and the baby smell that was partly shampoo and lotion but something else that was just unique to babies, or maybe to this particular baby. He could also see the older children. Ben was standing beside Emma, leaning on her arm as he watched what she was doing with absolute concentration. Tilly had somehow wriggled onto Emma's lap to get closer to the action but she wasn't watching the foil

being folded around the points of the cardboard star—
she was looking up at Emma.

And Emma, well, she was looking at Max and, while
the scene couldn't actually be any more different to the
drama of the rescue scene this afternoon when Emma
was folded inside that wreck of a car and he was assisting
her with that life-saving intervention, there was something similar in this connection. They were a team and,
in this moment of time, they were succeeding in what
they were trying to achieve.

But there was more to it than that. A whole lot more.

This... Max had to swallow the lump in his throat that
had just become oddly uncomfortable. This was a *family*
moment and it took him back in time. To when he still
had his younger brother in his life. And the mother he
had adored so much. A time when they might well have
been doing something together, in this very kitchen. A
time when this house had been such a happy place. A
real home...

Suddenly—shockingly—Max could see right through
that barrier he'd started creating as a young boy. The barrier that made him believe that he never really wanted
what he'd once had as part of a loving family. That life
would be far less painful and much more fun if he just
skated across the surface when it came to relationships
with other people. If he could turn away from things that
were so big they were terrifying and he could simply
shut them away in a place he never really needed to visit.

He became the son who loved his father very much
but never strayed into the private, sad space that James
Cunningham had retreated to after his beloved wife's
death.

A big brother who thought he was being kind by telling Andy that Father Christmas didn't exist and that they needed to grow up and look after themselves so that they didn't make things worse for their father.

An uncle who was quite happy to play with the members of a new generation of the Cunningham family but was never tempted by the idea of having children of his own.

A lover who could recognise the moment a woman was falling in love with him and wanted more and took the first opportunity to end things as kindly, but finally, as possible.

And, in this rather shocking moment, he could see that behind those barriers was someone who actually, desperately wanted precisely the things he had spent a lifetime protecting himself from. He wanted the kind of committed, loving relationship his parents had had. He wanted to watch his children grow up. To protect and guide them.

To love them. To have a partner by his side who would also love his children. Who would love *him* and choose to be with him for the rest of her life.

Someone like… Emma…?

As if she had sensed that astonishing thought, Emma broke the eye contact with Max.

'It's your turn now, Ben,' she said. 'You can put the silver foil on the star you cut out.'

Max could have smiled at the wonky star with rather round points that Ben had made but he didn't. It was partly because he wouldn't have wanted to hurt Ben's feelings but it was more to do with the shock of that insight and the idea that he might have got things terribly wrong all those years ago. Thankfully, he could sense those barriers becoming rapidly cloudy again so that he was losing the impression of what he'd seen behind them. He had taught himself well to push those things that were emotionally too big to deal with into the space where they could be locked away.

He might be being forced to have the family he'd never imagined he'd ever have, but that didn't mean he had to take the risk of including anyone else in his life. Good grief…he only had to remember Andy's anguish when his marriage had failed to know that trusting the romantic kind of love was even more of a risk than opening your heart to being a loving father figure. He'd never know whether driving into that tree at high speed had really been accidental but the grief from his brother's death had been devastating enough anyway. He'd lost half his family now. A bit more than that, perhaps, because his father had never been the same since his mother had died so he'd lost a part of him as well.

It was too much loss for anyone.

Max let his breath out in a sigh of relief as Alice finished the last drops of her milk. He set the bottle on the table and moved Alice so that she was upright against his shoulder and he could rub her back to encourage a burp. That barrier was solid again, he realised. He was safe. Maybe it was partly that relief that made him turn his head so that he could press a soft kiss to that silky baby hair. Okay, the barrier had clearly shifted a little and he knew he could make space for these children in his heart. But that was all. His father had never recovered from losing the woman he'd given his heart to and Max knew that the failure of Andy's marriage had been the cause of his death, whether it had been deliberate or simply the fact that he'd been so devastated it had been enough to make him do something he'd never have normally done and get behind the wheel of a car when he was drunk. Marriage—or any kind of long-term commitment to a partner—was still well off Max's radar.

Emma was as safe as he was from anything more than a professional relationship and/or friendship.

James Cunningham didn't approve of the Christmas tree in the drawing room.

Not that he'd said anything, but Emma could sense his shock when he'd walked in when she was helping Ben tie his homemade stars to the branches of the tree that Max had brought inside and set up on one side of the fireplace under Ben's direction.

'It has to be close to the chimney,' he'd told them. 'So that Father Christmas doesn't have to go looking for it. He doesn't have time to do that when he's got so many chimneys he has to go down.'

When James came into the room, Max was holding Tilly up to put her fairy/angel on the top of the tree and Emma had her arms around Ben, gently guiding his small fingers as he tried to tie a bow in the string that they had threaded through the hole in one point of his star.

Max's father had frozen—just for a heartbeat—and, for Emma, it felt as if the world stopped turning for that instant in time as well. She could see what James was seeing. A man with a small girl in his arms, smiling as he watched her stretch out to put the skirt of the angel over the uppermost branch of the tree. A woman almost cradling an older child and a baby asleep in a pram to one side. The fire was crackling softly beside them and it didn't matter that the small number of homemade silver stars, even with the tin soldiers Ben had chosen and the angel for the top of the tree that had been Tilly's choice, still left the tree looking virtually devoid of decorations—this was a snapshot of a family Christmas and all it needed now was the grandfather looking on from the comfort of his leather chair, with his cute dog at his feet.

And Emma could feel something expanding inside her chest. She knew it wasn't physically possible that her heart could be changing size but that was what it felt like. It was getting rapidly bigger. Too big, because it was starting to crack. And bleed...

This... This feeling of family and Christmas. Of having different generations coming together to celebrate something special. Of having children dependent on her for as much love and protection that she could offer and having a partner that she could share the journey with...

She still wanted this. She wanted it so badly it was making her heart ache as much as if it had really split open.

And, maybe, Max's father was aware of a similar sense of yearning. Or loss, perhaps. Because, after that single heartbeat of time, he turned on his heel, snapping his fingers for Pirate to follow him out of the room and his spoken words were only for his dog.

'Sorry,' he muttered. 'I forgot. It's time for your walk, boy.'

Pirate hesitated for a moment, as if he was also contemplating the scene in front of him and would rather stay, but then turned and followed his master out of the room.

Emma had to take her hands away from where they were touching Ben's because she knew that he would notice they were shaking. She needed to gulp in a breath of air as well, because it might have only been an instant in time but it felt like she hadn't taken a breath in quite a while.

This was exactly what she had feared might happen if she became any more involved with the Cunningham men and these children. That she would be reminded that she still didn't have what she'd wanted most in life for almost as long as she could remember—to have a family of her own. She'd taught herself to live without it. To be okay with the idea that it might never happen, in fact, because the walls she had built around her heart and her new lifestyle of never being in one place for a long time had been how she'd coped so well for so long. But she was safe, because that wasn't about to change. Or not yet, anyway. Not when she would be leaving this part of the world in a matter of days. Not for children who belonged to another family or a man who'd never been interested in her.

Except…that wasn't quite true, was it?

He'd been interested enough to kiss her that one time.

And Emma was almost sure he remembered that kiss as well as she did. She also knew they'd both changed enough for curiosity to be part of a feeling of connection between them and…after the intense way Max had been looking at her over the top of the Christmas tree strapped to his car this afternoon, she had a sense that the increased attraction she was so aware of could very well be mutual.

She let out the breath she had taken slowly. A sexual attraction was completely different to the minefield of emotions that came with the notions of family and forever. That was something she could cope with, even if it wasn't something she'd included in her life for a very long time. And she didn't have to think about it right now because there were more important things to focus on.

'Good job, Ben,' she said aloud. 'That's a beautiful star.'

CHAPTER SIX

THE WALK WITH Pirate seemed to have given James whatever inner strength he needed to get back on track with coping and he helped with getting the children fed, bathed and into bed. He excused himself as he stood up from the kitchen table after dinner, however, to retire to his room instead of sitting by the fire.

'It's been a long day,' he said.

'You sure you don't want a nightcap?' Max asked. 'I'm going to have one. Emma? Would you like a glass of wine?'

'I would,' Emma said. 'Thank you.'

'You deserve a chance to wind down properly,' Max said as he went to the fridge to collect the bottle he'd opened the night before. 'You've had a pretty big day as well.'

They had told James about the horrific accident outside the hospital and how they'd worked together at the scene. Emma had wondered if the topic of conversation had been of such interest to James due to professional reasons or because it was a relief to stop talking or even thinking about the three young children under his roof. He was looking so tired now that it was clear he was struggling with the changes in his life as much, if not more than his son and Emma's heart went out to him. It was no surprise that he needed some time on his own and refused the offer of a drink or further company.

Max was silent until he'd put a glass of wine into Emma's hand and then poured himself a small glass of whisky in the drawing room.

'It's this tree,' he told her. 'I can understand why it's upsetting Dad so much. We haven't had a Christmas tree in this house since Mum died.'

'It can't be easy,' Emma agreed quietly. 'But it's important, isn't it? For the children. And...' She stepped closer to the sparsely decorated tree to touch one of the crooked stars, looking up at the angel/fairy who was listing badly to one side at the top. 'And it's a beautiful tree.'

Max sounded as if he was suppressing a snort of laughter as he put his glass down and reached up to straighten the angel.

'It's a bit sad compared to what I remember our Christmas trees being like. Mum was a true fan. She loved fairy lights and candles and had so many boxes of decorations her trees were works of art. It was always a special evening when Andy and I were allowed to help decorate the tree.'

'I think Ben will remember making that star and tying it onto this tree. His first Christmas with the new part of his family.'

Max was silent for a moment and then cleared his throat as if he was intending to change the subject. 'The last time I remember seeing you was at Christmas time,' he said, as if an amusing memory had just surfaced. 'Must be ten years ago? It was at that party...'

Oh...*help*...

Emma could feel spots of bright colour appear on

her cheeks and she couldn't meet his glance. He *did* remember their kiss. For a heartbeat, she couldn't think of anything else. The distance of time had vanished and it might have been only seconds since he'd lifted his lips from hers. That tingle was back, dancing through her body before settling into a tight, hot knot somewhere deep in her gut. To try and cool it down Emma made herself remember what had happened next. That Max had laughed that kiss off as meaning nothing at all and she had followed his example a heartbeat later.

Max's tone was a little more hesitant when he broke the silence again. 'Do you know why I kissed you that night, Emma?'

It was her turn to suppress a sound of laughter. She turned away, heading for one end of the couch. 'You were carrying mistletoe,' she reminded him. 'You were kissing every woman at the party.'

'But you were the first. You were the reason I picked up that silly plastic mistletoe so I had an excuse.' He had picked up his glass again. 'Have you got any idea why I might have wanted to do that?'

Emma sat down on the soft leather cushion.

Did she want to know?

No. She didn't want to know that Max might have been as attracted to her as she had been to him. Because that might put a match to any residual attraction that might be there and…and something might happen…

Which actually meant—if she was really honest with herself—the answer to her silent question was yes. In fact, Emma wanted to know so badly she lifted her gaze when Max remained silent for a long moment, her eyebrows raised to encourage him to tell her.

'Tell me,' she said.

'I saw you crying.'

Shocked, Emma remained silent as Max came to sit down in his father's chair, between her end of the couch and the odd-looking Christmas tree.

'You didn't see me,' he continued quietly. 'And I wanted to try and make you smile again because I knew why you had been crying.'

Emma swallowed hard. 'Did you?'

'It was the day that little boy died. I've forgotten his name. The one who had such a severe case of hypoplastic left ventricle syndrome that the only way to save him would have been a heart transplant. We had just put a PICC line in a few days earlier to give him medication for his heart failure but it hadn't been enough and you'd been there when he—'

'Tyler,' Emma interrupted. 'His name was Tyler.'

'He was special to you.'

More than special. Emma had been totally in love with that ten-month-old baby who had a smile that lit up the room, despite how sick he was.

'He changed my life,' she whispered. 'More than you would believe.'

Max was giving her that look again. The one that made her feel as if he was seeing her properly for the first time. The one that made her feel as if she was the only person in the world that mattered at this very moment in time.

'I knew something big had changed the moment I saw you again in the Royal.' Max hadn't even blinked as he held her gaze. 'It took a while to recognise you. But what did it have to do with Tyler?'

Emma took a sip of her wine. And then another. This wasn't something she talked about. Or even thought about very much if she could help it. It was well in the past now and she was moving on as best she could. But Max's life had just changed as monumentally as Emma's had all those years ago and that gave them a new connection. That fragile new trust was still there as well, and trust always deserved a chance to be nurtured. She would be trusting him with an important part of her own heart if she did tell him her story but there was something in those astonishingly blue eyes that made her feel safe. That said she mattered enough to make her story important. Vital, even…

'I got pregnant,' she admitted. 'A few years after we worked together on that paediatric rotation.'

That didn't seem to surprise Max. 'We all knew you were destined for motherhood,' he said. 'You just loved being with those babies on the paediatric ward so much. Did you get married, then?'

'No. But I was with the person I believed I was going to marry. A paediatric surgeon called Richard. The pregnancy killed our relationship completely.'

'He didn't want children?'

'Oh, he wanted children. That baby wasn't going to be one of them, though. It became obvious during my second trimester scan that she wasn't going to survive. She was anencephalic.'

'Oh, my God…' Max drained his glass. 'I'm so sorry. That must have been so hard to have had to choose a termination at a late stage like that.'

'But I didn't.' Emma's voice was little more than a whisper. 'That was the problem. Richard wanted to get rid of the problem as fast as possible but I chose to carry my baby until she was due to be born. Because of Tyler.'

The pain was still there, wasn't it? The sense of betrayal. That someone who'd said they loved her wasn't prepared to support her in a challenge that was always going to be heartbreaking but felt important enough to be something she had to do in order to be true to herself.

Max was still staring at her so she could see the moment that comprehension dawned. His jaw visibly dropped. 'You carried a baby that you knew could never survive so that she could be a donor for babies like Tyler?'

Emma nodded, blinking hard to make sure she didn't let any tears escape. 'I thought I knew what I was doing. That it wouldn't be as hard as it turned out to be. Losing my relationship because of my choice made it harder, but, in a way, that was probably a good thing because it became obvious that we were too different to ever be happy together.' Emma drew in a shaky breath. 'What broke my heart even more was that she was born on Christmas Day. She only lived for a few hours.' Emma had to swipe away a tear that she hadn't fought off. 'I called her Holly.'

Max said nothing. He got up and went to the sideboard to pour himself another drink from the cut glass decanter. He stood there looking down at the amber liquid as he swirled it in his glass for a long time before he looked up at Emma. It was a look that went straight to her heart and she could feel its intensity in every cell of her body. This wasn't sexual in any way. It was respect. Admiration. Something that felt as if it was wrapping the threads of the connection they already had in a material that was strong enough to be impermeable.

'You're amazing, Em,' he told her. 'You know that, don't you?'

Emma shrugged off what seemed to be an over-the-top compliment, even if it was one that made her feel truly proud of the choice she had made. 'If I hadn't known Tyler maybe I would have made different choices. I might still be a paediatrician instead of a locum. I might be married to Richard and have had three more children and be spending my Christmases in Italy so that they could play with all their cousins...'

But Max was shaking his head. 'I'm glad you didn't,' he said. 'If this Richard couldn't support your choice to do such an incredibly brave and selfless thing then he wasn't someone you would have wanted to spend the rest of your life with, believe me.'

Emma blinked. He thought she was brave? Selfless? Amazing, even...? Would *he* have supported that choice? She had the feeling that he would have and that sparked something that was even more powerful than any physical attraction she was aware of for Max Cunningham. Stronger than friendship, in fact. You could fall in love with a man who could support you to do the really difficult things in life.

More than a little shocked by the thought, Emma had to break any eye contact with Max. Fortunately, she had an excuse to move because she'd just noticed that the bow in the string of the star Ben had tried so hard to attach to the tree had come undone and the star was on the floor. She stooped to pick it up and reattach it.

'I can't imagine how hard that Christmas Day must have been for you,' Max said, moments later. 'I'm really sorry you had to go through that alone.'

His voice was unexpectedly close as Emma straightened up from tying the string, so she wasn't really surprised to find that Max had moved to come and stand beside her. Her body seemed to be startled, however, because it was waking up with an acute awareness of his proximity that was so powerful it was actually painful. More like a stabbing sensation than any pleasant tingle.

'I knew it was coming. I knew I'd be able to cope even though it was hard. And…there was a kind of joy to be found there, as well, knowing that other babies were going to get to go home because of what Holly could give them. One like Tyler, even, who got a heart that was going to work. And, later, I heard that her kidneys had been used…and her liver…'

Emma's voice trailed away. It was still such a bittersweet balance to think about, let alone say aloud. She cleared her throat. 'You've had Christmas Days that were just as tough,' she added. 'Losing your brother last year. Losing your mum when you were so young. That must have cast a shadow over every Christmas since then.'

'We just didn't do Christmas,' Max agreed. 'And that's why this is so hard for my dad.'

It wasn't just hard for James, though. This was just as hard for Max. A part of him had to be missing his mother all over again as he watched Ben and Tilly and Alice struggle to adapt to their new family. And was this year the first he'd ever put up a Christmas tree? Given the way he'd dismissed the whole seasonal celebration as 'commercial hype', she suspected that he had always avoided anything to do with trees or decorations. She also suspected that his avoidance had far more to do with grief than anything else. It gave them another connection but it felt different to her own experience of grief. Max's had started so long ago, when he was no more than a boy and, looking at it from the point of view of an outsider, Emma could see how sad it was. That a father and his sons had been so lost and there clearly hadn't been anyone to help them through their grief. They probably believed they could never change how they felt about Christmas, but how sad would it be if their aversion to celebrating was transferred to yet another generation?

Emma wished there was something she could do to help because this was a lot bigger than her own sadness that was associated with Christmas. This was all to do with three innocent children.

'Do you think he can cope?' she asked. She was referring to James but she held Max's gaze in the hope that he would realise she was asking about his own ability to manage an emotionally difficult situation.

'He'll have to,' Max said—and he could have been speaking for both his father and himself. 'The children are here to stay and…well…it would appear that there are rules when it comes to Christmas.'

Emma smiled. 'There are rules,' she said. 'And I expect Ben knows them all.'

Max was smiling back at her. A small smile that grew. And then grew a bit more.

'What?' she asked. 'What's funny?'

'Nothing,' Max said. 'I'm just pleased to see you smile. The last time I wanted to make that happen for you I had to kiss you.'

Emma could feel her own smile fading. The mention of that kiss again made the intense subject of their recent conversation start to fade instantly into the background and then it hung in the air between them.

Like a suggestion. As if they were both wondering what it would be like to do it again. As if they were both realising that perhaps they really *wanted* to do it again. They were standing so close together it wouldn't take much for one of them to move and if they held this eye contact any longer, that was what was going to happen.

One of them would move and then Max would bend his head or Emma would stand on her tiptoes and they wouldn't need any mistletoe because they didn't need any reason to kiss other than that they were two single adults who happened to be attracted to each other. Possibly seriously attracted…

In that split second of time, however, as the ghost of their first kiss pulled them together like the most powerful magnet imaginable, a sound broke the moment. A crackle of sound that was coming from the handset of the baby monitor as Alice woke and began to cry.

'I'd better go and get her.' But Max seemed reluctant to move.

Emma opened her mouth to offer to help but no words came out because her thoughts were moving so fast they were getting tangled. Warning bells were ringing very loudly as she remembered the moment earlier this evening when that old longing for her own family had resurfaced. She couldn't afford—and didn't want—to get any closer to these children herself than she already was. And what about that moment when she'd realised how easy it would be to fall in love with Max? That should be enough to send her running all on its own because what she remembered most about this man was that he was a playboy. He'd never had the slightest interest in a relationship that was anything more than fun. Short term fun.

But it wasn't just the three bereaved children upstairs that Emma was thinking about right now. It was the two small boys who had lost their own mother decades ago and whose father must have been too wrapped up in his own grief to be able to know what to do and the end result was that they didn't know how to 'do Christmas' any more. Somehow, they needed to get past the ghosts of past Christmas tragedies, but that might not be possible without help from someone who hadn't been a part of that past.

Someone like Emma, who could understand how difficult it was but could also see how important it was for the sake of the children. She could do that if she was brave enough. The safe thing to do would be to remove herself from this house—to stay away from any more reminders of what was missing from her own life and away from the increasing pull she was feeling towards Max, but if she didn't run away—if she stayed here and helped both the Cunningham men and the children—it could be the foundation for a new family to form and bond. For a new life to be possible.

That would be a real gift, wouldn't it?

Not totally dissimilar to the choice she'd made more than five years ago, to do something hard in order to make new life possible for others. Max thought she was amazing for doing that.

Maybe she wanted him to think she was still amazing?

Emma took a deep breath. 'You go and get Alice,' she told Max. 'I'll get a bottle ready for you but then I really need to have a shower and get some sleep. I've got another early start tomorrow.'

Max still hadn't quite moved. 'And tomorrow?' he asked quietly. 'Will you come back here after work and help us put some more decorations on our tree?'

Oh…the warmth in those eyes. A mix of the new trust between them that had grown considerably this evening, shared memories of the past and the remnants of a kiss that hadn't quite happened. And behind what was there between herself and Max, Emma was aware of the needs of others. Of three children who badly needed something special to make them feel safe. Of a sad older man who was still suffering because his memories of Christmas were too painful. What James needed, as well as Max, was to be able to trust in family enough to open their hearts again. Emma could understand exactly why they had shut themselves off but she could also see how much better life would be if they could let go of the past and embrace a new future. And, if she could help them do that, she would be helping herself at the same time. She hadn't actually celebrated Christmas in any meaningful way herself since the day Holly had been born and died.

Maybe fate had brought her here because it was time for a new start. For all of them. It hadn't really been a mistake to come back here today. The mistake would be to leave before they had all taken that new step forwards.

Emma didn't trust herself to say anything aloud, though. All she could manage was to nod before she headed for the kitchen to make up the bottle of formula for Alice, but it was a definitive answer to Max's question nonetheless.

She would be here again tomorrow. And the next day.

And Christmas Day.

This was definitely getting a little easier.

Yesterday, in this very room, Max had been trying to feed a baby who wanted nothing to do with him. Now, he was sitting in his father's favourite chair, holding a baby who was almost asleep again before she'd got halfway through her bottle of milk. He should probably take her back upstairs and put her in her cot but he didn't want to move again just yet.

The shape of Alice in his arms was already becoming familiar. The smell of her, as well, as Max bowed his head to get closer to that small head cradled in the crook of his elbow. Imagine holding a baby like this, he thought—your own baby that you'd just given birth to—knowing that, in a blink of time, she would be taken away from you for ever. Max had been totally blown away by hearing Emma's story and his respect for her had gone completely off the scale. He'd never met a woman like her. He'd never met *anyone* like Emma Moretti, in fact.

He could understand now that it really had been fear he'd seen in her eyes the other night when Emma had come into the room to see him holding a miserable, hungry baby that he couldn't cope with. And what had he done? Simply shoved Alice into her arms, that was what, and he felt awful about that now. He wanted to gather Emma into his arms and tell her how sorry he was. Not just for forcing her to take Alice but for everything that had happened to her in the years since they'd gone on separate paths. For the grief she must have gone through. For the broken relationship, although he was quite confident that that Richard had not been good enough for Emma.

She was someone incredibly special. Astonishingly attractive, for that matter. He'd almost *kissed* her again, for heaven's sake. How had that happened in the wake of listening to her tragic story? And why had he longed to do it even more than the first time when all he'd wanted to do was to see that gorgeous smile appear again?

The reminder of that Christmas party made Max wonder if dealing with the aftermath of the grief of losing her baby Holly had contributed to her walking away from the career she had chosen because she loved children and babies so much? She was clearly very good at her locum work, fitting in instantly to new environments and being able to function brilliantly, but it didn't feel like the right fit for someone like Emma. In some ways, she reminded Max of his own mother—someone so clever and capable, with so much love to give the people lucky enough to be within her immediate circle.

It was weird that, even after decades, it was possible to feel a beat of that loss all over again, but it was muted enough that Max could easily refocus his thoughts. Emma was flitting from one job to another now, avoiding commitment to anything. To anyone? Did Christmas Day bring her any joy or was it only filled with unbearably sad memories?

He could understand that.

But…she'd said she was going to come back after work tomorrow and help with some more decorations. That she would stay until Christmas day, in fact. What if…?

Max gently removed the teat from Alice's now slack little rosebud of a mouth but he paused for a long moment before putting the bottle on the table beside him.

What if he could somehow make this Christmas something joyous for Emma? A time when she could smile and enjoy being with children and babies—a family, even? That might help her to take a step forward into a future that she really deserved, where grief could be outweighed by joy. Where sadness could be dimmed by the kind of light that laughter and love could create.

It wouldn't just help Emma. How good would it be for his father? For himself, perhaps, as well. It might not be easy but look at the way he and Emma had worked together today. If he could get her on board, by making it all about the children—or perhaps his father—they could help each other get past any personal issues. He could bury his distaste for the commercial hype of the season and hopefully Emma would get a glimpse of a future where she could see herself celebrating the family bonds that she believed Christmas was all about. A future that she could embrace with no restrictions or fear.

Not being at work meant that Max would have plenty of time to remember the way his mother had made the house come alive at Christmas time. He could go shopping— online, if necessary—to find gifts he could wrap up to go under the tree. He could ask Maggie to do a bit of Christmas baking so that the house would be filled with those delicious aromas he had a faint memory of. He could go up into the dusty attics of this house and drag out those dozens of boxes that contained miles of fairy lights and candles and every kind of decoration you could imagine.

Max looked down at the baby in his arms. He touched her cheek with his forefinger with the softest stroke.

'That's what I'm going to do,' he told Alice. 'For your big brother and sister. For my dad. For Emma. And don't worry, we'll take lots of photos so that it won't matter that you're not old enough to remember your first Christmas and it might be a good thing. This will be kind of a practice run and we'll be really good at it by the time you are old enough to remember.'

He got slowly to his feet, so as not to wake Alice, and carried her upstairs to her cot. It felt good that she was comforted enough to sleep again. It felt good to pass the door of the room not so far from his where he knew Emma would be tucked up in her bed and possibly also asleep.

And it felt really good that he had a mission for the next few days that might help Emma. And his father. Max had always worked hard and played hard. This mission was neither work nor play but the effort he was going to put into it was going to be a hundred and one per cent.

Because it mattered to everybody in this house and Max wanted to protect them all and give them the gift of joy. It might be focused only on one special day for now but it was a beginning and he was determined to make it the best one possible. For everyone, including Emma.

Maybe—given what he'd learned about her today— *especially* for Emma.

CHAPTER SEVEN

LOOPING HER STETHOSCOPE around her neck as she walked into the emergency department of the Royal early the next morning, Emma's steps slowed and almost stopped. Okay, it was Christmas Eve tomorrow, but what the heck were so many people doing in here wearing Santa suits? There had to be about ten of them—a sea of red and white in the cubicle area for injured or ill patients that weren't serious enough to need to be in one of the re-suscitation rooms.

Senior nurse Miriam was trying to keep a straight face. 'Seems like it was rather a good Christmas party,' she told Emma. 'There were too many people dancing on the table and a leg broke.'

Emma's eyebrows rose. 'A table leg or a person's leg?'

Miriam's smile escaped. 'The table, but there is a guy with an ankle injury, a woman with a possibly fractured wrist and quite a few bumps and bruises. The others are their partners or colleagues so we couldn't tell them to go away.'

'Who needs to be seen first?'

'Ankle Santa, I think. He's the boss. He's also rather drunk so he might be injured more than he realises.'

The middle-aged man was still wearing his red hat

with white fur trim. Having glanced at the chart on the end of his bed that told her his vital signs were all within normal limits, Emma introduced herself and then asked how he was feeling.

'Never better,' he told her. 'It was the best party ever. Gonna need a new table in the boardroom, though.'

Several Santas, including one that called from the next cubicle, seemed to be in agreement that it had been a memorable party.

'It must have been good,' Emma agreed, 'if it went on till nearly dawn.'

'Oh, I don't think it's finished yet.' A woman wearing a red dress with white trimming and a headband with a small red hat in the middle was holding her arm cradled against her chest, which suggested she was the patient with the wrist injury. 'There was a new case of prosecco being opened when our taxis arrived to bring us here.'

'Hmm…' Emma was already assessing the ankle injury of the man lying on the bed. It was certainly swollen enough to be either a serious sprain or a fracture but his toes were a good colour and she could feel a peripheral pulse on the top of the foot. 'Can you try and wriggle your toes for me, please?'

She watched the movement and heard the groan that told her it was causing pain but Emma was not quite as focused as she would normally have been. It wasn't just being surrounded by an unusual number of people dressed like Father Christmas who were all inebriated to some extent. It was more the mention of the Italian bubbly they'd been drinking, in combination with knowing that it had been a Christmas party. Because it immediately made her think of *that* particular party. That particular kiss.

The kiss that had very nearly happened again last night.

How much she had wanted it to happen had been the reason she'd left Max to cope alone with feeding Alice and why she'd slipped out of the house early this morning before anyone else was up. Things were complicated enough in the Cunningham household without letting a sexual attraction get out of hand. Emma wanted to help weld the new family of James, Max and the children together but, at some point in her almost sleepless night, she had decided that even the casual type of relationship that Max Cunningham was famous for would only be a distraction from what he needed to be focused on—the children—so her mission needed to be to keep him on task. If that wasn't exactly what she wanted, she was prepared to deal with it for the sake of everybody else involved.

She needed to keep herself on task as well.

'Have you ever injured this ankle before?'

'Nope. Mind you, I've never done the floss dance before, either.'

'You were really good at it.' A much younger Santa poked his head around the curtain. 'I'm still trying to figure it out.' He straightened his arms and held them out, staring at them as if he was trying to decide which one to move.

'Move your hips first,' someone called. 'Get the rhythm.'

'Uh-uh…' The firm voice belonged to Miriam. 'No dancing in here, folks. If you're well enough to dance, you need to go out to the waiting room. We've got sick people in here.' She tilted her head in Emma's direction. 'You need any help, Dr Moretti?'

Emma shook her head. 'But call me if anything major comes in.'

'I'm major,' her patient told her. 'Don't leave me, darlin'.'

'Do you have any medical conditions I should be aware of? Heart disease or high blood pressure? Diabetes or lung problems?'

'Nah. I'm as fit as a fiddle. Or I will be. I've asked Santa for a gym subscription this year. In fact, I think I asked several Santas.'

A ripple of laughter came from adjoining cubicles. 'Wasn't me,' someone called.

'I don't remember being asked,' someone else shouted. 'But I can't remember much at all right now, come to think of it.'

Emma was examining the ankle more closely. She put her hand under the foot near the toes. 'Can you push your foot against my hand, please?' She shifted her hand to the top of the foot next. 'Pull up against it, now?'

'Ouch.'

'I don't think it's broken,' Emma told him a short time later. 'But we'll send you off for an X-ray just to be on the safe side.'

The woman with the wrist injury was also sent to X-ray, but the other injuries were deemed minor and the crowd of red and white patients gradually dispersed, some beginning to complain of headaches and feeling rather unwell.

'Christmas parties,' Miriam muttered, shaking her head. 'More trouble than they're worth most of the time.'

'Mmm.' Emma needed to stop thinking about Christmas parties.

About Max and being thoroughly kissed by him.

Her next patient, coming in by ambulance already intubated and being ventilated after what appeared to be a serious stroke, was more than enough to give Emma complete focus on her job and that continued for the rest of her shift, with one case after another that required rapid assessment and treatment to stabilise them. There was an elderly man with septic shock, a drug overdose, pulmonary embolism, two heart attacks and a ten-year-old child with a severe asthma attack who needed transferring to the intensive care unit for close monitoring when she was finally out of immediate danger.

Emma was still thinking about that last case as she drove back to Upper Barnsley. The child's mother had burst into tears when told that the worst seemed to be over.

'She'd just been writing a reminder list for Father Christmas,' she sobbed. 'And I was feeling so smug because I've already got everything hidden away but…but I've just had an hour to wonder what it would have been like if they'd never been unwrapped…'

Those gifts would get unwrapped and that made it a good note on which to have finished her day. It had also reminded Emma that Max had asked her to find out what Ben and Tilly might have asked to receive for a special Christmas gift. Maybe when she got home she could help them write a list to put up the chimney. She was all ready to suggest this to Max the minute she walked through the door, but she didn't get a chance to say anything.

'Come with me.' It looked as if he'd been waiting for her to get home. 'We haven't got long.'

He grabbed Emma by the hand and started to head upstairs. Towards the bedrooms? Emma thought about tugging her hand free and trying to find out what was going on, but the warmth of Max's hand around hers and the determination of his forward movement was irresistible and all Emma could actually think about was that she'd probably go anywhere with this man if he wanted her to—even to a totally unknown destination. It was exciting. Thrilling, even. Especially the feeling of his skin against hers as they hurried upstairs. Her resolution to stay away from any intimate involvement with him seemed to be fading rapidly as the heat and feeling of strength in the hand holding hers made her curl her fingers tighter to make sure the connection wouldn't be lost.

They went past the bedrooms, into another hallway Emma hadn't seen before, with old portraits hanging on the walls, and then up a smaller staircase.

'The servants' quarters were up here long before my family moved in,' Max told her. 'It's where we used to hide when we were kids, Andy and me.'

'Is that what we're doing? Playing hide and seek with Ben and Tilly?'

'No.' They were up the small staircase now and leaving footprints on dust-covered floorboards. 'They're in the kitchen with Maggie and her daughter Ruth. Ruth's just gone on maternity leave from her job as an infant school teacher and she's brilliant with the kids. They're icing Christmas cookies at the moment. Alice is asleep. Dad's out on a house call. It's the first chance I've had all day to do this.' He stopped to peer up yet another staircase that was steep and narrow enough to be more like a ladder. Then he grinned at Emma. 'The main attic's up here,' he added, letting go of her hand as he started to climb. 'And there should be enough Christmas decorations to sink a battleship, if they haven't been eaten by mice or something. I need some help getting them downstairs but I didn't want Ben trying to get up and down these stairs. And I didn't want Dad to know what I was doing because he would have tried to stop me. He won't like it but if we can start putting them up I figured he would see how much fun it is for the kids and…and…'

'He won't want to disappoint them.' Emma nodded as she followed Max up the narrow stairs. 'A bit of emotional blackmail, huh? Well, it certainly worked on me.'

'What? When?' Max sounded appalled.

'When you reminded me about telling the children I'd show them how to make stars. Or getting them to remind me…'

'Oh…' Max disappeared through the hole in the ceiling and then turned to offer his hand to help Emma as she reached the final stairs. Having been holding it so recently, it felt completely natural to take it again, allowing him to pull her into the attic space. He was still smiling as he tugged her forward.

'Do you forgive me?' he asked. 'For emotionally blackmailing you?'

'It was for a good cause.' Emma realised that if she kept that forward momentum going she would end up bumping into Max's body. He'd probably put his hands on her shoulders to steady her and it might very well be an opportunity to pick up where they'd left off last night. To step back into that 'pre-kiss' moment if she wanted to.

She did want to. Very much. But, at the same time, it was making her nervous. Emma put the brakes on that forward movement unconsciously and, for a heartbeat, she stood completely still. She was now aware of the faint light coming from dormer windows in this highest level of the house. It was crowded with boxes and furniture and any amount of objects and it smelled musty and secretive. Even without kissing Max, it was still exciting because she'd never been in a real, storybook kind of attic before and they were here together and... and, well...

It was fun. And how long was it since Emma had done anything just for the sheer enjoyment of it?

'Look...there's one.' Max let go of Emma's hand to open a box. 'It's the fake greenery,' he exclaimed, moments later. 'I remember that Mum used to wind it through the bannister posts on the main stairs. And this one...' He pulled open another box. 'It's fairy lights. We need fairy lights on our tree, don't we?'

'Absolutely.' Emma was reaching for another box on the stack. This one was full of objects wrapped in tissue paper. 'Decorations,' she exclaimed. 'Oh, look... it's fruit. Little silver and gold apples and pears. And red cherries.'

'Don't open them yet.' Max caught her hand as she delved further into the box. 'Let's take them downstairs and the kids can help us.'

The touch of his hand, yet again, was more than enough to stop Emma. Turning her head, she found she was just as close to Max as they'd been last night beside the Christmas tree when she had been sure they would have ended up kissing if Alice's cry hadn't interrupted the moment. There was no baby's cry happening right now and they were possibly in the most secret part of this huge old house but, as Emma's gaze locked with Max's, she knew that they weren't about to steal a kiss. It felt as if they were making a kind of silent pact in this moment. That this was about the children and they were equal partners on the same team. Which was pretty much the conclusion Emma had reached last night, however tempting it might be to explore this unexpected revival of a seemingly mutual attraction between herself and Max. And it would appear that Max had decided the same thing.

She shouldn't be disappointed, Emma told herself firmly. She wasn't. Not really…

If she told herself that often enough, maybe she would actually believe it.

Oh, man…

He wanted to kiss Emma so much. Had she noticed that he couldn't seem to stop himself touching her? She'd been perfectly capable of climbing those stairs or getting up into the attic all by herself and here he was, holding her hand again, under the pretext of stopping her unwrapping any more decorations.

And the way she was looking at him. As if she wanted him to kiss her?

Well, he couldn't and that was all there was to it. Giving in to the temptation was the way the old Max would have responded. The one who was happy to play with any number of beautiful women. To love them and leave them and give himself a reputation that he was, finally, rather ashamed of. He had far more important responsibilities now and, besides, he respected Emma far too much to think that she might be happy to indulge in a casual affair.

She seemed perfectly happy to play Christmas decorations with him, however. Together, they ferried box after box downstairs and, as Max had been hoping, Ben and Tilly were so excited about what was inside all the boxes that they were almost unrecognisable compared to the silent, scared children who'd been sitting on the couch in the drawing room only a few evenings ago.

Maggie and her pregnant daughter Ruth were staying on to help—as curious as the children about what was being unearthed from decades of storage. Alice lay, still sleeping, in her pram near the couch as they spread out the boxes and opened them all.

'Look at these cute bunches of bells.' Ruth held up a trio of tiny golden bells, tied together with a loop of red ribbon.

'They went on the doors,' Max told her. 'So they would jingle every time someone went in or out of a room. And that really big wreath? That's for the front door.'

'There are so many candles.' Maggie had opened another box. 'And what's this? A tablecloth? And Christmas serviettes?'

'I don't think we'll need them,' Max said. 'I'm not sure I'd know where to start making a Christmas dinner.'

Maggie and her daughter shared a glance. 'Perhaps we could help,' she said. 'It was only going to be me and Ruth at our house and we've got a turkey that's far too big for just the two of us. We could come here and do dinner for everybody if you like.'

'What do you think, Ben?' Max asked. 'Are there rules about Christmas dinner?'

Ben nodded. 'Pigs in blankets,' he said. 'And red jelly for pudding.'

Maggie laughed. 'I think we could manage that.' She looked at Emma. 'You'll be here for dinner, I hope?'

'It sounds great,' Emma said. 'I'm covering a night shift on Christmas Eve so I'll definitely be back in time for dinner.'

Max wound a long string of fairy lights all over the tree in the drawing room but told Ben and Tilly to stand back while he plugged them in and turned the switch on. 'I'm not quite sure what's going to happen,' he told them. 'These lights haven't been used for a very long time.'

'Why not?' Ben asked.

'Because they were my mum's—your grandma's—special Christmas things and…well, she died and we were very sad so we never used them again.'

'Why not?' Ben was frowning. 'You've got to have lights on your Christmas tree. It's a—'

'—rule. I know.' Max flicked the switch and the lights came to life, making the tree sparkle as they flashed on and off sequentially. Instead of having bulbs that didn't work any more, or wires that caught fire because they had deteriorated over the years, it looked as if these decorative lights were as good as new. Max decided he was going to take that as a good omen. That everything was going to work and sparkle with a bit of Christmas magic.

'My mummy's died too.' Tilly's bottom lip was wobbling. 'And *I'm* sad.'

'I know, sweetheart.' From the corner of his eye, Max saw Emma start to reach out to Tilly but then he saw the way she stopped herself—the way her hands curled into soft fists—as if she was just too afraid to let herself follow her natural instinct to comfort this small girl. So he was the one who went to Tilly to scoop her up and cuddle her. He resisted the urge to draw Emma into the hug as well. If he tried to force her to open her heart to these children she might change her mind about staying to share Christmas with them and run away. He could only hope that some of that sparkly Christmas magic would wrap itself around Emma and she could find the courage to step past the perfectly understandable fear she had and that, by doing so, she would see what a new future could offer her.

'Can you help me?' he asked Tilly. 'You could unwrap all the ornaments in that box and then we can all hang them on the tree.'

'There's this green stuff too,' Emma said, pulling at loops of the long, thin length of artificial foliage of ivy, mistletoe and holly with red berries. 'I could go and put that on the bannisters, perhaps? And hang the bells on the doors?'

If it was time away from the children that she needed, it wasn't going to work. Ben's eyes widened as he saw the impressive amount of greenery appearing.

'I want to help,' he said.

'Me too.' Tilly wriggled out of Max's arms. 'I like bells *and* stars.'

She was almost running in her haste to get closer to Emma when it happened. The doorframe of the drawing room was filled with the tall figure of James Cunningham and the furious vibe radiated from him with the speed of light.

'What the *hell* is going on here?' he roared. 'Where did you get those boxes?'

'From the attic, Dad.' Max kept his tone carefully neutral. 'We needed more decorations for the tree.'

But his words could barely be heard over the sound of children crying. The angry roar had made Ben cower behind Emma's legs, still holding one end of a garland of greenery. Tilly had burst into tears and even Alice had woken in her pram and started howling. Maggie and Ruth both moved towards the baby. He saw the way Emma instinctively stretched out her arms as if creating a safe circle for the two children close to her. She was glaring at his father, as well, looking both horrified and angry that he was scaring everybody.

Max was angry too, even though part of his heart was breaking for his dad. He'd known his father would be upset at having his wife's precious decorations appear again with no prior warning but it wasn't fair to take it out on the children like this. Even Pirate was looking worried, slinking away from James to hide beneath one of the chairs.

'You've got no right.' James's voice was still loud enough to qualify as shouting. 'Put them back. Ben... put that down. Right now.'

The garland slid instantly from Ben's hands.

Max cleared his throat. 'If Mum was here, this is exactly what she'd be doing,' he told his father.

'I want *my* mummy,' Tilly sobbed, sinking into a puddle of miserable child on the floor. Ben came out from behind Emma and crouched to put his arms around his little sister. Pirate came out from beneath the chair and went slowly towards the children. He sat down close to Tilly and pressed his nose to the hands covering her eyes. Perhaps it was the surprise of seeing the little dog as she opened her eyes that made her stop crying.

Maggie was rocking baby Alice and successfully soothing her. Ruth had her hands protectively on the impressive bump of her belly and was staring nervously at her mother's employer. Max shifted his gaze to Emma to find she was staring straight back at him. If he'd had any doubts at all about her level of commitment to help him make this Christmas special for the children, they evaporated instantly. In the face of opposition she had just become as determined as he was to make this work

She was going to do whatever it took to protect these children, even if she had to do it alone, but she wanted his help. She needed him to be by her side and that made him feel remarkably fierce.

He would do whatever it took to protect Emma, as well as the children.

'It's what Mum would have wanted us to do, Dad,' he said firmly. 'You know that. You know how much she loved Christmas. How much she wanted everyone to be happy. I know it's been a very long time but we are going to have a proper Christmas in this house this year.'

James was staring at the boxes. At the huge wreath that Maggie had put to one side to take out to the front door. At the bunches of bells and the tissue-wrapped decorations.

'Oh…do what you want, then,' he snapped. 'You're obviously going to, anyway. I'm going out.' He snapped his fingers. 'Pirate…come with me…'

But Pirate didn't move. If anything, the little dog pressed itself closer to Tilly and Ben's hand moved to rest on the small white head. For a horrified moment, Max wondered if his father was about to march further into the room and drag his dog away from the children but James just stared for a moment longer, made a sound that was a frustrated growl and then turned on his heel and marched out of the room.

For a long, long moment, there was silence in the drawing room. It was broken by Ben's small voice.

'I don't think Grandpa likes Christmas,' he said.

Max walked over to his nephew and crouched down beside him. 'He used to,' he told Ben. 'It was the best day of the year for all of us when I was a little boy like you. He's just forgotten, that's all. But we can help him remember. He's not cross with you. He's just…'

'Sad.' Ben nodded. 'Because his mummy died.'

Max didn't bother trying to correct his interpretation of a former generation's relationships. 'It's always sad when someone you love dies,' he agreed. 'And it's okay to be sad but it's okay to have fun too. Why don't we all have fun now and see how pretty we can make everything with all these decorations? Do you think you and Tilly can pull that long rope of leaves and berries all the way up the stairs?'

Max caught Emma's anxious glance as the children headed for the door.

'It's all right,' he said. 'Dad will have gone out for a walk or something. He just needs time to get his head around this.'

Emma didn't look convinced.

'It's been a very long time,' Max added. 'I suspect he's healed far more than he even realises but he's never going to find out if that plaster doesn't get ripped off. Having a proper Christmas with his grandchildren might be the best thing that could ever happen for him.'

Emma was still frowning. 'As long as he doesn't hurt the children. Don't you think Ben's going to be a bit scared of him after that outburst?'

'Maybe.' Max was holding Emma's gaze. 'But I think he's going to be fine. Even the scary stuff isn't too bad as long as you've got someone on your side and Ben's got me. He's always going to have me.'

Would Emma pick up on the silent message that he was there for her as well? That she had him by her side as she faced what was probably her first real celebration of Christmas for a long time?

Maybe she had. There was a sparkle in her eyes that looked as if a tear or two was gathering.

'He's a lucky little boy,' she said quietly. 'And I think you're right. He's going to be fine.'

'He'll need help with that green stuff. Why don't I come and show you how Mum used to do it and then we can all do the decorations for the tree?'

It was much later that evening that Emma went down the stairs, admiring the greenery woven through the bannister railings, heading for the kitchen to get a glass of water. To her surprise, she found Max sitting at the kitchen table with his laptop open in front of him and the handset from the baby monitor to one side. James was also there, an empty plate in front of him that told Emma he'd eaten the meal they'd left in the oven when he hadn't come home in time for dinner.

'I owe you an apology too,' he said gruffly.

Emma nodded her acceptance. 'The children missed you at bedtime,' she told him. 'They wanted you to read them a story. Ben said that it might make you feel better because stories always make *him* feel better.'

James stared at her for a long moment. 'You always know the right thing to say, don't you, love? You're like my Hannah was, like that.' He got to his feet. 'I'm off to bed,' he said. 'But I'd better take Pirate out first. It's starting to snow and he doesn't like it when it gets too deep on the grass. Do you know where he is?'

'Lying beside Ben's bed,' Emma told him. 'I think he's decided it's his job to protect the children.'

'He's not the only one, is he?' James put his plate in the sink. 'It's okay... Now that I'm over the shock, I know I was wrong and I'll tell the children that tomorrow. It's time for Christmas to happen again here. Time for a new beginning.' He smiled at Emma. 'Maybe I should write my Christmas wish on a bit of paper too, and you could put it up the chimney. Max told me about you doing that for the children this evening.'

'It's what I'm working on now,' Max put in. 'Seeing if I can find exactly what they want online and get it delivered secretly tomorrow.'

'Didn't Ben say he wanted a blue bicycle?' Emma reminded him. 'That might be a bit hard to keep secret.'

'There's some rooms that aren't being used above the clinic. Extra bedrooms and a bathroom or two. It could make a good suite for live-in help for a housekeeper or nanny later, maybe. In the meantime, it'll be easy to get things delivered out of sight and hide them in there, wrap them up tomorrow night and put them under the tree for Christmas morning.'

James was heading for the door. 'Don't forget the stockings.' His voice was a growl. 'The ones your mum always hung up above the fireplace. They must be in one of those boxes.'

Max waited until his father had left the room. 'He's trying hard,' he said quietly. 'It's not easy.'

'I know. For you too.' Emma had been watching Max as they'd decorated the tree earlier. She'd seen the way he'd held some of those decorations so reverently— like the gorgeous glass angels and wooden gingerbread men—as if he was remembering the last time he'd done this, when his mother had been there as well, and her heart had ached for that little boy who must have dreaded Christmas for so many years afterwards.

She pulled up a chair to sit close beside him so that

she could see the screen of his laptop. 'How are you going on finding things?'

'Not bad. Derby's has a great toy department. I've found a bicycle for Ben and a football and a tent.'

'A tent?'

'It was something that Andy and I used to do—put a tent up in the woods and pretend we were miles from anywhere. I thought Ben might like to try that.'

'It's a great idea.'

'I'm not sure what Tilly meant by "fairy stuff", though.'

'Oh… I can help with that.' Emma leaned closer so that she could use the mouse and scroll through the available items. 'Look…a tutu, wand, tiara and wings all in a set. There's even a pot of fairy dust, which is probably glitter and will make an awful mess. That's what "fairy stuff" is all about.'

Emma looked up, her smile full of the delight of imagining the look on Tilly's face when she discovered exactly what Emma had helped her write on her scrap of paper that had gone up the chimney. She hadn't realised just how close she'd got to Max as she leaned over the laptop, however. And she hadn't expected him to be grinning down at her, as pleased as she was to have found the perfect gift.

And there it was.

That moment again, as their gazes locked and their smiles faded as they both found they couldn't look away from each other. That the magnetic pull was simply too powerful to resist.

'Thanks.' Max's voice was a little hoarse. A deep, sexy growl. 'I wouldn't be managing this if I didn't have you to help.'

'Oh…it's my pleasure.' Emma's voice was more like a whisper and her last word was the one that tipped the balance of control. *Pleasure*… It hung there between them and she knew that Max was thinking exactly the same as what was going through her own head. That real pleasure was also hanging there, just waiting for one of them to make the first move.

Maybe both of them did, because a split second later their lips were touching. So softly at first that Emma had to close her eyes so that she could feel it properly. And then she felt the movement of Max's lips on hers and her own lips parting. The kiss wasn't so soft now but it was when she was aware of the touch of his tongue on her lip before meeting the tip of her own tongue that Emma stopped even thinking about what was happening and fell into a forgotten sensation.

Sheer pleasure, that was for sure. So intense that nothing else existed. This was nothing like that public kiss under the mistletoe at that long-ago Christmas party. This was nothing like any kiss Emma had ever had in her life. She didn't want it to stop but the need for oxygen made it a necessity and her first breath was a gasp. She opened her eyes to find Max staring at her, looking as stunned as she was feeling.

Oh…*help*…

This wasn't supposed to have happened.

Emma braced herself for what was about to happen next. Laughter, perhaps, to dismiss the kiss as no big deal? The reassurance that she had nothing to worry about because she was 'so not' Max's type?

As he opened his mouth to say something, Emma closed her eyes so that she could hide her reaction to whatever he might be about to say.

CHAPTER EIGHT

MAX HAD NO idea what to say but felt the need to express appreciation for what had to have been the most memorable kiss of his lifetime and that was saying something, given how much practice he'd had.

There was something very different about Emma Moretti. It wasn't just the softness of her lips, or the incredible taste of her mouth, or the way she responded to him as if they were having a conversation in a language they were the only two people in the world who could speak. It was bigger than that. Because he'd come to realise that Emma was the most extraordinary woman he'd ever met and he had huge respect for her, professionally but even more on a personal level.

That she had chosen to go through such a traumatic experience as carrying a baby for months that was never going to survive only to help others was something he felt put Emma way out of his league in terms of humanity and kindness and the kind of virtues that nobody would associate with someone who had his kind of reputation with women. It made him feel curiously shy to even think that she might be interested in him but that kiss had just revealed that she was possibly just as attracted to him as he was to her. That she might, in fact, be just as desperate to take it a lot further than just a kiss.

Just a kiss?

Ha! The words that finally escaped Max's lips were not ones he normally used in public but he needed something very succinct and powerful to sum up his reaction. His words certainly startled Emma. Her eyes flew open and then widened in shock.

'I thought you were going to laugh,' she said. 'Not say…*that*…'

'Why on earth would I laugh?'

'That's what you did the last time you kissed me.'

'Did I?' Max searched his memory. 'No… I think it was *you* that laughed and I was pleased that you were looking happier again because that was what I wanted to happen.'

'You laughed first,' Emma insisted. 'And then you told me not to worry because I was so not your type.'

Oh…that was true. But not true at the same time. Even then he'd known precisely how attractive Emma Moretti was but she definitely wasn't his 'type' because she was dangerous. Or he was dangerous as far as she was concerned. She wanted such different things out of life and he would have ended up hurting her if he'd acted on that attraction. How ironic was it that he was the one who'd ended up with a bunch of kids and Emma was footloose and fancy free, roaming the world and perfectly entitled to work and play wherever and with whomever she chose.

Another thought that was a little disturbing was that if Emma had remembered his exact words after all this time, was it because he'd managed to hurt her anyway when he'd been trying to make sure he didn't? Max held Emma's gaze.

'No man in his right mind wouldn't have fancied you, Emma. I said that because I knew I wasn't *your* type. Maybe I wanted to say it before you did.'

'You weren't my type,' Emma agreed. There was a tiny smile tugging at one corner of her mouth. 'You were the "love 'em and leave 'em" bad boy of that group of registrars. But no woman in her right mind wouldn't have fancied you.'

Max found it suddenly rather difficult to swallow. Was she saying what he thought she might be saying? That she had fancied him? That she still did? He could find that out, he thought, if he kissed her again. If Emma wanted him to kiss her again. And, if she did, then he could scoop her up into his arms and take her…where… to his bedroom?

Where Alice lay sleeping in her cot?

His head turned to where the baby monitor handset was sitting beside his laptop. Emma had followed the direction of his gaze and he heard the sigh as she let her breath go. The reminder of the close proximity of three children was creating enough of a problem even theoretically. The small voice they both heard at the kitchen door a second later made it even more of a reality.

'Uncle Max?'

He turned swiftly. 'What is it, Ben?'

'I woke up.'

'I can see that, mate.' Max shut the lid of his laptop before Ben could see that he'd been surfing the toy department of Derby's. 'Did you have a bad dream?'

'Pirate's run away.'

'No, he hasn't.' Emma was smiling reassuringly at

Ben. 'Your grandpa just took him outside for a little walk. He'll be back any minute.'

Her gaze snagged Max's and it was another reminder of how difficult it was going to be to find time to be alone in the near future, if ever. It wasn't as if Emma was even going to be here for very long, either. Was he crazy to think that getting to know this amazing woman on a more intimate level was possible, let alone a sensible idea? It felt like Emma was thinking along the same lines. It also felt like she was reaching the same conclusions.

That it was no more crazy than this set of totally un-expected circumstances they had found themselves in, temporarily living together in this old house with or-phaned children, their grandfather and his dog and with a Christmas celebration to orchestrate when they'd both been avoiding doing something like that for many years. That they were both single adults and, if they wanted to, they could choose to indulge in a sexual attraction that wasn't going to hurt anybody else. And that the attrac-tion between them wasn't about to vanish any time soon and perhaps they both needed to find out if it could live up to its promise of being one of those experiences that you might only find once in a lifetime.

Not that they were about to get the chance to find that out right now. Max needed to get Ben settled back into his bed but, as he led his nephew out of the kitchen, the front door of the house opened and his father and Pirate came inside. He felt Ben's hand clutch his fingers more tightly but the brave little boy straightened as he stood beside Max, as if he was getting ready to be growled at again by his grandfather.

Emma had come out of the kitchen as well so, for a moment, they all stood there holding their breath. It was Pirate who broke the tension, trotting towards Ben with his tail wagging. Ben let go of his uncle's hand and dropped to cuddle the small white dog.

'I think Pirate wants to go back to bed,' James said into the silence that followed. 'Shall I come and tuck you both in?'

This silence was even more tense and Max let his breath out in a silent but very relieved sigh as, after staring at his grandfather for a long moment, Ben nodded solemnly and started walking towards him. He had almost reached him when there was a loud thumping on the door behind James.

'What the—?' James opened the door. *Jenny...?*

'Oh, Dr Cunningham—I'm so sorry to disturb you at this time of night but I saw you walking past. It's Terry. I think he really is having a heart attack this time...'

Both Max and Emma were moving towards the distressed woman. Emma reached for her coat on the rack near the door. 'I'll come,' she told Jenny. 'Have you called an ambulance?'

'Yes, but it's really snowing hard now and I'm not sure if they'll get through.'

Max didn't bother finding his coat. 'I'll get our first-aid pack from the clinic,' he told Emma. 'And the defibrillator. I'll meet you there in a minute.'

He turned back to find that his father was holding Ben's hand. 'Don't worry,' he told Max. 'I've got this. You go with Emma. I'll look after the children.'

'You sure?'

'Yes. Take your phone. I'll call if I need you. Go...'

Max must have run very fast, both to collect the equipment and then get down the long driveway, up the road and into the neighbouring property so quickly. Emma had only had minutes to start assessing Terry.

'The pain came on about twenty minutes ago,' she told Max. 'Central chest pain, radiating to his left arm. Ten out of ten, with vomiting and profuse sweating. Unrelieved by his spray. Radial pulse palpable but faint.'

They were classic symptoms of a heart attack and nothing like the pain he had presented with after his muscle strain the other day. He also had other symptoms that made it far less likely to be anything muscular. Max opened pouches on the defibrillator pack and began unrolling wires and snapping electrodes onto their ends.

'There's an IV roll in the pack,' he told Emma. 'And a small oxygen tank in the side pocket.'

'Onto it.' Emma put a reassuring hand on Terry's shoulder. 'Max is going to do what I did the other day and put the electrodes on your chest so we can see what's going on with your heart. I'm going to give you some oxygen and put a small cannula in a vein on your arm so that we can give you something for the pain. We're going to give you some fluid through that line as well, to help your blood pressure. Is that all okay with you?'

Terry nodded. He was looking terrified. So was his wife.

'Do whatever you need to,' Jenny whispered. 'Please...'

Emma opened the IV roll and found everything she needed to put an IV line in. There was a separate pouch that contained drugs in both ampoules and packets. She popped a tablet from its foil strip.

'I'll get you to chew this up for me first,' she told Terry. 'It's an aspirin tablet. Jenny, maybe you could get a sip of water to help it go down?'

Jenny looked relieved to be given a helpful task.

Emma focused on gaining access to a vein on the back of Terry's hand with a needle and then sliding the plastic cannula into place and taping it down securely. Max was working around her, sticking electrodes to Terry's shoulders and each side of his abdomen and then in a pattern across his chest and around his heart. They were working together, as smoothly as they had the day they had been treating the victims of that multi-car pile-up outside the Royal, but it felt different now. The professional trust they already had was coloured by a far more personal connection. Not that either of them would have been giving that kiss a moment's head space but it was there, somewhere in the background, and it had brought them a whole lot closer.

'Are you allergic to any medications?' Emma asked.

'No…' Terry's voice was slightly muffled behind the oxygen mask that was now in place.

'Is the pain still ten out of ten?'

Terry closed his eyes as he nodded. Jenny was hunched over the back of the chair her husband was slumped in, one hand pressed against her mouth, the other stroking Terry's head.

'I'm going to give you some morphine,' Emma told him. 'As well as something else to stop you feeling sick. You should notice a difference in the pain very soon.'

'And I need you to keep as still as possible, Terry,' Max said. 'I'm going to take a recording of your heart now.'

He looked up to catch Emma's gaze as the graph paper began to spill out of the monitor. He knew she had seen the big picture of what was going on already on the screen and that Terry was, indeed, having a heart attack.

'ST elevation leads two, three and aVF,' Max confirmed as he showed Emma the printout. 'T wave changes starting.'

'Inferior infarct,' Emma agreed quietly. Heart attacks in this region had a better prognosis than other regions but it was still time critical to get Terry to hospital for the definitive treatment that would reopen his coronary arteries.

'I'll ring the hospital,' Max offered. 'They can get the catheter lab team on standby for angioplasty.'

'Can you find out how far away the ambulance is?' Emma asked. 'And do they have transmission ability so we can send the twelve-lead ECG through first?'

Max nodded. 'Yes, and yes.'

Emma turned back to their patient. 'How's the pain now, Terry?'

'Better.'

'On the scale of zero to ten?'

'Maybe five.'

'That's great. I'm going to take your blood pressure and a few other measurements now. Try and relax. We're going to get you to hospital very soon.'

'So he is really having a heart attack this time?'

'It looks like it, Jenny. But try not to worry too much, okay? The treatment of angioplasty will stop the damage that's happening. You did exactly the right thing in calling the ambulance and then coming to find us so quickly, which meant we could start the treatment faster.'

'Ambulance is only a few minutes away,' Max reported as Emma wrote down the set of vital signs she had just taken. 'Apparently the road's not too bad with the snow yet and the call's gone out to the cath lab. They're expecting Terry in Emergency as well.'

'Jenny? Could you go and pack a bag for Terry? Just

his pyjamas and toothbrush and things he might need for a day or two in hospital?'

Again, Jenny seemed grateful for something useful she could do and she had accomplished her task by the time the paramedics arrived with a dusting of snow on their shoulders and a cheerful ambience that was immediately reassuring.

'How lucky are you to have doctors living next door?' they said to Terry. 'Looks like they've done all the hard work for us too. We just need to put you on our comfy stretcher, change you over to our monitor and oxygen and we'll be at the hospital in no time at all.'

'Can I come with him?' Jenny asked anxiously.

'Of course you can, love.'

'I can come as well.' Emma picked up her coat from where it had been thrown over the back of a couch.

'No need, Doc. You've done everything already and all we need to do is keep a close eye on Terry here until we get him into the Royal.'

They both knew that the only real danger was that Terry could go into a cardiac arrest en route but it seemed unlikely given how stable his cardiac rhythm was looking despite the changes happening with the heart attack and they were going to get Terry into the safety of the emergency department as soon as possible. They were already rolling the stretcher towards the door. These paramedics were just as capable as Emma of dealing with a cardiac arrest and, if she went in with the ambulance, how would she get home again?

Max was winding up the wires for the defibrillator. 'You go with Terry,' he told Jenny. 'We'll tidy up the mess we've made and then lock up. I'll leave the key in the usual place, yes?'

'Oh…thank you, Max. I can't tell you how grateful we are… You and your dad… Well, we're just blessed to have you in Upper Barnsley, that's what…'

'I'll call the hospital in a bit to find out what's happening.' Max had paused in his task to smile at Jenny. 'He's going to exactly where he needs to be,' he said gently. 'Try not to worry.'

Emma went with Jenny to see her climb into the front passenger seat of the ambulance, which had its lights flashing in the drift of snowflakes as it drove away. She went back inside to help Max tidy up, picking up packaging from the IV supplies and the plastic squares that had come off the ECG electrodes. He was rolling up the IV kit and slotting it back into place in the first-aid pack.

It was only then that Emma realised they were alone again for the first time since they had shared that astonishing kiss.

Since Max had pretty much admitted that he'd always fancied her. Since she had told him pretty much the same thing.

The silence was suddenly a little awkward.

'It's really snowing out there,' Emma finally said. 'I might have to put chains on my car to get into work in the morning.'

'They'll clear the roads fast.' Max zipped up the pocket that held the small oxygen tank in the kit.

'Should I have gone in with Terry, do you think?'

'He didn't need you.' Max's tone was reassuring. 'I know those paramedics and they're great. He'll be safely in the cath lab within an hour and I reckon he's going to be fine. It might muck up their Christmas plans but Terry will probably end up being a lot healthier than he's been for a long time.' He stood up. 'Besides… I need you.' He offered her the ghost of a wink. 'There's too much gear to carry.'

Emma's heart skipped a beat but her mouth was suddenly too dry to supply the obvious comment that he had managed to carry everything here by himself not so long ago. The look he was giving her was intense enough to make her quite sure that Max was not referring to any help with returning the clinic's gear. No… That look had made it feel as if Max was thinking about that kiss again. About what it might be like to do it again. To take it wherever it might lead—and they both knew exactly where that was. They were also about to head to a part of that huge house that was well away from the children and any threat of interruption. If Emma wanted to reinstate her resolution not to distract Max from his new responsibilities as a father figure by making herself available, this was quite probably her last chance.

But would it be such a bad thing if they both gave in to the simmering attraction that was on the point of boiling over? It wasn't as if it was going to change anything. In less than a couple of weeks, Emma could be almost anywhere in the world taking up a new locum position. She might never see Max again. How weird was this, that she was talking herself into being with a man she had steered well clear of years ago because he lived his life thinking along those same lines—that it was perfectly acceptable to give in to physical desire with no intention of it ever being anything more than that?

And if she didn't, Emma might never know if what she was imagining was true. That Max Cunningham could give her a night that she would remember for the rest of her life.

'I'll take the kit,' she said, turning away because if

she kept eye contact with Max it might make her so nervous she would change her mind. 'It looks lighter than the defibrillator.'

They walked past the front door of the main part of the house.

'Looks like it's all quiet on the western front,' Max said.

It was a bit of a relief for Emma to find something new to talk about. They had already exhausted how thickly the snow was falling and whether Terry might already be out of the emergency department at the Royal and on his way to the catheter laboratory.

'I thought the clinic rooms were in the west wing. And they're around the corner.'

'True. But it wouldn't sound right saying it looks like it's all quiet on the southern front, would it?'

They turned the corner of the house. There were downstairs lights still on so it was easy enough to see where they were going. Emma could also see snow gathering on the ivy that scrambled over the old stones and even a curl of smoke coming from one of the many chimneys.

'It's a gorgeous house,' she said aloud. 'What a magic place to have grown up in.'

'It was,' Max agreed. 'But it was never the same after Mum died. I was glad to get away when I went to med school, to tell the truth. There were sad shadows everywhere and I don't think any of us knew how to shine a light to get rid of them. Andy got the closest. He set out to create a family of his own. To celebrate Christmas again.' Max shook his head as he opened the door of Upper Barnsley's general practice. 'That gave us a whole new level of sad stuff, what with the failure of his marriage and then his death and now three kids who are going to grow up without any parents.'

'They've got you.' Emma put the first-aid pack down in a corner of the waiting room. 'And I think they've got their grandpa now, as well. Did you see the way he was holding hands with Ben when we left the house? The way Pirate was right beside them? He's given them a bond, that little dog.'

'I think you might be right.' Max put the defibrillator back where it belonged on the bench. 'I hope so, anyway. I was old enough to help take care of Andy when Mum died but these kids really need him and that might well be enough to bring him out of his shell. He's been hiding for far too long.'

Emma opened her mouth. She had been about to say that James wasn't the only one who'd been hiding. That maybe Max himself needed to learn to trust in love again—enough to be able to commit to making that love a significant part of his life. That loving his nieces and nephew would be a very good place to start.

But that was something he needed to discover for himself, wasn't it?

'It's not easy,' she said, instead. 'Letting anybody into your heart when you know how hard it is to lose a person you care about that much. I think your mum must have been a wonderful person. She certainly loved Christmas. I can't believe how many decorations we've put out today.'

'You know what?' Max was smiling at Emma. 'I love seeing them out again. There are happy memories to be found now and they're even stronger than the sad ones. We kept the smallest decorations that we could find and put them on that little tree that Ben was carrying with him when he arrived. I put it in their bedroom.'

Emma's smile was meant to be encouraging but she knew it was wobbling a bit. 'That was a sweet thing to do. That tree was special.'

'I want to remember what Christmas used to be like when I was a kid,' Max added. 'I want Ben and Tilly to feel like that too. And Alice, when she's old enough. I want to get that blue bike for Ben and have it waiting under the Christmas tree for him so that he comes down and just knows that the magic is real. That Father Christmas is real and got his letter—the way I did when I got my first bike.'

Emma's smile felt even more wobbly, now. Maybe Max was already well on the way to opening his heart again. It was quite possible that he didn't trust the idea of marriage after his father was so devastated by his wife's death and then his brother by his broken marriage, but if he changed his mind he wouldn't have any trouble finding someone who would want to love him back. Someone who could end up being a mother to those three children and give him the kind of family he'd once had himself? He deserved that.

'I know he'll find out the truth one day but that can wait, can't it? He can have a bit of time to believe in magic?'

Max had stepped closer to Emma as he was speaking and now he was close enough to touch her face. To let his fingers and thumb slide so gently down her cheeks and then to cup her chin softly as he bent his head ready to cover her lips with his own.

'This is magic I can still believe in...' he said softly. Emma's weight was on her toes and she tilted her body to touch his as she returned that kiss and felt his hands move to trace the shape of her shoulders and slip between them to touch her breasts. Emma could only gasp at the spear of sensation that coursed through her body and the movement of Max's hands stilled instantly, as though he was afraid she didn't want this.

Which couldn't be further from the truth. Emma had never wanted anything in her life as much as she wanted the escape of sinking into a timeless bliss that would make anything else in the world irrelevant. She wanted that magic…

'Don't stop,' she whispered, lifting her face to kiss Max again. 'Please don't stop…'

CHAPTER NINE

HAD SHE REALLY believed that giving in to this over-whelmingly powerful attraction between herself and Max Cunningham meant nothing would actually change?

How wrong had Emma been?

Everything had changed.

She couldn't stop thinking about it. About every touch of his hands. Every kiss, from those so tender they could bring tears to her eyes to ones so passionate they made the world tilt on its axis. Almost falling asleep cradled in his arms in the aftermath of their lovemaking, feeling the steady thump of his heartbeat beneath her cheek, until he'd reminded her gently that they needed to leave this secret room above the practice clinic. He had to be in the main part of the house in case the children needed him during the night.

She'd lain awake in her own room for a long time, reliving every moment of their time together. She'd been absolutely right about one thing—she'd experienced something she would never, ever forget. Something which had made her feel as if she was stepping out of ordinary life into a place that felt very different. A bright place where colours were more intense, where food tasted better and something as simple as the scent of a pine tree in the house was special. A place where laughter was the most beautiful sound in the world, the excitement of watching snow falling thickly was so strong it took her back to her own childhood and even the chore of getting the chains onto her tyres so that she could get to work this afternoon was not nearly as tiresome as it could have been.

It was a place that Emma finally recognised, even though she'd never experienced it to this kind of level.

At first, it was a surprise to be getting frequent text messages from Max as she attended to one task after another during a busy Christmas Eve shift in an emergency department. She received images of Ben and Tilly standing in the snow in their gumboots, with carrots in their hands that they were going to leave out for the reindeer, when she snatched a few minutes to go and visit Terry on the cardiology ward and catch up with the great news that he'd received several stents in his coronary arteries, fast enough for the damage from his heart attack to be minimal.

There was one of Pirate with some tinsel tied to his collar, being cuddled by Ben, that arrived in the minute or two between Emma sending an eighty-year-old woman off to X-ray, knowing that she'd broken her hip when she'd slipped in the snow on her front step, and going to stitch up a nasty laceration on a young man whose Christmas party had gone seriously awry.

The best thing about that image was that the small boy was sitting on his grandfather's knee when the picture had been taken and Emma had to blink away a tear, knowing that at least one of the barriers in the Cunningham household was beginning to crumble.

The one Max had sent much later, when the children

must have been settled in bed and he'd been able to sneak back to the rooms above the clinic where the gifts had been hidden had broken her focus quite noticeably.

Was Max remembering what had happened in that room last night in as much detail as she was? His attempt to wrap Ben's bicycle in Christmas paper did make her laugh, though, and that eased the emotional tension that she could feel building.

She texted back.

Great effort. Just leave it like that with the pedals and handlebars sticking out. It's not as if Ben's not going to recognise it instantly—he asked Father Christmas for it, didn't he?

Things got really busy in the department as it got closer to midnight. A stabbing victim from a pub brawl meant that Emma was tied up in Resus for a long, difficult time. When they'd finally sent the critically ill patient up to Theatre, finding the selfie Max had taken wearing the sparkly tiara that was part of Tilly's fairy supplies had made her smile rather than laugh.

She'd spent long seconds just staring at the face that filled her screen and remembering what it had been like to have those beautiful, dark blue eyes staring into her own when they'd been as physically close as it was possible for two people to be.

She texted back again.

Wish I was there. Looks much more fun than being here.

Max's text came instantly.

Wish you were here too. More than you can imagine.

Oh…she could actually imagine it only too well if it was anything like she was feeling and it was when the physical tingling in her body morphed into a longing that was intense enough to steal her breath that Emma finally recognised what was going on.

She was in love with Max Cunningham.

It wasn't just that he'd given her the best sex she'd ever experienced in her life. The sex could only have been that amazing thanks to the connection that had already been there. Because the trust had already been there between them—a mix of familiarity from knowing each other long ago, respecting each other in both professional and personal capacities and shared experiences of dealing with tough things in life. Because there was a possibility that she'd always been a little bit in love with Max, she'd just never let herself go there because she didn't belong in his kind of world.

She still didn't belong here with a new family just trying to glue themselves together, so being in love with this man was only ever going to be a problem—especially when it made her feel as if she wanted to stay in exactly this part of the world and not move on to a new position in the very near future. When it made her feel as if she could quite easily open her heart to the generations of Cunninghams on either side of Max and have an instant family of a size that her Italian relatives would approve of heartily.

Even if Max wasn't taking the first steps to try and piece together a new lifestyle when his old one had exploded around him, he had never wanted the same things in life as Emma. She could understand why he'd thrown around that catchphrase of being here for a good time not a long time, given the early tragedy in his life, but the truth of the matter was that Max was never going to give his heart away. Not in the way that Emma could with the person she might want to choose to spend the rest of her life with.

Oh, he would love the children who had unexpectedly come to share his life—he already did—and he would take the best care of them and of his father, but that was far more responsibility than he'd ever planned to take on and, eventually, he would sort out the current chaos around him. He would employ a full-time housekeeper and nanny and be able to come back to his job in the Royal's emergency department in the very near future. He would get his apartment repaired and most likely keep it on, despite living in the manor house, because it would be the perfect place to find private time with the women who would always be eager to be chosen even though they knew—like Emma did—that it might only be a one-off night to treasure. He might be even less likely to consider a long-term relationship—not only because he'd seen his brother's marriage end in misery—but because it wouldn't be fair on three children who'd already experienced far too much disruption in their lives.

Being in love with Max was her problem, Emma realised, and it would be far better if nobody else knew anything about it. Max probably wouldn't notice, especially tomorrow when it was Christmas Day and would be all about the children. Or make that today, she thought, as she checked her watch to find midnight had come and gone a while back. That meant she was closer to being able to escape before Max had the chance to notice anything different about her. She'd only ever promised to stay long enough to help create a magical Christmas Day for Ben and Tilly and Alice. Only one more day and that had started already. She had a day off rostered for Boxing Day and Emma could use that to find somewhere else to stay. There was only one more week after that until New Year's Day and that was when Max had told her the new nanny was due to arrive.

So that would be that. Maybe they'd stay in touch and Max would send a Christmas card every year with photos tracking the changes as the children grew up. It was just as well you could send digital cards now because goodness only knew where in the world Emma was likely to be.

She tapped the screen to enlarge the photo of Max in the tiara again. To soak in the expression in his eyes and that smile.

'Dr Moretti? We've got a Status One patient arriving by ambulance. Electrocution from faulty Christmas tree lights but someone had started CPR before the paramedics got there and they've got a perfusing rhythm again. ETA two minutes...'

'Resus One clear?'

'Yes.'

'Activate the trauma team, please. And get whoever's on call in Cardiology down here stat.'

Her phone slipped back into the pocket of her scrub suit. Goodness also only knew when she'd get the next chance to check on the progress of the gift wrapping and that was a good thing.

Emma needed to try and step back.

To keep things under control so that nobody got hurt, including herself. It was Christmas Day and she was going to play her part to make it as perfect as possible for the Cunningham family and as little as possible about herself. It was a strategy that had worked for years now.

She was good at it.

She was also good at her job and right now she had the challenge of dealing with a post-cardiac arrest due to electrocution. This person wasn't going to die in the early hours of Christmas Day. Not if Emma Moretti could do anything to change that.

Max was the first person awake in the Cunningham household on Christmas Day which surprised him, not only because he'd been up in the night with Alice and should have been tired enough to sleep through all but a major disturbance but because he remembered the way he and Andy would get up while it was still dark and tiptoe past their parents' bedroom to go downstairs and see if the Christmas magic had happened again this year.

He could hear soft snuffles coming from the cot in the corner of his room but that wasn't the sound which had woken him. It was the light tapping that was coming from the hallway beyond his open door—the sound of a small dog's toenails on the wooden floorboards on either side of the carpet runner. So he wasn't really the first person awake, after all. He had to smile when he heard Ben's whisper that was even more audible than Pirate's toenails.

'Shh, Pirate… Don't wake up Uncle Max. Let's find Grandpa first because we have to have a Christmas cuddle… It's one of the rules…'

Oh… Max knew who he'd like to be having a Christmas cuddle with right now. How horrified would Emma be if she knew just how much she'd been on his mind since they'd made love in the early hours of Christmas Eve? He wanted to do that again. As soon as possible.

As often as possible.

For the rest of his life…

Good grief… Max was properly awake now, that was for sure. How on earth had that thought surfaced again? He'd already sorted things out in his head after he'd had that disturbing glimpse through his personal barriers and thought, for a heartbeat, that he wanted the kind of partnership his parents had had when they'd created their family. That Andy had thought he'd found with the woman he'd fallen so deeply in love with.

Was that what was happening here?

Was Max falling in love with Emma?

No. He didn't do 'falling in love'. Never had, never would allow himself to take that kind of risk. It was what women did with him and it had always been enough to make him end things rapidly. Falling in love was a magic you only believed in until you learned that the truth could be very different and he'd learned that at a very young age. It was like Christmas magic, until you discovered Father Christmas didn't actually exist. Ben still believed. And Max wanted to be there when the little boy went downstairs and saw his bike under the Christmas tree because he wanted to remember what it had been like for himself all those years ago. He wanted to feel *that* magic, just for a heartbeat.

Max pushed the bedclothes away and reached for his clothes. A pair of jeans and a tee shirt and an extra warm woollen jersey because he could feel that the central heating was already struggling this morning. There was also that odd feeling of silence that only came when the world was blanketed thickly enough by snow. Would Emma make it home safely after her shift ended this morning?

And there she was again. In his head.

In his heart, as well, judging by the squeezing sensation he was aware of in his chest even though he knew that the heart was not an organ that was capable of either thinking or feeling. That was disturbing too. A kind of magic all of its own.

He had to get a handle on this. He wanted this Christmas Day to be special for Emma so that she could get on with her life and find joy again. He wanted it to be special for Ben and Tilly and Alice. For his father as well, because it might be a struggle for him to cope today. How had he reacted to a small boy and a dog climbing into his bed for a pre-dawn Christmas cuddle? Taking the handset of the baby monitor with him, Max left his room to go and find out.

'I got a *bike*, Emma. A blue bike—just like I asked for...'

'Oh...that's amazing, Ben.' It was impossible not to return the happy smile that Emma had received full blast when she'd finally arrived back after a shift that had gone overtime.

'Did he make it?' Max came out of the drawing room a few seconds after Ben had run to meet Emma at the front door. He had Tilly perched on one hip and she was in her full fairy outfit with the tutu and wings and tiara. 'The Christmas lights guy?'

'He was sitting up and talking by the time I left. He's not going to get home for his Christmas dinner but I don't think his family's too bothered.'

'I'm sure they're just delighted he's still alive.' Max nodded. He was holding Emma's gaze and he looked delighted as well, she thought. Because of a successful case in his department, or was he as pleased to see her as she was to see him again? The warmth that was coursing through her body made it urgent to get her coat and hat and scarf off and hang them on the hooks.

'I'm a fairy,' Tilly told her.

'I can see that, sweetheart. You're the prettiest fairy I've ever seen.' Emma pulled in a deep breath. 'Something smells gorgeous,' she added.

'That'll be what Maggie and Ruth are cooking up. Turkey and bread sauce and Brussels sprouts and roasted potatoes—the whole nine yards. Pigs in blankets for Ben too. They got here before it started snowing again, which is lucky. How did you find the roads?'

'A bit dodgy around here. They must have cleared them this morning but it was just as well I had chains on. It's still snowing hard.'

'But I want to ride my bike,' Ben said sadly.

'How 'bout we make a snowman instead?' Max suggested. 'After we've had our dinner? It might have stopped snowing by then. Otherwise, we might be stuck inside for a while yet.' He gave Emma just the ghost of a wink. 'We'll have to think of other ways to entertain ourselves if that happens.'

Emma had to drag her gaze away from Max. That gleam in his eyes told her exactly what kind of entertainment he had in mind and it felt wrong to be thinking about that in the presence of two small children.

'I'll go and see if Maggie and Ruth need my help in the kitchen,' she said.

'Come in by the fire for a minute first. Dad insisted on opening some champagne,' Max told her. 'There's a glass with your name on it.'

'It's a rule,' Ben told her. 'Grandpa said it was one of Nana's rules but it's only for grown-ups. Come on, Emma. Come and see our new toys. And there's new stories too…'

'Yes…' Max was smiling. 'Come on, Emma. We're having a very special Christmas but we've all been waiting for you to come and share it.'

The floor of the drawing room was littered with crumpled wrapping paper. Alice was asleep in her pram near James's chair and Pirate was lying at his feet chewing happily on a dog treat bone. The lights on the Christmas tree were sparkling and the fire was glowing. Emma watched Tilly slide to the floor from her uncle's arms so he could pour the champagne and then she went to climb onto her grandfather's lap as if it was the most natural thing in the world to do. Ben picked up a picture book from a pile and handed it to James, curling up on the floor beside Pirate as the most senior member of the Cunningham family started reading the story.

She was already a little spaced out from working a night shift and it felt as if she had stepped into a Christmas card scene so she sipped her celebratory drink cautiously as Max came to stand beside her near the fire. This was exactly what she'd imagined when she'd told Max how important this Christmas was to these children and the opportunity it was providing for them to bond as a family. This was perfect and it was a pleasure to be a part of it and to be watching it happening. And, according to Max, even better news was waiting in the wings.

'Do you remember that I told you that Maggie's daughter Ruth is an infant school teacher?'

Emma nodded. 'You said she was wonderful with the children.'

She'd been looking after them when Max had taken Emma up to the attic to find the boxes of decorations. It seemed a long time ago already that James had been so upset to see them being used again. He had a grandchild on his lap right now and another one leaning on his leg and he looked like a man who'd had his heart well and truly stolen.

'She is. And Maggie says she wants to come and live in Upper Barnsley so that her mum can help after the baby's born. They've cooked up a plan between them that Ruth could be our nanny and Maggie can stay on as housekeeper as well as helping to look after Ruth's baby. It sounds like a good plan, doesn't it?'

Emma's head was definitely spinning now. 'It sounds perfect,' she agreed. 'You'll be able to go back to work. You might not even need to wait until the New Year?'

Which meant that Emma wouldn't be needed as a locum any longer. If she left the manor house tomorrow, she might never see it again. Or see James or the children or Max again and that simply felt...wrong...

Very wrong...

'Dr Cunningham?'

'What is it, Maggie?' Both Max and James turned towards the anxious voice at the door, where their housekeeper was wiping her hands on her apron.

'Would one of you have a minute? Ruth isn't feeling terribly well.'

Emma put her glass on the mantelpiece, turning back swiftly, but Max was well ahead of her as she left the room. Glancing over her shoulder just before she pulled the door closed behind her, Emma could see that Ben was climbing up to join his grandad and Tilly in the roomy leather chair and that James was nodding, quite prepared to take responsibility for the children.

A short time later Emma wished she had stayed where she was and sent James in to assist his son. It had taken Max only minutes to find out why Ruth had started feeling so awful she had gone to lie down on the old couch at one end of the huge kitchen.

'You're in labour,' he told her. 'You're far enough along for it to be safe for the baby but it looks as though you might already be close to the end of the first stage and that means that it's happening very fast. I'm not happy to try driving you to hospital and risk you having your baby on the side of the road. I'll call for an ambulance but there's no guarantee it'll get here in time with the amount of snow on the road.'

The way Emma's head was spinning now had nothing to do with fatigue or the sip of champagne she'd had. This was more like an adrenaline overload. A fight or flight response and all she wanted to do was flee.

Another baby was about to be born on Christmas Day?

No…no, no, no…

She couldn't do this.

But now Max was standing in front of her and his gaze was telling her that she *could* do this. That she had to because he needed her to.

'You know where the kit is in the clinic,' he said. 'Could you go and get it, please? There's an obstetric pack right beside the drug cupboard too. Maggie's got a key. She'll go with you to get what we need, but we need it fast.'

Getting out of this room was good. Getting out fast was even better.

Emma turned and ran.

CHAPTER TEN

THIS HAD TO be the most unusual management of an emergency that Max had ever been in charge of. Here he was, in the kitchen of his childhood home, the aromas of a traditional Christmas dinner beginning to fill the room, and he was about to help a new baby into the world.

An ambulance was on its way to the house but he was pretty sure it was not going to arrive in time for the crew to be present at the birth of this baby. He hoped that was the case, anyway, because a long delay at this stage of a delivery could mean there were complications so a smooth transition and fast birth were preferable.

Ruth must have been having contractions for some time. She'd told Max that she'd put her discomfort down to an increase in the backache she'd been aware of for a couple of days, due to being on her feet since early this morning helping her mother cook the Christmas dinner they'd all been planning to share. By the time Emma and Maggie had come back into the room with the kit and Max had pulled gloves on, he could feel the bulge in Ruth's perineum that meant that crowning of the baby's head was imminent.

Ruth wasn't his only patient here. There was a baby

that was about to come into the world a lot faster than usual, and that was a worry due to increased risks of haemorrhage or tearing for the mother and aspiration of amniotic fluid for the baby, or infection due to a less than sterile environment for the birth.

'Grab some clean towels, Maggie. We'll put some under Ruth right away. I'm surprised her waters haven't broken already.'

Maggie was pale but composed. 'I'll be right back... Oh, my...that's the bread sauce boiling over. I thought I could smell something burning...'

Max wasn't the only doctor here either. Emma had opened the kit. She had also put gloves on and she was unrolling the IV pack. She knew that IV access was a priority. Not for intravenous pain relief because it was probably already too late for that, but they might need to be able to give fluids if Ruth started losing too much blood.

But Emma was even paler than Maggie. She was doing what she needed to do but Max could feel how difficult this was for her. He could almost see the pressure that she was fighting against.

And he understood completely just how hard this had to be for Emma.

Her own baby had been born on Christmas Day and, while Holly had been born alive, it had only been a short time later that Emma had lost her daughter. This had to be taking her back to the pain, both physical and emotional, and Max could feel a piece of his own heart tearing.

It was unbearable to see Emma in such pain. He wished he could have protected her from this but he hadn't been able to. The urge to offer comfort now was so strong it had the potential to interfere with what he needed to focus on, and it was in that split second that Max realised just how important Emma was to him.

He wasn't in danger of falling in love with this woman.

It had already happened. In the space of only a few days, with his world as he knew it crumbling into chaos around him, he had found a human rock who had anchored him. Who had shown him a future that he could embrace. Someone who had touched him on levels he'd never experienced before and he knew he could never find with anyone else. Max was a better man for having had Emma Moretti in his life for only a matter of days. Already, he couldn't imagine his life without her in it.

So he was feeling her pain but he knew that, somehow, she had to face it or she would never be able to move on and embrace a future of her own—whether it was with him or not. And, because he loved her, he had to help her.

The thoughts flashed through his brain as more of an awareness than any conscious analysis. His focus had to be fully on his patients and, as Maggie arrived with soft, clean towels that were put in place merely seconds before Ruth's waters broke, Max only had a heartbeat to catch Emma's gaze. To try and let her know that he understood. That he was going to do whatever it took to make sure that Emma could cope. That everything was going to be okay.

You've got this...

His message was silent but he knew that it had been received because he could sense the contact. As if she had accepted an outstretched hand. As if his strength was welcome.

* * *

It seemed as if every new situation that Emma saw Max dealing with increased her respect for this man and filled her heart with a mix of emotions that felt limitless.

Like how proud she was of his abilities. Like how much she loved how gentle he was trying to be but how uncompromising he was in doing what needed to be done, like cradling the back of the baby's head as it appeared and putting pressure on it to prevent an explosive delivery. His hand looked huge as he supported the tiny head as the forehead and then the face and finally the chin and neck were delivered and then helping to deliver each shoulder by careful downward pressure for the first and upward for the second.

'You're doing great, Ruth. Almost there...'

Dear Lord, it was hard to try and keep a totally professional focus, here. Emma could feel the pain of every contraction Ruth was having and she could remember exactly what it felt like to have the rest of a baby's body slither out after the shoulders were delivered. That moment, suspended in time, when you were listening for the first cry of your child. That moment had been so much worse for Emma, because she'd known there was a very good chance she might never hear a first cry but oh...she could have wished to have had Max present at the birth of her own baby.

The way he'd looked at her, only minutes ago, when she'd returned to try and assist him in this unexpected and precipitous birth. As if he understood exactly how hard this might be for her but he had complete confidence that his admiration for how she could cope with difficult things was not misplaced. It felt like the way he'd looked at her when she'd first told him the tragic story of Holly's birth. As though the threads of connection between them were becoming so strong they could be trusted to take any amount of weight.

But perhaps he was wrong…

It was that first cry of Ruth's baby that tipped the balance. It took Emma straight back to that delivery room five years ago. To the mindset that she could cope because she'd known what was going to happen but…but then *she'd* been wrong. It might have looked to others as if she'd coped and carried on coping but that was only because she'd been hiding. She'd run away emotionally and built protective walls that had just come crashing down with the single warbling cry of a newborn baby.

'I'm…sorry…' The words came out as a whisper as Emma pushed herself to her feet. 'I… I have to go…'

Where was she?

It was nearly an hour later that Max could finally focus on what had been an increasingly urgent concern. Emma hadn't been seen since she'd fled the kitchen after the birth of Ruth's baby. He hadn't been able to go after her then, of course. His responsibilities lay with caring for his patients, even though it appeared that everything had gone as well as he could have hoped it would. The baby's Apgar score was good at one minute and perfect at ten minutes. Ruth experienced only minor blood loss and her placenta was delivered without any problem. When the ambulance arrived, along with a police escort and a snow plough waiting at the end of the driveway, Ruth's tiny son was already nursing well and a proud grandmother was ready to accompany them to hospital.

'Just to be on the safe side,' Max told Maggie. 'I'm sure they'll have you all back home by this afternoon.'

'I can't thank you enough.' Maggie brushed back tears. 'I've just helped Dr Cunningham to change Alice's nappy and given him a bottle for her but I think your Christmas dinner might be a bit ruined. The turkey and potatoes have been in the oven a bit too long and that bread sauce is inedible.'

'It doesn't matter.' Max was smiling. 'It was your Christmas dinner as well and I'm sure you're not worried about missing it.'

'You could heat up the pigs in blankets for Ben. And there's red jelly in the fridge. I'm sorry, Max. I wanted to help make this Christmas perfect for all of you.'

'We'll be fine. You go and take care of your family, Maggie. I can take care of mine.'

'But where's Emma?'

'That's what I'm about to find out.'

He checked the drawing room but hadn't expected to find her with his father and the children. That heartbreaking look in her eyes when she'd heard Ruth's baby cry for the first time had told him that she was facing a ghost she thought she had to grapple with alone.

But she was wrong.

She needed him. Or maybe it was that Max needed to be with her.

He checked her room but it was empty.

He went outside into a world that was silent and white, with a fresh burst of fat snowflakes drifting slowly down to cover the tyre tracks of the emergency vehicles that were now long gone. The biting cold nipped at his skin and Max stared towards the woods on either side of the driveway but then he shook his head. Emma was far from stupid and she hadn't been dressed for being outdoors. Besides, there were no footprints in the snow leading towards the woods.

There were, however, footprints that led around the corner of the house. A lot of prints, but was that because they'd been made when Maggie and Emma had gone to fetch the medical gear he'd asked for? With the new snow falling, it was hard to tell whether there were any more recent tracks but Max kept following them.

Because he was remembering walking this way with Emma when they'd brought the emergency kit back from the neighbours' house and where they'd ended up, later that night. He was remembering not the mind-blowing sexual encounter but what it had been like afterwards. When he'd held Emma in his arms, skin to skin. Heart-beat to heartbeat. How it had felt like the most perfect place in the world to ever be.

If he was in pain, or scared, or he simply needed comfort, that would be the place he would want to be, wouldn't it? In Emma's arms. But, if that hadn't been possible, he might well have chosen the next best thing— to be in the place that he *had* once been in Emma's arms, so that he could imagine that comfort and wrap himself in it like the warmest blanket on a day exactly like today.

Max let himself into the clinic and then headed for the stairs to the room above.

Those agonised tears had finally stopped a while back.

Emma had curled herself into the smallest ball and pulled the old eiderdown that had been rolled up on the end of this antique brass bed over herself. She'd heard someone coming up the stairs from the clinic rooms and she'd known that it would be Max, because he was the only person who would know that she knew about the existence of this room, but she was too exhausted to move. So utterly drained she thought she might never be able to move again.

He didn't say anything when he came into this room. What he did do was to lie down on the other side of the bed, beneath the eiderdown and behind Emma, to not only take her into his arms but to wrap his whole body around hers. His warmth seeped into her skin with far more effect than the feather-filled cover over them both and she could feel his heartbeat against her back. A steady ticking that was an affirmation of life.

Of caring…

It felt like love…

His words, when they came, were soft against her ear.

'I know it hurts. I've got you. It's going to be okay…'

Emma's words were shaky. 'But it's not. I thought it was. I want it to be but… I'm scared. I thought I had it sorted but I didn't really. I've been hiding—all this time. It broke me, Max, hearing that cry. I would give anything to hear another baby of mine cry, but how could I ever go through that again when I know how much it can hurt?'

'You can't hide for ever.' Max was stroking Emma's hair. 'Well, you can, but I hope you don't. You have so much love to give, Em. So much love that others will want to give you. If you keep hiding, they won't be able to find you and you'll miss out on both giving and receiving that love, and how sad would that be?'

Emma turned in his arms so that she could press her face against the reassuring beat of his heart.

'Nobody's trying to find me,' she said quietly. 'I've made sure I never stay in one place long enough for that to happen.'

'It doesn't always take a long time.' Emma felt Max's

lips press against the top of her head. 'I've found you—and I wasn't even looking.'

Emma's breath caught.

'I didn't want to look,' he continued softly. 'Because I guess I was hiding too. Even when it was right in front of my eyes I couldn't see it properly. Like that night when you were making stars with Ben and Tilly and I was feeding Alice and I felt like…like we were…'

'A family?' Emma whispered into the silence. 'I know. I felt like that too, when we were decorating the tree. Until your dad got so upset. Until I remembered how much safer it was to step back. To hide…'

'I didn't believe in Christmas,' Max said. 'I knew the magic wasn't real. That it had died when Mum had gone but, you know what?'

Emma pulled back just far enough to be able to see Max's face. 'What?'

'You've made me believe in a different sort of Christmas. And a different sort of magic. Not the sort when you believe someone comes down the chimney and gives you the bike you've wanted for so long, but it's still magic. The family kind. My dad's probably still sitting in front of the fire, playing with his grandkids or reading them another story. Maybe he's gone into the kitchen to heat up those pigs in blankets for Ben or maybe they've just gone straight for the red jelly. But what he's really doing is letting those kids into his heart and that means he's going to start living again. Really living…and that's magic, isn't it?'

Emma could feel her eyes filling. A single tear escaping to trickle down her cheek. 'It is… It's real magic. Like love…'

'I tried to make you stay with us because I knew that

couldn't have happened without you. We need you, Em. We all need you but I need you most of all. I love you, Emma Moretti. I'm *in* love with you and I never thought I'd ever say that to anyone because I didn't believe in that magic either and I know that you're the only woman in the world that could make me believe in it. I want you to stay for the rest of this Christmas. And next Christmas. For every Christmas to come for as long as I live.'

Tears were falling freely now. Max had come out of the place he'd been hiding in for most of his life. He was risking his heart. For the children who had come into his life but for *her* as well.

Could Emma be that brave?

'I love you too, Max. I need you. I want to stop hiding but I can only do that because you make me feel a lot braver than I really am. I want to be here for every one of those Christmases and...'

And then Emma had to stop talking because Max was kissing her. There were tears mixed into that kiss. A bit of laughter too and a great deal of love. And then, with their arms wrapped tightly around each other, they went back into the house.

To the family that was waiting for them both.

EPILOGUE

Two years later...

IT WAS JUST as well that the Cunninghams' manor house had so many bedrooms because it seemed like the house had to cater for more visitors every year.

'Sorry, Maggie…' Emma eyed the huge pile of tiny sausages that were having strips of bacon wrapped around them and secured with toothpicks. 'I'll have to start limiting how many of my relatives come over here from Italy for Christmas before it gets to be way too much work.' She went to the sink to wash her hands so that she could start helping with the preparations. 'I wonder what they'll think of these pigs in blankets? I tried translating the idea but my *nonna* looked very dubious.'

Maggie laughed. 'I'm sure she'll love them. And I love how full the house is and how many children we've got running around. I loved that we had the feast of the seven fishes last night too. And that your mum brought your family's gorgeous nativity scene. Ruth's loving it all as well. She was so impressed with your star making class yesterday.'

It was Emma's turn to laugh. 'We've got so many wonky stars now, I think I'll have to make a string to put across the ceiling next year or we won't have room for all the other decorations on our tree.'

'Ruth will help with that. She says her job is like she's running her own little school and the best bit is that she gets to take her wee Joseph to work with her.'

Emma peered out of the window as she dried her hands. Ruth's two-year-old son was as much a part of the crowd of excited children outside as her Italian nieces and nephews.

'Ben's got him in the wheelbarrow,' she said. 'Along with Alice. I hope he can cope with both of them. They're a bit like twins, aren't they? There's six months between them but they're inseparable.'

'Maybe it's because we celebrate Joe's half-birthday so it doesn't get lost in Christmas. Tilly is convinced they're both the same age.' Maggie started a new row of the wrapped sausages on the oven tray. 'Is Ruth out there supervising?'

'Ruth *and* Max.' Emma was still looking out of the window. 'They look like they've got everything under control for the moment. Pirate's out there too but he's probably as eager as everyone to get back inside. What made us decide that the kids could only open their stockings before breakfast and we'd do the gifts under the tree before dinner?'

'Oh…that reminds me. Ben was worried about where his little tree was. You know, the one he brought with him when he first arrived and that we save all the tiniest decorations for?'

'I put it up high to keep it safe,' Emma said. 'The toddlers were getting into everything. It's a circus around here at the moment.'

But she was loving it. Every moment of it. Because

every day brought so much love, along with something new and special into her life. Today one of the special things was that this was the first Christmas for the newest member of the Cunningham clan. Emma forgot that she was about to help Maggie create the army of pigs in blankets. Instead, she walked towards the pram parked on the other side of the Aga stove, to gaze at her four-month-old daughter. Hannah had been named after her paternal grandmother and was currently dressed in the cutest stretchy suit ever—a tiny green elf outfit, right down to booties with curly toes and a green and red hat. She was awake in her pram but not crying and when she saw her mother her little face lit up with the widest smile and she held out her arms to be picked up.

The kitchen door opened as Emma gathered her baby into her arms. Max's face lit up with the same kind of joy as Hannah's and he went straight to his wife and daughter to wrap his arms around both of them.

'Where's Dad?' he asked Maggie.

Maggie's face softened with a smile that made Max and Emma share a knowing glance. They suspected that something might be going on there and this looked like another clue.

'He's upstairs, putting on that Santa suit so he can distribute the presents. Shall I go and see if he's ready?'

'Good idea.' Max nodded. 'I'm not sure how long Ruth will manage to keep the troops out of the way. I don't think we'll be getting any kind of white Christmas this year but it's pretty cold out there.'

He waited until Maggie had gone out of the kitchen before he bent his head to kiss Emma—a slow, tender kiss that tapped into everything she loved so much about her husband and about their life together which was only getting better with every passing month. How had they not known, when they'd first met all those years ago, that they were so perfect for each other? That they could meet every challenge in life as long as they faced it together?

'Champagne?' he asked. 'I do believe it's one of those Christmas rules.'

'After the presents.' She smiled. 'As the other half of Upper Barnsley's general practice, I think I have a duty to cover any calls until your dad has changed out of his Santa suit.'

'I guess I'll wait too, then—so we can share that first toast to a happy Christmas.'

'It's already happy.' Emma smiled up at Max. 'I don't think it could be any happier.'

Except it could.

The kitchen door opened again and a stream of small children came rushing in.

'Mummy… Daddy…' Six-year-old Tilly was bursting with excitement. 'You've got to come… *Father Christmas* is here…'

Ben was by her side. He and Max exchanged a grin and Emma knew what that was about. As the oldest child, Ben was now in on the secret—that it was the family that made the magic happen at Christmas time but that was fine by him. He knew how important a part of this family he was and he was going to help make that magic happen from now on.

This Christmas was going to be the best yet.

Until next time, of course…

* * * * *

A PUPPY AND A CHRISTMAS PROPOSAL

LOUISA GEORGE

MILLS & BOON

CHAPTER ONE

'DAMN SNOW. THE weather forecast said this Arctic vortex should have ended by today.'

Alex Norton locked Oakdale Medical Centre's front door and turned up his coat collar against the flurries that were now falling thick and fast, covering Oakdale village in a glistening white blanket. Winter had arrived with a vengeance with Christmas hot on its tail. And all he had to do was keep sane through the madness of the next month and then he'd be able to breathe properly again.

All? With the memories of Christmases past haunting him at every turn in this tiny claustrophobic village he'd be lucky if he stayed sane until the end of next week.

'Hasn't snowed this much in December for years.' His colleague and business partner Dr Joe Thompson grinned as he fell into step with him up the path towards the main street. 'Going to be a white Christmas, do you think?'

White? Blue? Yellow with orange spots? Alex didn't rightly care what colour Christmas was going to be, but he managed a half-decent, at least polite, reply. 'Who knows? It's three weeks away. This will all be murky slush before you can blink.'

Joe's eyes narrowed. 'I hope not. I promised to take Katy tobogganing tomorrow.'

Alex checked himself. Okay, so perhaps murky slush wasn't polite. Not everyone disliked Christmas, especially not the father of a pre-teen girl. Maybe Christmas might actually be fun with a kid around. *As if he'd ever know.* 'Oh, yes. First day of your holidays. Have fun. See you on the other side of New Year.'

'I'm grateful you've agreed to stay here to cover the clinic for us. Rose is looking forward to her first Oakdale Christmas and Katy's beside herself with excitement about the New Year's skiing holiday. For the first time in years I'm going to be able to get to all the school things they have at the end of term; the kids' disco, the Nativity... And she's going to love the pantomime in Lancaster next week.' Judging by the shine in Joe's eyes he was fairly keen about it all too. Which, as far as Alex was concerned, was a long time coming. Joe had been through a rough few years and it was good to see him smile. He figured Joe's new partner Rose had a lot to do with that too. 'It'll be good to be able to enjoy it all as a family without worrying about rushing back for work.'

'You deserve the time off. Happy to do it.' With a bit of luck he could bury himself in his job and forget it was the time of year that everyone seemed to go just a little bit crazy. Alex hated December. He hated Christmas. He hated the reminders of everything he'd lost, and at this time of year he was usually on holiday somewhere far away trying to drink away the memories.

But there would be no holiday this year; their other practice partner, Jenny, was off sick with a nasty leg fracture and their new partner wasn't starting until next week, and with Joe having pre-booked leave right through December there hadn't been anyone to step up but Alex.

Joe stopped as they reached the turn-off that led up the hill to his house. 'Coming to the carol concert later?'

'No. Not my idea of fun.'

'Good job you don't have kids, mate. You'd go mad this time of year with all the Rudolph the Red-Nosed Reindeers going on. Katy's been practising and let's just say that, although I love my daughter to pieces, even I have to admit she does not have the voice of an angel.' Joe laughed. 'Seriously, you should come.'

'With that recommendation?' Alex ignored the stab in his chest. It wasn't just a good job he didn't have kids; it was a physical impossibility. He dug his hands further into his coat pockets. 'No. I'm fine. A warm fire and a cold beer beckon.'

'The pub? Friday band night?'

'No. I'd like to keep my eardrums intact into old age. I'm just heading home. Just me, and not a red-nosed reindeer in sight.'

'Okay. So basically it's "Bah, humbug" and all that?'

'Yeah. Something like that.' Joe clearly wasn't getting the 'don't push it' vibe Alex was sending him. 'Enjoy the concert.'

'I'll try…' Joe grinned and waved his phone earbuds '…not to listen too hard.'

Then it was just Alex and the crunch of fresh snow as he stalked across the empty village square. Each footstep a beat…warm…fire…cold…beer… Warm…fire. Cold… beer. Nothing better after a busy work week.

Despite the streetlights it was dark and fresh and he wished he'd dressed more suitably for a blizzard. Every shopfront had some sort of festive display or Nativity scene and someone had strung bunting made out of silver stars zigzagging from the post office to the butcher's and over to the newsagent's. There was a small and slightly gravelly snowman outside the little supermarket, its carrot nose lying on the snow-covered ground. Alex picked it up, stuck it back onto the large white head and tightened the woolly scarf round the join between head and body. 'There you go, mate, whole again.'

He tried hard not to think how that might feel. But at least he'd fixed the snowman. See? What was that if it wasn't embracing the Christmas spirit? *Bah, humbug, indeed.*

He made his way down the icy path towards the opposite end of the village to where Joe was heading, to the house he'd grown up in, his thoughts tumbling between the usual tumult of GP life and that one Christmas eight years ago when his life had changed for ever.

He tried to push the memories away but there was something about those Nativity scenes that seemed to lock them in his head; the doctor's office decorated in tinsel for festive fun, diametrically opposed to the hot panic that had consumed him. The phone call. Tears. So many tears. And then navigating an entirely different landscape from the future he'd been planning.

From somewhere he heard a little whine, then an excited yelp tugged him back to today, the past receding a little. Behind him was a fluffy bundle of fur on four legs. Not a red-nosed reindeer but a dog…a puppy to be exact. It stopped walking when he did. When he started again it let out another yelp then bounded through the drifts and caught him up, tangling between his legs.

Huffing out a breath, Alex disentangled himself from the pup. Along with huge soppy eyes it had a long snout, big paws completely out of whack with its body and a tail that stood up like a spike. Cute. If you were the dog-loving type. Alex wasn't. Especially when they hindered your journey home after a long day looking after particularly difficult patients. He stepped over the mutt. 'Whoa, puppy. It's too slippery out here to be doing that.'

It didn't move. 'Go.'

Nah. Nothing. He picked it up, turned it around and plopped it back onto the snow, hoping it would return to wherever it had come from, then he set off in the direction of home. *Warm fire. Cold beer. Warm fire. Cold beer.*

Another yelp. A little bark. Did that one sound like, *Hey, Mr Bah Humbug, I'm freezing*?

'Look, stop following me. Go home, boy…or girl…' He couldn't tell from this distance. But the puppy just tipped its head to one side and looked at him. 'Go. Shoo.'

Pointy ears pricked. Well, one did; the right ear had a floppy fold. One up, one bent.

Not cute at all. Really. Not cute.

And lost. He looked at the trail of puppy paw prints in the snow and sighed as he bent down. 'Okay, okay. Let's have a look at you.'

No collar. *Great.* A boy pup. And very happy to be given attention. 'Someone, somewhere is going to be missing you. How about you turn right around and go back where you came from?' But he couldn't help sinking his fingers in the fur at the back of the pup's neck and giving him a good scratch. The puppy nuzzled against his arm and something in Alex's chest squeezed.

No. 'I am not going to be bamboozled by big soppy brown eyes and cold paws.'

No. Nope. No way. *Niet.*

As soon as this silly season was over he was booking a holiday. A climbing holiday perhaps where he could put all his energy into something physical. A holiday fling maybe? That could be good respite too. A something with someone who didn't want for ever. He noticed his fingers were still fur-deep and his palm was wet with over-enthusiastic licks. It actually felt kind of nice. When was the last time he'd made a meaningful connection?

He didn't want to think about that, because making connections deeper than the ten-minute appointments with his patients was something he avoided at all costs. Dragging his hand away from the fur ball, he tried to sound authoritarian. 'Don't go getting attached to me. Off you go.'

He started to walk away. *Don't look back. Don't look back.* Words he'd repeated over and over to himself so many times in his life; in the darkest times, when he'd faced an uncertain future, he'd known that looking back at all those unfulfilled plans he'd made would have given him no solace at all.

But the puppy ran along next to him, sinking deep into the snow, then pushing with those huge paws and jumping out and into the next drift. 'A puppy with authority issues. I see. Just my luck, right? Look, mate, this isn't going to work. I'm just not that into you.'

The wind picked up as he reached his cottage, swirling snowflakes faster and thicker. He slid the key into the lock and pushed through into the cold and dark, pausing for a moment to stamp the snow from his boots. Wishing he'd left either a light or central heating on, he flicked on a switch, flooding the hallway in a soft cream glow, and caught a spiky tail disappearing into his kitchen. 'What? Hey! Houdini! You don't live here.'

The damned thing had snuck in with him and was now, he discovered as he rounded the corner into his large kitchen-dining room, lying on his grandparents' heirloom rug in front of the dining table, chewing on Alex's best, top-of-the-range and shipped-all-the-way-from-the-States climbing shoes.

'Hey! Hey! No! They cost a fortune! Let go.' A throaty, playful growl came from the dog as Alex took hold of his shoe and tried to tug it out of its mouth. 'I only just bought them. I've only worn them once.'

But the dog stuck his bottom in the air and laid his enormous paws out in front and kept on tugging back, that tail wagging back and forth like a metronome on heat.

'This is not a game.' Alex needed to distract it. 'Food? What could you have? Water? Yes. Water.'

He filled an old porcelain Willow Pattern bowl that had belonged to his grandmother and put it on the floor, then microwaved the sausages he'd planned to eat for dinner and chopped them up. 'Your last supper, matey. Then you're back out there.'

He looked out of the window at the whirls of snow-flakes, heavier and thicker than he'd seen in a long time. Then he looked at the puppy, who was devouring the food as if it hadn't eaten in days. Maybe it hadn't. 'Who do you belong to?'

One tentative sniff of the sausages and Spike gob-bled the lot—okay, so the name just came to him. It fit-ted the mutt perfectly, especially with the tail that stuck straight up. And so much for not getting involved. As a rural GP he'd been around enough farmers to know you didn't name things you didn't want to get attached to.

Then *Spike* bounded over to him, dragging the now

mauled and mangled shoe. Alex used his best authoritative voice. 'Drop. Drop.'

But Spike went right on chewing at Alex's feet. Whoever owned him scored very low in the puppy-training ranks.

'You must belong to someone. Surely? How would I find out? A dog like you shouldn't be out there in the freezing night—oh? Ugh.' His words stalled as a warm and wet sensation trickled down his ankle.

'Oh, great. Just great. A puppy with authority issues and a weak bladder. Brilliant.' He looked down and his eyes met those dark brown soulful ones. He ignored the squeeze in his chest. 'Spike, my man. Just what the hell am I supposed to do with you?'

Sometimes folks loved their pets more than people, and Beth Masters understood that more than most. Pets didn't break promises or let you down. Pets never gave you the cold shoulder or silent treatment. Except for the one she was examining now; the poor farm dog was so ill, and exhausted from being sick, she could barely move. 'How long has she been like this?' Beth asked Meg's owner, local farmer Dennis Blakely.

The old man just shrugged as he stared down at his lovely old collie and stroked her muzzle. 'Help her, Beth.'

Beth recapped what he'd told her when he'd rushed through the door a few minutes before, frantic for help. 'So, we have a history of vomiting and shaking…like a seizure?'

'Yes. No. Well…she was shaking and coughing and then she was sick. It was dark-coloured.'

'Blood perhaps?' Beth did not like the sound of that. 'And now she's just completely exhausted. It could be a bug, or something she's eaten. Or any number of things.' Or, most likely some kind of tumour in a dog of such advanced age. But Beth knew better than to jump to conclusions and she couldn't feel any obvious mass.

Mr Blakely tore his eyes away from the dog and looked over at Beth. 'Something she's eaten? Do you think so? What kind of thing?'

Beth listened to the dog's heart. 'At this time of year it's usually chocolate. People leave it wrapped up underneath the Christmas tree and forget it's dangerous to dogs. Oh. Oh, dear, poor you.' She rubbed gently as the dog vomited onto the counter. This wasn't looking good. But she could see it wasn't chocolate that had made the poor pooch sick. Meg whined and laid her head onto her paws, her eyes looking deep into Beth's heart. Wait... there was a tinge of yellow in the dog's sclera. Liver problems maybe?

Her phone vibrated on the desk in the corner of the room. She ignored it. If it was urgent they'd call back.

They did. Her heart thumped as the vibrations made the phone dance across the wood. 'Excuse me, I need to get this.'

But it was just a text from her mother reminding her about the carol concert they'd planned to go to later. Well, that plan was about to go south; she couldn't leave poor Meg like this. 'Mr Blakely... Dennis... I'm so sorry that Meg is so sick. I'm going to run some tests and, in the meantime, keep her as comfortable as I can. It could take a while to get her stable...if I can even manage that.'

'Aye.' He nodded. His pale eyes filled. 'Do what you can, love. But save her, whatever it takes. She's all I've got now Nancy's gone. It doesn't matter how much it costs. Just save her.'

Beth's heart twisted. Poor guy. A widower of only two years and, judging by the scruffy whiskers and the unkempt hair and dirty clothes, he wasn't coping well. But caring for a very sick dog overnight would mean she'd have to miss the concert and she'd be letting her mum down. Again.

Because the progressive rheumatoid arthritis had eaten away at her mum's joints and rendered her unable to drive without a lot of pain she was relying on Beth to get her to and from the school hall. Beth felt torn; promises were something she always tried to keep, but she couldn't not treat a sick dog.

'Let's see how she goes, Dennis. She's very sick and you need to know...' Her throat was raw. God, she hated this part of her job. She put her hand on his arm. Despite the thick old coat that hung from his thinning frame his papery skin was cold to the touch. 'I can't promise she'll make it through the night.'

The man just nodded and looked as if his heart was breaking. She put a drip up through one of Meg's veins and bandaged her paw. The poor thing barely flinched. Then Beth popped her onto a blanket in one of the holding cages and made sure she was comfortable and safe while Beth ran the tests. 'That should start rehydrating her and hopefully she'll feel brighter. I've taken some blood and will do some X-rays and see if they come up with any clues.'

Someone banged on the surgery front door.

'We're closed!' she called out. 'Dennis, you go on home. Try to get some rest.'

'Hey!' The person outside rattled the letterbox. 'I can see you're in there.'

'Still closed!'

No rest for the wicked. She tried to remember when she'd done something wicked and came up blank. Sure, she'd wanted to be wicked...lots of times. But she was far too sensible to throw caution to the wind. As a child she'd always been a little devil-may-care but being her mum's carer and then having her heart stamped on had curbed that a little. And now she was a very responsible professional, who could hear canine yelping and human huffing.

She sighed, because sometimes she was her own worst enemy, but she couldn't let another animal suffer if she didn't have to. She just hoped it wasn't another serious emergency. 'Okay. Give me a minute.'

Focusing back on the situation in hand, she double-checked Meg was stable then walked Dennis to the door. 'I'll call you if things change.'

'Good lass. I just hope I got to her in time.'

'Fingers crossed.' But she had a sinking feeling that it was going to need a lot more than luck to get Meg well again. She unlocked the door and opened it to let Dennis out.

'Hey, Dennis. How are you?' A very familiar voice had her heart jumping. And not in a good way.

Alex Norton. *Great.* She breathed out slowly, trying not to let her body overreact, or her brain for that matter. She had more important things to concentrate on than Alex Norton.

Dennis sighed long and deep and shook his head. His movements were slow and infused with grief. 'Not good, Dr Alex. Not good at all.'

'Oh? Anything I can help you with?' Alex smiled. There he was with the smooth, kind and concerned doctor tone. *If only they knew.*

He was holding a puppy, which was licking his neck. And he was smiling.

Alex Norton and a puppy and a smile. How could the universe be so cruel?

'I doubt you can help this time, Doc. Not unless you know about four-legged patients.' There was a crack in the old man's voice. 'Meg's taken a turn. She's not doing well. But Beth here's a good 'un. If anyone can make her well again, she can.'

'Yes, I'm sure Beth will do her best. I'm hoping she can help me out too.'

No. Please, no. The last thing she needed right now was a conversation with the man who'd stomped on her heart all those years ago and—unfortunately, for Beth—the only man to date who could affect her with a simple look.

Not that she didn't want to see him per se; in fact, he was lovely to look at. From being a good-looking adolescent he'd grown into a damned fine-looking man in his expensive wool coat and jeans. His dark hair was shorter than he'd used to like it and the odd grey strand was creeping in. His blue eyes were darker than she remembered and had developed one or two lines around them. He was broader too, his shoulders more powerful-looking and he was, possibly, taller than back then. But with him being six feet two his mouth had always been a tiptoe to reach.

She was not going to think about his mouth. Or his kisses. Or him.

So, while she didn't mind looking at the gorgeousness that was Alex Norton she just didn't want to lay her eyes on him. Because whenever she did she was filled with such a heady mix of emotions she couldn't sort through them. Although she knew sadness and anger were definitely the dominant ones.

'Hey, Beth.' His smile was still there…and something else. He wanted something and, because she knew him so well, she knew that whatever he wanted was going to cost her.

'Alex.' She aimed for the same amount of ice that coated the path outside the vet surgery.

He didn't seem to notice. 'I wasn't expecting to see you here. I thought you might be going to the carol concert or Friday band night at The Queen's Arms.'

'Interesting. You thought I wouldn't be here? Or hoped?' He'd actually thought about where she might be? That was unusual; thinking of someone other than himself. Despite her better judgment she let him in but only because he was holding a pet, and pets were her business, not his.

But she didn't have the time to play nicey-nicey with him, even if just looking at him sent her heart into apoplexy. Stupid heart to keep hammering a tattoo for someone who dumped her and disappeared into the ether with not a single look back.

'I did wonder whether you might be here.' He lugged the puppy up under his arm. 'Or whether you'd even be open this late.'

'We are officially closed. And I did promise to take Mum to the concert, but I can't leave Meg now—she's really not well.' Beth hurried back through to the hospital area so she could keep an eye on the old dog. The poor thing lay with her head on her paws, breathing steady. No more vomiting, so that was something. But she didn't look right. 'I need to run some tests. Like… now.' She hoped he'd take the hint.

'Would you like me to arrange for someone to take your mum to the concert? Joe's going. I'm sure he'll be able to take her down.'

Not good at hint-taking, then. For a second she thought about saying no to him just because that was how she was feeling. But saying no to her mum having a nice night out when she rarely left the house was plain mean-spirited. So, it looked as if she was going to be beholden to Alex Norton tonight. *The first and last time.*

She managed a brief smile. 'Okay, yes, if you could give Joe a call that would be lovely.'

As he called his business partner she took the chance to check on Meg again. She was holding on, but very weak as Beth did her vital signs. She didn't move an inch when she was put in the X-ray sling. Didn't so much as whine as Beth drew more blood.

Alex came back as Beth was finishing up another round of observations. 'Okay, done. Joe will take her to the concert and drive her home afterwards. He was more than happy to do it. He said he'd make sure she got back into the house safely.'

'Thank you.' That was something to feel less guilty about, at least. One good thing about being in Oakdale was that everyone looked out for each other, even though it could feel claustrophobic at times. Like, when everyone knew when you'd been dumped at Christmas and you had to endure those pitiful stares and sad smiles and you couldn't wait to get the hell out and never come back. Except, of course, when your mum needed you. 'I'll give her a call and explain why I'm still here.'

'I'll wait. Er…*we'll* wait.' Alex cradled the puppy against his chest and stroked its back until it fell asleep.

Beth refused to let the sight of gorgeous man and dog do anything at all to her emotions.

When she'd finished calling her mum he asked, 'Was she okay about it?'

'Not really. We were both looking forward to going together like we used to do years ago, but she knows my work here is demanding and that I often have to stay late, or even overnight. She's used to me making promises I can't keep. But then…we all know how that goes, right?' *Ouch.* That was probably unnecessarily harsh. But when you broke off a relationship—an *engagement*—by phone call with no explanation, you had to expect the odd barb, right?

Geez. Beth closed her eyes for a second as she found some calm. It had been eight years. Eight damned years. She needed to let it go. In fact, she'd thought she had, until she'd come back to Oakdale to help her mum and found herself bumping into Alex at every turn. Ironic really, given that eight years ago, when she'd so desperately wanted to talk to him, she hadn't been able to find him, and now she didn't want to see him he was front and centre of Oakdale life. The sooner she went back to Glasgow, the better.

When she was able to breathe slowly again she turned to him. 'So, Alex, why are you here, exactly?'

His jaw clenched and she wasn't sure whether it was a reaction to her short manner or whether it was something else. 'I seem to have a new friend.'

And why do I care? Oh. Why *did* she care? Because she knew deep down she still did. Cared enough about him that he made her heart hurt. Just a few more weeks and then she'd be gone and Alex wouldn't be part of her life again.

Then she realised he meant the adorable puppy in his arms, who had woken up and was licking Alex's chin and making him squirm. She scrubbed the back of the dog's neck and it turned to look at her, large eyes brightening at her touch. 'He's gorgeous.'

'He? You can tell the gender without looking?' Alex's eyes grew bigger too. 'It took me a few minutes to figure that out.'

'I can tell the gender by the way you're holding him.' She tried not to laugh. 'But, if this is just a show and tell about your new pet then I haven't got the time.' Or the inclination.

She had to keep telling herself she didn't have any inclination towards Alex Norton. Except anger. Was that an inclination? There had been many times, particularly in the first few months after he'd dumped her by phone, that her inclination had been to force-feed him the engagement ring he'd so beautifully proposed to her with. That was, if she'd been able to find him.

Alex shook his head. 'He's not mine. He just followed me home, snuck into my house and ate my shoes.'

'All very lovely, I'm sure. And you want me to…?'

'Take him.' With the kind of smile that had once melted her heart, and now did absolutely nothing to her at all—*at all*—he handed the puppy out towards her. 'He doesn't belong to me.'

'Nor me.' Shrugging, she looked at the cute little dog who had a silky coat and bright eyes that were adoringly fixed on the man she'd once looked at like that. But he was distracting. They both were, and she had to deal with Meg. 'He looks perfectly fine. Healthy and alert.'

'He is.' Alex craned his neck away from the puppy's tongue and grimaced. 'Too alert.'

'Alert is a good thing, Alex.'

'I need to find his owner.'

'Of course you do, and I'm sure they'll be very grateful.'

'Has anyone reported a missing puppy to you or anyone here?'

She quickly flicked through the notices in the large clinic diary on the desk. 'No, not in the last few days. A white rabbit, rather unoriginally named Bugsy, is currently AWOL, as is a Siamese cat called Marg, but no dogs.'

She threw him what she hoped was an über-efficient and over-officious smile that she knew would definitely not reach her eyes or exude any warmth or encouragement for them to stay. Whimpering came from the treatment room. Meg.

Damn. 'Look, I have to go. Meg needs me and I need some answers.' And not just about what was ailing the dog. 'You know where the door is. Goodnight, Alex and friend.'

CHAPTER TWO

BUT HE DIDN'T LEAVE. He just stood there open-mouthed, shaking his head and cradling the dog to his chest as if protecting it from her. Great, and now she was Cruella de Vil.

'Beth? Really? You can't just send us out into the snow.'

'Yes, I can. That's exactly what I'm doing. You live a five-minute drive away, Alex. You are not going to die of cold just going back to your house in a fancy-pants Mazda cabriolet.' And, okay…yes, she was far too aware of Alex's life and his penchant for red cars that zoomed too quickly down the winding Lake District country roads.

'But…what about this little one?' He held the dog towards her and looked at her almost as dolefully as the dog did.

Steeling her heart against them both, she peered closer. Maybe she'd missed something. 'Is he sick?'

'No. He's a handful.'

It was just a ruse. He'd come here to dump the poor pooch on her, but she was in no position to take on a puppy. 'Do you have a fire or central heating at your house so the two of you can be warm until you find his owner?'

Alex's hopeful smile faded. 'Of course.'

'Right. And you're a grown man and a medical professional to boot. You'll manage.' She couldn't hold back the sigh. 'This is not an emergency, Alex. I am not needed here.'

'Yes, this is an emergency, Beth. I don't want a dog. I don't know how to look after them. I don't have the time. I need to give him back to his owner. Think of the poor little girl who is missing her puppy so close to Christmas.'

He was standing under a swathe of the cheap tinsel they'd strung across the clinic ceiling in an effort to be festive. His eyes locked onto hers and for a minute she was thrown back to a Christmas years ago when they'd come back from their separate universities for the holidays and they'd decorated his bedroom and made love for hours. Then he'd made her a crown out of gold tinsel, kissed her hard, told her she was the queen of his heart and asked her to marry him.

And she'd been the happiest woman on earth for a whole year, until he'd unceremoniously knocked her off that throne and broken her heart with a single phone call. Then had gone travelling…without her. In breaking up with her he'd not only cut her off from him, but from his parents and sister too…the extended family she'd always craved. Because, of course, when she'd come back home in the holidays and he wasn't around she'd questioned them about why he'd disappeared from contact. They'd rallied behind their beloved boy. With a gentle sadness in their eyes, admittedly, but they'd rallied.

We're so sorry, but it's what he wants. We're sorry, Beth.

For breaking her heart?

He could deal with the dog on his own. 'Feel free to find the owner and be the hero of the hour. Why do I need to be involved?'

He shrugged. 'Because I don't know what to do next.'

'Have you developed an allergy to phones or something?' She shook her head. 'Call the rescue centre.'

'I did. No one's reported a missing dog and they're full so they can't take this little one. No room at the inn, right?'

She rolled her eyes at the very bad Christmas pun. 'The animal pound in Kendal?'

'Same. Full, no missing reports filed.'

'The police? Here—' Raising her eyebrows, she thrust the surgery's laminated card of emergency numbers towards him. 'Call the local station.'

He took the card but shook his head. 'You know, you're not being very helpful.'

Say what? He had a nerve. 'Alex, I am always helpful in times of need. This is not one of them. I'm in the middle of something very important. I have to go to Meg—'

'But you know about dogs.'

'I know about sick ones.' That was a little disingenuous. She knew a lot about animals in general, she just didn't feel a need to abandon her sick dog to help Alex.

He shrugged. 'I don't know anything at all. He's not mine and he needs to go to his rightful owners. He hasn't got a collar so it's not just a case of picking up a phone. Maybe he has a microchip? Or what if he hasn't? What if he hasn't got anyone?' He almost—*almost*—looked genuinely concerned. 'What do we do then?'

'*We?* Oh, no. That is not going to happen.' She was not going to get embroiled in this.

'Me,' he corrected. 'What do I do with a lost puppy? I'm working all weekend. I haven't got time for this. Oh.' Alex's mouth crumpled as a stream of liquid left the dog and hit the counter, splashing Alex's jeans en route. 'He keeps doing that.'

'At least we know his urinary system is in good nick.' It was getting late and she needed to check the blood results and generally tend to Meg but she also had a duty of care to the puppy too. Or, at the very least, she needed to make sure it was safe and cared for, and that the person responsible for it had an inkling of how to keep a dog alive. 'Look, if you can give me an hour or so to get Meg sorted then I'll be able to concentrate on this little one. Why don't you go home and bring him back later?'

'I'd prefer to stay here. You have all the equipment. I have nothing suitable for a pet at home. Plus, he doesn't like cars, he howls like I'm trying to kill him. I tried to soothe him with some classic tunes from the nineties but that didn't work, and neither did Rihanna, which I don't understand at all, because when Rihanna sings I'm all ears.'

'Okay, okay. That's enough.' She didn't want to know any more, she didn't want to hear his voice or see his face or be subjected to his bad puns, because those were things from her past and she was working forward now, not looking back. She dug out a bowl and filled it with water, and another one with puppy food. 'Give him something to eat and drink then go through to the staff room and make yourself a coffee.'

And she'd make sure she stayed safely at least two doors and a corridor away from him.

'Thank you.' He breathed out slowly, relief flickering across his eyes, and then he smiled.

God, that smile did her in every time. *No.* She stood tall. She was immune. She had to be.

'It's okay, I'll just add it all to your bill, which is growing by the minute.' She watched in amusement as Alex put the dog on the floor and then proceeded to follow it around, growling every time it started to get frisky or inquisitive. He clearly had no idea how to look after dogs.

She closed her eyes and counted backwards from ten, wishing that seeing Alex Norton in charge of a puppy—or, rather, completely out of control with a puppy—didn't make her knees weak and her ovaries prickle. 'Why do I get the feeling that I'm going to regret this?'

'How's she doing?' Alex lowered his voice to a whisper and crept into the treatment room, almost fearful of disturbing Beth as she was so completely focused on the collie. But he'd waited and waited and now he was worried the old dog had passed on and she was in here grieving and dealing with it all on her own. But no, both vet and patient were holding on. 'I've brought you a cup of tea, Beth. Thought you might need one.'

As always, the sight of her made his heart stutter. Her long honey-coloured hair had fallen over her face as she titrated the IV drip attached to Meg's paw, but he remembered every detail of her pretty features; the dark brown eyes that were warm to everyone, but him. With good cause, he knew. The perfect nose and mouth that had a generous smile…mostly. Not tonight, obviously.

Yes, this was difficult. He hadn't wanted to bring Spike here, but he'd run out of options. And he'd hoped Beth had had the day off. No such luck.

It had been hard enough for the few weeks she'd filled

in as the general practice receptionist when their regular one had suddenly taken ill, but he'd always managed to skirt past her and had tried to avoid any lengthy conversations about anything other than work. He'd breathed a sigh of relief when she'd left to take up a vet position here because time and distance, it appeared, didn't make you forget. Strange, how the body instinctively remembered.

She looked tired, but as beautiful as ever. Capable and professional and forthright, and still angry with him. Beth had always worn her heart on her sleeve and he knew he'd stamped all over it, so had no claim on her time or generosity. But for the zillionth time in his life he wondered whether he'd actually done the right thing all those years ago.

Yes. He had. He'd had to set her free rather than lock her to him and an uncertain, potentially very dark and bleak future. And now? Even though things had gone a lot better than either he or the specialists had hoped, he still couldn't give her what she wanted or deserved. But it didn't hurt any less to have lost her. Never mind aching for the body he knew that fitted so well against his, the mouth that was made for his kisses. He fought against the rising regret. He'd done the right thing.

Forcing himself to not look at her, he focused on her patient. It was easier that way, because looking at Beth made his heart hurt. And sing. And beat hard and fast to her rhythm. Life had definitely been easier without her around, but he didn't want to think about not seeing her when she decided it was time to move on.

He didn't know anything about dog care but Meg's breathing seemed less laboured than before. She appeared calmer and less stressed. But that could have been his imagination.

Beth straightened and drew her gaze from the dog. Her eyes were soft and kind almost as if, for a moment, she'd forgotten to be angry with him. She took the cup he was holding out and had a sip. 'Lovely, thank you. I'm parched actually.'

'I wasn't sure if you still took it white, no sugar.'

'Yes. Oh.' Beth blinked and just like that she slipped back into the woman she'd grown into whenever she was around him: guarded, professional, distanced. She swallowed and put the cup down on the counter.

Damn. He shouldn't have alluded to the past. 'How's Meg?'

Beth breathed out and he could see she was shutting him out. The warmth in her eyes slowly seeped away, her back straightened and she turned away from him. 'She's holding her own. Just. She's had a hell of a ride. But I've run the tests: full blood count, biochemical analysis and urinalysis. Done an ultrasound of her abdomen and then an endoscopy and it looks as if she's got gastrointestinal bleeding and some liver damage.' Her voice was measured and professional, as if she were giving a report to someone she didn't know. 'She's been in a few times recently, with the odd cut or weird symptom that led to nothing, and has no other significant morbidity, so I'm thinking she's eaten something. I can't be sure, but with the damage to the gut it's classic signs of ibuprofen poisoning. And if that's the case we need to keep a very close eye on her over the next few days.'

'Poor Dennis. It would be terrible if he lost Meg so soon after Nancy.' As if the guy hadn't been through enough already, having nursed his wife through cancer. 'He's not really coping, is he?'

'No, he isn't and it's so sad.' Beth gave a sharp shake

of her head. 'I know grief eats away at you and some-times makes you distracted, so I need to have a chat with him about whether he may have left any tablets lying around that Meg could have got into. People don't realise how dangerous some medications humans take are for pets.'

'I'm his GP. From memory, he isn't on ibuprofen but I'll double-check at work tomorrow. It's easily bought from most shops, so he might have some regardless. I haven't seen much of him recently, but he's clearly lost a bit of weight and he looks a bit dishevelled compared to when Nancy was alive. He always made an effort for her.' He wondered how it was to have a love that lasted decades. Then stopped himself from going down that track because it wasn't going to happen to him. 'Maybe I could be there when you have that chat. Give him a bit of support, you know?'

Beth raised her eyes and looked at him. He could see she was thinking hard about this. Was that because she didn't want to spend any longer than necessary in his company? Were things so bad between them that they couldn't even do a joint professional consultation? But she eventually nodded. 'Okay. Yes. That's probably a good idea. You know him better than I do. It'll be good for him to have someone there that he's familiar with.'

'Good. Let me know when you're planning to chat to him. Now, it's getting late and I wondered if you've got time to just wave your magic wand over that little guy out there and see if he has a family who are miss-ing him. And I don't want to leave him too long on his own.' At her wide eyes he reassured her, 'I popped him in one of the holding cages with some biscuits and a toy duck. Yeah, I know, just add it to the bill, right?'

She looked at her watch. 'Shoot. I've been in here over two hours? I'm sorry. Poor pup. But I needed to deal with Meg.'

'I know you did. But if there is a family out there, they're going to be frantic. I called the police and there are no missing-dog reports. I'm stumped. You're my last hope, Beth.' He tried the smile again, hoping she'd at least smile back. Or even laugh. Because if they had to spend time together then he'd prefer it without the daggers and sharp words.

'We won't be long, old girl. Hold on for me.' She gave Meg a quick stroke then whipped round to Alex. 'Come on, then, let's get this sorted.'

Wow. No smile. Definitely no laugh. She really hated him, and he didn't blame her one bit. He walked through to the place where they kept the large crates. The little pup jumped up as they entered the room, tail wagging, paws thumping, and yelping so enthusiastically it tugged at Alex's heart. 'What kind of dog is he?

Beth opened the cage and helped Spike jump free onto the ground. She bent down and ruffled the back of his neck. 'This beautiful boy is the best kind there is. A pure-bred mongrel.'

He was so out of his depth here. 'Is that a thing?'

'Alex, really? It means he's a cross. I think there might be some Labrador in there. He has huge paws so he's going to be big, but he hasn't got a lab tail. This is more beagle. He's got the tricolour patching, but...' She frowned and ran her hands over Spike's ears. 'The ears are wrong...'

'Wrong?' Alex felt strangely protective all of a sudden. 'There's nothing wrong with his ears.'

'I mean the ears are wrong for a beagle. Look, these

are pricked. Beagle ears are pendant. Well, actually...'
she smiled and held up one ear '...he has one of each. I
guess we'll know more when he's older and grown into
himself.'

'I don't really need to know as I'm not keeping him.'
He absolutely could not have a pet. They were too tying.
You couldn't take a puppy climbing up a mountain. Hik-
ing, yes, but not rock climbing. And nothing was going
to stop Alex from doing the things that kept him sane.
'Does he have a microchip?'

She ran a scanner over Spike's neck. Finally. Then
she frowned. Repeated the scan. 'No. Nothing.'

'So, he's a stray?'

'Well, I'd say he's at least three months old and the
law now says a *keeper*—not an owner—has to microchip. If he hasn't got one then either the keeper hasn't
got around to it yet or chances are he's a stray, or lost
or...' she shrugged sadly '...dumped.'

'Dumped? What the hell?' He wasn't going to keep
the dog but, hell, dumped? 'In winter? At Christmas?
What happened to goodwill to all men and men's best
friends?'

'It happens. Rather more than you'd think. Sometimes
the dog is too fussy, or too difficult to train. Sometimes
circumstances change and they have no room for a puppy
any more. Sometimes they just fall out of love with the
idea of having a pet.' She pushed the pup's mismatched
ears back and rubbed his muzzle. 'You are so gorgeous.'

She was rewarded with a lick on her cheek and smiled.
Finally. But it had taken a dog and not this human to
crack that. It bothered him that even after all this time
he still wanted to see the pretty smile that lit up her
face and made her eyes dance brightly. He should have

moved on. He had to move on, because he'd given up his chance with her and, besides, she wouldn't want him again once she knew the truth he'd been hiding from her. From pretty much everyone.

She stood and wiped her palms down her trousers. 'You're going to have to take him home, at least for tonight. Bring him back in the morning and we can see if anyone's reported him missing by then.'

'I can't take him back there. He's already weed on the carpet and nibbled a hole through my best climbing shoes.'

'Oh, no? The horror! Really? That's nothing compared to what I have to put up with in my job.' Her hands hit her hips and her head tilted a little as she stared at him. 'A nibbled shoe? Poor, poor Alex.'

'Say it like you mean it.'

'I mean every word.' She shot him a look of disdain, but it was laced with a faint tinge of humour that gave him a powerful thump to the chest. Because he wanted her to forgive him for hurting her. He wanted things to be okay between them instead of this difficult defensive manner she took whenever she was with him. A smile was a good first step.

But the smile quickly faded. 'You know, Alex, I really haven't got time for this. You tried the pound in Kendal, right? I'll call the one in Ulverston. I know it's a long shot, being so far away, but who knows?'

He watched as she made the call and was thrown back eight years. How, when she was on the phone checking in on her mum, he'd wrap his arms round her waist and hold her close. How he'd run his fingertips over her freckles and try to count them, and she'd laugh and tell him that infinity was the number of freckles on her body and that he'd never, ever be able to count them all. How he'd nuzzle his face into her hair and tell her she was the most beautiful girl in the world. And she still was, without a doubt. Not just in the way she looked, but in her compassion and good-heartedness...if not towards him.

He jumped when she said something and he realised she'd ended the call and was now talking to him. 'The Ulverston pound is full too. They said they're often the first place people ring when they're missing a pup, but they've had no one call them over the last few days, and definitely not for a puppy matching this one's description. They suggest you take him home and we'll try again in the morning.'

'We?' He couldn't suppress his grin.

Her eyes blazed irritation. 'You. I mean *you'll* have to try in the morning. After you've taken him home.'

'I've just told you, I won't have anything left if he spends the night at my house. Can't you have him? You have everything set up here for a puppy. Food, beds... you.' A night with Beth? One more night?

No.

'No.' Her lips pursed and he was glad that was something they both agreed on. 'I stopped doing you favours a long time ago, Alex Norton. I can't have a boisterous puppy in here stressing Meg out and distracting me from giving her all the love and attention she deserves. That's just not fair. She needs peace and quiet.' She gave him a look that seemed to say, *Like me. I need peace and quiet away from you.* 'Maybe it would be good for you to think about someone other than yourself for a change and take—'

'Hey, I'm a doctor. I think about other people all the time.'

But that was what she thought. She believed he was selfish and self-centred. And he was. He'd had to be just to get through the months of debilitating treatment and recovery. But letting her go had been the single selfless act in the whole damned episode. He couldn't have let her go through what he'd endured when his cousin had been sick; the long hours at the hospital desperately hoping for a miracle, the despair at Mikey's suffering, the prayers and then…the loss of hope. He'd watched his family drowning in grief that had been raw and unending and all-consuming and had known the moment the specialists had sat him down and explained his prognosis that he wouldn't put Beth through that.

Clearly not wanting to hear any more, she went to the shop section and pulled supplies out for him. 'Here are some training sheets if you can't cope with a bit of wee. Put them on a floor where you don't have carpet. Your kitchen, perhaps? Here's a bed for him, a couple of toys. Some food. A soft cage you can put him in while you're not able to watch him. Don't worry if you don't have the cash, we take all major credit cards.' She scratched the back of the puppy's neck. 'There you go, Button. Do your worst at Alex's.'

'How about "be a good boy"? Or, "don't wee on the heirloom rug or eat Alex's favourite trainers"?'

She eyed him wryly. 'I thought you wanted me to say it like I mean it.'

'I've changed my mind. And Button? His name is Spike.'

'He is so far from a Spike it's a joke. Look at those eyes—they're like little dark buttons.'

He couldn't argue with that. 'But Button is a…a feminine name and he's not a girl. And that tail is all spiky.'

'No way. It's a sickle tail not a spike.' She drew shapes in the air; one arcing and one pointing straight up. 'Sickle. Spike. See the difference?'

He ran his fingers up the fluffy tail. 'It spikes if I hold it up.'

'Whatever.' She rolled her eyes. 'We'll just have to agree to disagree. Okay. Time to go, Button.'

'Spike.'

'Button.' She held his gaze for longer than they'd managed to look at each other these last few weeks and his body prickled with heat at her fiery indignance. Yes, she still was the most beautiful woman he'd ever met. Why was his body reacting to her like this when he knew, rationally, that wanting her was the least best idea he'd had in a long time? Eventually, she drew her eyes away and sighed. 'I can hear Meg whimpering. I have to go.'

'And tomorrow morning?' He tried to think about Spike and not about the prospect of seeing Beth again as soon as possible. 'I've got a clinic booked from eight. My patients need peace and quiet, not a boisterous puppy distracting both me and them.'

The corner of her mouth twitched as she registered the same words she'd used against him earlier. 'You're not giving up, are you?'

'No. Beth, Spike needs you.'

Both man and dog stared at her and he saw the softening in her eyes and the moment she finally relented. 'Okay. Okay. Drop him off here first thing, before your clinic. I'm hoping Dennis will be here too so we can have that chat.'

'Okay. Sure.' He whispered to Spike, 'See? She's

nice really. I'm *persona non grata*, but you're not dog non grata.'

He got an ear lick for that. And an eye roll from Beth. 'And there'll be reinforcements to keep an eye on Button while I try to get a little bit of rest between clients. And hopefully we can reunite him with his owner.'

'Thank you.' Without thinking he pressed a kiss on her cheek and immediately regretted getting close enough to inhale the familiar fresh scent. 'I mean, Spike thanks you.' He held the dog up to her and was relieved when it gave her other cheek a lick that made her smile— a damned sight more than his kiss had done. 'You're a star.'

'No, I'm a sook with a soft heart for a lost puppy. It's just babysitting, that's all. I'm helping Button. Not you.' Pressing her palm to the spot where he'd kissed, she shook her head, and he could see the warring in her eyes. She hated him but there was something else there too. This was as hard for her as it was for him, but that didn't make him feel any better. 'That. Is. All.'

CHAPTER THREE

ONLY IT WASN'T ALL.

Being so close to Alex was a whole lot of everything. A whole lot more than Beth wanted. The temptation to rail at him about the way he'd so callously broken up with her was sky-high, but she wasn't in the right head-space to hear she'd been somehow disappointing as a girlfriend, or that he'd grown bored of her, or that he'd found someone better... There were hundreds of reasons why people broke up, she was just a statistic and she'd do better than to analyse something that had happened so long ago.

So she wasn't going to let him get to her and she certainly wasn't going to allow thinking about him to interfere with her caring for Meg. She would ask him when the time and place were right. Or maybe she wouldn't give him the satisfaction of letting him know how much she'd cared.

So she did what she'd done for the last few years and shut down the part of her that still ached for him and didn't allow herself to think about the press of his mouth on her skin and how, despite her anger and confusion, he made her heart race and her body tingle, and she set about saving a life.

It was a long night. Too many times Meg's blood results had shown her to be the wrong side of critical, and Beth had fought hard to keep her patient from slipping away, but she'd held on. They both had and gradually, in the early hours, the dog's stats started to improve.

It was still dark outside when the front door bell jangled, alerting Beth to the new day and waking her from a light and very disturbed sleep that had been punctuated by regular alarms to check on her client. She tossed the blankets aside and sprang up from the recliner chair they kept in the hospital room, checking Meg for progress. She was stable. Which was more than could be said for Beth. A combination of sleep deprivation and an endless intake of coffee to keep her alert when needed made her jittery. Not to mention the Alex factor.

'I'll be out in a minute!' she called through to Reception, and quickly glanced in the mirror. 'Ugh. You've definitely looked better, girlfriend.'

Her hair was a halo of tangles, and sleep lines etched deep into her cheeks. Her eyes were bloodshot and her skin blotchy. Did it matter? What mattered was that Meg's owner was here for an update, having already called twice in the darkest hours to see how his beloved pet was.

She quickly brushed her teeth and patted water over her eyes then marched into Reception, gluing a smile to her face.

'Sorry to keep you!' But her already jumping heart skipped a couple of beats as she found, not Dennis, but Alex and Button waiting for her. 'Oh. Hello, you two.'

Alex's hair was rumpled, his eyes were as sleepy as hers and he looked even more gorgeous than yesterday, reminding her of those heady early mornings they'd shared after long, late, sexy nights when they'd visited each other at university. In one hand he held his work bag, in the other was Button. He smiled, although it was a little wary, and put the puppy onto the floor. 'Morning, Beth. You look terrible.'

She couldn't help laughing at his audacity. 'Gee, thanks. You don't look so good yourself.'

'I had a very interrupted night. You? How's Meg?'

'Touch and go. Poor girl had a hell of a ride. She hated the activated charcoal, but it was essential to stop her absorbing the drug and damaging her liver and kidneys further. She was quite anaemic from the gastric bleed, so I had to give her a transfusion too, which kept us both on edge for a while as she didn't react well to it.' She bent to the puppy and gave him a good old tummy rub. He really was the most beautiful, happy boy and it was affirming to see something with so much vibrant life instead of Meg, who was possibly reaching the end of hers. 'How did you two get on? Did he settle okay? Did he sleep at all? What did he eat? Look at me, I sound like a worried mother. God help my kids when I have them, I'll be your typical helicopter parent constantly fussing over them.'

'Right. Kids. Yes, I bet you will.' Alex swallowed and his smile faded.

Had she said something wrong? Maybe the dog hadn't settled or he'd had as restless a night as she'd had. It would serve him right for all the sleepless nights his abrupt break-up and subsequent silence had given her.

But then he shook his head and looked down at Button, who, despite having no lead, was sticking very close to Alex's ankles and looking up at him as if he were some sort of superhero. 'He chewed a hole in my favourite beanie, did his business on my work bag and wouldn't sleep unless lying here.' Alex pointed to his chest, and she wished he hadn't. His shoulders were definitely broader than years ago and, covered in that thick wool coat, looked just about the perfect fit for her sleepy head. She imagined how it would feel to snake her arms into that coat and slide them around his waist...

He harrumphed. 'The soft cage was a joke. I put him in it, but he just howled and howled until I picked him up. He won't take no for an answer and I'm pretty sure he's completely untrainable.'

'Going well, then.' She laughed, even though he didn't. 'You'll be glad to get him off your hands.'

'Er... Absolutely.'

'Indeed.' She wanted to repeat, *Say it like you mean it*, but didn't think that was fair. Anyone would fall in love with Button and she had a feeling—just by the way Alex looked at the puppy when he thought no one was watching—that he was a little way down that path. Although he'd never admit it. 'His owner will be worried sick by now.'

'I called everyone again this morning. The police, the pounds, the rescue centre. No one's reported anything overnight. I've made some posters.' He pulled out some coloured pictures of Button with the word 'FOUND' and Alex's mobile phone number on. 'I'm going to leave some here and get the shopkeepers to put them up in their shops between here and Bowness.'

'Excellent idea. And I'll put the word out to the other vets in the Lakes area. Oh, and Mum rang and said she really enjoyed the concert, so thank you for organising it.' Beth mentally kicked herself—she sounded too prim and too polite, as if she'd never known him or loved him. But she couldn't help it; keeping her distance from him emotionally as well as physically was pure self-preservation.

He shrugged. 'Don't thank me, thank Joe. He did the chauffeuring. I hope she wasn't too upset about you missing it.'

'She knows my work commitments sometimes mean I don't get to keep family commitments.'

'So, is this job here permanent?'

Weird question. Although, maybe he was just passing the time of day. She didn't want to spend any more time than necessary talking to Alex, and definitely not about her personal life, but one conversation with anyone in the village would give him answers, so she decided she might as well tell him. 'I'm helping Mum sell the house. She's moving into Bay View rest home in a couple of weeks. The whole process has taken longer than we initially thought and I had to extend my stay here, which is fine by me, but I have to keep paying my mortgage somehow.'

'You've bought a place? Here?' Was she mistaken or was that a flare of interest in his eyes?

And by way of a very misguided reaction her skin heated in response. *No.* She was angry with him. He'd already dumped her once. She wasn't going there again. Pets were definitely preferable to men who broke hearts, a zillion times over. 'Not in Oakdale, no. I have a house in Glasgow and I'm heading back there on Christmas Day after I've spent the morning with Mum. She should be well settled by then and I'm keen to restart my life. Besides, my old boss is heading off to Australia for a sabbatical and he needs me to take charge. I had to let my job there go when I came to look after Mum, so I'm thrilled I can go back.'

Alex nodded. 'So, you like Glasgow?'

'I love it. Give me a busy city over boring old hills and The Queen's Arms Friday band night any day.'

A little frown settled over his forehead. 'You used to love it here.'

'People change, right? Let's just say I've grown out of Oakdale.' She hoped that by saying these things out loud it would put a halt to any further feelings she might have for him or the place she grew up in. It would definitely give him the impression that she wasn't interested in staying. She needed to get away, from here and from him, as soon as she could. When the front door bell jingled relief skittered through her. 'Ah, here's Dennis. Let's have that joint chat. I'll pop Button in the little pen over there so he can't get into any mischief. Molly's due in any second. She can keep an eye on him while we take Dennis through to see Meg.'

Dennis looked as if he'd aged ten years overnight; he'd clearly had as little sleep as she and Alex had had. 'How's my girl?'

'About the same as when we spoke earlier. She's not out of the woods yet, not by a long way. The poor love is old and tired and she needs all her energy to fight.' Beth's heart squeezed at the love Dennis had for his dog and she glanced quickly over to Alex. She didn't know why she did it, maybe she just wanted…what? Camaraderie, a sense of something shared. He held her gaze for a little longer than she'd expected and she saw something flit across his eyes. A softening, for sure. Sadness perhaps? And she knew—she just knew by the way he was looking at her—it wasn't all because of Dennis.

But then what? So Alex had feelings? She'd never doubted that. He'd just somehow cut them off for her and given her no explanation whatsoever.

She opened the cage and watched as Meg lifted her head slightly and sniffed Dennis's hand, then she rested her muzzle in the old man's palm and the two of them just looked at each other. There was an understanding between them, man and dog, that she'd witnessed often between pets and their people. She believed that dogs sensed emotion and they were hard-wired to try to ease the burden, by their nestling, nuzzling, or just by sitting stoically at your side through whatever life threw at you.

Meg and Dennis definitely had that connection and it broke her heart to think it could end sooner than any of them had expected. Her throat seemed to close over but she managed to squeeze her words out. 'She missed you. Look how she's perked up now you're here.'

'Come on, old lass, get better quick. I need you home.' The old man's voice sounded as rough as Beth's. 'Did you get to the bottom of what's wrong with her?'

'I'm fairly sure she was poisoned.'

The old man stroked the dog's ears, but his shoulders tensed. He said nothing but gave the slightest nod.

Beth carried on explaining in case he was just waiting for more details. 'Ibuprofen. It's a painkiller. I can't be one hundred per cent sure, but I think she ingested ibuprofen somehow.'

Dennis went very still. Poor guy, it was a lot to take in.

'I-bu-pro-fen,' Alex repeated the name slowly as he spoke to Dennis's hunched back. 'It's a very common medication that humans take, but can be toxic, even fatal, to dogs.'

Dennis still didn't reply.

Beth tried. 'Do you know if you have any of it at home, Dennis? Anything that Meg could get hold of?'

He rubbed his palm across Meg's back and made little grunts to her. But then he replied gruffly, 'Don't know.'

Alex frowned. 'I checked the surgery records and Nancy had some prescribed for her when she was sick.'

Dennis shook his head again. 'I don't know.'

'I imagine you threw out all her old meds?' Beth tried, gently. 'Or did the community pharmacist collect them? Sometimes they do that.'

Dennis shrugged and kept his eyes on the dog. The poor man was grief-stricken.

She caught Alex's eye and shook her head, trying telepathically to tell him to leave it. They weren't achieving anything here. She tried to infuse her voice with positivity. 'It's a good job you brought her in when you did. Any longer and she might not have made it. I reckon your quick action gave her a good chance of recovery.'

'Did it?' For the first time since Dennis had rushed in with Meg his eyes brightened, but not before a tear ran down his ruddy cheek. 'Did I save her life?'

'Well, she's not out of the woods yet, but you certainly gave her the best chance.' She put a hand to his shoulder and gently coaxed him away from Meg. 'I think we need to let her rest now. I have to do some more checks on her, so why don't you go home? I know you were up in the night, so you're probably shattered.'

'I'd like to stay if I can.' He looked so stricken she almost relaxed the rules about visiting.

Almost. 'I have a few things I need to do for her and the clinic's about to start so we're going to get busy in here. How about you pop back at lunch time?'

'Aye, I suppose. A farm doesn't run without a farmer. Although sheep don't move so well without a sheepdog.' His gaze lingered over his old friend.

Beth sighed. Living miles away from her home town, she knew how hard it was to be on your own, but she did have a large circle of friends she knew she could call on, any time. 'You have no one to help you with the farm? Family?'

'No. No one.'

So, he had no one to share this worrying time with either. 'Very well. You do what you need to do and I'll call with an update in an hour or so.'

They watched him go and Beth closed her eyes. 'Sometimes this job is so damned hard.'

'He certainly loves that dog.' She was aware of a change in the air and then sensed Alex getting closer. In times gone by she would have reached for him and had a hug but now she just clenched her fists and tried to put that single tear out of her head.

She opened her eyes and took a deep breath, stepping away from Alex and his familiar scent of sandalwood and fresh Oakdale air. 'Right. I'm going to keep Meg alive if it means I get no sleep at all for the next few days.'

But Alex shook his head. 'Something's not quite right.'

'What?' She bristled at his assertion. 'It's textbook poisoning and I'm implementing appropriate therapy. She's improving. Small amounts, I know, but at least she's not getting worse.'

'Hey.' His voice was suddenly soft and conciliatory but his frown told her he was trying to put his finger on something that didn't sit right. 'I didn't mean your treatment, or even about Meg. I'm sure you're doing everything right there. I mean there's something not quite right about Dennis.'

Oh. That would serve her right for jumping to conclusions. 'I don't really know him. I mean, he's been in Oakdale for as long as I can remember, but he's always just been the grumpy old man up at Oaktree Farm.'

'He can be very direct and forthright, I admit. But he's always had a sharp mind and he nursed Nancy at home for the last six months of her life, right up until the end, refusing to let her go into hospital or even respite care because she wanted to stay in the place she'd lived for the last forty years. And at the same time he was running a working sheep farm when many men his age have sold up and retired years ago. There are no children to support him, no relatives. He took sole responsibility for his sick wife and he did it very well with our support.'

'What are you saying?'

'If he was so involved in her care, he would know the names of her tablets, right?'

Beth wandered out into the reception area and waved to Molly, who was talking on the phone. 'He's probably forgotten or trying to put all that behind him. And the names are confusing, aren't they? They're never easy to remember especially when you're as stressed as he is.'

'You're probably right.' Alex shrugged and walked over to the pen where Button was gnawing on a puppy teething ring. He absent-mindedly stroked the mutt as he said, 'I was just thinking, maybe he did leave some medication out and he's too embarrassed to say, but worse… what if he's getting a little confused or forgetful? What if he just didn't realise he'd left it out? Forgot he'd even had the tablets?'

'Are you thinking general forgetfulness or something worse, like early signs of dementia?'

'I don't know and I'm certainly not going to jump to conclusions. He's not the kind of man who'd respond well to me asking him to make an appointment to come to the clinic, so I'll pop by the farm on the pretext of wanting to buy a fleece or something and try have a chat and see how things are going up there.'

Surprising. 'I didn't think Oakdale GPs did house calls unless it was a medical emergency. At least, that's what the rules were when I filled in as receptionist.'

'Normally we wouldn't. But sometimes rules are made for breaking, right?' Now he was scruffing Button's neck and playing with the mismatched ears with a lot more fondness than he'd ever admit to. 'Poor guy's been living it tough and he's never going to ask for help, so we have to make it easy for him to accept it if he needs it.'

'Alex Norton, what with this and looking after Button I'm starting to think you do have a heart after all.'

'What?' His gaze collided with hers and he looked shocked, embarrassed and uncharacteristically off balance. 'No. I don't. I'm just trying to save the practice a whole lot of work down the line by helping Dennis now before it's too late. You've got to be proactive, right?'

'Aha. And sleeping with Button on your chest? How's that fit into your heartless excuse?'

He let go of the pup and stood up. *Caught in the act of caring.* 'Actually, it was more a case of *not* sleeping with *Spike* on my chest. Haphazard dozing, propped up with pillows and at high risk of being licked to death.'

She imagined him on a pile of pillows snuggling with the dog and her heart kicked hard against her rib cage. She ignored it. Tried to. What she wanted to do was ask him what the hell he'd been thinking eight years ago. Why he'd disappeared and treated her so cruelly, and why he was showing her now that there were still remnants of the man she'd loved…why? *Why?*

But this was not the time or the place and, even though she wanted answers, she didn't want to hear that he'd simply fallen out of love with her, so instead she tugged her vet hat back on tightly. 'Don't tell me you let a puppy onto your bed? That is not a good idea for either you or him. You have to set boundaries.' As she was trying to.

But he smiled sheepishly. 'What choice did I have? It was either that or be kept awake by the howling downstairs.'

'So, you'll be glad if we find his owner today.'

'Absolutely.' He gave Button a quick pat and didn't look glad at all.

'And if we don't? You'll pick him up after your clinic.' It wasn't a question, just an affirmation.

But he stepped back. 'It's Saturday night. Me and the lads from the climbing club are going to go to the indoor climbing wall in Kendal.'

'Now you have commitments you're going to have to rethink that.' She noted he hadn't said he had a hot date with a woman and chose not to note the shiver of relief skittering through her. 'If I have him all day then you're going to have to take him tonight. That's only fair. I can't have him bothering Mum and her place is a mess of packing boxes that he'll get into. Our house just isn't set up for a puppy.'

'Can't I just have him tomorrow?'

'I thought you were working the whole weekend? Surely it's better if I have him during the day and you have him at night.' And sure, she was setting herself up for seeing him at each handover, but there was a puppy here who needed caring for.

A hopeful eyebrow rose. 'Tomorrow night, then?'

'*And* tonight.' Button had started to whine so she picked him up and held his front paw out to wave good-bye. 'Alex, this is a baby. You can't drop him just because you want to go out with your friends. Imagine if you do that when you have human babies of your own.'

His jaw set at that, his eyes darkened and he shook his head, and for a minute she thought he was going to growl at her. But he took a deep breath and ground out through a very tight mouth, 'That, Beth Masters, is a scenario that will never happen. I'll cancel my plans. Just try to find the owner in the meantime.'

Then he grabbed his bag and stalked out of the clinic, leaving her confused and stung by his tone. For a little while she'd been impressed by his generosity and compassion, but she was seeing the true side of Alex Norton now.

And for the first time in a few long years she was starting to think their break-up had been a very good thing indeed.

CHAPTER FOUR

KIDS. KIDS. KIDS.

Every time Beth mentioned them Alex's gut knotted. He'd reconciled that he wasn't going to be a father and he'd worked through all of that over the years. But now, whenever she mentioned them she had such a wonder-struck look in her eyes that it brought back all their plans and promises, and he found himself reeling back to before the diagnosis.

She'd wanted a football team because she'd been an only child and he'd agreed to it because he'd loved her so much he'd wanted to give her whatever she wanted. Even now she talked about children as if they were a definite, as if conceiving was going to be a walk in the park. She talked about them with a certainty. She was going to be a parent.

He wasn't.

He wasn't going to let her distract him any more, either. The morning clinic had dragged on and on and all he'd been able to think about was the way she'd looked when Dennis had cried, and how much he'd wanted to comfort her.

'What a busy morning, Alex. I can't believe the rush we've had on. All those winter colds and flu. Looks like you're fully booked this afternoon too.' Out in Reception Maxine handed him some papers to sign. It was good to have her back, happy and well, following her heart operation. Things at the practice were running smoothly. Not that they hadn't when Beth had helped out, but at least he could breathe for a few hours every day now. 'You look exhausted already. I hope you're not burning the candle at both ends? I know what you young, free and single men are like.'

He laughed. If only he had the chance to burn the candle at one end, but work and Spike had him otherwise occupied. 'Actually, I had a very sleepless night trying to entertain a particularly perky young thing.'

'Oh! No! I do not want to hear about your escapades.' She put her fingers in her ears and laughed too, because not a lot could shock their seasoned receptionist.

But just in case… 'It was a puppy, Max. Don't worry.'

'Oh? Taking on a puppy is a big commitment. Does this mean you're settling down? About time too.' Something glittered in her eyes, something that made Alex panic slightly.

'No. It's a temporary thing until we can find the puppy's rightful owner. Actually, talking of dogs and owners, have you seen much of Dennis Blakely recently?'

'I haven't, but then I was off work for a while so I could have missed him.' She tapped on the computer keyboard and read from the screen. 'Not since Nancy passed away, not really. He's picked up a repeat prescription for his blood pressure tablets a couple of times, he saw Joe a while back for a cut on his hand…'

'Yes, I saw all that. I don't suppose you know of any friends or people around here who'd be able to look in on him every now and then?'

She frowned. 'Why? Is he okay? Is something wrong?'

'I don't know. Just a hunch I have. Could be nothing.' But Beth had thought along the same lines too.

And there he was, thinking about her again.

Maxine tapped on the keyboard. 'I'll ask around. He's never been one for friends, to be honest. Nancy was the one who did the socialising. He's always been a bit of a loner. Sad, really—he doesn't look his best these days.'

In that case he'd definitely drive by and check in on the old man. 'Okay, thanks, any information is good.'

Maxine smiled gently. 'Oh, and the new doctor called to say he'll be arriving in Oakdale next Saturday and will be ready to work sometime the week after. So, there'll be some relief for you.'

'Yes, once I've done the orientation, which is enough work on its own. Let's hope he's as good as Joe says he is.'

'I've heard he's wonderful. You all are. Mostly...' She grinned, because pulling people's legs was her speciality. 'And, last question—if we get a quiet moment can you give me a hand to get the Christmas decorations down from the top shelf in the staff room? It's about time we made it festive in here.'

He tried not to prickle at the thought. 'Sure.'

'And bring the tree in from the back door. Ralph dropped it off earlier but he had to make a few more deliveries so I told him to leave it there and we'd sort it out.'

'Sure. Decorations. Tree. Yes.' It wasn't as if he had an aversion to the actual tree or the tinsel per se, just the memories this time of year brought, bombarding him with emotions he preferred not to have.

But it wasn't until the very end of the clinic that they both had time to catch breath and fetch the tree and box of decorations. As Alex carefully lowered the fir into a prepared stand, Maxine stood back to make sure it was straight. 'Can you give me a hand to decorate it?'

He fought the rising memories of Beth and tinsel and her wonderful smile as he'd proposed, and wondered how he could extricate himself from this without offending his receptionist.

But before he could open his mouth the door swung open. Frank Entwhistle, one of their regulars who had the farm next to Dennis, shuffled in. 'Doc! Please… Can you help?'

Frank's colour wasn't good. He was pale and breathing too fast and too shallow. Alex ran over and helped him into a consultation room. The very last thing he wanted was to decorate a tree, but he didn't want Frank to have to be wounded just as an excuse.

And he'd driven down from the farm to the clinic in this state? Those farmers were so damned stoic. 'What's happened? Take your time. Take a deep breath.'

'I… I…was…rammed by a bloody ram.' The man held his arm tight across his chest and it quickly became clear taking a deep breath wasn't possible. 'Hurt.'

Alex gently prised the man's arm away and undid Frank's wool shirt. 'Let's take a look at you. You're saying you were attacked by a ram?'

'Aye.' He grimaced and rocked forward, biting his lip. 'Grandson…was teasing it…charged.'

Frank's chest and abdomen were covered in bruises showing extensive blunt force trauma. Alex sucked in a breath. Nasty. 'Made a pretty pattern.'

'Tupping season's over…aggressive.' The old man closed his eyes. 'I'll be okay. Give me a minute…' He slumped back against the pillow.

'Frank? Frank.' Alex tapped the man's hand and got barely a weak murmur as a reply. He checked his pulse. Thready. Blood pressure dipping too low. Time was running out. 'Frank. Frank.'

'Everything okay?' Maxine was at the door. 'I heard you shouting.'

No. Everything was not okay. 'Phone for an ambulance. Tell them we have high velocity blunt injury trauma. Probable internal bleeding. No, make that definite internal bleeding. I'll put in a line. Bring the resuscitation trolley and ECG. This would be a very good time to have an ultrasound scanner.' And another pair of hands that weren't Maxine with her recent heart stent operation and arthritic legs.

'Right you are.' She rubbed Frank's hand. But the man was still barely responsive. 'Hang in there, Frank.'

As he waited for the siren Alex slipped an oxygen mask over Frank's face, put up some normal saline and administered pain relief while monitoring his patient's labile blood pressure. Just when he thought he'd managed to get it stable with the added fluids, it started to drop again. Which told Alex his patient was bleeding somewhere that Alex couldn't see.

He was preparing to insert a chest drain when the paramedics rushed into the room. Relief rushed through Alex. Many hands helped in these circumstances and this was a basic rural GP clinic, not a hospital. He didn't have the right equipment or enough qualified staff here to deal with such severe internal injuries.

He described what had happened and his observations so far. 'He's had a serious chest and abdominal injury. He's hypotensive. In a lot of pain, although I've administered pain relief. He has ipsilateral decreased breath sounds so I suspect a tension pneumothorax. We need to do a needle decompression asap.'

'Got it. Righto. Let's do it.' Andrew, the lead paramedic, set up and between them they slid a large bore angiocatheter into the left midaxillary fifth intercostal space. Blood drained into the chest drain and Andrew grimaced. 'Let's get him to Lancaster double quick.'

Alex nodded. This was not looking good. 'I'll phone ahead.'

Within minutes they'd transferred their patient to a trolley and closed the ambulance doors and Alex finally managed to breathe properly himself. Even if Frank survived the journey to the hospital he had a fight on his hands. These Lakes farmers were hardy, but he certainly wouldn't be dealing with sheep for a while.

As he watched them head off Alex wondered how Dennis managed on his own up at the farm—especially if his mental clarity wasn't as acute as it once had been—and how Alex was going to deal with the sticky conversation that might eventuate. And then his thoughts drifted from Dennis and, somewhat inevitably, to Beth.

As he made his way back inside the clinic he allowed his mind to wander, in a moment of pure selfishness and respite from the intense hour with Frank, to the gentle ribbing she'd given him over letting Spike sleep on his bed. She'd smiled and laughed, and things had slipped a little way towards how they'd once been and, with it, so had his mood. Simply, she made him feel better. She made him feel a lot of things: happy, hot, calm and yet desperate. For her kisses. For her heat.

And he realised with a sharp pang of regret that he'd never got over her. And never would.

But he had to, otherwise he'd go mad being around

her. He shuddered as Maxine closed the door on the cold air and said, 'Just when you thought it was safe to put the closed sign up we have an emergency. It's a good job you were here.'

Alex refocused. 'Did you manage to get hold of his wife?'

Maxine nodded. 'She's out of her mind with worry, but got her son to take her over to Lancaster General. Thank God for family.'

'Indeed.' Unless you were Dennis, and didn't have one. He made a mental note to suggest the old farmer came down to the pub more often, or joined in some of the community activities—at least that way there'd be more people looking out for him. Alex knew only too well what staring at the same four walls day in and day out could do to a man's brain.

'Hi there!' Beth called as she breezed through the front door, and Alex's heart rate trebled at her breathless smile. She looked even more exhausted than before and about three times more beautiful. 'We didn't arrange doggy handover, so I wasn't sure what time…is now okay? I've finished and am finally heading home.'

She let the puppy down on the floor. It careened over to Alex and barked and barked at his ankles and didn't stop until he bent down and gave him a big stroke and lots of fuss.

Maxine clapped her hands in delight. 'How gorgeous. And Beth! Lovely to see you. How's your mum?'

As they chatted excitedly and petted the puppy Alex made plans for a quick getaway. 'Right, well, I'll be off now.'

But Maxine frowned. 'You were just about to help me dress the Christmas tree.'

Finally, he had the perfect excuse. 'Not with a puppy. Look at him—he's going to destroy every last bauble.'

Beth lifted the box onto the desk. 'Now he can't get at it. Look, I really need to go. Mum's waiting for me. And I can't wait to get out of these clothes. I've been wearing the same thing for two days. I need a long, hot bath.'

The thought of a naked Beth sinking slowly into a steam-filled bubble bath was not the kind of image Alex needed in his head right now. 'Can we do the tree tomorrow, Maxine? Seriously, I have to get this little fella home and sorted. He's had a long day and he needs his rest. Like me.'

Maxine grinned. 'There's a man with the right priorities. Of course, we can do it another time. Puppy comes first, right?'

'Say what? Priorities? You've changed your tune.' Wide-eyed, Beth stared at him before slipping her hand into a large brightly coloured crocheted bag she had slung over her shoulder. 'Okay, here's a lead. I thought it was time we taught Button to walk to heel. Or, at least vaguely in the same direction as you, with a reasonable amount of control so he doesn't venture into the road. Good luck.'

'Whoa. You want me to do this? A lead?' He tried to attach it to the smart black collar Beth had put on the mutt but Spike was having none of it and playfully turned in a circle, chasing his tail, every time Alex went near him. 'Hey! Come here, you rascal.'

Way to make me look totally incompetent, dude. Why couldn't you have been here when I did the chest drain? I'd have looked a damned sight hotter then.

'Why don't you show him, Beth? Alex has to walk past your mum's to get to his house—why don't you walk the dog on the lead together?' Maxine had a grin that told him she was enjoying watching the interaction. She must have known about their past history—everyone in the village had known. His parents had reported back to him that their break-up had been hot gossip for a while. And yet here she was, pushing them back together.

'Oh.' Beth bit her lip and looked from Maxine to Spike and then at Alex. She shrugged, looking as if a romantic snowy dog walk for two was the last thing she wanted to do. But her cheeks pinked under the gaze of himself and Maxine and a very happy puppy and she eventually nodded. 'Okay, walk me to my house and then you're on your own.'

They fell into step as they crossed the quiet village square. A very slow step, as coaxing Spike to walk with the lead instead of gnawing it was proving difficult. Plus, he needed to sniff every step, plant, electricity pole...

The snow crunched under their feet and Alex searched for something to say that would generate easy conversation. He finally plumped on, 'How's your mum doing?'

Another shrug. 'She's deteriorating. This recent flare-up hasn't abated and it's really taking its toll. It's so sad, it's like she's fading in front of me. It's not just the physical, but emotionally she's fragile too.'

He knew well enough how dependent Beth's mum had been from time to time and how much Beth had had to give up to care for her. She'd almost given up the idea of going to university, but the specialists had found a new drug that her mum had responded well to, which had meant Beth could at least have a life of her own.

But clearly that drug had only been effective for a while. The pain in her eyes speared his heart and he wished he could do something to help. 'And you? How are you doing?'

She sighed. 'I feel guilty about leaving her. I feel guilty about living in Glasgow, but when I tried to come back after graduating she was adamant she didn't want me here. But physically she was so much better then, she'd even got a man friend who was helping her and they were coping really well.'

It was the first time in a long time that he'd felt Beth open up and he encouraged more. 'How did you feel about her not wanting you here? That must have been tough after everything you've done for her.'

'Honestly? I did feel a bit hurt not to be needed, but also relieved. It meant I had a chance to do some living.'

He thought about the kind of living he'd been doing: working, climbing, random sex with women who just wanted to hook up—and that suited him just fine. He grimaced at the thought of Beth having random sex with anyone other than him. 'I don't want to hear about that.'

'Alex, *you* broke it off.' She harrumphed. 'I'm not a nun.'

'I know.' He wanted to tell her he regretted it all. He wanted to tell her how much he still wanted her. But he couldn't take that step, not when they were just starting to communicate again. 'There's eight years to fill in.'

She took hold of the lead and miraculously Spike walked by her side as if compelled by some sort of weird magic. Then she sighed. 'It's a long time.'

'We could try to fill in the gaps.'

'Why?' Her eyes crinkled as she frowned. 'Why do you want to know what I've been doing?'

'It's called being civil. Polite. Plus, don't dogs pick

up on hostility? Spike's only a baby—he needs a har-
monious atmosphere.'

She almost smiled at that. 'I'm not being hostile. I'm
just minding my own business.'

'Beth. Come on. I just want us to try to get along.' He
knew he didn't deserve anything from her and he was
touching a nerve here, but he couldn't bear being close
and not being…close. 'Spike wants to know all about
you. Don't you, boy?'

She looked from him to Spike and rolled her eyes.
'Okay. I don't know where to start. Oh, yes, I do.'

Her eyes met his and for a moment he thought she was
going to ask him why. Why? Why had he broken something so good? Their conversation back then had been
inadequate and brutal, but he'd been too shocked to be
gentle, too scared to be anything other than quick. His
heart banged hard as he hunted for the right words, but
she asked, 'Why did your parents go to live in Spain?'

Unexpected. But they'd always got along with Beth
and he'd felt terrible when he'd asked them to stick with
his plan to protect her from his illness. They'd protested
that it was unfair, but he'd pulled out the desperately
sick son card and they'd eventually agreed to abide by
his wishes.

'After Mikey died my aunt Carol and uncle Seb
moved to Malaga.' He didn't need to remind Beth who
Mikey was: she was Alex's girlfriend when his cousin
had been diagnosed with testicular cancer; she went to
the funeral; she saw the fallout of grief. 'They needed
to escape the place that reminded them of their son and
start somewhere afresh. Their marriage was rocky and
Spain patched them up. Then two years ago my folks
decided they liked it there and moved over too. I bought

their house because it's been in the Norton family for four generations and I wanted it to be somewhere Melanie could bring the kids in the holidays.'

'Malaga's nice. I went there after uni. Funny, I might have bumped into them all.' Her eyebrows rose wryly. 'Wait. Your sister has kids? I somehow missed that. My mum's Oakdale gossip's not as reliable as it used to be.'

This was good. This was chatting on a level they hadn't reached for a long time. Although the light in her eyes when talking about his sister and her children gave him a little pause. 'Yes. She's got a two-year-old boy and a six-month-old baby girl. She's doing great. Her husband, Jon, is something to do with media in Manchester.'

'No kids or anything for you?' Beth's eyes grew bigger. 'I guess I'd have seen them around.'

'Not on my radar.' Was putting it mildly. 'You ever get engaged again?'

'No. You?'

'Nowhere close.' He shook his head, shocked by the relief at her words and yet lost as to where to put that relief, because it wasn't as if he could offer her a future she'd want. 'What's been happening in your eight years?'

She shrugged. 'Vet school. A stint in America at an animal sanctuary. Back to Glasgow for post-graduate study. A job. A house. The usual things. Mum's relationship fizzled out. I came back to see her just for a weekend a few months ago, and I'm still here. She'd pretended things were okay for too long and got herself into a mess. A bad mess, Alex. It was terrible seeing her in such a state.' She stopped walking and looked up at him. 'I just wish people were honest. It would save a lot of heartache and hurt in the long run. Right?'

He knew she didn't mean just her mum. 'Beth—'

'Oh, here's me.' She turned away from him and pointed to the house he knew as well as his own. How many hours had he spent there after school? In the long summer holidays when her mum was still managing a part-time job they'd hang out together there all day. He knew that the wallpaper in the lounge had been ordered from Liberty in London. That the back garden was paved because it was easier to maintain.

That he'd pressed Beth against every wall and kissed her until he couldn't breathe for wanting her. That they'd made love in the kitchen, the lounge and the bathroom as well as Beth's pretty bedroom that had a clear view of the lake. Of course, she wasn't thinking any of this as she said, 'I'll see you tomorrow morning for handover. You want to drop him here? Or at the surgery?'

'Beth—' He wanted to say…what? That he was sorry. That he'd been an idiot and handled things badly, but if he were in the same circumstances again, looking down the barrel of that same gun, he'd do exactly what he'd done eight years ago. He would let her go. And wish for ever that things could have been different in every damned way.

She was looking at him expectantly, for an answer, but he couldn't remember the question. She huffed out a breath and handed him the lead. 'The vet clinic is easier for me. Bring him down for eight o'clock. Thanks.'

Then she turned to go and without thinking he put his hand on her shoulder. 'Beth. Stop.'

She wheeled round to him, the cold night turning her breath to smoke that dissipated into nothing. 'What, Alex?'

'I'm sorry I hurt you.'

She flinched away from his hand. 'It was a long time ago.'

'I wish...'

She lifted her chin. Daring, proud. Her eyes blazing. 'What exactly do you wish?'

So many wishes—most of them involved Beth. Some were attainable, many just weren't. 'That things were different.'

She pressed her lips together and raised her palm. 'Don't do this now. Please. I'm exhausted and I can't... I don't understand what you're saying.'

Neither did he. What the hell was he doing? The last thing either of them needed was this. He tugged gently on the lead and brought Spike close, then turned away from her haunting eyes and the mouth he ached to kiss. 'I'll see you tomorrow.'

CHAPTER FIVE

THE BATH WAS WONDERFUL. Beth's heart, not so much. Questions and emotions see-sawed through her. Why hadn't she just grabbed the chance to ask him what the hell had been going on all those years ago? Because she'd spent years building herself back up. She'd done well, too. Until she'd come back.

Never go back—that was a hard lesson learnt.

What had he meant by he wished things were different?

And why the big heartache now? Why did he have to say that when she was already emotionally vulnerable? What with wrapping up her family home, looking after her mother and holding down a job that involved beloved pets her life was wrought with too many emotions as it was, without adding Alex into the mix. But ever since she'd come back home she'd tumbled from delight at seeing him, to sadness at what they'd lost, then anger and a desperation to move forward.

She'd soaked for an hour just to get some personal space and to de-stress after the trauma of Meg and Dennis. And Alex. But eventually the water had turned cold and she shivered as she went downstairs, wrapping her dressing gown tightly round her. She hated being cold.

That Christmas when he'd broken things off she'd felt as if she was cold for months. She hadn't been able to stop shivering and shaking, not for a long time.

Her mum was in the dining room surrounded by boxes.

'What about this lovely dinner service from Grandma Masters? I'm sure it's worth something…you could sell it if you don't want to take it with you.' Beth's mum tearfully nosed her wheelchair round the dining table, which was covered in the contents of the old pine dresser, while Beth fixed a smile on her face. Downsizing from a three-bedroomed eighteenth-century cottage to a one-bedroomed modern apartment in Bay View rest home was hard work.

Sure, it was a nice dinner service, but for twelve people? How was she ever going to fit twelve bodies round her tiny table in Scotland? The last time the service was used was when her father had been killed in a work accident when Beth was six, and ever since it had been taken out three times a year, cleaned and then put back in exactly the same place to collect dust.

All she remembered was sitting in this room after his funeral, not understanding why her daddy wasn't coming back and staring hard at the dainty pink and blue flowers willing herself not to cry. Every time she'd looked at it since she'd had a feeling that life was unreliable and that the rug could be well and truly ripped out from beneath you at any given time.

It was difficult enough sorting out the remnants of her childhood without going through every single item and reliving the memories. 'It's tempting to say yes to taking everything, but I'm not sure it will all fit into my two-bedroomed terrace in Glasgow.'

Her mum wiped her eyes on her cardigan sleeve. 'I've always loved my china collection. There's pieces from both sides of the family and mementoes that people brought me from all over the world. If I knew you had it then it would make me happy.'

But would it make me happy? Beth didn't want the oddly painted china doll from Russia and didn't have much need for the porcelain Picasso mugs from Malaga—from Alex's parents, maybe? But she didn't need her mother's heart to break along with her own either. 'I don't know. Let's put it in the not sure pile.'

'Beth, love, the only pile we've made so far is the not sure pile. I'm hoping for a keeper pile soon.'

She was right. Beth had hedged about taking any of it. 'Oh, Mum. I'm sorry. I'm tired. Maybe we should do this tomorrow after work, when I'm feeling brighter.'

Her mum covered Beth's hand with her own very misshapen one. 'It's not just tiredness, Beth. I can see that it's something else. Something's bothering you and I'm fairly sure it's not just sorting through a load of old stuff.'

Oh-oh. Beth wasn't in the mood for a heart-to-heart with her mum. When Alex had put his hand on her shoulder earlier and said he was sorry and wished things were different her chest had felt as if it were squeezing so tightly she was going to stop breathing.

Worse, part of her—a big part—had leaned in to him, melting at his words and the soft pain in his eyes. She'd genuinely thought he'd meant it. For one split second. Then she'd reminded herself what it had taken for her to recover from him last time. She wasn't going there again. She found her mum a smile. 'I'm fine.'

'I know packing your life up is hard. You should look at it as a chance to declutter. I've been watching a TV programme about it. You can't move forward until you let go of the past.'

How to tell her that just handing it all over to some-one else to deal with wasn't exactly the solution? Beth laughed. 'Hmmm. The only thing stopping me from moving forward will be the hours I have to spend on eBay selling all this stuff.'

But her mum gave her an 'I know you better than that' kind of look. 'It's Alex, isn't it? That's what's up-setting you, not this.'

'No.'

'Love, I see the way your eyes light up when anyone mentions his name. I also know what the break-up did to you. That Christmas you came back and barely spoke, you barely ate, I was so worried about you. You just sat in your room and stared out of the window.'

Beth didn't want to be reminded. 'Now you're mak-ing me sound like a sad case. I was a lot younger and naive then and I got over him eventually.' And vowed never to let a man make her feel so empty again. 'I was over him a long time ago. I'm a different person now.'

It was just that seeing him all the time was frustrat-ing in the extreme.

'I know you are,' her mum said gently. 'You're strong and brave, and how you hold yourself together when you're dealing with those sick animals is beyond me. But you've got a soft heart, and all I'm saying is that it must be hard being around him again. Sharing custody of that puppy means you're getting too close.'

'I'm working hard to find a home for him. The puppy, I mean, not Alex.' Although rehoming her ex to Outer Mongolia was a pretty good idea right now. 'I've put adverts on all the community social media pages and hopefully someone will come forward and claim him. Once he's settled things will get back to normal again.' Whatever that was. And there was the other thing— when she wasn't with Button she worried about him. It was getting harder to stay detached. From them both.

Her mum smiled. 'There are a few boxes in the attic with the things Alex gave you. What are you going to do with them?'

She couldn't even face looking at them. It was stuff she'd thrown up there in her anger, hoping it would never see the light of day again. Did she want his eighteenth birthday card? The teddy bear he'd bought her to sleep with when he wasn't around? That beautiful engagement ring? Up the ladder, out of sight but not always out of mind. 'I'm tempted to just throw them all away. Fresh start, right? Moving forward.'

'Really? Even that lovely ring?'

'Definitely the ring. Just throw it all away.' Beth swallowed, pushed his face away from her memory banks and picked up one of the six white porcelain jugs her mum owned. All very similar, all very pretty, slightly different sizes, but six? There'd only ever been a maximum of three people living here at any one time—why did they need six milk jugs?

She'd come here for one weekend visit and now her whole life was upside down. Beth put the white jug down on the piece of paper marked 'SELL' and took a deep breath. Result. Maybe her mum had a point: she felt better just decluttering one thing. 'Right, then, the only decision I need to make right now is whether to have a glass of Chardonnay or a bucket of Shiraz. Want to join me?'

'I shouldn't…not really…not with the tablets I'm on. But…' Her mum pressed a button on the chair and an electric hum took her towards the door. 'Okay, darling, Chardonnay it is. And shall we watch the tidying programme to get some tips?'

'Definitely. I think we're going to need them. Some of us more than others.' Beth grinned, grateful her mum hadn't pushed her more on the Alex issue.

If only you could declutter emotions too.

Oaktree Farm was four miles out of the village. Up into the low-hanging snow-filled cloud and beyond. As the car wove higher through the hills the snow got deeper and the air colder—even with the very efficient heater in his *fancy-pants* red Mazda.

Alex smiled at Beth's description of his car. There was something about a woman who had no problem speaking her mind that kept him interested. She was a challenge, but then she always had been. That was what had attracted him to her in the first place. He'd been waiting for her to ask him about that phone call and he wondered why she hadn't. Had she groomed her heart against him so completely?

For the last four days it had been going round in his head and he'd wanted to broach the subject again somehow, but puppy handovers had been swift and curt and she'd found an excuse to leave every time they'd met.

His full body smile quickly morphed into discomfort. He should have kept his guard up around her instead of muddying things further. He shouldn't have opened his mouth and said what he wished, but there was something about Beth being finally willing to have a conversation that had lulled him into giving her more than he'd planned. He should have—

Suddenly the world swerved. *No.* It wasn't the world.

It was the rear of the car sliding out of control. Black ice. *Shoot*. Heart hammering against his rib cage, he took his foot off the accelerator and focused on the road ahead, steering the car into the slide. Trying to. *Trying...* He dragged road-safety messages from somewhere in a deep corner of his brain. *Focus on the road. On the road.*

He was travelling sideways towards an oak tree. The road was lined with the damned things.

Faster...sliding...was this the last thing he was going to see? Oak trees and ice? Not Beth's pretty face? Not the infinity number of freckles that kissed her skin?

Focus on the road.

A dip in the road, then a rise. The ice. The tree. The road. The road. And...he came to a sliding halt.

Alex sat for moment and breathed deeply. Holy hell, that was close. He should have been focusing on the damned road. But Beth, it seemed, was with him everywhere. All. The. Time.

And now it was getting dangerous. So, he needed to be honest with her once and for all—maybe then he'd be able to offload some of the guilt he'd been carrying around about the way he'd finished things between them. Maybe she'd forgive him. Maybe she wouldn't. Probably not.

But even so, he needed to address the huge elephant in the room whenever they were together. He needed to tell her the truth. Then maybe he'd get her the hell out of his head.

Glad when he safely reached Dennis's farm along ever narrowing and increasingly icy lanes Alex stepped out of his car and breathed in the rarefied air. There'd been no other footprints or vehicle tracks on the snow and he wondered how often anyone other than Dennis ever came here. The farmhouse was made of similar materials to most of the houses round Oakdale—walls made of whitewashed, locally quarried large stone boulders, and blue-green slate roofs. Although Dennis's roof had some slates missing and the whitewash was blackened in places by dirt and neglect.

Alex rang the doorbell and was greeted with a loud barking. So, Meg wasn't the only farm dog to keep Dennis company. That was something at least. Even though Alex sometimes hated living in the claustrophobic confines of a small village and he often craved the solitude of the hills, he couldn't imagine being permanently this removed from people. There was nothing and no one for miles around, just an endless undulating landscape of white. Of course, it would be a different view depending on the season, but right now he reckoned the starkness of it would be enough to drive him just a little bit crazy.

As he waited for Dennis to answer the door he glanced right, across the slate courtyard to a large barn. The doors were wide open, giving him a good view of the contents: two large green tractors, a farm quad and trailer and what Alex thought must be various shearing tools. He didn't know much about farming, but it was clear the machinery was old and well on the way to rust.

Over to the left there was a sheep-dipping pen that looked like some sort of weird maze with its own moat, and beyond, ewes wandered in a patchwork of paddocks that stretched down the hill towards Oakdale village. After Frank's accident Alex hoped the rams were all fenced off somewhere. *Baa, humbug.*

'June. Heel.' The gruff voice made Alex jump and whip round. The door had opened and a collie with a lot more energy than Meg ran around Alex's legs, sniffing and whining as Dennis appeared in the doorway. June was a dog?

'Hey, girl.' Alex patted the mutt's head. 'Hello, Dennis. Good to see you.'

'Aye.' Dennis gripped the door handle. Knuckles white. Face red. Chest heaving. A little breathless, unkempt, red cheeks, which could be a sign of rosacea or polycythaemia, or just not enough sunscreen. 'Is it bad news, Doc?'

'No. I was just passing and thought I'd pop in to see how you were.' Truth was, the chances of Alex just passing were very, very slim and they both knew it.

Dennis frowned. 'Meg?'

'As far as I know she's doing okay. Discharge tomorrow, I understand.' Alex looked hopefully beyond the front door. 'Can I come in?'

Dennis glanced behind him, then back at Alex, clearly uncomfortable at his question. 'Why?'

Alex stepped forward. 'No reason. I was just wondering how you're doing. I know you must be worrying about Meg. Thought you might need some company.'

'Not really.' The old man pulled the door closed behind him, and blocked Alex's path. Perhaps the place was a state. Perhaps Dennis was embarrassed. Perhaps he was just a man who protected his privacy from nosy GPs who turned up on spec.

Alex tried to deflect attention away from his client. 'To be honest, I'm parched. Any chance of a cuppa?'

'No. I'm on my way up the hill.' Dennis scuffed dirty hands down grubby, baggy trousers that looked as if they'd been around for fifty years.

'Did you hear about Frank Entwhistle?'

'Aye. Rum business. But he should have known not

to mither a ram after tupping. Sheep Rearing for Beginners.' The old man's eyes narrowed. 'You're not here to talk about Frank.'

Okay. Alex took his chance. 'Just wondering about the ibuprofen.'

'What about it?'

'Did you find any?'

'Come on, June, heel.' Dennis clicked his fingers and the dog ran to his side.

What was this dog-control wizardry? And what was with the question-dodging? Was there or wasn't there any ibuprofen?

'It's okay, Dennis, you're not in trouble or anything. We just want to help.'

Dennis shook his head and waved his hand as if all this was just a waste of time. 'And I just want to get on.'

It looked as if Alex wasn't going to get his answers today. 'Okay. If you need to chat then you know where I am. Any time.'

'I don't need a doctor. I just need Meg back.' Dennis's chin rose a little and there was a glimmer of light in his eyes. 'I saved her life...'

'You did. If you hadn't acted so quickly, she definitely would have died.'

'Aye. Now she needs to come home.' He stalked towards the quad bike, climbed wearily onto it and then called to his dog. 'Come on, Juney.'

As if tugged by some imaginary force the dog did exactly as Dennis asked and Alex wanted to question him about his training skills, because so far his puppy had done pretty much the opposite to whatever Alex told him to do. But Dennis revved up and steered the quad out of the barn, took a sharp left turn and off up onto the hill.

Alex watched him disappear but not before Dennis turned back to look at him. Twice. Something wasn't right and he needed to talk his thoughts through with someone who knew him.

Luckily, he knew just the person.

CHAPTER SIX

BETH WAS PUTTING the 'Closed' sign on the door as Alex arrived at the clinic. Her stomach did the same kind of funny little flip it used to do whenever she saw his face—anticipating his kisses or just one of his warming hugs. She reminded herself it was just a Pavlovian reaction, that was all. It would wear off once she was out in the snow and with distance between them. Distance, she'd decided, was the best way to deal with Alex.

But there was no avoiding him, so she searched quickly for an excuse not to have a prolonged conversation as she stepped aside to let him in, taking extra care not to inhale his scent or stand too close. 'Hi there. I'll just get Button. He's having a nap in the staff room.'

'Really?' Alex laughed as he stepped into the clinic. He had a way with him that was almost lazily confident. He wasn't easily fazed; he was comfortable in most environments. He seemed comfortable around her most of the time. There was little of the trembling she had when he was close, none of the breathless dizziness. There was little to show he was affected by her at all. So why did he wish things were different? 'The staff room? Has Spike been promoted?'

One day they might even decide on a name they both

agreed on. 'No, he's just spoilt rotten. Everyone who works here thinks of him as the "clinic puppy". He has more mummies and daddies than any animal should have.' She escaped as quickly as she could and called Button out of the room.

The pooch barked excitedly at the sight of Alex standing in the shop area of Reception, looking at the toy section. Man and dog greeted each other like long-lost relatives and she dreaded to think how all of them were going to be when this puppy-sitting jaunt finished. Or when she went back to her real life in Glasgow without them. Or, without Button at least.

Alex crouched and scratched behind Button's ears. 'How was he today? He seemed a bit off his food this morning. Did he eat anything?'

'Pretty much everything in sight.' She laughed, pretending her chest wasn't aching just by looking at them. Not just her chest either; watching his hands move across the dog's fur reminded her how assured he could be... which led onto other thoughts about those hands. The way he'd make her feel as he stroked her skin. The hours she'd spent just delighting in him and what they'd had together. The sex that had been so delicious, so damned good.

Stop it. There was no point thinking backwards; she had to keep going forward. She swallowed and found her words. 'Right, got to dash, I'm helping Mum again tonight.'

Alex stopped scratching. 'Still packing? It's taking for ever.'

'Tell me about it. It's a whole life to sort through—these things take time. Plus, she's pretty indecisive.' Beth handed him the lead and the poop bags. 'You probably won't need them as he's already performed today. Okay, got everything? Bye, then.'

She couldn't believe she was talking to Alex Norton about their shared puppy's bowel habits.

Their puppy? How had her life gone full circle so that she was back talking to her ex-fiancé about *our* and *we*? The sooner they found a home for Button, the better. And geez, could she be any more obvious about getting them out of the room? She headed towards the door.

But Alex didn't move. 'I went to see Dennis today.'

'Oh?' News on Meg's owner was important enough to stay a bit longer for. She tugged her handbag straps up her shoulder and waited.

Alex rocked back on his heels and stood up. 'He's got another dog up there. June. Collie. Younger than Meg, I think. Certainly more energetic.'

'That's hardly surprising after what Meg's been through. But, yes, I looked them up on the computer system here. She's Meg's daughter apparently, and she's been in a few times too with weird symptoms, nothing concrete. No diagnosis. Just random things.'

Alex shrugged. 'She seemed happy enough. But he was acting a bit strange.'

That wasn't surprising. Dennis Blakely had always been…different, but her mother had always said that it took all sorts to make up a world. 'Maybe because you turned up uninvited?'

'Okay, I realise not everyone is happy to have me around these days—' He raised his eyebrows at her and she knew her attempts at avoiding any further meaning-ful contact had hit home. It wasn't that she didn't want him around—hell, having him around did things to her that only Alex could do. It just hurt to be so close, to pretend this was fun and normal and that their past didn't rush up in her chest every time she saw him. The good bits as well as the bad.

She raised her hand. 'Guilty as charged.'

He smiled. 'I am so misunderstood.'

'Yeah. Really?' Now would have been a good time to talk about that Christmas, but she needed to hear about Dennis and make sure Meg was going home tomorrow to a safe place. And she was looking forward, right?

'Seriously, I was trying to give the guy a chance to offload and to have a quiet look around to see if he was coping up there on his own. It's about ten degrees colder on that farm, I swear.' Alex tugged his coat collar up around his neck and she was overwhelmed with the same sudden urge she'd had the other day to wind her arms inside his coat and press her body against his.

This couldn't be happening. She couldn't think about sex every time she looked at him. She couldn't think about how good the sex had been. She couldn't keep doing this to herself. 'Did you find anything to sway you either way? Is he managing? Is he safe?'

'His house needs some TLC and his machinery is decrepit, but I can't say he's in danger. He whizzed off on his quad bike like a seasoned pro. I just think he's a bit gruff and very private. Not everyone wants to socialise—even though it's proven to be good for mental health and mental agility.' He smiled as Button nuzzled into his palm. 'One thing, though. Dennis might not be great with humans, but he has complete control over his dog. One click of the fingers and she's at his side.'

'What? Like this?' Beth could barely hide her smile as she showed Alex the new trick she'd been working on with Button. 'Boy! Boy, come here.'

Alex's mouth opened as the pooch padded straight over to her. 'Boy? Since when...?'

'I'm trying not to confuse him by using Button or Spike. When he goes to his for-ever home they'll still call him Boy somehow. Like we do. Hey, boy. Lovely boy...you know. I just thought it best to keep our chosen names out of the equation. Now, boy, sit!' *Please.* 'Sit.'

Alex's chin almost hit the ground as Button sat on his back legs. 'Magic. Witchcraft. Sorcery.'

Now she did smile. Getting one over on him had always been fun. 'Yes. Pretty much.'

'Where's the wand?' He looked behind her back, turned one hand over and then the other, standing so close she could feel the heat emanating from him. She clenched her muscles to try to stop the whisper of desire spiralling through her as his skin touched hers.

'Don't need one.' Turning her back to Alex, she covertly took a dog treat from her pocket and slipped it to Button, then gave him a fuss. She wasn't going to admit to spending every spare hour here teaching Button. She certainly wasn't going to admit to the clutch in her heart every time the clinic phone rang and she thought it might be someone claiming the pup she'd grown so fond of. 'Give it a go.'

One of Alex's shoulders rose and he patted his thighs. 'Okay. Boy, come here. Come.'

But Button just sniffed around Beth's shoes and paid him no attention.

Alex laughed. 'I think I need your invisible wand, Beth. He's certainly not bewitched by me.'

'Aww, one teeny, weeny hiccup and you're giving up?'

He took the bait, lowering his voice. 'Not a chance.

He just needs a firm command. Right? Boy! Come here. Come.'

Button tilted his head to one side, one ear pricked, one floppy, and didn't move one inch. She could have kissed him. The dog. Not the man.

Okay, maybe the man.

Definitely the man.

'Boy!' She grabbed a handful of treats and closed her fist, called Button over and he came at her first command. Then she opened her fist and showed Alex. 'Not magic. Bribery.'

His smile grew. 'Cheating, more like.'

'Also known as training. This kind of thing takes time—you have to repeat and repeat and repeat until it's Pavlovian.' Like her tummy flip whenever he was close. Okay, so that had taken years to perfect...and she couldn't expect it to diminish just because her head told her body to stop. 'I bet Dennis has spent literally hours, days even, training his dogs. I bet it's not something you could do, you're too impatient. You always wanted everything *now*.'

'Beth Masters, I am not impatient.' He stroked Button's head then lifted the floppy ear and whispered, loud enough for Beth to hear, 'Don't listen to her. It's all lies. I am patience personified.'

She rolled her eyes and laughed. 'Really? I remember that spring bank holiday when you'd been given a surprise weekend off. Within minutes of leaving the ward you decided to visit me in Glasgow. You were supposed to be coming up the weekend after, but you just appeared on my doorstep saying you couldn't wait another week.'

'I needed to see you. Three-day weekends are the

best.' He smiled some more…this time it was open and unguarded and sexy as hell. 'Best—'

'Spent in bed.' She finished the phrase for him and then wished she hadn't. Her chest felt as if it were cracking open as she remembered opening the door to him holding a bunch of drooping daffodils and a bottle of wine. Before she'd managed to say a word he'd pressed her against the front door and kissed her so hard she'd thought she was going to die of lust right there, in his arms. She'd never been so pleased to see anyone in her life, and she'd never been so turned on. Just the thought of it had desire prickling over her skin. She tried to swallow it away and rubbed her palms down her thighs to feel something other than a sensual ache. 'Anyway. That's how you train a puppy. Reward him for good behaviour.'

'Is that how you train humans too?'

'It would take a whole lot more than treats to make your behaviour fit my standards, Alex Norton.'

But instead of being taken aback by her tongue lashing he stepped a little closer, eyes glittering. 'What kind of more?'

She couldn't find her voice in her tight throat. He was here and close and she couldn't think straight. Her senses seemed on overdrive; there was a heady sensual scent in the air, her body sensitive to where he put those amazing hands now, wishing they were exploring her instead of shoved in his pockets.

She wanted him and she shouldn't. She'd immunised herself against him. She'd reeled from his words, nursed a broken heart. 'A lot more than you've got.'

'I can do more.' He wanted to kiss her. She knew him too well to not misinterpret that misted look in his eyes. It had been a long time but she hadn't forgotten. And hell, she wanted to kiss him too. Just once. Just to feel his lips press on hers, just to taste him one more time. Then she'd turn and walk away from him. This time, she'd do the walking.

His palm cupped her cheek and his mouth was so close all she'd have to do was tiptoe up as she used to.

It was easy. So easy it was as if her body had learnt it by rote. She put her palm on his shoulder and raised her heels. Touched her head to his. Heard the sharp inhale as he put his lips to her forehead. Relished the tight rasp of his jaw on her cheek. His scent was almost a taste in the air.

God, she wanted to taste him. Couldn't stop now... the memories flooded her. His caress. His mouth. Him. The core of her heart. The beat. The rhythm of her life. Her everything. She brushed her lips against his cheek then stopped a breath away from his mouth. She raised her eyes to his, so dark, dangerous and piercing. Urging her on. Because after all that had happened they both knew this had to be her move.

She wet her lips with her tongue, felt his shudder. Heard the groan. Then she closed her eyes and brushed her mouth on his. Not a kiss. Not quite.

Neither of them moved, but she felt the thud of her heart mirror his. Could she do it? Could she push harder, take more? Could she kiss him the way she'd done back then? Could she let herself fall?

Then she heard her name in his throat, felt the way he offered it like a prayer against her lips, and she opened her mouth to him. He tasted the same and yet something new...of mountain ice and warm winter sun, of regret and hope that she felt settle into her skin and her belly and her heart. His scent, so familiar, enveloped and anchored her. It was like slipping softly into the past and stepping into a bold new future at the same time.

He put his other palm to her cheek and deepened the kiss, his tongue slick against hers, intense and intimate—only Alex had ever kissed her with such passion and it made her belly ache with need. She was kissing him again. As if the years in between hadn't happened. As if nothing mattered but this.

He slid his arms round her waist and pulled her to him. She wound her arms inside his coat and for the briefest moment she let herself fall into the feeling... muscled arms, broad chest, Alex Norton was more than before.

Before...before he snapped her heart in two and went loco.

He'd left her broken.

It was utter madness, going back there. Some sort of collision course of masochism. He'd already damaged her once. She was not going to let him do it again. She stepped back, struggling to catch her breath and pressing a shaking hand to her face, trying to take the heat out of her skin. 'Once upon a time I would have loved to kiss you a whole lot more, Alex Norton. But not now.'

He shook his head, running his fingers across his scalp. 'I know. I'm sorry. I shouldn't. We shouldn't—I just...'

Now. She needed answers now. Before she did something else stupid. She needed to hear he'd got over her and that this was just a little out-of-control lust that would fade the second she walked out.

She took another deep breath that eased a little of the shaking in her limbs. 'Okay. It's time... I've got to get a handle on what's going on here. You said the other day that you wish things were different. How? That you'd dumped me in a different way? That you'd been kinder? That you'd hung around long enough to explain a little more why the supposed love of your life wasn't for life, she wasn't even for damned Christmas? What?'

'Oh, Beth.' He held his palms up. 'You have every right to be angry with me.'

'Too right, mate.' The rage of old started to rise up in her chest, mingling with the rush of pure desire she'd had being wrapped in him. And now she was so conflicted. She wanted to kiss him, but she was, deep down, still angry with him. How could you want to kiss someone who made you feel all mixed-up inside?

She fought it, because she didn't want him to see what he'd done to her and she wasn't sure she wanted to hear what he had to say. Closure was one thing, but actively putting yourself in the line of fire was something else altogether. But she needed to draw a line under the past so she took a moment to control herself then said, as calmly as she could, 'You dumped me just before Christmas and then went travelling. You broke promises and I'm still not sure exactly what I'd done wrong. Basically, you broke my heart, Alex. Why wouldn't I be angry about that?'

His eyes flickered closed. When they opened again they were haunted and dark. 'I didn't go travelling, Beth.'

'Yes, you did. Your parents told me. Thailand or something. I can't remember the details. Hard to listen when your heart is breaking.' She'd briefly seen them when she'd come back from university for the Christmas holidays. They were heading off now, they'd said as they'd bundled suitcases into their car. *We're so sorry, it's what he wants.* And she'd been left with a zillion unanswered questions and had gone back to university none the wiser, and growing angrier by the day.

'I didn't go travelling. I was in England. London, actually.'

'What?' That wasn't true. 'Please don't lie. Your mum said Thailand, I'm sure. Anyhow, you were travelling. You were taking a term off or something… It was so sudden and so unlike you that I thought you were having a breakdown or something. I thought it might have something to do with losing your cousin and you feeling guilty or depressed. But they were adamant you just wanted time out to travel.'

He breathed out heavily. 'Well, if you call being wheeled from the ward to Theatre and back again, then to Oncology, then to chemotherapy ad infinitum *travelling*, then I guess you could say I was fully immersed in the experience.'

What the hell? He'd been sick? Her heart contracted. 'Oncology? Chemo? What are you talking about? Your parents told me—'

He pulled out a chair from behind the desk and slumped down on it. 'I know what they said, Beth, because I told them to say that. I didn't want you to know the truth.'

'But…' She didn't even want to say the word, never mind think through the implications. 'Oncology?'

'Testicular cancer.'

'Oh, my God.' Her heart collapsed in on itself and she went to put her arms around him. But stopped, because she didn't know whether holding him now was a good thing or not or where it might lead or what to do generally. While her mind reached out for explanations and reasoning her body ached for him. She didn't know how to act, but she sure as hell knew how to feel. Right now, she was a mix of so many emotions she lost count. 'Alex, I'm so sorry. It must have been so frightening—and now? Are you okay?'

He nodded and there was a dim light in his eyes that told her he'd been through too much and he was welcoming the relief to be able to say, 'All clear.'

'Thank God.' She breathed out, not even realising her breath had stalled in her throat. He was okay. He was okay. So many questions bubbled around her head and it felt as if there were a heavy weight on her chest. 'But… like Mikey? You had the same thing as your cousin?'

She'd been there through Mikey's treatment, watched a vibrant young man who loved playing football and basketball, who loved music and hanging out, who had been just a regular teenager, be ravaged by the disease. She'd watched the family implode in grief. She'd stood by Alex's side through it all. It had brought them closer, that was what he'd said, and that she'd been his guiding light in the dark.

Then, when he'd needed her he'd snuffed the light out and lied?

He put his hands to his head. 'Sucks, right? Who would have thought that kind of lightning could strike twice in the same family? But, apparently, with some types of cancer there is a familial link. Only, I survived and he didn't.'

Certainly not for the lack of wanting, hoping, bargaining with whatever higher force might listen. Alex had been glued to his older cousin's bedside, had all but moved into the hospital to help him. He'd attended every appointment with him, asked all the difficult questions and had been there when Mikey had railed at the unjustness of it all. He'd sat up with him for endless nights, distracted him with computer games and talk of the future. But in the end, nothing had helped. Mikey had been diagnosed too late and not even his cousin's strength and hope could save him.

And Alex had been through that and told his parents to lie to her? She couldn't stop her hands from shaking. She suddenly felt sick. He'd been ill, so very ill and he hadn't wanted her to know? 'You had cancer and you didn't tell me? Your girlfriend? Your fiancée? The woman you declared to be the love of your life? You kept that from me? Who even does that?'

His features flattened. 'I did.'

'It doesn't make any sense. Why? Why didn't you say anything?'

He reached out and touched her arm. 'I had my reasons. I was trying to protect you.'

She shrugged away from him. 'That really is not how it works. That is not how love works, Alex. Not at all. You stick with them, you trust them to look after you, you let them love you. You don't lie and get your parents to lie.'

'I was in a panic. It was a shock and I didn't know what to do.'

'So you pretended you were going on holiday instead of telling me you were in hospital? Wow.' She needed to breathe fresh air. She needed to get the hell away and work out what this all meant. 'You broke me. I thought you'd found someone else. I thought you'd got bored. I thought I wasn't enough.'

'You were enough, Beth. You were everything.' He shook his head. 'I'm sorry.'

'That's really not going to cut it.'

How could she have been enough if he hadn't been able to tell her the most intimate thing he was facing?

Biting back the sting of tears, she stumbled towards the door, almost tripping over Button. And whatever else Alex might have said, she didn't know. She didn't want to hear. She slammed the door behind her and crunched across fresh snow, trying to breathe, trying to understand how anyone could do such a thing.

He'd been having chemotherapy. He'd been in hospital and she hadn't known. She'd imagined him on a beach with another woman, having lazy sex under a hot sun. Laughing, kissing, stroking. Loving. Only not with her. But the hard reality had been that he'd faced something utterly frightening and he hadn't looked to her for support.

He'd lied to her. He'd not let her in at the most difficult time of his life. It was cruel. Just cruel. He hadn't given her the chance to care.

That was all she needed to know.

CHAPTER SEVEN

SHE HADN'T LET him explain.

He tried. He chased after her, but she refused to speak or listen or stop. Since then, at every doggy handover she'd turned down any chance at communication and only gave him reluctant eye contact. He could see that even this morning, days later, she was still seething. She had good reason, but he didn't want it to go on any more without making her listen; he just had to work out how.

Which was impossible when he was currently the only glue holding his GP practice together and he had to focus here and not on her and his past. But his head kept on going there. Too much and too often. The kiss still lingered on his lips; he could still remember the taste of her, the way she'd fitted back into his arms as perfectly as before.

Kissing her had been stupid because it had woken something up inside him. Something that could never be a reality so he'd be better leaving her to stew and to let her hate him. But even if he couldn't offer her anything before she went back to Glasgow, he wanted to be honest and truthful and open.

'This is Dr Fraser Moore and his daughter, Lily. The cavalry in our hours of need,' Maxine joked as she introduced Alex to them in the clinic reception area during his Monday lunch break, such as it was—if he was lucky, he'd get five minutes before the next patient strolled in. He noted the clinic was now bedecked in Christmas glitter and tinsel and that the Christmas tree had been decorated. Thankfully, Maxine had steered away from asking him to help a second time. But just the sight of the tinsel had him thinking of Beth all over again. Maxine glared at him and gave him a 'go on, smile' kind of look. 'This is Alex Norton. He'll show you both round the practice.'

'Good to meet you, Alex. Not sure I'm cavalry material but I'll do my best at patching up the injured.' Fraser smiled and shook Alex's hand. He seemed okay. About the same age as himself…maybe a bit older if he had a teenage daughter. 'We're keen to get stuck in and get to know the community here, aren't we, Lily?'

The girl slouched forward and nodded. She was like a Fraser female mini-me although where her father had short dark hair, hers was long and pulled into a scruffy ponytail. She had large dark eyes that, also in contrast to her father's, were not at all amused or brimming with enthusiasm. She wore a thick woollen jumper that was so big on her it looked as if it belonged to her dad and skintight jeans and trainers. The typical uniform of all the teenagers round Oakdale. As was the grouchy look on her face. No smile. No handshake. She just rolled her eyes and managed, 'Er…yeah. Hi.'

He wondered if there was a mum around, but it didn't feel appropriate to ask so Alex just walked them through the clinic, showing Fraser his consulting room, the treatment spaces and nurses' rooms. 'It's your average rural GP clinic, but things are getting a bit hectic with the usual winter colds and flu. There's only me at the moment, so I'm very glad to have you here.'

'Is tomorrow good for me to start?' Fraser looked keen. A good thing indeed.

'Tomorrow is great. We'll arrange a cut-down clinic after a morning orientation. Maxine will run through the software with you, although I think I read you used the same one in your GP practice in London?'

'Sure did. I've also done a fair bit of locum work over the years, so I'm used to fitting in and working things out on my own.'

'Have a cuppa before you head out into that cold.' Maxine brought a tray with tea and biscuits into the staff room and Alex shoved back a groan. He needed to get back to work, but he also needed to be polite.

It was both a blessing and a curse to be so busy that he could barely breathe, let alone think. The weekend had been a washout, both weather and mood wise. Dark heavy clouds had emptied more snow over the roads and mountains, which had meant his usual weekend activities of hiking and climbing had been cancelled. Normally he used the discipline and concentration of climbing as a form of meditation to clear his head so, being stuck inside with a frisky puppy that seemed to have as much tense energy as Alex did had almost driven him crazy.

The only outside time he'd managed had been to take Spike out for short walks, between snow falls, around the low-lying hills. But, maybe sensing Alex's mood or the impasse between him and Beth, their dog had been particularly disobedient, except at their handovers where he'd been exemplary in front of Beth.

Which had made everything worse.

Not that much could be worse. He didn't know how to make it right apart from more talking and she wasn't having any of that.

He turned to Lily, who was squirrelling away the custard creams. 'Will you be going to Bowness High School?'

The girl shrugged. 'The same place my dad's going to run the evening outreach clinics? Great. Can. Not. Wait.' Her accent was southern, London maybe, longer-stretched-out vowels, no northern bluntness. Except for in her tone. She did not want to be in Oakdale.

It was Fraser's turn to grimace. 'Sorry, yes, she will, after the holidays, no point in her starting just as they're about to break up for Christmas. She's going to be helping me out with sorting our things in the cottage.'

'You've bought? Renting?'

'Bought,' Fraser explained. 'Thought it might make us feel more settled.'

'As if.' Lily sighed and rolled her eyes. 'What's the Wi-Fi like around here? It's been rubbish all weekend. In Clapham it was brilliant.'

'Sporadic at best.' Alex caught the new GP's eye as he winced.

'But you won't be needing it as much, I'm sure, Lily. There's lots to do here.' Fraser sounded hopeful and Alex smiled to himself. If you liked the outdoors the Lake District was brilliant, but if you were forced to move here from a busy city—and he wondered if that was why Lily was so grumpy—and you didn't much like hills and countryside, then it was going to be a bit of a struggle.

Alex tried to help. 'There's a great climbing wall in Kendal if you like that kind of thing. And there's some very cool cinemas in Ambleside. Pop into the tourist information centre at Bowness—they have lots of ideas of things to do and they might know of some school-holiday activities going on.'

Lily sighed again and shook her head and Alex felt for both father and daughter. He didn't know their story, but there clearly was one.

Fraser put down his cup. 'Right, we're heading off to the school to sign Lily up then we've a few more things I need to tick off the list. Registering at the doctors' is easy, clearly. We need to take Jasper to the vets...do you know any good ones round here you could recommend?'

Did he? The best. He couldn't forget the image of her haunted face as he'd told her the truth. The hurt he'd caused then and now that was etched in her features. The swirl of tears that she'd steadfastly blocked away. And the pain under his rib cage that never seemed to abate. He'd do anything to take all that back, but she wasn't giving him the chance. He looked at Lily, who was staring at him as if he were crazy. 'Oh. Jasper?

'A dog?' she said, making it sound more like *duh*?

'Is he sick?'

'No.' More *duh*. 'He needs a haircut.'

And for the first time ever Alex was a little relieved that kids weren't going to happen to him.

Beth didn't want to talk to Alex because she was finding it damned hard to forgive him—or to even understand what the hell he'd been trying to achieve by lying to her—but here he was strolling into the clinic as if he owned the place and she had nowhere to hide.

Angus was holding the door open and chatting to him and she wanted to shout out to her boss not to leave her here with Alex because she wasn't sure what she was going to do with all the bottled-up anger, but she also didn't want to sound like a crazy woman.

She casually waved as Angus left and then pretended she was busy on the clinic computer, simultaneously trying to stop her hands from shaking and giving her away. She'd wanted to kiss him one last time and walk away unscathed, but instead she felt as if she'd been hit by a two-ton farming truck. And yet there were parts of her that still ached for his touch. Go figure. Maybe she was a crazy woman.

He came and stood on the opposite side of the reception desk, a face of smiles and sorry and all kinds of sexy. The kiss they'd shared, right here, was a spectre looming between them. 'Hi, Beth.'

'Button's in the soft cage in the treatment room.'

'Oh? Not the staff room today? He's been demoted?'

'Turns out he's a bit more stubborn than I originally thought.' Or maybe she'd been a little stretched and short-tempered today. The last few days, if she was honest— even her mum had commented on her bad mood. 'He kept trying to pull the food bags off the shelves and even got into one of them, so I had to put him somewhere safe while I worked. Anyway, you can go through and get him. I've got notes to write up.'

'Beth, we need to—'

'No.' She cut him off without giving him the pleasure or advantage of being in control of any of this.

She watched him disappear into the treatment room and put her head in her hands. This was too hard. Made harder because she wasn't only angry at him, but she also couldn't forget the way he'd looked at her when he'd kissed her...as if he actually cared. As if he wanted her the same way he'd wanted her all those years ago. And the ache in her chest, through her body, just wouldn't shift.

Too soon man and dog were back in front of her, making a fuss of each other and of her. Alex smiled again and it did something to her tummy. It felt as if he was trying to break through her defences by smiling that beautiful, sexy 'I want to kiss you again' smile. It wasn't going to work.

It. Would. Not. Work.

He leaned casually on the reception desk, opposite her. 'Did the new doctor and his daughter come in today?'

Beth stood and slapped Button's lead into his hand. 'Yes.'

'They have a dog.'

'Yes.'

She sat down and stared at the desk, noticing the air around her still, and she knew he was looking at her. Waiting. She didn't, couldn't look at him because she was barely holding onto her self-control. That kiss had muddied everything, because now she was cross and turned on and confused and conflicted.

'Beth, does this have to be so awkward?'

Eventually she gained enough strength to raise her eyes, just enough so she could see the buttons on his coat. She wasn't ready to give him eye contact yet. 'Yes.'

He threw up his hands and let Button run off down the pet-shampoo aisle. 'Can we be civil? Maybe try a little conversation? I recommended that Fraser and his daughter come here. They seem nice, right? I hope so, because I'm going to be working closely with him while Joe is on leave and Jenny's off sick.'

Her mother had always told her that if she didn't have

anything nice to say, she shouldn't say anything at all. She kept her mouth shut.

Alex didn't. 'What kind of dog do they have? Maybe we could arrange playdates for Spike. They've just moved up from London, so I thought I'd show them some short walks around the place.'

The elephant in the room was lies and betrayal but he wanted to talk about his new workmate. Okay. She directed her focus back on the monitor. She had no idea what was on the screen but she stared at it anyway as she said, 'They have an Old English sheepdog.'

'Beth, please look at me.'

She didn't want to. Couldn't.

'Please. We need to talk. About everything. About the kiss.'

She closed her eyes and tried not to think about it and how good it had felt.

And she hated the difficult atmosphere and wanted the ache in her chest to go. What would it hurt to hear him out? What would it hurt to look at him?

She raised her head and caught the full heat of his gaze. It made her feel off balance. More, she saw pain in his face as he shook his head and that hit her hard in the chest. 'You lied to me.'

He shook his head. 'I'm sorry, Beth. I was young and confused. I was trying to do the best thing I could by you.'

'By leaving me out of the most difficult and significant thing in your life?'

'Yes. Absolutely.' His eyes were dark, but determination shone through them.

And that was the thing she couldn't get her head around: he was adamant he'd been right to do it. 'I don't understand. I just don't understand. I've been going through it for the last few days and no... I just would not have done something like that to you.'

'I gave you a future.'

'What does that mean?'

He huffed out a breath, then came round to sit on a chair, facing her. It looked as if he was trying to find the right words, or choosing carefully, at least. 'It was December the eighteenth. I'd found a lump and it was big enough for me to know it needed to be seen as soon as possible. On the morning ward round I spoke to the surgeon I was on rotation with. He called his friend, a urologist, who said if I could get to his morning outpatients clinic he could see me straight away. It's unheard of, I know, but sometimes, if you're lucky—or unlucky to need it in the first place—things fall into place.'

She wasn't sure where this going and what it had to do with her future, because she felt as if it had been ripped away and she hadn't had a say. 'And there wasn't a five-minute gap where you could have called me?'

'I wasn't thinking straight and my mind was whirling with possibilities—none of them good. I wanted facts before I called anyone and all I could think of was Mikey and how it was going to be for me and how I was going to tell everyone I was going to die.' He took a breath and she could see some of the fear he'd been experiencing in the tightness of his shoulders and the haunted eyes. 'So, I had a consult and ultrasound and CT scan that morning, rushed through because the surgeon agreed it was probably malignant...and he'd had a cancellation that afternoon so could fit me in for surgery. Either that or wait three weeks until after the holidays and New Year.'

'You don't want to wait for something like that.'

Alex shrugged in agreement and turned his head a little as he talked, taking his gaze elsewhere—she didn't know where. The past? That hospital? 'It was late afternoon and he was telling me the diagnosis and… prognosis. It wasn't good. The ward had been decorated in Christmas stuff and as the doctor was telling me the diagnosis my eyes drifted to a Nativity in the corner. A man, a woman and a baby. And all I could think of was that that was not going to happen to me. I didn't even know if I was going to make Easter. I couldn't stop thinking about that scene and how we'd shaped our lives to that and how much you wanted it.'

'It wouldn't have mattered to me. I would have stood by you.'

His gaze settled back on her. 'You can say that now, but you don't know how you would have reacted as a twenty-one-year-old. You had a lot of living to do and all those plans.'

Plans she still had. Yes, she wanted a family but so far the chances of that happening were literally zero. Generally, a family didn't happen without a partner or a child, neither of which existed in her life right now. 'Plans can change, though. I like to think I would have stayed with you, whatever happened. I would have fought with you, for you.'

He rubbed his hand over his head. 'And that's the whole point, Beth. I didn't *want* you to, can't you see? I'd watched Mikey fight and die. I watched him give up. I fought and fought on his behalf and it didn't work anyway. I watched him change and I changed along with him. It was hard to see someone you love go through that and then to lose them. You know how it was…'

She remembered the whispered behind-the-door arguments about how to deal with the prognosis. How everyone had a different opinion about keeping hope or being honest and accepting fate, Mikey's folks splitting up for a while because they didn't know how to cope with a child dying. She remembered Alex railing against the boundaries his parents had set for him—coming in late, drinking more, arguing back. The anger-fuelled guilt at not being able to help his cousin in the end. 'Your family did some hard grieving.'

'We didn't know how to cope—there are no lessons on that and everyone reacts differently. After Mikey died, we were all so tired and broken by it and I just couldn't do that to you. Besides, more than anything I didn't want you to see me like that. I didn't want you to make promises that you'd feel compelled to keep even if you changed your mind. I certainly didn't want to offer you a future with me that was either pretty damned short or...infertile. I didn't want you regretting your promises and looking over your shoulder for a different life with the family you'd always craved. You'd spent a lot of your life looking after your mum and I saw how much that took out of you. I didn't want you to see me as the same burden.'

'So, you told your parents to tell me you'd gone travelling.' That explained the rush for them to get the suitcases in the car and the guilt that had been written over their faces. And the worry, now she knew why they had been so anxious to get away.

'It had to be something definitive and final so you wouldn't be able to find me and see what was happening. Even though they didn't want to lie they had to do what I asked. They needed me to concentrate on fighting and getting better...if that was possible. Remember, in those first few days we didn't know how long I had. It had spread.' It looked as if it was breaking his heart to tell her this. She slid her hand over to his and squeezed tight. It didn't feel like nearly enough and, more than anything, she wished she'd been with him at the time.

'I'm so sorry. You must have been so scared.' It was devastating to hear this but, even so, she couldn't let him off the hook. 'But what does it say about our relationship that you couldn't share this with me?'

'It says I loved you.' His eyes burnt hot and he looked at her with such affection that she couldn't stop the surge of emotion rising through her. She was briefly tempted to cover his mouth with hers and kiss away the pain she knew he must have had. But there, hammering hard in her head, was the fact that he'd already broken her heart once and she couldn't let it happen again.

She slipped her hand out from his and sat back. 'Weird. Because I always thought that love meant sticking together through thick and thin.'

'You were twenty-one years old, for God's sake... No one needs to care for their lover like that at twenty-one. And...there was a very high possibility that I wouldn't come out of it down the track and that you wouldn't get the family you wanted or even the man you'd fallen for.'

'Wasn't that something I should have decided? I am so bloody angry with you. You didn't give me a choice.'

'I was trying to protect you. Protect us both from a whole lot of heartache.'

'How's that working out for you?' Because her heart felt as if it had been blown wide open.

His eyebrows peaked. 'I've had better days. And worse, to be honest. A lot worse.'

She imagined him at twenty-three years of age, so

young and yet sick in hospital, staring at a possibly bleak future or no future at all, with no girlfriend to comfort him. And her heart contracted around a hot fist of hurt, regret and sadness. 'Alex, this is madness. I don't know what to say.'

'I had to let you go. I wanted you to have the future you'd always planned for.'

'Without you? We were together for six years. We were engaged to be married. You couldn't trust me with this?'

He huffed out a hollow sound. 'I couldn't bear for you to look at me, at what I was going to become and what I was going to lose. And I knew you'd still want to honour your commitments regardless of how things changed. A pity marriage, Beth? That wasn't what I wanted for either of us.'

'Pity?' That was the furthest from her mind. 'I would never pity you. I loved you.' Her heart squeezed with a too-familiar ache.

Alex's eyes shuttered closed for a moment. When he opened them the irises were black. 'You are loyal and loving and have a beautiful soul, Beth. You would have followed through on your promises no matter what. No matter the consequences to you...or me.'

'I thought we were each other's rocks—through thick and thin—and yet you snatched all that away from me. You didn't give me a chance to care for you. *Care* for you, Alex, care about you. Not pity you. There is a difference.' Her throat was raw with the sting of unshed tears. 'I don't believe this. I thought I knew you as well as I knew myself. We were Alex and Beth for so long it took me years to learn how to be just Beth.'

'You could never be *just* Beth.' He leaned closer

and for a moment she wondered if he was going to put his arms around her and whether she would let him. Whether they could possibly develop anything—even friendship—after this. But he just shook his head. 'Don't ever think that. You're amazing. Beautiful. Funny. Sexy. That's why I said I wished things could have been different.'

'So why didn't you come looking for me once you'd finished your treatment? Why didn't you come and tell me what you'd been through? That you were okay and...' *That you wanted me back?* Suddenly the image of a future with him—the same image she'd designed years ago—started to form in her head. He still cared for her, she knew. 'Why wait eight years to come clean about it?'

'Because, in the end, I still can't offer you any future.'

'But you said you got the all-clear.'

He held up his palm again and the look on his face told her that he was not travelling along the same idea path she was. 'You won't get your two point four plus a dog with me. I can't have kids, Beth. Okay?'

'But—'

The door rattled open and she realised she'd forgotten to lock it or put the closed sign up. Alex did that to her: made her forget things and flustered her. But, once upon a time, he'd made her spirits soar too.

He was infertile.

No kids. No family.

She hadn't even thought through the ramifications of his treatment. She hadn't even wondered whether he still wanted the same things. Because she knew damned well that she still did. She hadn't thought past a delicious kiss and this...this mess of lies and some sort of weird idea of protecting her. His weird idea of what love meant.

Dennis Blakely stormed through the door cradling a dog, a beautiful but very sick-looking golden retriever. He was breathing heavily and panic flickered across his face. 'Beth. Beth, can you help?'

She glanced over at Alex. The conversation was over. She had to think and digest what he'd told her and work out what to do next. If anything. But not now.

She ran over to Dennis. There was no blood, no obvious injury to either of them. 'Who is this? What's happened?'

'It's Frank Entwhistle's dog, Alfie. I found him on my farm.'

'What's wrong with him? Bring him through.' She nodded goodbye to Alex and gave Button a quick stroke then bustled through into the treatment room.

He laid the panting dog onto the examination table. 'Same thing as Meg. Vomiting.'

'Okay.' If it was the same symptoms she knew exactly what the treatment would be, but she couldn't assume anything. 'Why was he at your place?'

'Frank's a stickler for keeping him up at his farm, but he's still in hospital and his family aren't always so careful. My Juney's on heat and I think Alfie's keen. Was keen. He must have got loose and run over the fields.'

Alfie wasn't quite as lethargic and exhausted as Meg had been so chances were he hadn't ingested as much as she had. *If* that was the cause. She couldn't jump to any conclusions despite what her gut instinct was telling her. 'Did you see him eat anything?'

Dennis's back was turned but she saw the lift of his shoulder as she felt Alfie's abdomen. 'No.'

'And June and Meg are fine?'

'Meg's quiet.'

'That's as expected. She's been through a harrowing experience. And your other dog?'

'June's flighty. Same as always.'

'But okay?'

He nodded. No sound.

Beth put Alfie in a holding cage until she'd finished with Dennis. From past experience she knew he'd want to watch over her shoulder so the only way she was going to get him out from under her feet was by walking him out. 'Right, I'll do an examination. You know how it goes... I'll do my best here, Dennis. Go on home and I'll call you when I know more. Can you call Mrs Entwhistle and let her know her boy is here? Thank goodness you acted so quickly.'

His eyes glittered. 'Aye.'

She ushered Dennis out into the reception area and found Alex and Button waiting for her. Alex jumped up from his seat as soon as he saw her. 'Are you okay? Do you need a hand?'

'I thought you'd gone.' She wasn't sure how to talk to him now. The last few days had been beyond intense. 'I can manage. You need to take Button home. It's getting late and he needs his sleep. Routine works best for babies.'

But Alex shook his head, resolute. 'We're staying. If this is anything like Meg you're going to be up all night. I'm not going to let you do that on your own this time. We're not going to let you, are we, Spike?'

'I don't think that's a good idea.'

'We won't get in the way. We'll wait in the staff room, hot drinks at the ready. When you need one just pop your head in.'

It was a kind gesture but she needed space, not an entourage of helpers getting under her feet and wheedling their way further in her heart.

'I don't want you to stay. I can't deal with this right now, Alex. I need time to think.' And breathe and do all those mindless chores that would help settle her head and her heart. She glanced over to Dennis and wondered what he was making of all this, and decided she didn't care right now. She bent and gave her beautiful puppy a good rub then stood to face Alex again. He was looking as if he wanted a good rub too. 'And actually Angus is on call tonight, not me. He'll be back in a few minutes. I'm just covering for him while he does a house call. So, thanks, but I won't be needing you.'

If Alex was stung by her manner he didn't show it. He just nodded. 'Okay. As long as you're okay. We'll talk tomorrow.'

She wanted to say no and that she never wanted to see him again because the more he talked the chasm between them grew.

And she wanted to say yes, because the thought of never seeing him felt like a wound deep in her soul that would never heal.

CHAPTER EIGHT

'SO THAT'S THE last of it. All boxed up ready for the removals men tomorrow.' Beth stepped back and ignored the catch in her throat. All that was left of her home was a huge pile of boxes, one comfortable chair in the lounge and a large stack of full black bin bags ready to be thrown out. Upstairs, in the room that had been her bedroom sanctuary on and off for nearly thirty years, was just her bed and a suitcase of clothes.

'Didn't we do well?' Her mum grinned as she wheeled her chair around the large empty space, looking a little flushed and possibly with slightly more swollen feet than usual. Beth made a mental note to mention that to the rest home manager when she moved her mum into Bay View tomorrow morning. 'You were certainly a woman with a mission tonight, Beth.'

'Tomorrow's deadline kept me focused.' Amazing what a good dose of anger could do. She'd attacked the last of their possessions in a frenzy, trying to do something to get rid of the ache in her chest. Decluttering had helped a bit but the reason for the decluttering had shifted the ache sideways, infusing it with sadness that her mum had become debilitated enough to need daily care. But she tried to be cheerful for her mum's sake.

'The truck will be here at eight, so we need to be up early.'

'I'll set an alarm.'

'I won't need one. I'm bound to be awake.' Sleep had been pretty elusive ever since she'd kissed Alex. Of course, she couldn't tell her mum that was the reason. 'I'm probably going to be worrying about the golden retriever that Angus is looking after tonight. He was pretty sick.'

'You overthink, you always have. Let Angus do the worrying. And thank him for letting you have the day off to help me move.'

'Hey, I'm just the locum helping him out for a few weeks. He owes me for taking the pressure off at a busy time of year.' Beth bent down and wrote on the box lids with a thick black Sharpie.

Kitchen Glasgow
Lounge Glasgow
Photos Bay View
Bedroom Glasgow
Lounge Glasgow 2

Okay, so she'd clearly agreed to keep more than she'd intended, but at least her mum was sorted. 'I'm so happy you're looking forward to moving into your new place.'

'Change can be good. I'm going to make sure it is. Oh, I left the little Christmas tree out for you. I thought you could dress it. Something to make the place look festive until you leave.'

'I thought you were going to take it with you for your room.' Beth looked over at the three-feet-tall Christmas tree on the floor next to the boxes. 'I'm not much in the mood for a tree.'

Her mum wheeled over and, wincing with pain at even the slightest movement, picked it up and straightened out the branches. 'You should make an effort, Beth. It will make you feel good to see the glitter and the trimmings. Christmas is a funny time of year… There's always so much anticipation. But I've had good ones, bad ones, boring ones, funny ones, ones where the turkey was off and we ended up opening a tin of corned beef…'

Rocking back on her heels Beth joined her mum in the trip down Memory Lane. They'd been doing that a lot recently. 'I remember that one. It didn't seem to matter what we ate in the end—we had fun anyway.'

'Exactly. It was the company that made it special. That first Christmas with you. Oh, my. That was the very best. Always.' Her mum's eyes filled with tears and, unlike Beth, who tried hard never to be seen crying, she let them fall. 'The first one without your dad. That was hard.'

So shocked by her father's sudden death, Beth could hardly remember a Christmas celebration even happening that year. 'Did we go to Aunty Jackie's in Leicester?'

Her mum nodded and swiped at her cheek with her cardigan sleeve. 'And she got drunk and ended up shouting at the Queen when she was doing her speech. Every Christmas is different, Beth, that's what I'm saying. In the end it's what you make it. I have no idea what it's going to be like in Bay View, but I have no doubt we'll all try to have fun.'

'They seemed a lively bunch when we went to the viewing. Are you sure you're okay about going? Really, really sure?'

'Darling, I never wanted to move from here, and you know that. This has been my home for thirty-five years. It was a huge admission that I couldn't cope any more, and it took me a long time to be okay with it, but sometimes you have to pull on your big girl's panties and get on with it. Like you giving Alex a chance to be your friend or at least get some peace with what happened.'

She hadn't mentioned the kiss, but while doing the packing Beth had told her mum about what had happened to Alex and between them they'd tried to make sense of it.

'There's a lot of water under the bridge…many, many years. You don't want to be carrying all that hurt around with you and letting it give you sleepless nights.' She gave Beth the kind of knowing look only a mother could give. 'You're grown-ups now, you're different people from who you were a decade ago.'

'I had got over him, until…' the kiss '…until he told me the truth. I just can't get over the fact he lied to me.'

The anger she'd worn as a badge and a barrier had been cracked open by that kiss. He'd thought letting her go was a gift. He'd broken things off because he'd thought that was best for her and not for him. It was cockeyed logic, but she could see how, in extremis, you might turn your thoughts inside out. If he really did believe he'd been doing the right thing she couldn't hold that against him, could she? But she was bruised that his parents had been complicit in keeping it from her. She hadn't just lost her boyfriend, but also the family she'd come to love and see as her own.

'He might not have handled things the way you would have, but he did it with a good heart. He is a good man, Beth.' Her mum straightened the tree branches out, fluffing up the green strands that hung sadly as if empathising with Beth's mood. 'Obviously I knew him as a young adult who loved you so much, and then when he came back to take over his father's place at the practice a couple of years ago I saw how good he is with the patients and the staff. He's always willing to listen and help. He even did a house call on Dennis Blakely, and, trust me, only a saint would do that. And he's kind. Look at how he's taking care of that dog. I just think you should listen to what he has to say.'

Which wasn't helping Beth at all, because she preferred being spectacularly cross...that way she didn't have to acknowledge the other feelings swirling in her gut. The ones that took notice of the way he'd offered to help her with Alfie and the way he'd kept on talking about anything and everything just to break down the barriers she'd built. The way he'd kissed her.

Oh, that kiss.

'And I wanted to tell you one more thing, Elizabeth Grace Masters.'

'Oh-oh. Full name.' She smiled up at her mum while guilt wriggled through her. Parents could do that to you. It was the same kind of feeling Beth got when she was pulled over for a routine police check. 'What have I done now?'

But her mum was beaming. 'Amazing things. Selfless and wonderful things. You were eight when I was diagnosed with this horrible disease and with every flare-up you slipped into being my carer with no complaint. Ever. You were always there for me.'

'Not true. I went to university.'

'Only because I made you go.'

And if she hadn't Beth wouldn't have the qualifications and experience she had now. An ease to be able to do the job anywhere. The opportunity to make a difference to the lives of, not just animals, but their humans too. But she'd give it all up in a heartbeat if it meant her mum could be pain-free and reclaim some of her independence. 'You know I'd do it all again.'

'I know you would. But now I'm going to have help twenty-four-seven, so when you come down we can do nice things instead of you always having to do boring chores for me. And you need to put yourself first. Let your hair down. Take chances that are offered to you without thinking about me.'

'Ha! Chances? In Oakdale?'

'Anywhere you want to go, my girl. Glasgow. South America. Asia. Or yes, right here in Oakdale.'

The way she was feeling about being around Alex, the moon wouldn't be enough distance away.

Her mum put the tree on the floor and reached out for a hug. Beth went into her arms the way she'd been doing since she was a little girl. 'I love you, Mum.'

'I love you too, Elizabeth Grace.' There was a little wobble in her voice. 'Right, grab the wine. Put some music on. Let's get the tree decorated.'

It was surely one of the scrappiest trees ever made and, as it had sat on Beth's drawers in her bedroom every Christmas for over two decades, it was a little battered and worn. It should probably have been put in the bin bags along with the other rubbish, but her mum wanted to do this and she had no real excuse as to why not. Plus, it wouldn't take long to hang half a dozen baubles on it anyway.

She rooted in the box marked *Xmas Decs*. The first bauble was one her grandmother had given her when she was a toddler, a wooden reindeer with red antlers. As she hung it up she remembered her grandma's smile and the lovely hugs she used to give. With the next bauble she remembered her dad, and the way his Christmas hat always fell over his eyes just as he was about to carve the turkey, and she'd laugh so hard and tug it up so she could see his dancing eyes. And then, Aunty Jackie singing karaoke. Badly.

Beth was surprised to notice her chest wasn't quite as tight as she hung bauble after bauble on the tree. She even managed a smile as she found the sparkly angel Alex had bought her one year. She'd been so happy then and, yes, she could be again. Geez, she had been happy many times in the last few years without him.

So, her mum was right, each Christmas was different and it was up to her to make them the best they could be. This year Beth would be sitting with her mum, sharing food with a bunch of lovely people. Who knew where she'd be next year and who she'd be spending it with? She could look at that as a challenge or as an exciting secret yet to be unwrapped. Anyone would choose the unwrapped secret, right?

And if she was capable of thinking happy thoughts about next year, then she could think happy thoughts about now. Her mum was going to be cared for so that was one less worry. She had a job in Glasgow and a house she loved. She'd reacquainted with Alex and even managed conversations. He'd told her about his darkest times and she'd looked at it all from her point of view and not his. So, if she truly had loved him, she could at least wonder how it had been for him, if nothing else. She could be kind and compassionate—all the things she was in her job and to everyone else. She could listen to the man who had once been her whole world.

Listen. That was all. Because she couldn't trust herself, or him, to do the kissing thing again. That was a step further than she was ready to take.

By the time they'd finished hanging the baubles she had a little warm glow. She stood up and stretched, glancing round at what else needed doing before bed. 'I'll just put these bags in the rubbish bin outside.'

Her mum nodded. 'Then we can watch the last of the tidying programmes on my tablet.'

'I'm not sure we need to watch them any more. Our job here is done. We are the declutter queens.' Although Beth still hadn't found the right place to put her emotions.

Her mum looked at the bags that numbered almost as many as the boxes. 'Are you sure you want to throw so much out?'

'Fresh start. For both of us, right?' Beth hauled the bags up and shuffled out to the front door.

The night sky was bright with diamond stars and the air was crisp and fresh. There wasn't a sound, and with the icy white blanket over the roofs and paths and the little strings of lights crisscrossing the village square it looked quite magical, like a scene from a children's Christmas book. She stopped to lean on the gate, half expecting Santa Claus and his sleigh to appear out of the sky, the way she'd wished he had and dreamt he would for so many years growing up.

This house, this view, this garden had been her safety net. This home with her mum, that she'd come back and forth to over the years, had always been here for her. In a week or so she'd hand in the keys and go back to

Glasgow. It was as if she was closing a door on her past. She breathed deeply. Yes, that was what she needed to do. Close the door and start looking forward again.

She was just shutting the gate when she heard a man's voice. She turned quickly to her left and there he was.

Alex. *Of course.* Out walking Button, their backs to her as they meandered down the street. Their footprints were in the snow right in front of her...shoes and paws in a scudded mush of slush. And she wondered if they'd paused when they got here, or hurried past. Whether Button had caught her scent and sniffed and whether Alex had thought about her, about them. About where to next.

She considered calling to them, but instead watched for a moment as they waded through the snow side by side, his long legs making easy strides and the quick hop-bounce of Button's baby steps. Then the pup abruptly stopped. As dogs did. To sniff or wee or chew on something. She smiled to herself as Alex gently tugged on the lead and Button kept right on sniffing. He tugged again and Button took no notice. Eventually, Alex crouched, tickled the dog's neck and said something she couldn't hear.

And as she watched she absent-mindedly scooped up some snow from the garden wall and ran it through her fingers. Damn, it was the kind of cold that burned. The kind of snow that made perfect snowballs.

She ran her palm along the wall and scooped up more snow. Crushed it into a ball. And she watched Alex, crouched to the dog, and her heart did a little wobble. She tried to tell herself it was because she'd become too attached to the puppy and she was going to have to leave it behind when she left, but it was more than that.

It was Alex. Why did everything have to be so confusing? She'd come here with a clear vision and things had got messy in her heart and her head. Even when she reaffirmed her purpose he was still there, muddying everything. Why did Alex make her feel so much?

What she needed was something to get all this pent-up emotion out of her system. Sex? Not a good idea because the only man she could imagine having sex with was Alex and that was simply out of the question. Getting drunk? Perhaps. But she only had a half-bottle and she was going to share that with her mum. She compacted the snow in her hand. The perfect snowball.

Oh. She smiled to herself. Here was just the thing.

Target practice.

Alex took a deep breath and let it out slowly, watching his breath curl into the air and then fade away, and wondered what he'd done to deserve a puppy who took absolutely no notice of him and yet seemed to snap to attention whenever Beth was around.

Beth. Yeah. That last conversation hadn't gone as well as he'd hoped, but his cards were on the table now.

'I did the right thing, Spike. I've finally been completely honest and I feel just a bit more...freed up.' He was talking to the dog as if it was his confidant. Go figure. But, judging by the way Spike was sniffing at the electricity pole, he had a feeling this man's best friend wasn't listening. Something had caught his attention. Probably something dead. But the dog wouldn't budge so Alex had bent down to see what, if anything, was so interesting. Nothing. Just snow and stones. 'She won't want to love me now, so that's good. There won't be any more confusion or unnecessary emotion.' Just a few more days until she left. He could deal with that. He could deal with being close to her if he knew she wasn't going to be here for ever.

If she was going to stay here for ever then he'd have to move somewhere far away; he had a feeling the moon wouldn't be far enough. Spike gave him a big lick on his cheek then bounded away, the lead dragging behind him making a little trail in the snow.

'Hey! Spike! Come ba—' As he straightened and started to turn round to see where Spike had run off to something hard thudded against his shoulder. What the—? Clumps of snow fell from his coat. A snowball?

He whipped round and saw Beth leaning on her gate, fist in the air. *Gotcha!*

Spike at her feet.

She looked victorious and animated and breathtaking and was already patting snow in her hands for another snowball shot. He walked directly into the line of fire, chancing that she wouldn't throw if he was actually walking towards her. 'Hey, crazy girl, you could have hit my puppy.'

Crazy girl. She wasn't the girl he'd fallen in love with back in his teens, she was a stunning, independent, staggeringly beautiful woman and, even if he hadn't been mad about her a decade ago, nothing could have stopped him from being attracted to who she was now.

She smiled, and it was the first time in days that he'd seen it. 'Not a chance. I'm not that bad at throwing and do you honestly think I would have missed you? I've been sharpening my skills for long enough.'

At least she was talking. 'Truce?'

'Tempting, but no.' She stuffed more snow into his neck and the ice slithered down his spine. Cold, but not cold enough to douse the need building inside him. He'd closed himself off from wanting anyone for years, but she made him want. She made him hot. She made him need. She made him wish for things out of reach. And yet he kept on wanting them.

'Right. You asked for it.' He scooped snow into his palm and rubbed it on her neck, making her scream. She squirmed and turned into him, so close her scent was in the air, making him inhale sharply—he just couldn't get enough—and wish he were buried deep inside her.

'Okay, truce! Alex. Truce.'

'Don't like your own medicine, eh?' He bent and clipped Spike's lead onto his collar and lifted him up to see her. 'Spike says hi and please don't throw snowballs at my nice daddy.'

'Hello, lovely boy. By which I mean the dog. Obviously.' As she fussed over Spike her eyes were shining and she seemed brighter, happier, more relaxed than she'd been before. 'And hello, Alex.'

Still, he stuck to safe subjects. 'How's Alfie? Have you heard?'

She wiped her hand over her forehead, missing a bit of snow that was stuck to her hair, but he let it be and let her talk. 'I got a call from Angus an hour or so ago. He's pretty sure Alfie has ingested something. It's not a systemic illness, there's no temperature, no obvious disease process. An acutely inflamed gut. An unhappy dog. Not as ill as Meg, but enough to be kept in overnight.'

'So, whatever it was, he's eaten the same thing? Is that what you think?' Spike was chewing Alex's coat sleeve. 'Spike! Stop that.'

'He's bored. Puppies chew when they're teething too,

so it could be that. Put him on the ground and let him have a sniff around.'

'He probably needs to walk. As do I. My feet are getting numb.' He stamped his feet as Spike pawed at Beth's leg. 'And he wants you to come too.'

A corner of her mouth lifted. 'I said I'd sit with Mum. It's her last night with me. She's going to Bay View tomorrow.'

Of course. 'Totally get it. No worries.'

'Okay, I'll see you in the morning for handover.'

'Sure.'

She turned and clicked the waist-high gate behind her but stopped. Then she looked back at him. 'Actually, I do need to talk to you quickly about something.'

'I'm all ears.' His heart spasmed. Whatever she wanted to say, he'd listen. He'd take on board what she thought, because, even though he still totally believed he'd done the right thing, he could see how badly he'd hurt her in the process.

'About Alfie and Meg and Dennis… I just need to talk things through…you know, theories, ideas…possible causes…' she clarified.

Right. Not everything was about him. She'd made that very clear more than once. 'Sure. Of course. Now? Or tomorrow?'

'I don't…' She frowned and gave a little shrug. 'It's just a feeling I've got. It's probably nothing.'

'Or…? Maybe it's something. Can it wait?'

She pursed her lips, breathed out. 'You know, no. I want to talk it through with you and morning handovers are always busy, especially tomorrow as I'm going to drop Button with the team at the clinic for the morning and then take Mum to Bay View. So… I'll just grab my coat and let my mum know I'm walking with my boy for a few minutes.' She kissed Spike. 'That is still you. Still not Alex.'

'Hey, I'm getting the message, loud and clear.'

Within minutes she came running out, a turquoise puffer jacket billowing behind her as she shoved her arms into the sleeves. They headed out on the path up towards Oak's Top, a little hill of oak trees that gave the village its name.

And as they trudged she talked. 'So, I'm thinking that if both dogs have eaten something we need to find out what it is before any other pooch gets hurt. It's a puzzle. I was sure Meg had ingested some tablets she shouldn't have got into, but how could Alfie have eaten the same thing?'

'Unless it's a plant or something they're attracted to. Or something to do with things they use on the farm, perhaps? Fertiliser or insecticide?'

'Everything's covered in snow and I'm pretty certain they don't use those sprays until spring. I'm not sure there'd be anything for them to get at. What else could it be? Not chocolate—you see that in the stuff they bring up. Maybe it's antifreeze. It's sweet and dogs like to drink it. Maybe one of Dennis's trucks is leaking, or he's being careless with the bottles and leaving them around the farm where the dogs can get into them.'

'Maybe.'

'Could be Dennis's water supply?'

'He's okay though.'

'It's likely not the water. I'm going to have to have another think.' She sighed. 'Have you heard anything about Frank?'

'He's sore but off the critical list. They removed his

spleen and his liver was badly bruised along with three broken ribs, but he'll be okay. Lesson learnt, Beth, keep away from tupped-out rams.'

'I'll bear that in mind.' She grinned at him. 'But here's something else. When I went back through June's notes I found that she's been in with a series of weird symptoms too—she saw the previous clinic owner a couple of times and then the locums. Angus has had two different locums. Dennis also brought in a cat that he said had been staggering and acting strangely but on examination they found nothing of any consequence. So, he's brought in four pets with similar symptoms, seen by four different vets.'

'That's the problem with having locums. They don't see patterns of behaviour.' Something previously fractured and blurred started to take shape in his head. 'Patterns of *owner* behaviour. Do you think…' the notion that someone could hurt their own pet was so troubling he was starting to doubt himself '…it's some sort of attention-seeking thing?'

Her eyebrows rose. 'He's been reporting symptoms no one else could see.'

'Until now. Meg was really sick. Alfie too.' He didn't want the piece of the jigsaw to fit. 'Do you think…? No. No.'

'What?'

He felt sick. 'That Dennis is doing it? Making them ill and then bringing them in? Escalating the urgency with poisoning?'

'No. Why would he do that? He wouldn't, would he?' She shook her head, her eyes widening as she thought more. 'It must be accidental. It's more likely he's forgetting things or misplacing them. You know, like people with early dementia. Unless…unless he's having some sort of breakdown.'

'In either case he needs help. Urgent help.' Alex looked at his watch. It was late and this kind of thing needed to be dealt with carefully. Turning up in the thick of night would only put Dennis on the back foot. And it was all just a whole load of supposition and ideas with nothing substantial to tie them together. 'I'll go to see him tomorrow.'

She stopped walking and put her hand on his arm, genuine concern in her eyes. 'Are you sure?'

'Of course. We need to get to the bottom of this.'

'You shouldn't go on your own. Take someone…the new guy? What's-his-name? Fraser?'

'He's got a Well Child clinic all morning, then a training thing in the afternoon. Besides, it's not exactly the best kind of welcome, is it? Can you come and help me suss out whether a patient is hurting his animals?' It was an improbable idea.

They were still climbing the hill and her breath came fast, puffing little whorls of steam into the air. 'What about Joe? Could he go with you?'

'He's on leave with his family and I'm not going to bother him with this. I'm booked up all day, but I can scoot up there on my lunch break.'

She nodded, resolute. 'I'll go with you. I should be done with moving Mum by then and she'll be wanting her afternoon nap.'

'Are you sure?'

'Absolutely, this is my case, these are my clients. I'll come with you.'

He reminded himself she was leaving; that was the

only way he could convince himself to keep away. 'How's the packing going?'

Trudging through the snow was hard work, and she had a sheen of moisture on her forehead. She wiped it away with the back of her hand. 'Finished. In the nick of time. The removals people are coming early and I'm going to drive Mum over and get her settled. She's at that point where she just wants it to happen.'

'How do you feel about it now?'

Her nose crinkled as she grimaced. 'Oh, you know, weird. Happy that she's found somewhere she likes, but a bit strange that I won't have a home to come back to any weekend I want to see her.'

'You could stay with me.' The words blabbed out before he could stop them.

She blinked and looked at him with a zillion questions in her eyes. And a very definite no.

He corrected himself. 'Just offering, as a friend. I have plenty of rooms. Too many.'

Rooms she'd have filled with kids and animals. Rooms that were now empty spaces.

They were at the top of the hill now, looking down at the village below. It had been their favourite walk when they were younger, and he wondered whether she was thinking that too. In winter they'd drag toboggans up here, in summer they'd lain in the long grass and whispered promises to each other in between kisses. He wondered if she remembered, if she was thinking the same things, and whether she was wanting to revisit those kisses the same way he ached to.

Because no matter how much he told himself to rewire and stop wanting her, it wasn't happening. He still wanted her. He tried rewiring again. She was leaving.

He'd have to get used to being here without her again. 'And then…you'll be going back to Glasgow.'

'Going home, yes. What should we do about Button? No one's come forward to claim him and he's getting more and more attached to us.' She didn't add that it worked the other way too but Alex had to admit he was likely to miss the little terror once he was gone to his new family…whoever that was. She bent and gave the puppy a stroke. 'I'm leaving in a few days and there's no way he can stay at mine. I'm sole charge of the clinic, it's too busy and I have no home back up.'

'Likewise. I'm not sole charge now, but my life isn't geared to a dog. I work long hours and he'd get bored at home on his own. It's just not fair on a lively puppy.'

'What will we do?'

'I've put adverts everywhere. Someone's bound to reply soon. We'll have to make sure whoever has him knows what they're doing. I don't want him going to just anyone.'

Her eyes grew big and she laughed. 'Someone who has no idea how to look after a puppy would be terrible, right?'

'You talking about me?'

'Of course. But I have to say you're a fast learner, and not everyone would be willing to house a boisterous puppy.'

'He has his uses.' Like, an excuse to come walking. Like, a reason for him to meet up with Beth twice a day. Spike had been the best way of breaching the yawning gap…even if it had meant a sad goodbye to his best climbing shoes. 'He makes for a good hot-water bottle,' he explained, quickly.

'Do not tell me you still let him sleep with you?'

'There's no one else there to mind. What's the harm?'

'Alex Norton, if I was sharing your bed I'd mind a lot if there was a puppy there too. Oh. I didn't mean…' Even in the dark he saw the heat in her eyes and the bloom on her cheeks. 'Oh, you know what I mean. I wasn't talking about us.'

'I know. Beth, I know.' But the thought was there. The temptation to pull her to him and kiss her senseless was almost overwhelming. Because this was perfect. This. The three of them, here at the top of the hill, the clear black sky, the promise of snow. The silence filled only by them. It was like it had been years ago and yet, different. Because they were both different now. And he wondered how things might have been before his body had let him down and pulled his dreams down with it.

Could he reach to her? One more time?

But she turned away and wrapped her arms around her chest. 'Come on, let's get home. I'm freezing to death. And Mum's going to wonder where I've got to.'

And just like that the moment was gone, along with his chance.

CHAPTER NINE

BETH TRIED TO focus on her mum all morning but sometimes—like now, as her mum made the life-affirming
decision as to which drawer to put her nightwear in,
and then perfected the folding technique they'd seen on
TV—her thoughts drifted.

Could it be possible that Dennis was knowingly giving contaminated food to the dogs?

No. No, she wouldn't entertain that thought. But even
so, going up to Oaktree Farm to play detective made her
a little uneasy. Not physically, not at all, but she wasn't
confident at dealing with confused or defensive patients.
She was glad she'd have Alex with her. Safety in numbers would be best.

Her heart gave a little jump at the thought of him.
And she had to admit that last night had been a step in
the right direction. Being on Oak's Top had felt right.
Until she'd almost suggested that sharing his bed might
happen, or be a good thing or…

She checked her watch. Twelve fifteen. He should
have called her by now. His afternoon clinic started
at two, so he was fast running out of time to get up
to Dennis's and back. She called the clinic and, after
lengthy 'How are you?'s back and forth with Maxine,

she was put through. 'Did you forget we were going up to see Dennis?'

'I'm sorry. One of the Archer kids is having a serious asthma attack and I'm waiting for the ambulance. I can't leave, not yet.'

'No, of course not. Stay there.' There was no choice. He was the doctor; she was the vet. 'I have to pick up Button from the clinic. I can't take advantage of their generosity any longer. I said I'd be there at twelve and it's now almost twenty past and I haven't left yet. I'll get him and then I'll go see Dennis.'

'No. Absolutely not. I don't want you going on your own. We'll go together, later.'

His voice was firm and commanding, and for a millisecond she thought about agreeing. But she couldn't wait. Who knew how long Alex was going to be dealing with a sick child? And if Dennis really was hurting his animals, he needed to be stopped.

It was a slithery, slippery journey up an icy road flanked by oaks and too many times she skidded. But finally up at Oaktree Farm Beth parked in the courtyard, took a big deep breath and climbed out.

'Stay here, Button. I won't be long.' She left a window slightly open, a blanket in case he got cold and a bowl of water on the floor of the car, then walked across the courtyard.

On her right the barn doors had been drawn open and there were fresh tyre tracks in the snow. If he wasn't here then he was out, somewhere, on his farm. God knew where.

Maybe he'd been out and returned already. She hammered on the door. No answer. She pushed it open and called again, 'Dennis! It's me, Beth, from the vet's.'

There was a bowl of fresh dog food on the floor by the front door. She looked closely and it all looked normal but…wait. Was that powder in there? Or snow? Or was it her imagination conjuring things up? Not quite believing she was doing this, she scooped some of the food into a plastic bag and stuffed it into her handbag. She'd send that off for analysis when she got back to the clinic. As she straightened a collie appeared from a room further in the house.

'Are you June?' The dog looked up at her then whined and came slowly over to sniff Beth's hand. 'Are you okay, girl? Where's Dennis? Dennis? Dennis?'

But the dog just lay down on the hall floor.

'What's the matter, old girl?' She stroked the dog's head and bent to take a better look at her when she was barrelled from behind, almost toppling over.

It was Meg, barking and rubbing her nose into Meg's hip.

'Hey, Meg. Hey, girl. How're you doing?'

The dog looked as if she'd recovered from her ordeal. She let Beth fuss her and check she was okay and then ran outside. And back inside again. Beth breathed out. The old mutt had got her energy back at least. Meg ran to the door and stopped, looking back at Beth. Then bounded over and tugged on her coat. Then back to the door.

'Where's Dennis?' Beth asked as Meg ran back and forth, barking. 'Do you want me to come with you?'

What to do? June looked exhausted and melancholy and there was definitely something not right with her. *Thank God I left Button in the car.*

Meg nuzzled against Beth's leg then sank her teeth

into Beth's coat and tugged. 'You want me to come with you? Is…is it Dennis? Where is he?'

Something skittered down her spine. Ice. Fear. Meg was running in circles, frantic…to the door, to Beth, to the door, to Beth.

It was eerily quiet. Where was Dennis? She looked at her phone. The reception signal bars dipped and then rose and then disappeared altogether. Further down the hall she found an ancient landline and picked up the receiver. No dial tone. Damn. It had been working the other day when she rang him. Maybe the recent heavy snow had brought the lines down?

She tried to control her panicky heart as she thought. She couldn't call Alex to discuss what she should do. She was on her own. Did she bundle June into the car and take her to the clinic? Did she go with Meg to find Dennis? And why was Meg so frantic? That was not a good sign. Meg? June? Or Dennis?

The lethargic collie was at least safe and warm in the house and wasn't having seizures and there was no sign of vomiting. And Meg was frantic. She made her decision. 'Okay, girl. Show me.'

After shoving the bowl of food outside and then closing the door to make sure June couldn't get to it, Beth followed the collie out to the right of the farm and along tyre tracks that veered off up a hill.

The dog clearly knew exactly where she was going and kept running ahead and then back checking Beth was following. But Beth wasn't as fit or as agile as a collie and the uphill hike whipped the breath from her lungs. It was as if ice hung in the air, thick and heavy, making everything slippery. Up and up they went following fresh thick tracks. A tractor or quad?

They topped the hill and she tracked across the landscape looking for something. She didn't know what. But as she peered down to her left she spied something that jarred. Something red and metal.

She started towards it and as she got closer saw it was a quad bike, tyres uppermost.

'Oh, my God, he's fallen off the quad.' She started to run but it was too hard to maintain a grip and the next thing she knew she was tumbling over and over down the hill, ricocheting off small stones and rocks, wincing at pain in her shoulder, the small of her back, her left thigh. Eventually she came to a stop face first in the snow and still metres from Dennis. *Damn.*

Her heart thumped hard and she tried to suck frigid air into her lungs. She was here, alone. There was a sick dog back at the farm and Dennis underneath a quad bike. She needed to be calm and not put herself in danger too. Wasn't the first rule of emergency rescue to make sure the rescuer was safe?

Okay. Big breath. And another.

Putting all her weight through her arms, she shoved herself upright, put her foot out and pitched forwards on the ice.

She didn't have time to care as she stumbled and slid down the hill, placing her feet in the tyre grooves in the snow to give her boot tread something to grip on. She was tired and aching and breathless when she reached the upturned quad.

Dennis was there, his leg wedged underneath the engine. The snow around his head was a red halo.

Head injury? Leg crushed. She knelt down, ignoring the cold and wet spreading through her jeans and into her bones. She took off her thick jacket and laid it over him in some vain attempt to warm him despite the snow, then investigated the head injury. He had a large gash across the back of his head caused, she imagined, by a jagged rock sticking up through the snow. She gently shook his arm. 'Dennis? Dennis? Can you hear me?'

He didn't move.

Pressing freezing fingers to his neck, she searched for a pulse. 'Come on, Dennis. Please.' *Please.*

There. There it was, faint and thready and slow. He was barely clinging on, but alive. She put her weight against the quad, pushing as hard as she could. But it didn't move. How long had he been here?

She shook him again. Then tapped his cheek. It was like ice, his skin like parchment and his lips a pale blue. 'Dennis. Can you hear me?'

Okay. What to do? With shaking fingers she fumbled for her phone, tried again for a signal. Nothing.

She breathed as slowly as she could and worked through things logically. Unconscious or fast slipping away? 'Dennis, talk to me. Dennis.'

A gurgle came from his throat and his mouth opened a fraction.

'Dennis, it's Beth.' There was no way she was going to be able to lift the quad from his leg, not on her own. She needed help.

She needed Alex.

More than ever, she needed to see him. To see his steady and unshakeable calm. She didn't want to admit it right now, but the thought of him warmed her through. More. The thought of him made her body prickle with heat and longing. But he wasn't here, he was stuck with a sick child back at the village and that was where he should be. Damn. No phone signal. No Alex. She was on her own.

Even if she could get him out from under the quad she wouldn't be able to get him up and over that hill. The only way Dennis had a chance was if she got help. Maybe…maybe there'd be some phone reception on higher ground? Failing that she'd have to get in her car and drive until she got a signal.

'Dennis?' She rubbed his arms and legs in a, likely vain, attempt to get his circulation going. 'Dennis, I don't know if you can hear me, but it's Beth. I'm here. I'm going to get help. Just hold on for me, please. June and Meg need you to hold on.'

The dog whimpered at her name and she came and licked Dennis's cheek. His eyes flickered open. 'I'm…'

'I'm going to get help, Dennis. Meg's here. Meg, come here.' She got the dog to lie on his chest, hoping she'd infuse warmth into him and a will to survive. 'Stay, Meg. Stay, girl.'

His lips moved again and she leaned close to hear. 'So…sorry…'

'It's okay. I'll get help, Dennis. Please. Meg needs you. June needs you. Hold on.'

Alex pulled into Oaktree Farm courtyard and cranked the handbrake. Beth's car was parked askew. She was here, then, despite the fact he'd told her to wait for him.

He jumped out of the car and looked around. Knocked on the front door. Twice.

'Beth? Dennis? Anyone here?' He pushed the door open and nearly tripped. June was lying on the hall floor and she raised her head as he barrelled in. 'June? Where's Dennis? And Beth?'

But the dog just lay at his feet and whined.

This didn't feel right. He didn't like the whining. He didn't like the silence when the whining stopped. Surely, he should be hearing Beth and Dennis talking? Surely, they'd come to his calls? Where was Meg?

He wandered outside and saw footprints heading off behind the barn so he followed them, his pace fuelled by the uneasy feeling in the pit of his gut.

'Beth? Dennis? Beth?' he called out to the wet blanket of mist that was quickly descending. Damn, it was so cold. How did Dennis live up here? Why? And where the hell were they? Why hadn't she called him? Why hadn't she just damned well waited?

He breached the top of the hill and saw a small figure heading down away from him into the distance, trudging through knee-deep snow. His heart jumped in relief that she was okay, and also in a sudden need to beat to her rhythm. Where was she going? 'Beth? Beth?'

He started to move towards her, but his foot slid on a sheet of ice and his arms cartwheeled to keep his balance. 'Beth!'

She stopped and turned. 'Alex?' Her voice was thin and whipped away by the wind.

But she ran back towards him, stumbling and slipping, reaching to the ground to get purchase through the steeper parts, and he ran towards her, fighting to keep upright and fighting to stop the crazy relief that she was safe overwhelming him and making his steps stutter.

She was breathless, her cheeks pink with exertion, and she looked spooked as they met somewhere halfway. 'Alex. Thank God.'

'What's happened? Where's your jacket? You must

be freezing.' He slipped his coat off and put it round her shoulders.

She looked surprised as she slid her arms into his coat sleeves, as if she hadn't realised she wasn't wearing one. 'It's Dennis, he's had an accident on the quad. It's bad. His head's bleeding and his leg is crushed. He has a pulse and he's vaguely conscious, but I'm not hopeful. He's down there, looks like the quad might have skidded or something, anyway it's on top of him and I couldn't get it off.'

As he peered in the direction she was pointing he could see a red stain in the middle of white. From memory the quad was ancient and rusting and probably weighed a whole lot more than she did. 'Call an ambulance.'

'I just did. I had to run to the top of the hill to get phone reception. They're on their way but…oh, Alex.' Her face crumpled and she looked as if she needed a hug. Without thinking he put his arms round her and felt her momentarily sag against him. 'I got Meg to lie gently on him, in a place I didn't think he was injured, so she could keep him warm. I hope that was okay.'

'It's fine, Beth, you've done everything right so far. We'll do what we can to help him.'

It was the first physical contact they'd had since the kiss and he couldn't help notice, through the rush of adrenaline, how perfectly she fitted against him. Her hair was cold against his cheek but he pressed his face into it, just damned glad she was okay. He wanted to kiss away that tension in her body, to comfort her in more ways than this. He wanted her to not have seen what had happened to Dennis. Whatever that was.

She pushed away from him but held his gaze. 'Thank you, I needed that. But come on. Quick.'

The old man was in bad shape. Alex untied his scarf and used it to stem the bleeding from the head wound while he did a quick assessment. 'It's not just the blood loss I'm concerned about, there's hypothermia and the weight of the quad on his leg is compromising his blood supply. Any idea how long he's been out here?'

'No idea.' She shook her head and put her hand over his. 'I'll do this, you look at his leg.'

From what he could see it was a mess, but he couldn't assess the full extent of the damage without lifting the quad off his limb. 'Dennis, can you hear me?'

The old farmer's eyes flickered open, then closed again. Good. A reaction at least.

'I'm going to lift the quad, okay? It's going to hurt but I'm going to be as quick as I can.'

Beth slid her hand into the old man's. 'Dennis, I'm here. Hold my hand. I'm here. Alex is here. He'll get you safe, okay? Just hold on.'

Alex took off his trouser belt and tied it around Dennis's thigh. 'I can see there's a lot of blood loss there too. If I need to I can tighten the belt and stop any more bleeding. I just have to get eyes on the injury asap. I have to move the quad.'

'Okay. Do it.' She looked up at Alex and he felt her trust in him to save this man as a punch to his heart. And also a heavy weight in his chest, because if he didn't raise the quad and save their client he'd have failed her. But he used the force of her trust to power up the strength in his body. He pressed his shoulder against the quad and pushed hard. Pushed again. And with an ominous creak the machine lifted.

Beth inhaled sharply and he could see the grip on her hand tightening. The old man was gripping on.

He couldn't risk aggravating any potential damage Dennis might have done to his back by moving him at all, so somehow he managed to shift the angle of the quad and release it off to the side with a sickening crunch.

Dennis's leg was indeed a mess. 'It's a complicated fracture and I'm worried he's compromised the blood supply to his foot. He needs urgent surgery.' Where the hell was the helicopter?

He tightened the tourniquet and packed ice around the leg. And then the distant whir of blades set off a rush of relief through his veins.

The two paramedics brought pain relief, oxygen and blankets and while they worked on getting Dennis ready to be transferred onto a stretcher Alex handed over. 'His veins are thin and collapsing. We should do an intraosseous infusion in his left leg to get some fluids into him.'

The lead paramedic nodded. 'I'll give you a hand with that and Sam here can radio ahead.'

Alex blew on his hands to get some circulation working; he was going to need good dexterity to manipulate the drill and insert the cannula directly into the bone marrow.

Meanwhile Beth wouldn't let go of Dennis's hand. She turned her head away as Alex got the drill out and winced at the sound.

But as they transferred him to the warmth and safety of the helicopter she blew out slowly. 'Do you think he's going to be okay?'

'If he is, it's thanks to you. But why did you come on your own when I told you to wait?'

She shook her head and her eyes blazed. 'Because I had to make sure the animals were okay.'

Now they were safe the reality of what had happened started to sink in and he fought the rising emotion born out of worry for her safety. 'You had a suspicion that he was feeding something nasty to his pets and you were going to confront him, right? Didn't you think for a moment that it might be dangerous?'

'I wanted to see for myself what was going on. I had to come, okay?'

'You should have waited.'

'What?' She blinked.

'You should have waited for me.' As he said it he saw the change in her demeanour; a shift to defensive and guarded. And he wished he could somehow take the words back. She was a professional and she'd been acting on a hunch. He had no doubt she would have dealt with the situation appropriately. It didn't mean he couldn't be worried about her, though.

'No, Alex. You don't get to tell me what to do. I didn't know how long you were going to be and I had to do something.' Her hands were shaking. They watched the helicopter rise and covered their faces from the dusting of snow. When the chopper had disappeared into cloud she sighed again. 'Turns out it was a lot more dangerous for him, not me.'

He touched her arm. 'I was worried about you. I didn't know where you were or what had happened.'

'Now you know how it feels. And that was just for a few hours, not eight years.' She pressed her lips together and started to walk up the hill, her back taut and her feet stomping through the snow.

They'd both just been through something traumatic and intense and he knew she was spitting adrenaline-fuelled talk as a pressure release. But he also knew if they couldn't draw a line under what had happened then they'd never move forward. He'd thought they were moving forward. Technically, they were…but, just like on this ice, it was more like one step forward, three slips back. He caught up with her. 'Beth, please. For God's sake. I can't turn back the clock. I can't make what I did any different. I did it. I'm sorry. We don't have long before you head back to Glasgow. Can we please…*please* just have some time when you're not going to throw the past back at me?'

She stopped and turned to him. 'You hurt me.'

'I know. I know. And I'm trying to make things right.' He opened his arms wide, ignoring the whip of wind that brought the chill factor way below zero. And the fact she was wearing his coat, and his scarf had disappeared into the paramedics' detritus. So yes, he was standing on a hill, ankle-deep in snow, in a thin jumper and jeans, fast turning into a snowman, but he didn't care about any of that, because he cared too much for her and needed them to get past this. 'Want more target practice?'

She huffed out and pulled a face. 'It's no fun when the target is offering to *be* a target.'

'Okay, well, I'll walk ahead and you can take joy in the element of surprise. If that makes you feel better.'

'Stop being reasonable. It's annoying.' She fought a smile but not before he saw it. She'd always loved that he hit arguments head-on—that was probably another reason why she'd been so discombobulated when he'd backed right away all those years ago. What it meant, too, was that she still cared enough for him to be angry even now. He wasn't sure whether that was a warning or a gift but it certainly made his heart ache. Her shoulders sagged a little and he saw the chink in her armour that was shaped like him. 'I shouldn't have said what I said, Alex. I'm sorry. It was definitely mean after everything that's happened over the last few days. I think I'm a bit stressed out and emotional.'

'Understandable. Me too. But fighting each other isn't going to help.'

'I know. But the thing is, I don't know where I am with you. I don't know how to feel. I like you. A lot. I'm just trying to work it all out.'

I like you. It was something. It was something he needed to think carefully about. He didn't want her getting ideas about things that simply couldn't happen, but he did want to smooth their relationship into something more than prickles. 'I'm at the point where feeling something is a distant memory. I'm numb. Completely numb.'

She scanned his face and upper body and winced. 'Oh, God, you're shivering.'

'Hypothermia tends to do that to a guy.'

Now she did smile. 'And you're joking about it. Here, have this.'

She went to slide her arms out of his coat but he stopped her. 'Keep it, there's no point in two of us freezing. But for the record, I don't know where I am with you either. I didn't intend for things to get complicated. I didn't intend to kiss you, but I'm bloody glad I did. And I want to do it again, if I can ever get my lips to defrost.'

'Here, you need to get warm.' She cupped both his hands in hers and blew on them until he wiggled them at her to show it was working.

'Beth, we need to talk about this. About what's happening.'

'Yes, we do. But not now. Not here. We need to get

you somewhere warm.' She fastened her hand around one of his and started to trudge up the hill.

But he wasn't going to let this go. They needed to mark a line somehow on their past. 'Then when?'

'I don't know.' She opened and closed her mouth a couple of times as if trying to work out what to say and then, 'When you lifted that quad bike my heart was in my throat. You were bloody awesome.'

'Climbing gives you good upper-body strength.' He went to flex his muscles but couldn't make a fist; despite all her attempts at defrosting his hands were still pretty frozen.

'You've got good inner strength. That's what's even better. You make me smile, even when I'm trying to be cross at you. You didn't argue back, you just tried to take the sting out and it worked. And you gave me your coat.' She stopped walking, pulled his hands back to hers, looked deep into his eyes and smiled, pressing their hands to her heart. 'I know we need to talk about it and we will. But right now, before you freeze to death, I want you to know that even though I was very angry at you, I liked kissing you, too. A lot.'

He couldn't take his eyes off her. Standing here with water dripping from her hair, her cheeks burned with cold, her nose red, she was the most beautiful thing he'd ever seen and the frustration that she'd come up here to see Dennis on her own revealed itself to be because he cared for her. So much. Too much.

She smiled and then tiptoed so she was face to face with him. Mouth to mouth. Lips to lips. Her eyes misted and she brushed her cheek against his. 'In fact, I liked kissing you so much I'm going to do it again.'

'Good. It might help de-ice my mouth.'

'Oh, you know me, anything to help.' She slipped her arms around his neck and pressed against him. Then her mouth was on his, lips like ice but so damned sweet to taste.

He felt the outline of her body against his, the curve of her breast, the press of her hip, and the biting cold that had seeped deep into his bones was replaced with a heat so intense he struggled to control it. Fired by the mewl in her throat and the moan of pleasure on her lips he pushed her hair from her face, tilted her head and deepened the kiss, his tongue sliding against hers.

And she gripped his shoulders, fingernails deep as she raked down his back. As if the last eight years of wanting and aching and longing were wrapped up in this moment.

Whereas their last kiss had been a gentle exploration and reacquainting, this was electric and desperate. Greedy, open-mouthed, wet. And all he wanted was more of it. He ran his hands down her coat, inside her coat, pressing his palm over her breast.

'Alex.' She said his name like a plea and a promise and then she tugged away. Pressed her hands to his face and kissed his jaw, his cheek, his mouth, her breath coming in frenzied gasps. Then suddenly she was sliding and slipping away from him and he had to haul her up, clasping her against his side.

'This is treacherous.' She clung to his shoulders and he wondered whether he meant to her balance or to her heart. 'Damn ice.'

'I've got you.' And as he wrapped his arm round her waist to keep her upright he wished that were true. He wished he had her. He wished he could promise her all the things he knew she wanted.

But she laughed and shook him away. 'I'm fine. Honestly. I've got a grip now. I'm okay. We need to go.'

He tilted her chin so he could see her eyes. 'Are we good?'

'We're good. No more barbed comments.' She put her finger to her mouth and he noted her hand was shaking almost as much as he was. Then she tugged his coat round both their shoulders, wrapped her arm round his waist and started walking with him as if kissing as if your life depended on it and sliding ankle-deep in snow with an ex was perfectly routine in her life. She called out, 'Come on, Meg. Let's go get your girl.'

And he let it go. Because he had trouble keeping up with how they'd gone from her shooting metaphorical arrows at him to kissing, but trying to analyse something so impulsive and intense would break it.

Eventually, they made it down the track and back to the farm and she slid her hand out from his back, the cosy atmosphere broken by barking dogs and a sense of having to jerk right back into professional mode again. But he knew, and she knew, that out there on the hill they'd shared something precious.

She hurried towards the front door. 'Hey, I'll do you a coat swap if you can grab my jacket from the boot. I'll just get June and we can take her down to Angus along with Meg. Someone's going to have to look after them while Dennis is in hospital.'

'Sure thing.' It had been a hell of a day, and it was only three o'clock. His head was all over the place with the thought of Dennis's life-threatening injuries and then that scorching kiss. He couldn't keep the hell up. He took out his phone to call Maxine and explain why he was missing his clinic. He looked at the screen. No reception. Maybe it was worth a try anyway. Miracles did happen—Beth's kiss proved that.

As he tried to scroll through his contacts with fingers so cold they could barely move he opened Beth's car door with his other hand and something darted past him and out across the courtyard.

'What? Hey! Spike?' He stuffed his phone into his trouser pocket, bent to grab the pup but he'd already bounded well beyond his reach. 'Come here. Come back. Wait—'

As he ran to the door, Beth came running out of the house, saw Spike and screamed, tugging their puppy away from a bowl of food. 'No! Button, stop. Oh, Alex—'

The food. *Damn.* His gut contorted as a wave of nausea rippled through him. The only reason they'd come here was because they were concerned about the dog food and now Spike had eaten some.

'Oh, God, Beth. I didn't know he was in the car. I just opened the door and he jumped out.'

'I should have said. I was just distracted by everything.' She shook her head as tears glittered in her eyes. 'June's sick, Alex. I think maybe the food is contaminated. And now…did he…? Did Button eat any?'

Alex could barely swallow past the nausea but he wasn't going to sugar-coat the truth because she'd hate him if he did that. 'Some, I think. Before we managed to stop him.'

'He's a baby.' She pressed her lips together and for a moment he thought the entente between them was broken but she tugged on his hand, squeezing the way he imagined Dennis had squeezed before. As if her life depended on him. 'We need to get all three dogs to Angus.'

CHAPTER TEN

'I SHOULD BE in there.' Beth had spent every minute of the last two hours pacing the vet clinic reception floor while Angus assessed Button in the treatment room. Meg was fine and in a safe pen. June was very sick and Beth had been allowed to take her bloods and X-rays but she'd been ushered out when Angus had started the charcoal stomach washout on Button.

'I'm the vet; you're the owner,' he'd said. 'Trust me to do my job.' And she was trying to, but she didn't know what to do with her hands and she found herself literally wringing them together. 'What if he needs me?'

'You're going to wear a hole in the carpet.' Alex stood up from the plastic chair and came over to her. He put his hand on her shoulder and she stopped moving, even though her thoughts still whirred a mile a minute. 'Angus said it was better that you weren't in there to see Button in distress. He's got a good team with him. Come sit down.'

'But what if—'

'I'm not playing the what if game, Beth. Don't go there.' Having called his surgery and asked Fraser to cover the rest of his clinic, Alex hadn't left her side, as worried about the pup as she was.

For the millionth time today she fought the onslaught of tears. 'Hopefully, we got to him in time.'

'We did.' He looked into her eyes and smiled softly. 'Breathe, Beth. You're not going to be any use to him if you wear yourself out.'

He was right. She was going to need all her strength if their precious pup was sick...or worse. Following Alex's lead, she inhaled and breathed out slowly. Then she shook her hands out to try to relax them. 'It feels like a very long time since I set off this morning to take my mum to Bay View.'

He huffed out. 'Damn. I never even asked. How did it go?'

'She's happy as anything. She loves the room and the view and made fast friends with the lady in the room next to her. I ended up feeling like a spare part.' Which should probably have been a good thing, but Beth felt a little displaced. 'I mean, I'm glad she doesn't feel like a burden any more but is it bad to feel just a little bit... adrift? Like my roots have been dug up and exposed. That everyone's got a life and I'm catching up.'

He walked her over to a chair, pushed her gently into it and sat next to her. 'I felt the same way when my folks upped and left. But you're strong, you'll deal with it.'

'After the day we've had I feel a lot more wobbly than strong, to be honest.'

'I'm never going to forget seeing the way you helped Dennis and willed him to hold on. Everything you did today was for someone else. You're amazing, Beth.' He tucked her hair behind her ear and whispered, 'But I already knew that. You've always been amazing.'

'So have you.' She'd watched in amazement as he'd lifted the quad bike from Dennis's leg. The calm, measured way he'd manipulated the drill and inserted a line that would surely have kept Dennis from slipping away. And she would never forget the look in his eyes of apprehension and relief when he'd run down the hill to her and the steadfast way he'd put his arms around her then. The way her heart had jittered and panicked and then calmed just at being in his arms.

Today had been a roller coaster of emotions but none so heightened as the desire she felt for this man right now. Things were getting back on track between them and they were developing a new way of being. And she liked it. She liked that they'd found each other again, but for eight years she'd wondered what had happened to him and why he'd so brutally cut her adrift. She'd discovered he'd been quietly facing the darkest part of his life, getting treatment and then growing into a good man, just as her mum had said. And she'd missed it.

That was what hurt the most. She'd missed those parts of his life and she would never get them back. She would never get the chance to show she could stick by him in times of duress. He'd taken that away from her.

So she could have railed against him the way she had on the hill, she could have made some snarky comment about the way he'd treated her. She could have said a million different things, but right now just being here with him was all that mattered. Holding each other up, taking comfort where it was offered.

He put his arm round her shoulders and she leaned against him, letting the tension ebb slightly. She snuggled closer into his arms, relishing the warmth of his body against hers, and wasn't surprised when she felt the press of his lips on her forehead. She turned her head and looked up at him. Saw the confusion in his eyes, but also the heat and the affection. They hadn't mentioned the kiss and she didn't know what to say about it now anyway. She'd gone with her gut, but ever since then her gut had been all messed up with her worrying about poor Button.

'Right, Beth, you have a choice.' It was Angus, bursting through the door in his usual brisk and efficient manner.

She jumped up, heart hammering against her rib cage as she looked at his empty hands. 'Is everything okay?'

'He's groggy and not at all pleased with me for the gastric lavage, but I think we've got everything out and his blood work was okay. I've repeated it and there's nothing to worry about…so far. But I don't have to tell you how quickly things can change, especially in babies. Right?'

She gripped Alex's hand. Tight. 'Right.'

'So…' Angus held the door open for them to walk through to the treatment area. 'I have my hands full with the overnighters we already have and now June too, and she's very sick so she's going to need a lot of my attention. Your choice—you can leave Button here with me to monitor him, or I'd be fine if you wanted to take him home to watch him yourself. Not something I usually allow, but because you're a vet it seems like a good plan.'

'Yes. Yes. Great plan. Let's take him.' Relief flowed thick through her veins and she couldn't move quickly enough. They found their boy fast asleep in one of the cages. She looked at his observation chart—everything was fine, as Angus said, *so far*. But if he'd absorbed any poison it could still be in his system. He wasn't out of danger yet.

Angus opened one of the cages and checked on June. Her observation chart told a very different story from

Button's. 'I'm going to keep the other two here. June's still critical. Once she's better...' he gave a look that said *if* rather than *when* '... I'll foster them together until we know the outcome with Dennis.'

'Excellent.' Alex nodded and cautiously lifted a groggy Button out of the cage. 'Come on, then, boy. Time to go home.'

Angus laughed. 'Careful. He's tired and grumpy.'

'I know how he feels.' Alex smiled, relief in his features.

'And remember, even though his blood work's fine now, things could change. It's not as if we know what he might have ingested.'

'It doesn't bear thinking about.' Beth shuddered. Things could have been very different. 'Thanks for everything, Angus.'

'Not a problem. You've done enough for me these last few months.' The senior vet raised his stethoscope by way of a wave. 'Excuse me while I do another check on my charges.'

Beth walked with Alex and Button out into Reception. 'Okay, as there's no room at this inn for the night I'll take him to mine.'

'Your furniture-less house?' Alex frowned. 'Absolutely not. If we're staying up all night we need some home comforts.'

'It's fine, I'll just keep him in my bedroom. Thankfully, my bed's still in there. That's about all, to be honest, but it means I have more space for him to run around.'

'No, Beth.' The pup was in the crook of one of his arms. Alex tilted her chin with his free hand, so she could see his eyes. That meant trouble. For her tummy if nothing else. Looking into his eyes made her hot and bothered and all kinds of jittery. 'We can't all squeeze into your childhood bed.'

'We?' The thought of them all in her bedroom gave her hives. Not that spending the night with Alex hadn't crossed her mind…it had. Many times. But not under these circumstances. 'It'll be just me and Button.'

Alex shook his head vehemently. 'No, no. I have custody of him at night, that's the arrangement. He's used to falling asleep on my chest—er…bed. Besides, my house is closer to the clinic in case we need to dash back over with him. He has to come to mine.'

Infuriating man. She shook her chin free from his fingers. 'But I'm the vet, Alex. He's been released into my care, not yours. I need to monitor him.'

He was cradling the dog against his chest as if it was the most precious gift he'd ever been given. 'Then maybe you can come too. What do you think, Spike?'

The pup sleepily nuzzled against her hand. She decided it was an overwhelming yes. 'Well, thank you.' She laughed. 'That will work.'

'Just don't distract us. We have a routine.'

'Okay, I'll try to keep low-key.' She rolled her eyes. Infuriating, sexy man. Funny too.

They walked out into the dark evening. Alex bundled the puppy into his car then turned to her, placing his hands on her shoulders, relief morphing into serious. 'Listen, I'm sorry, Beth.'

'For being a royal pain in the backside?'

'For letting him out of the car.' He looked, as he'd looked on and off since they'd found Button nose down in the food bowl, bereft. Without second-guessing herself she reached up to him and put her hand to his cheek. 'It's not your fault. None of it.'

He shook his head. 'I should have thought he'd be in the car.'

'I should have said. We were both distracted by Dennis's accident. Let's not play the blame game, eh?' She needed him right now—he was the only person in the world who cared for Button as much as she did, no matter how much they'd both decided not to get attached. Alex was the only person she could share this worry with.

'Thank you.' He cupped her face and dropped a kiss on the tip of her nose. 'We should get that boy home.'

'Wait.' She looked at his kind eyes and that sexy mouth that she knew so intimately and the swell of emotion in her chest was almost too much to bear. The bond wasn't just with Button, it was with Alex. A bond that had been broken but not irrevocably. There was hope. There was desire.

Then, she was kissing him, pressing her body against the length of his. Being in his arms was safe and comfortable and yet felt as if she were stepping into somewhere exotic at the same time. Familiar but exciting. She felt his arms snake around her waist and he pushed her back against the car. And thank God he did, because her legs were like jelly and her head dizzy with the sensation of his mouth on hers. It felt as if she'd been eight years in the wilderness and she'd finally come home. This was her homecoming gift: this kiss. This man. It didn't matter what difficulties they'd overcome or those they were going to face, this moment mattered more.

When he pulled back he was breathless. He ran the backs of his fingers down her cheek. 'Hey, you're shivering—you still haven't thawed out properly?'

'Just call me Ice. Ice baby.' She was only half joking, because her clothes were still damp from kneeling
in the snow, although not as damp as his. She put her
hand under his jumper and pressed it against the heat
of his belly.

'What the hell, Freckles?' He squirmed away from
her. 'What is it with you and the hot and cold treatment?'

And she couldn't help smiling because he hadn't
called her Freckles for such a long time and it was right
and perfect and she didn't want to stop the way she was
feeling: comfortable with him, proud of what they'd done
to save Dennis, worried about Button and not just a little
turned on to have touched Alex's bare torso.

It took five minutes to reach Alex's house, five minutes of fighting the urge to make him stop the car and
kiss him again, but they had precious cargo and they
needed to get him home and safe.

Memories flooded in as she carried Button into the
cottage. How many hours, days, weeks had she spent
in here over her lifetime? How many dinners had she
shared with his family, laughing with his sister, talking
about her studies with his parents? She could draw the
timber framing with her eyes closed, describe the lay-
out of the kitchen.

And yet it was the same but different. 'You've painted
it. It looks great. Fresh.'

'Thanks.' He smiled and something kicked in her
chest. 'It needed a lot of work. My dad was a great doctor but he's not the DIY type.'

She hadn't thought Alex would have been either,
and yet there was a new window seat exactly where she
would have put one, although it woefully lacked cushions. And the wall colours were muted greys where she

would have chosen something a little bolder. It was a man's house. Smart and clean and...it smelt of him. Her tummy clenched. Spending the night here was going to be hell. And would test every part of her resolve.

Although, given the fact she'd already kissed him twice today she had a feeling she'd badly failed the resolve test already.

'Put him down here. I'll light the fire.' Alex stroked Button's head and pointed to a rug on the hearth. Just seeing that rug brought memories tumbling back.

'Is that your nana's old rug?'

The one they'd made out on many times when his family had been away, in front of a roaring fire; heat and heat and heat. There had never been anything wrong with the passion and attraction. Just the trust, it would appear. But she could feel that changing.

He bundled kindling and newspaper into the fireplace and threw a lit match onto it. The kindling sparked and little blue-orange flames erupted. He dragged a fireguard out and put it in front of the fire to protect Button from errant sparks. 'It's part of her rug, yes. The part Spike has allowed me to keep. I'm going to have to ask Joe's new wife Rose if she can do her crochet magic and fix it so it doesn't look so ragged.' Rose was infamous in Oakdale for her bright-coloured yarn bombs around the village. Beth decided that if she lived in this house she'd definitely be asking Rose for something to brighten it up. A stripy blanket and multicoloured cushions. And there she was, making plans she was never going to keep. Alex smiled. 'Or maybe I'll have to bin it like the rest of the stuff we used to have in here.'

'It's very minimal. Have you been watching that tidying programme on TV too?'

He laughed. 'I don't need to. When my parents moved overseas we had a big sort out. Although, I have to admit to being ruthless. What they needed for a flat in Malaga and what they wanted me to have didn't compute. It was like they wanted to keep all their old stuff here as a sort of shrine to them. I wasn't having any of that.'

'Sounds just like my mum.' She sat down on a smart charcoal-grey sofa that had some very un-puppy-friendly pristine white blankets folded up on the arm. The puppy tsunami must have been a big wake-up call for him. 'I like what you've done to the place. You were working in London, though. Why did you come back to live here?'

He rocked back on his heels and absent-mindedly stroked Button's back as he talked. 'It was my dad who suggested it. He was thinking about retiring and wanted someone to take over and asked if I'd ever considered coming home. Home. It hadn't felt like home for a long time. I'd keep coming back and you weren't here. Anywhere that didn't feature you wasn't my home.' He swallowed and smiled ruefully. 'I went through all that and couldn't have you anyway.'

'Oh, Alex.' This was getting to the nub of things. Honesty. Finally. Her throat felt raw.

He shuffled over to sit on the floor by the sofa, tugged off one of her boots and socks and started to massage her toes. 'I was adrift for a bit after the treatment. I was working in the East End and I just couldn't settle but felt like I'd been given a second chance and that I had to choose wisely. I needed to leave all those bad memories behind. I wanted to…indulge myself, I guess. I love the hills and the mountains and the fishing and boating. I figured if I hated working here I could move on again. Two years later, I'm still here.'

She was stuck on imagining him in treatment. She shuddered, suddenly very cold. 'Was it bad? As bad as Mikey?'

His hand stilled. 'Yes. And no. I knew what was to come. I'd walked it all with my cousin.'

A gruelling treatment regime. Surgery. Chemo. Radiotherapy. But Mikey had had Alex by his side all the way and Alex had done it on his own.

She wanted to reach out and hold him close but she got the feeling he didn't want her comfort for what had happened. He'd made his choice and he'd had to live with it. The only physical contact was his hand on her foot. Massaging her toes was something he used to do for her years ago after they'd been hiking and her boots had rubbed. Her mind seemed to be endlessly spinning from the past to the present. So much of her formative years had been spent with him she couldn't disentangle herself. As he'd been able to do with her. 'I'm sorry I wasn't there, Alex.'

He snagged her gaze. His was filled with regret and longing and a plea to forget it all. 'Beth, please—'

She reached for him now, clutching him tight against her. 'No, this isn't me being angry. This is me being genuinely sorry I wasn't there. For you. I wish we could rewind and change what happened.'

'Trust me, I wish that too. But you're here now. That's enough for me.'

A beeping made them both jump and, cursing, he pulled his phone from his pocket. 'The hospital. I'll just take this.' He looked at Button, who had stirred at the noise. 'In the kitchen, so I don't disturb him.'

He came back a few minutes later with two glasses of wine that he set on the coffee table, before sitting on the sofa next to her. He looked ashen and shaken and she wasn't sure whether it was because of the phone call or the memories of his dark days.

'Dennis?' Her heart thrummed and her gut tightened in readiness for bad news.

But Alex gave her a small smile. 'Yes. They called me because I was put down as a contact. They have no next of kin for him.'

'He really is all alone. Poor guy. But still alive?' The knots in her stomach eased a little. But she still had to reconcile the reason she'd been at the farm in the first place with the sick man in the hospital bed.

'He's in Intensive Care. They've had to amputate his leg. It's very early days and he's critical but they think he'll recover.'

'I don't suppose he said anything about his dogs and what was making them ill?'

'Nothing. They've put him in an induced coma. He won't be talking for a while.'

'Maybe we'll never know. I did some Internet searching yesterday and I read about Munchausen by proxy in pet owners and it *is* a thing. There have been some cases where people have made their animals sick to get attention.' Just the thought of it made her shudder. 'I don't want to say that was what he was doing, but hopefully we'll get the test results back from the food sample I sent off and we'll find out. We did good.'

He picked up his glass and drank. 'We make a good team. Medically, I mean. In small country places like this it's good for different health professionals to share information. You probably saved his life. Your trick of getting Meg onto his chest would have kept him warm.'

'He needed something to hang on for and I know

that—whatever he's done or not done to them—he does love his animals.' She wondered what Alex had had to hold on for. Because it certainly hadn't been for her. He'd decided to face it on his own. Geez, she couldn't imagine what torture that would have been. And instead of being angry with him she just felt a huge sense of sadness. And relief that he was here and well.

'And good news that Spike—' He put his glass on the table. 'He needs a proper name, Beth. We can't keep calling him Button and Spike. It's confusing. It's confusing me. We need a name everyone can call him, even when he goes to his new place. He needs his own name. Just one, right?'

Everything was confusing. That she was here in this house, that her foot was snuggled in Alex's hands. That she couldn't think of anyone else she'd rather spend the night with watching over a sick puppy. Anyone she'd rather spend the night with. Period. And now they were choosing a for-ever name for a pet they weren't going to keep. She'd already thought about this. 'Could we just call him Boy?'

'Is Boy a real name?'

As he said it the pup's ears twitched and he raised his head and looked at them. Alex laughed. 'That's decided, then. Boy it is. I like it.'

He took her other foot and pulled the boot off and his hands began their massage magic. For a moment she was lost in the rhythm of his touch. He removed her sock and began massaging her instep, each stroke sending shivers of desire up her legs and arrowing deep in her belly. She lay back and let his fingers explore her toes, her calf and she imagined his fingers higher and the pleasure he could give her. Not just with his fingers...

And then…and then what?

'What are we doing?' She pulled her legs up and hugged her knees.

He growled, his hands splayed as if asking *what the actual hell?* 'It's just feet, Beth.'

It wasn't just feet. They both knew damned well it wasn't about the feet. It was about the contact, about the touching and where it would lead. Not that she didn't want to go to bed with him, but what then? Would they do the long-distance thing as they'd done at uni? Would they—? Her ricocheting thoughts stalled as his hand ran up her leg, stopping just above her knee. 'Your jeans are still damp. You have to take them off before you catch cold. I have something you can wear instead. Wait here.'

He was back in minutes, having changed into some track pants and a clean dry T-shirt, and carrying a pile of freshly laundered clothes. She eyed him suspiciously and laughed. 'This is the scene in the rom-com movie where you hand me your clothes, I smell your amazing smell and then fall into bed with you, right?'

Okay, perhaps suspiciously *and* a little hopefully.

His eyebrows rose. 'If that's what you want. Sure. But, hand on heart, it wasn't what I was thinking.'

'Oh, no? What were you thinking?'

He handed her the clothes and sat down next to her. Closer than before. 'I was wondering if I had enough washing powder for our clothes and then I was calculating if I put the washing machine on now what time the cycle would be finished.'

'Really? So the foot massage wasn't…?' She'd been daydreaming about sex when he'd honestly been all about the massage?

'Beth.' He flashed a smile, his hand back on her leg.

'I was hoping you'd go for a shower to warm up, maybe invite me to join you. Then I'd hand you my shirt and you'd slide it on and look even more sexy than you actually do. If that was physically possible.'

Her mouth went all kinds of dry...and wet. 'Um, really?'

'And then, later, after we'd eaten oysters and drunk champagne, I'd get to peel it off you and you'd be so overwhelmed by my scent—not my smell. If you were overwhelmed by my smell then I'd have to use more deodorant—'

She giggled. 'You don't need more deodorant. You smell like Alex. I don't want you to smell like anything else.'

'And then we'd fall into bed.'

'You do want to go to bed with me.' It wasn't a question. She just had to say it out loud.

'Yes.' He put his hand to the back of her head and drew her to him, lowering his mouth to her neck. 'I have never stopped wanting to go to bed with you, Beth Masters. Not once in eight years. Going to bed with you is at the top of my bucket list. Only, I don't have oysters. Or champagne. Just this wine.'

'Wine works.' She'd be gone soon enough, then this would be over. Could they? Should they? Could they put the past behind them? She pressed against him, her hands on the cool cotton covering his taut plane of a stomach, wishing she were running her hands over bare skin. She swallowed hard. 'We can't.'

His mouth moved to her throat and kissed a trail to her collarbone that made her dizzy and heady and frantic for more. 'You're going to Glasgow and it's complicated and your life is there and mine is here and we should be old enough to control our sex drives, right?'

'I mean…' She could barely breathe for the rush of sensation over her skin, in her body, making her breath ragged. Needy, desperate. 'We can't go upstairs and leave Boy here. In case he's poorly.'

'He's sleeping now. We can leave him for a few minutes.'

'Is that all it's going to take?' She pushed his shoulder, wanting that mouth on hers. Hot damn, how much longer was she going to have to wait? 'Eight years and I get a few minutes?'

She couldn't keep up with the rapid-fire beat of her heart and the deluge of emotions rushing through her. It felt as if all the arguing, the missing him, the raging on the hill had led to this moment. She knew how he kissed; she knew how he made love. Rather, she remembered how he was then. How would he make love now? Would he be more confident? More skilled?

She wanted to know. Now. She sat up, put her hands on his shoulders and straddled him. She wanted to relearn him. This could be her last chance. Her only chance to be with him. She could do it. Let the embers flare and then douse them when she left to go back to Glasgow. If she didn't, she'd always regret missing this chance. She was going to do this. She was going to take what she wanted and she was going to walk away with her heart intact. Her eyebrows rose and she nodded towards the sleeping puppy.

'Boy,' she whispered, testing the viability of the plan.

The dog didn't flinch, twitch or move so much as a muscle.

She turned to Alex, drank him in, a sigh escaping her throat. 'He's fast asleep.'

'Good, because he's far too young to witness this.' Then he pulled her down to him and crushed her mouth in a scorching kiss.

This was no relearning; it was taking and giving. It was greedy. Demanding. It was a lifeline of hope, a prayer. And she melted into it. Into him. She felt his hands wrap round her, settling her higher onto his lap. She felt his hardness underneath her and rocked against it, wanting him inside her with a savage need she'd never felt before. His hands skimmed under her still-damp jumper and ripped it from her, then he was palming her breasts through her bra. 'You have no idea how much I have wanted this. How long I have waited for this. For you.'

She pressed herself against his erection, tugging at the waistband of his track pants, but he covered her hand with his. 'Wait.'

She pulled back, her mouth throbbing from the delicious roughness of his kisses. Was he having second thoughts? 'What's wrong?'

His eyes darted to Boy and he shook his head. 'I'm getting stage fright. Come on.'

And with that he slid his arms under her legs and lifted her, powering up the stairs two at a time. He kicked open the master bedroom door and she was momentarily afraid it would be the same as she remembered: all nineteen-eighties flowered curtains and chenille bedspread. But it was decorated in the same chic masculine tones as downstairs with a very modern bed and she breathed. 'I thought we were going to be having sex in chintz.'

'Kinky too?' His eyes glittered. 'Sorry to disappoint.'

'No way, Alex. I'm far from disappointed.'

'And I haven't even started yet.' He laid her on the thick cream faux-wool blanket and she felt as if she were sinking into heaven. More so when he unzipped her jeans and slowly peeled them from her. Her breath hitched as he climbed onto the bed, crawling over her body until his mouth was on hers again, stealing more hot kisses as he unclipped her bra.

Her thoughts blurred as he slid cool fingers over her nipples, his playful demeanour slipping into something serious. He looked at her as if she were a goddess, as if the pleasure was all his and he couldn't quite believe his luck. 'You've grown into one hell of a woman, Beth.'

He lowered his mouth and licked her nipple, making her moan in desperation and delight. He teased her by pulling his mouth away, making her cry out in desperation for more. Then he lavished both breasts with kisses until her thoughts fled and she could only feel. His touch. His mouth. The way every part of her body strained for him.

Rising up on her knees, she slid his trousers and then boxers over strong muscular thighs, releasing his erection. He groaned as she took him in her hand and looked down at the man he'd become. Half cautious, half curious.

'I...?' She didn't know what she'd thought. Maybe that he'd look different. But he was all there.

He took her hand and brought her to face him. 'Amazing what they can do.'

'Amazing indeed.' She went to reach for him again, but he flipped her on her back and kissed a trail of wet kisses down her abdomen. She writhed against him, anticipation of his tongue at her core making her crazy with need. He parted her legs and slipped his fingers deep and she clenched around them, fighting the rising release. But when she felt the scorching heat of his mouth against her nub and his fingers sliding she knew the fight was lost. Losing hold of her control, she sobbed out, 'Alex. I need… I need you.'

Not just this, but everything. She needed his strength. She needed his kisses. She needed him. Now and always.

'I need you too. You have no idea.' He gripped her tight as she shuddered against him, his hair in her fingers, his name on her lips. *Alex. Alex. Alex.* So many times she'd dreamt about this, believing it could never happen again. And here he was. Wrapped around her, clutching her tight against him as if she were his everything.

But it wasn't enough. She wanted him inside her, on her. With her. She tugged him up to her and kissed him hard, stroking his length. He groaned into her mouth. 'Wait. Slow down.'

No. 'I'm done waiting. I've waited too long.'

'Condom.' His hand flailed out to the drawer in the cabinet by the bed and he grabbed a foil.

'I thought…?' She watched him slide it on, confused. Desperate. Not wanting to think about anything except the next minute. She didn't know what she thought. Good. Condom. Good.

He laid her back on the fur and positioned himself at her entrance. His eyes blazed his truth, the same truth in her heart. The same truth she'd carried for over a decade. 'Are you sure?'

'More than anything.' She shifted beneath him, shocked and exhilarated at the feel of him against her. She wrapped her legs around him as he slid deep into her. At the first thrust he inhaled sharply, closed his eyes as if in prayer, whispering, 'Beth. My Beth.'

He smoothed her hair back and kissed her with such urgency she thought her heart might stop. He thrust again. And again, holding her hands above her head. 'I want to see you. I have missed you so much. My Beth. My beautiful Beth.'

She'd planned to do this and keep her heart intact. She wasn't going to let him have any of it. But it was too late. She bit back a sob, but couldn't stop the tears pricking her eyes. He was the beautiful one. He was divine; he was hers. It was the same. It was different. It was a new stamp on her heart. A soft bruise on her soul. An ache that would never be fully satisfied.

She arched and encouraged him deeper, learning what he liked now. Learning what made him groan with pleasure. And in return he teased and tormented, his rhythm tantalisingly slow then deep, then fast, and with each new stroke her heart accepted him more, her body shaped herself to him.

He wiped the tears from her cheek, pressed his mouth to each one, a sound in his throat equal to hers. A sob. A cry. Then his rhythm increased and he thrust fast and deep. Wild. Untamed. The grief and the need and the ache of eight long years written on his face, in his pace. She sat up and pulled him to sit facing her, wrapped her legs around his hips, gripping his shoulders so he could go deeper still. The intensity was like nothing else she'd ever experienced. His eyes locked onto hers, his fist wound into her hair. She let the tears flow freely, couldn't stop them when he called her name into the dark and shuddered against her, his loss of control stoking hers. They grasped, kissed, clung to each other as release bonded them closer. Tighter.

For ever.

CHAPTER ELEVEN

'THAT WAS AMAZING.'

Beth peeled herself away and lay, breathless, on his bed. Alex felt the damp of her tears as they dried on his clavicle. 'Amazing' didn't get near to describing how it felt. She'd brought light into his life, she'd pushed against his barriers, she'd made him feel, made him want. Made his heart ache.

He'd broken his promise—not to have sex with anyone who cared more than he did. Beth cared. He could see it in the way she looked at him: as if he was something good. As if he was beautiful too.

He couldn't remember anyone ever looking at him like that, as if he were an actual freaking superhero. It made the centre of his chest raw and tight as if there were light in there, and warmth. As if he could do anything. It wasn't the kind of feeling he'd had when the surgeon had said he'd successfully removed the lump, or when the oncologist had said he was cancer-free. This was a whole different kind of feeling, that someone believed he was good, that she believed in him. That everything he'd done and been through had been for this moment, for her.

And hell, he cared. Cared more than he wanted to

admit. Cared more than ever before. And he wanted to keep on having that feeling.

And yet…it was impossible. For him to be happy meant she couldn't be.

She stroked his chest with trembling fingers, which he captured with his. Tears still lingered in her eyes and she looked a mixture of happy and kind of weirded out. He kissed her forehead. 'Are you okay?'

She smiled. 'I think so. It's just been so…much. I'm having trouble dealing with it all. You?'

I don't know.

'Yes. Yes, of course. Intense. Exhausted, actually.' He cuddled closer and tried to push the nagging thoughts away.

She pressed against him and laughed softly, her palm on his chest, over his heart. 'Oh? You're a…what did Frank call it? A tupped-out ram. Do I need to be careful?'

'Trust me, your liver and spleen are safe. But I can't vouch for anything else.' He ran fingertips over her nipples, loving the way they budded at his touch. He ran his hands down her curves, and he looked at her skin in the shaft of moonlight fingering through the open blinds. If this was going to end—and they both knew it would— he was going to make it the gentlest ending ever. Not like last time. 'How many more freckles are there now?'

She giggled against his ribs. 'Infinity has no end.'

Like the feeling in his chest that was so intense he wasn't sure he would breathe properly again. He stroked down her side, stopping at a whorl of purple on her hip bone. 'What are these? Bruises?'

She shrugged. 'Must be from falling in the snow when I was at Dennis's farm. I was more on the ground than upright. I should have just gone roly-poly down that hill.'

'God, you put your all into everything you do. You always did.' She was so beautiful and he had to tell her, show her what he felt, just once. 'I didn't think we'd ever…get this chance again. I just wish we'd had more time.'

She tilted her head to look at him, her hair tickling his neck. Her eyes tear-stained but dry now and ardent. 'We have time, Alex. We have a few more days before I go back. Then…who knows what could happen? It's not far to Glasgow.'

He did not want to say this, but he had to. He'd told her enough for her to not get any ideas that this could be anything more than temporary. Even though temporary wasn't what he wanted. 'We both know this can't go anywhere.'

'It feels like you've already decided.' She kept on looking at him as if she could see the very depths of his soul. 'Tell me.'

This was the *talking about it* that they'd agreed on yesterday. She wanted to know about the treatment, about everything. She wanted to know about everything he wanted to forget. She wanted to know where they stood now and what the future held.

And ruin this moment? *No, thank you.* He pushed the sheets back and stood up, pulling on some boxers, suddenly too aware of the gaping chasm between what they wanted and what they could actually have. 'We need to go downstairs to check on Boy.'

But she kept on looking at him and they both knew he was stepping back from his usual forthright Alex and hedging.

'Okay. Yes. Come on, then.' She wrapped a blanket round her shoulders and wandered back downstairs clutching two pillows. He followed, carrying two more. She was naked, but for the blanket wrap, her hair hung down her back in loose honey curls and her mouth was bruised and swollen from kissing. She knelt to stroke Boy, who was clutching his saggy green and yellow toy duck in his front paws. Alex wondered if it was possible to die from feeling too much. Because if it was, he was probably in his last minutes on Earth right now.

'Is he okay?'

'Sound asleep.' She plumped up the pillows and put them at one end of the sofa, then threw the blankets down, devising a makeshift bed. She climbed in and beckoned for him to follow.

He climbed in next to her, slid his arm under her and tugged her to his chest. He could hardly believe it. She was here in his arms. Christmas come early. Christmas. His heart clenched.

Not now. Don't spoil it. Be gentle.

'This is even smaller than your bed.'

She wiggled her hip against him. 'Cosy. I like it.'

And he had to admit, the glowing space in his chest was filled with warmth and a feeling he didn't want to end. She breathed against him, hooking her arm over his abdomen. 'Given Mikey's history, didn't you do regular checks for lumps?'

So if he thought he was off the hook he was sorely mistaken. He knew her well enough that she wasn't going to give up. He stared into the darkness. Thinking about the past and the future that had been stolen from him. Her future too. He owed her this talk.

'I did checks, of course. Regular and thorough. Then I

got busy with the clinical rotations at the hospital. Working long hours with no sleep for days was hard and there was the studying on top. Routines become non-existent and it's just a case of trying to survive. You lose track of the days and…you get blasé. You see people who are sick and you know you're not like them. You begin to think you're bulletproof.'

'You should be able to think like that when you're young.'

'And then one day it occurred to me that I hadn't even thought about it. That should have been a good thing, right? That I was getting through the grief of losing Mikey. And so I did the usual checking…' The day he'd found the lump had been one of his darkest. He hadn't needed a specialist to tell him what it was. 'I just hadn't realised it could spread so quickly. It was aggressive.'

She squeezed against him and took his hand, lacing her fingers into his. 'Didn't they offer sperm banking?'

The real nub of it all now. Could she have the future she wanted and with him? Was this even a scenario she could imagine?

Had they mentioned saving his sperm? 'Everything from that day is a blur—except the diagnosis. It was as if the consultant had just said cancer, cancer, cancer, cancer and nothing else. I remember the panic that filled my whole body. The cold of the ultrasound jelly. The feel of the oxygen mask on my face. The taste of the anaesthetic as I drifted to sleep. I think they did talk about sperm banking…but I don't remember saying yes. I was too worked up to get the damned tumour out of me. I wasn't thinking straight. I was blinded by panic. I thought I was going to die, Beth. I thought I was going to face months of treatment and then things would get worse and then that would be the end. You have no idea the kind of things you feel—or don't feel—when you're staring at the prospect of dying. Of how much living you still want to do and you don't have time.'

He remembered the phone call he'd made, willing himself to stay calm and sound normal. Blunt but normal. Trying to stop Beth from crying when his own tears were streaming down his cheeks. The thought he might never see her again and that he was glad that he'd saved her from all this mess.

Then, the wait for his parents and feeling so alone.

'I would have been panicked too.' She kissed his knuckles. 'And now? Now the panic is over?'

'I haven't been tested in a few years, but the last test said I had zero chance of getting a woman pregnant. And the test before that. Every test, Beth. Post-treatment fertility levels vary and sometimes they recover. So far mine hasn't. There are no guarantees. I can't say what will happen.' He needed to get this through to her. This was why he'd refused to make meaningful connections with any woman. 'I don't want to make promises I can't keep.'

She stared into the dying embers in the grate. 'It doesn't all have to be your decision, Alex.'

'I'm not going to let anyone martyr themselves over me. Okay? I don't want pity.' He wanted her love. He wanted to be the man she wanted, deserved. And he just couldn't be.

'Give me a chance to prove that there is nothing like pity in here.' She put her hand on her chest. 'But there's a whole lot of something and I know you feel it too. Something good, something that's not going to go away any time soon.'

She pressed her lips together and he wondered if she was holding back more tears. When she turned to him he saw that she was and his heart melted all over again. He smoothed her hair back and kissed her cheek. 'Let's not talk about the future. Let's just do the present.'

She put her hand to his chest. 'I like the present.'

'Me too. I like you, Beth Masters. So damned much.' He didn't want to talk any more. Or think. He just wanted to lose himself in her. Cupping her face, he slid his mouth over hers. This kiss was filled with everything he wanted to tell her. His regret, his feelings for her, which were currently a lot more than like on the affection scale. He wanted to make the most of what they had left even though he knew spending more time with her would make it so much harder to walk away in the end. But, for now, he was going to live in the present and think about the future another day.

Just as things were getting interesting she jerked and kicked out her leg. 'Ugh! What the hell is that? Button— I mean, Boy? What the heck? He's nudging his nose on my hip.'

Alex laughed. 'He does that when he needs a wee.'

'I'll take him.' Sighing, she went to stand but he slid from the sofa and wrapped a lap blanket round his waist. 'No, I will. I'll let him out in the garden. Stay right there. Do not go to sleep. Do not pass go…we have more catching up to do.'

'I am far from sleep, Dr Norton.' She shivered and pulled the covers up to her shoulders. 'But what about our little puppy audience?'

He grinned, his heart full, a little panicked by the weight in his chest and a lot turned on. 'Didn't you know? That's why blankets were invented.'

* * *

'Alex—?' Beth felt about for his warm body and found nothing but space next to her on the sofa. He'd gone. Her heart trembled. Gone where? Was that it? Over so soon? She sat up and blinked, and the panic subsided. 'Oh.'

He was curled up asleep, at the far end of the sofa, his bare chest covered by a snoozing puppy. Soft dawn light filtered through the blinds, bathing them in a halo of gold. Oh, God, could he be any sexier? Her chest flooded with warmth just to look at them, so completely relaxed.

This was how things could have been—him, a pet or two and further down the line some kids. The family she'd always craved. Her heart felt as if it were turning in on itself. That wasn't going to happen, not with Alex. If he asked, would she put that dream aside?

She didn't know. She couldn't say. How did you stifle your ticking body clock?

They'd missed eight years, and yet would she have felt like this if she'd walked his cancer journey beside him? Would she honestly have stayed the duration? She liked to think she would have, but she didn't know. She'd have given up her course to look after him, the way he'd taken a six-month break to look after Mikey, but then what?

In the meantime, she'd finished her degree and got a whole load of experience. She'd grown independent, without him. She'd grown out of the break-up and now she knew what she wanted and what she was prepared to take and also what she wasn't prepared to give up. Could she give up her dream? For the man who'd already broken her heart?

Would he ask?

Alex stirred and uncurled, one hand clasping Boy to

his stomach. 'Beth. You're still here. Good. Very good. Sleep okay?'

'The best for a long time.' She stretched over and kissed them both, pausing to nuzzle into Boy's soft silk coat. 'You?'

'We had three wees overnight and a little play at four-thirty...until five fifty-two.' He didn't look cross, just mussed-up and sleepy and very much in love with his dog. 'There is absolutely nothing wrong with this animal.'

'Good. That's so good to hear.' Her heart was filled with relief. And yet a sadness she couldn't shake. 'But playing at night-time? Really? Why didn't you wake me?'

He stroked her leg and his eyes crinkled with fun. 'I need you to have all the energy you can muster.'

'Oh? What for?'

'You know what for.' He tiptoed his fingers up her thigh, making her gasp. She crawled into his arms, her breasts puckering against his bare skin. It was impossible to refuse him.

Because she definitely knew what for. He'd shown her what for, under the blankets. Twice. And she'd relished every stroke and every kiss. She loved the way he made her feel. She loved the way he looked at her.

So why break it all with questions? They had no idea what was going to happen. Who did? You could make plans and be knocked over by a truck tomorrow. She was going to enjoy this ride, for as long as it lasted. Which, she considered with an ache in her chest, was going to be until Christmas Day when she pointed her car towards Glasgow.

She snuggled against him, breathing in the man and

fussing over the dog. It was perfect. For now. She struggled with the catch in her throat. Damned emotions, she still hadn't worked out how to declutter them.

Alex looked quite pleased with himself as he said, 'I need you to be bright-eyed and bushy-tailed for a date.'

'Oh? Really?' That was a surprise.

He nodded. 'Boy wants to go to the Christmas markets in Carlisle, so I promised we'd take him.'

She couldn't hide her smile. 'So, it's a date for Boy really, not for me.'

'He said you could come. If you behaved yourself.'

She laughed, because how could she not? 'But you don't like Christmas. The same way I don't like Christmas. It has too many memories.'

His eyes clouded and he stroked her cheek. 'Oh, Beth. I am so sorry. I know that's my fault.'

She shrugged, telling herself it didn't matter any more. Trying to believe it. 'It's okay. Honestly. Each Christmas is different and it's up to us to make them good ones.'

'Exactly. And Boy doesn't have any experience of the festive thing, so we're going to educate him.' He leaned in and kissed her. 'And I want to make things better.'

She took a deep breath. 'They are better.'

'Good.' He jumped up and put the puppy on the floor, then tugged her to standing. He wrapped his arms around her and kissed her deeply until she was moaning his name and wanting more. But he pulled away and smiled. 'Right, you go shower. I'll make breakfast.'

'You cook too? That's new. I like the new you, Alex Norton.'

'It's muesli, don't get too excited.' He squeezed her bottom. 'And I like you more, Elizabeth Grace.'

She tucked that away and almost danced up the stairs. It was stupid to let her heart jump at his words. He'd broken her and he could do it again.

But forewarned was forearmed and she was stronger now. She knew not to invest too much and she was trying hard not to. She turned the shower tap on high and stood under the hosing water until her skin was red and the soft aches from their lovemaking were eased a little and she'd gathered herself together and got her head in the right space for a day at work.

When she sauntered back into the bedroom he was waiting for her. Her skin prickled at the sight of him, in anticipation of a smile, a kiss, sex. 'Oh? Wanting to join me? Sorry, I just got out. I can go back in…?'

'No. Beth.' He was holding the phone in his hand, his face pale. Something was wrong. Something bad. Her heart thumped and she clutched the towel tight around her, all thoughts of sex and kisses chased away. Ice slid into her chest. 'Was that the hospital again? Is it about Dennis?'

He swallowed. Shook his head. His eyes were sad. So sad. 'No.'

'Then what? What's the matter? Are you sick? Is it my mum?'

'No.' He took her to the bed and sat her down, stroking her cheek. 'It was someone asking to adopt Boy.'

'No.' Her heart slammed against her rib cage. 'They can't.'

'They can. We advertised. We asked everyone to put the word out.' He blinked, his lashes damp, his breathing uneven. He cleared his throat. 'A family. Two small children who desperately want a puppy for Christmas.'

'It's for life, Alex. Not just the festive season.'

He held her and rocked her close. 'They sound nice, Beth. They have a farm, so he has lots of space to play and run around.'

She clenched her fists, trying not to cling to him. She didn't want to be needy. She didn't want to feel so much about either of them. But it was too late. She'd fallen in love with Boy and...no. She wasn't going to admit that the way she felt about Alex was anything more than a crush. An infatuation. A sexy walk down Memory Lane. She wasn't in love with him. But her heart was still breaking. 'When? When do they want him?'

'They're coming to collect him tonight. After work. It's Christmas in three days and they want to have him as soon as possible.'

She fought back tears. 'So soon?'

'It's for the best, eh?' Alex's voice broke slightly and she realised he was hurting as much as she was. And yet was trying to be gentle with her. 'Better to let him go now before we get too attached.'

Which was what she'd thought about doing with Alex, but when it came to it, she knew it would be so hard to let him go too. 'But I'm on call tonight. I can't be here to meet them—' Or make sure they were the right fit for her puppy.

She swallowed through a raw throat, unable to find any more words. It was what they'd decided, back at the beginning. Neither of them could take on a puppy long term and when she was back in Glasgow he'd have no one to take over the day shifts when he was at the surgery. And who was she to deny two small children a loving pet like Boy?

But her heart felt as if it were crumbling.

CHAPTER TWELVE

HE DIDN'T KNOW what to do.

It was Christmastime and she was sad and she'd said she wanted to make happy Christmas memories. He didn't know how to make her smile. When he'd picked up Boy from her clinic the other day she'd pressed her lips together so hard he'd thought she might have drawn blood. Her brave goodbye to their puppy had splintered his heart. And even when she'd come to his place the next morning and they'd made love it had been heart-wrenching and desperate.

Yesterday had been the same. She was trying hard to be okay, but she wasn't. And now it was late afternoon on Christmas Eve and she'd had the day off to get ready for her move back…home. But she didn't seem happy about that either. He needed to make her smile. That was the thing about relationships, however burgeoning and new, or however old and familiar, however fleeting: you held each other up when needed. Beth needed holding up.

He found her at Bay View, sitting on her mum's bed looking at an old book, with a backdrop of so much glitter and tinsel and Christmas guff it made his eyes water. Someone here really, really liked Christmas. He was pretty sure it wasn't Beth.

'Alex?' The affection in her eyes made his heart contract into a tight ball.

'Ho. Ho. Ho. And all that.' Unable to stop himself, he went over and gave her a kiss that he knew looked a lot more than just good friends—which was the description she'd given her mother, apparently.

He kissed her mum too. On the cheek. 'Is it okay if I steal your daughter away for a few hours, Mrs Masters?'

'It's Hazel. You always called me Hazel before.' She patted his hand. 'Yes, I'm fine. Go. Go. We're just going through some old photos. I could sit here for hours and look at my little Beth. You want to see—?' She offered the book to him but Beth stopped her and rolled her eyes.

'Mum, no, he does not want to see what I looked like as a baby. I'm a grown woman.'

Hazel's eyes were filled with affection for her daughter, and a little motherly irritation. 'A grown woman who needs to get a life. Go.'

Alex managed the briefest of glimpses at the pictures. Beth sitting on her father's knee. A Christmas cracker hat almost covering his eyes. He laughed. 'I've seen those photos before. You were a very cute baby, but you're a hell of a lot cuter now.'

'What do you want?' Another eye roll. But her cheeks pinked and she smiled. Result! 'Where are we going?'

He walked her outside to his car, held the door open for her. 'I promised you a date. So here we are. Hop in.'

'It's so beautiful here in the winter.' She stared out of the window as they drove along the narrow winding road. It had stopped snowing a few days ago but was cold enough for the snow to stick. The leafless trees looked like strange eerie sculptures in a stark white landscape. She sighed. 'It's going to be a white Christmas.'

He wasn't going to think about what tomorrow was going to bring. 'Will you stay with me tonight?'

She blinked and looked at him curiously. Then nodded. 'Yes. Yes, I will.'

'And have you...' He didn't want to say it. Think it. Believe it. 'Packed everything for your trip back tomorrow?'

Her mouth tightened. 'Pretty much.'

Don't go. It was a selfish thought and he pushed it back. There were so many things he wanted to say, on the tip of his tongue. So many words. He was going to miss her.

It was for the best.

I love you.

What the...? That one punched his chest, staccato. Like shots fired. I. Love. You. The shock was the same and had his brain reverberating. But she was talking and he had to pay attention. 'Oh, before I forget. Two things: June's gone to the foster home with Meg. She's going to be okay. And...the results came back on the food sample I took at Oaktree Farm.'

'Did it find anything?' He registered that June was okay. Great. And there were results. But his thoughts swayed back. He loved her. He'd asked her to stay the night when in reality he wanted her to stay for ever. He wanted to make her happy. But he couldn't. She made him happy and he didn't want that to end.

Selfish.

She was animated as she talked. 'They found traces of ibuprofen. So Dennis must have put it there. Luckily, Boy didn't eat enough of it to make him sick and the lavage would have washed out any lingering traces. It makes me so angry and sad that he was doing that. Why? Why would you do that?'

Now he was focused but the hollow feeling in his chest lingered and his stomach clenched. 'My guess is that it was a cry for help. He was lonely and wanted to feel important. You remember how he perked up when we said he'd saved Meg's life? It made him feel useful. Will you report him?'

She nodded. 'I'll have to. Obviously.'

'If he survives the accident he probably won't go back to the farm. Chances are he won't be allowed to own any animals. It's an illness, Beth. Doing something like that is an illness.'

She shook her head. 'It's just so sad.'

'Poor guy, to be so desperate to do that. Poor animals.'

What else was pretty damned sad was that Alex had held back for eight years because he hadn't wanted to get to this damned point. Yet here he was. In love with her. Never stopped being in love with her. And he was still impotent to do anything about it.

They'd arrived in Carlisle and he pulled the car into the side of the road as soon as he found a decent parking spot. 'Looks like they've closed the road. We're going to have to get out and walk.'

She climbed out and when they rounded the corner she gasped. 'Wow. It's beautiful.'

Even he had to admit that the sight of dozens of little timber huts decorated in tiny white fairy lights and a carpet of twinkling snow was magical. 'I heard there was exceptional *glühwein* here. We have to find that stall.'

'Good plan.' She slipped her hand into his and they started to make their way round the stalls. They didn't get far before she'd slipped a red Santa hat, with flashing lights on the brim, onto his head and made him pose for a selfie. 'Say bah humbug, Alex.'

He got her back with a kiss under plastic mistletoe. And another under some of the real stuff. And another just because…

They ate mince pies and sampled limoncello and artisan fruit cake. A little brass quartet was playing Christmas carols and she started to hum so badly it made him laugh. Then he pressed her against a lamppost and kissed her long and hard and he had to admit that sometimes Christmas could be okay.

But he didn't wrap tinsel around her head and tell her she was his queen. And he certainly didn't propose as he had all those years ago. Although, the idea flickered in the background no matter how much he pushed it away.

He loved her and he was letting her know and letting her go. Again. That was his gift to her.

'This is the best *glühwein* I've ever had.' She licked her lips and turned away from the stall, accidentally bumping into a pregnant woman who was holding a baby that looked about a year old.

'Oh, goodness. I'm so sorry.' Beth cooed to the baby and smiled at the woman and made sure they weren't harmed. 'Oh, Laura, I haven't seen you for ages. How's things?'

'Beth Masters! Hello!' But the smiling woman rolled her eyes towards two-peas-in-a-pod toddlers who were running around and between their mother's legs. 'Oh, you know. Busy.'

'Twins? Lucky you.' Beth bent down and smiled at each of them, fishing candy canes out of her bag and, with the mum's nodded permission, handing them one each. 'They're gorgeous.'

'They are so competitive. You wouldn't believe.' Laura jiggled the baby on her hip. 'This one's learning to walk and I can't keep up with him. I hope this one's quieter.' She patted her swollen belly. 'A girl would be nice, but you can't choose, can you? How are you? You got kids?'

'No. No kids.' Beth's eyes darted over to him and he felt the burn in his chest. Her eyes were kind and yet tinged with sadness. 'I'm just here to play.'

'Lucky you.'

Beth ruffled the baby's head and beamed. 'No, you're the lucky one. Just look at that gorgeous smile.'

Then Laura headed away and Beth's eyes followed them as they wove through the market. Alex took hold of her hand and brought her to a stall selling organic soaps and candles, trying to reconnect with her. But she looked back again, so he asked, 'Old friend?'

'Someone from school. Can you believe it? She's my age with three kids and another on the way. Busy.'

'She doesn't know busy until she's got a puppy with authority issues.'

'Oh, Alex. I miss him.' She hugged him tight. 'I hope he's happy with his new family.'

'I'm sure he will be.' Not wanting to add to her worries, he didn't tell her about the three calls so far asking how to stop Boy chewing everything in sight.

Because, man, she had so much love to give, so much hope in her heart. She deserved to have a happy ever after filled with kids and babies and puppies under her feet. She deserved to fill her heart and her home with love and laughter and little ones. She deserved a row of stockings on the fireplace and late-night assembly of tricky plastic toys on Christmas Eve. She deserved all the love that came with excited squeals, and tinsel and glitter and Christmas magic. He didn't know what to do or say because he couldn't make her feel better about this. He was the wrong guy.

Thoughts tumbled and jumbled and reassembled in his brain and he put his hand to his head to stop them. But he couldn't. Truth was, this was just a game of trying to pretend there wasn't a massive elephant in the room. Playing at being a couple when it was never going to happen. He turned round, his boots making a dark, dirty circle in the snow. And another.

She caught his arm. 'Alex, what is it? What's the matter?'

'Nothing. I'm fine.' But he took her arm and gently steered her away from the crowds. He couldn't do this here. Not with the tinsel and Christmas music…

She shook her head. 'It's not fine. Stop. Talk to me. What's the matter?'

He stopped and put his hands to her face, wishing his heart weren't tearing open like a cheap Christmas cracker. Wishing it were May bank holiday or Midsummer's Eve and not bloody Christmas. 'I can't… Baby, I can't do this.'

She gripped his sleeve and stumbled back with him to the car. 'Don't. Don't, Alex. You promised me tonight. You promised.'

'Tonight and then tomorrow morning and then when would it stop? Glasgow isn't far away. We'd do the weekend thing, holidays. Then you'd move down here and we'd slide into something you wouldn't be able to say no to.'

He opened the car door and she climbed in. 'I don't understand. Are you asking me to stay?'

With a tight knot deep in his gut, he slid into the driver's seat, stabbed the ignition pad and pulled into the night. 'No, Beth. I'm telling you to go.'

She shook her head sharply, her mouth wobbling. She pressed her lips together. Then, in a small voice, 'Why?'

'If I asked you to stay, I get the feeling you might say yes.' Keeping an eye on the road, he touched her cheek. 'And, God, there is nothing I want more. We're good together. We both know that. So damned good. You make me feel things I never thought I'd feel again. You make me…hell, Beth… I…'

He wanted to tell her he loved her. It was shining brightly in his head and his heart. But if he told her that she'd stay, out of misguided loyalty to a dream they'd once had and hope they might actually have it some time. He tried to keep his eyes on the road but kept being drawn to look at her. Luckily, the traffic was quiet, everyone with their families, enjoying Christmas Eve. Having fun.

She blinked. Fast. 'But—'

'We'd settle into something nice and we'd get comfortable and then one day you'd look back…like you did just then. You'd look back and see what other people had and you'd wish and then you'd wonder why you'd given up your dreams, for me. I saw the way you looked at those kids. The affection. The longing. You've always wanted a family, Beth. Hell, you deserve one. Don't you dare give up on what you want.'

'We could adopt. We could… I don't know, we could see someone, a specialist.' Her breathing was as frantic as the look in her eyes. 'We could...whoa. Be careful, it's icy.'

The car skidded and he fought for control, trying to slow everything down, not quite believing he was back breaking her heart all over again. So much for being gentle. He turned left onto the Oakdale Road. 'You want your own family. Your own babies. Don't tell me you don't. Adoption is difficult and not guaranteed.'

'You wanted children too, Alex. I know it's the end of a dream for you, not just me. You don't have to pretend you don't care because I know you do.'

Of course he cared. Caring hurt like a sharp knife being jabbed into his heart. Over and over. For eight long years. 'You can do it, though. You can go ahead and have your dream. With someone else.'

She opened her mouth, closed it. Tears glistening in her eyes. Then one fell. Another. 'We could just have pets. Dogs. A puppy.'

He looked at her as his heart shattered, wanting to stop her tears, wanting to promise her everything. 'Clutching at dreams, baby. A puppy is never going to be enough. Not even two. Three. A whole damned zoo.'

She swiped her sleeve over her cheek. 'So, this is it?'

'It was always going to be it. You knew that. I was honest from the start. You need to pin your hopes on someone else. Someone better.'

'There you are again, making decisions for me. I can choose, Alex.'

He pulled up outside her cottage. It was dark. There was no jolly Christmas wreath on the door, no welcoming lights. 'Don't choose me.'

'So what? You're going to end up all alone? Like Dennis? On purpose?' she shouted at him. Angry. Magnificent. Beautiful. Her fists on his chest, pressing, pushing. 'For God's sake. I don't believe you are doing this. After everything we've been through. Everything we've shared. I should never have let you into my heart again.'

Then she climbed out of the car and slammed the door.

Slamming shut the last chance of happiness he'd ever have.

How bloody dared he?

How dared he saunter into her life and break her heart all over again? She stumbled into the cottage and leaned back on the front door. Her old home was pitch black and empty.

Just like the way her life felt right now. She'd given part of herself to Alex and to Boy, the parts she should have given to someone who would have treasured them. Treasured her. And not thrown it all back at her.

She took a deep breath and shuddered on the exhale. Tried to control her inhale. And out. Tried to calm down. She was done. Done.

No. She was nowhere near done. She was raging.

She flicked on the light and stormed into the lounge. The pathetic Christmas tree she'd decorated with her mum sat in the middle of the floor like a bad omen. She ripped the baubles off and stuffed them back in their box, then picked up the tree, snapped the branches off and stuffed them into the last black bin bag she had.

Gone. Done. Done. Bloody Christmas. Bloody men.

A tear dripped onto the plastic. Then another. And soon a torrent of them fell, making rivulets on the bin bag drizzling to the floor. Why did it have to hurt so much? Why did she pick the wrong men? *Man.*

It was only ever Alex. He was the only man she'd ever loved.

Her fist closed round the bag and her fingernails dragged holes in the plastic. The truth flickered starkly, blinking like the lights on the Santa hat she'd made him put on for the photograph. Why did he make her hurt so much?

Because she loved him.

After everything he'd done to her the first time around, and still she'd opened herself to more hurt. She loved him. How could she have been so stupid? How could she have been so reckless with her heart? Again?

Loved him without a shred of sensibility. Loved him with abandon. Had pretty much offered up her heart and invited him to stomp on it. She stalked upstairs to her room, tripping over her suitcases on the floor, adding stubbed-toe pain to the physical hurt in her heart. She kicked one over.

Thank God she was leaving this place. Thank God she still had a house and a job in Glasgow. Thank God she hadn't given up her dream for him.

But what use was a dream if the man you loved wasn't in it, sharing it, loving you back?

CHAPTER THIRTEEN

THERE WAS FRESH snow to greet Alex when he opened the blinds on Christmas morning with about as much cheer in his heart as the Scrooge character he was often compared to. Not surprising, really, given that memories of Christmases past had done their very best to haunt him into the early hours.

He'd done the right thing. Twice. And that was it. He was never getting involved in a relationship again. Climbing and hiking, doctoring and sleeping. That was what his to do list was now. Nothing else. No emotions, no feelings. Certainly not falling in love.

He peered through the wooden venetian slats and watched the Oakdale locals milling about the village square in heavy coats and red and white hats, smiling, laughing, hugging. He shivered and shoved his hands deep into his pockets. Happy Christmas? Just another one to chalk up to experience. Next year he'd definitely go somewhere else. Australia and sunshine sounded good. Anywhere where he'd miss this.

A rap on the door made him jump. Beth? She'd come back?

He flung it open and found Joe and Rose and Joe's daughter, Katy, standing there in terrible matching festive jumpers with reindeers on. Joe held out his hand. 'Just passing, thought we'd stop to say happy Christmas.'

Alex shook his hand. Surprised. Thoughtful of them. But the last thing he wanted was to pretend to be jolly when his heart was in pieces. 'Oh. Right. Thanks.'

Rose grinned and held young Katy under her armpits as the girl's legs slithered on the path. They were both laughing. Rose held Katy tight and pressed her head to her stepdaughter's. 'Katy wanted to try out her new roller skates. But they're not great on snow.'

'Not any better on concrete either. I don't think it's the roller skates, I think it might be operator error.' Joe laughed. Then his smile dropped. 'You okay, mate?'

'Oh, you know. Fine.' He wasn't fine. This was Joe's family's first Christmas together and Alex was watching them all huddled together and laughing and so…so much more than okay that it made him feel worse…and had him wondering how it could be that some people embraced the Christmas spirit and others just…didn't.

Then he thought about something Beth had said about making the most of it. Yeah. The only thing that would make him smile right now was seeing her face. It had been ten hours since she'd slammed that car door. Ten hours where he'd thought he'd feel better about breaking her heart. And maybe he did, just a little, because once again he'd done it for her own good. But not for his.

But the sad truth was, he didn't want to end up lonely. He didn't want to be alone. He wanted to love her. To have her in his life. Always.

He'd been too quick to dismiss her thoughts and suggestions. He'd mired himself in feeling sorry and spiritless and hopeless for so long he hadn't been able to grasp a chance at pulling himself out of it. He'd pitied

himself for what had happened to him and for the loss
of his dreams and had expected others to do the same.

He'd accused Beth of doing it when maybe…just
maybe, she actually was attracted to him the way he
was attracted to her. Their lovemaking hadn't felt like
something she'd been doing because she felt as if she
had to or because she wanted him to feel better. It had
been hot, electric, intense, giving and taking in equal
measure.

And he'd fallen for Boy within about two minutes
of meeting him. Okay, perhaps it had been love at first
sight. So maybe he could grow to love an adopted child
too. If he truly loved Beth he could at least try.

Couldn't he? The same way Joe and Katy had let Rose
into their hearts. The way she'd grown to love Katy as
her own daughter. His phone buzzed in his pocket. He
took it out, his heart swelling in the hope of seeing her
name.

It wasn't Beth. But he nodded to his unexpected
guests. 'Sorry, I'll just have to take this. Have a good
Christmas, guys, and enjoy the skiing.'

They laughed and waved as he talked and listened.
And when he flicked the phone back into his pocket he
smiled. Maybe…just maybe… Christmas was indeed
what you made it.

Beth had put on a brave face for her mother, but her heart
hadn't been wholly invested in looking for a twenty-
pence piece in her Christmas pudding, or singing 'Jingle
Bells' and drinking lumpy eggnog, so she'd slipped away
quietly after giving her mum a tender hug and promis-
ing to visit again soon.

To be fair, Bay View had put on quite a day of it and

with all her mum's new friends fussing and laughing Beth had felt like a spare part. She was glad to be alone in her car where she could…okay, wallow a little.

The drive to Glasgow was remarkably smooth and she pulled into her garage and sighed. She'd thought—hoped—that the sight of her house would make her feel better, that being back here would ease the ache, but it didn't. She was still angry that he hadn't been willing to hear her out. To consider options.

But at least the anger fuelled her muscles and she emptied the car of numerous boxes in no time. Then she switched on the central heating, made a cup of tea and sat in *her* lounge, in *her* house. *Her* home. One day it would feel like a proper home too. She was determined to make the best of it. One thing she knew she was good at was being kind to others and now she had to be kind to herself. She would heal in time. She had a job she loved. She had a lot more than some. A lot more than poor Dennis. Her heart twisted thinking about him and the dogs and her lovely Boy. And then, of course, her Alex.

Next Christmas she'd have a huge tree. She'd make it the best Christmas ever and put this one down to a memory she'd prefer to forget. Although, she would never, ever forget Alex. She just had to get over him. She sighed. She'd done it before. She closed her eyes and fought back the tears. No more. She was done.

Oops. Running a finger under her eyelid, she caught a rebellious stray tear. *Almost* done. She took a deep breath, blew out slowly and stood up. 'Right. Time to make a life.'

An hour or so later she was unpacking her suitcase when a hammering on her door had her heart racing. Who the hell would that be on Christmas Day? She didn't know the neighbours. Was it the police? Was her mum okay? She ran down the stairs and tugged open the door. Did a double take. Forced herself to breathe. 'Alex.'

There he was. By some miracle. On her doorstep, wearing the most ridiculous Christmas jumper, with embroidered red bells tied with a bow and the words 'Jingle My Bells' written above. And it wasn't fair, because even with that ghastly number on he looked so damned beautiful it made her heart stutter.

He smiled warily. Unsure. 'Er… Happy Christmas?'

'Christmas, yes. Happy? What do you think?' Her heart was now in overdrive and her body prickling with longing. She scooped some snow from the garden wall and cooled her face with it. His fancy-pants car was in the driveway and she could see something moving… no, jumping inside.

Her heart lurched. 'Oh? Is that…is that Boy? In the car? What's going on?'

Alex shrugged. 'It didn't work out with the family.'

'Why not? What was wrong?' Was he here just to dump the dog on her? Just the way he'd tried to a few weeks ago? Typical. It wasn't about her at all. It was about him. Business as usual.

'He wasn't happy, Beth. Not at all.' Alex's lips pursed and he looked as if his heart was going to break. 'He didn't settle. He just howled the whole time and scratched at the door. He chewed everything in sight and pooped on the Christmas presents.'

She bit back a laugh. Some people shouldn't have pets. 'They didn't give him much of a chance. Three days?'

'They tried everything but…well, he missed us and they didn't think it was right keeping him when he was so sad. They were so worried. But they've phoned round and found another puppy who loves them and does what he's told…at least some of the time.'

'And you've brought him here for me to look after, is that it? I only have a small place.' She pointed to her tiny hallway and imagined how quickly Boy would wreck everything within reach. 'It's not dog-proof. I can't—'

'Actually, I've decided I'm going to keep him. We kind of get along. I've given up all hope of ever having a pair of un-chewed shoes again. Or a rug that hasn't got teeth-shaped edges. I've arranged for Fraser's daughter to play with him while I'm at work. When she starts school I'll have a rethink. But I'll work something out. Frank's wife said he can go up there and play. Frank's home now, by the way—he called earlier to say thanks and to wish us all the happies for the season.'

'That's good. That's great. I'm happy for you all.' But her heart was breaking. It had been a kind of comfort to think he was hurting and alone too, but now…man and dog were together and she was… She took a deep breath. She was fine.

She would be.

'Do you want to see him? Before he claws holes in my fancy-pants upholstery?' Alex's gaze snagged hers and this time his smile was a lot warmer and hopeful and friendly.

'Of course. Yes. Of course.' What was this about, then? Had he come to show off? He'd got the dog and she hadn't? She watched as he walked to his car and as he opened the door a blur of brown streaked past and bounded towards her.

'Oh, Boy. Boy.' She knelt down and nuzzled into his

fur, her throat raw and sore. 'How was my baby on the journey? Did he howl and cry or was he a good boy?'

Alex's voice was pained. 'Howled, the whole way.'

She imagined that. And Alex trying to deal with it and drive. It would have been terrible. Boy could make a hell of a decent howl. 'Good. But at least he wasn't car sick.'

Alex's eyebrows rose. 'Ah…'

'Oh, good boy.' She fussed her puppy again. Fussed and scratched and rubbed and poured all her emotion into cuddles. Because here they were taunting her with her lost dream all over again and she didn't want to let it go. 'Vomiting on the fancy-pants car. Oh, who's a good boy? You're a good boy, aren't you, darling?'

Alex stood back and watched, a frown settled on his forehead. 'This is not going to plan. It seems like you're only interested in him.'

She stopped fussing and looked up at him. *Really?* 'Because he doesn't want to break my heart.'

He knelt down next to her. 'Neither do I, Beth.'

'It's a bit late for that, right?'

'Can we come in?'

Like hell. She wanted to scream at him, to show him her bruised heart. But he'd come all this way and he was smiling and there was just that little bit of hope and her hands were shaking and it wasn't all because Boy was here.

'I suppose so.' She scrambled up from the step, picked up Boy and walked through, hoping he'd follow. 'Five minutes.'

'That's all I need. Oh, and a lifetime.'

She whirled round to face him. 'What?'

He took a step towards her. 'I'm sorry, Beth. I was

spooked by the emotions. I'd taught myself to stop caring because I didn't dare to think I could live our dream. It wasn't possible. It isn't.'

'But we can try. We can talk about it. Talk to specialists. It doesn't have to be your way or no way.'

'I know. I'll do anything, anything to give you the family you want. Adopt. Surrogacy. IVF…a sperm donor. All of it, none of it. Whatever you want. I love you so damned much, Beth. I've spent eight years trying to get over you and I just never will. No woman has ever been a match to you. You're my best friend, my lover. My love. I just want you in my life.' His eyes danced. 'And not just for Christmas.'

'You love me.' She had never seen anyone look at her the way he was looking at her right now. He didn't have to say the words, she could see it in his eyes, in the hope glittering there.

'I love you, Elizabeth Grace, with everything I have. I adore you. I miss you and I hate it with you gone.' He picked up the puppy and waved a paw. 'Don't we, Boy?'

She slapped her hands to her hips. 'You're using the puppy to get me back?'

He winced and winked. 'Desperate times. What can I say?'

'You broke my heart. Twice. I don't think I can get over that.' But she was willing to try. Because this was her chance. Her dream.

He loved her.

'I am going to spend every second of the next thousand years making it up to you. I promise.' He circled his puppy-free hand round her waist, loosening her grip on her hips, and pressed close. 'Please come back to Oakdale. Please, my love. Come back to your for-ever home.'

'Oh, Alex. Yes. Yes. I want to come home.' A tear escaped just when she'd thought she was done with them. But these were happy ones, so she didn't fight them. And when he lowered his mouth to hers she let him kiss her, totally and thoroughly, and things were just starting to get interesting when she felt a wet slurp on her cheek. She pulled away from her man and pressed a kiss to her dog's head. 'I love you. I always have. And by you, I mean both of you.'

'We love you too. Even more than chewing on state-of-the-art climbing shoes. Well…almost.' Alex brought his mouth back to hers. 'Happy Christmas?'

She smiled, her heart full. 'Yes, my love. The happiest Christmas ever.'

One year later…

'Has he been? Has he been?' Little Leo tugged on Beth and Alex's blanket, breathless and so over-excited his feet danced over the carpet.

Beth opened one eye and her breath caught in her throat at the sight of her bright, funny, kind son. It had been a hard road but she and Alex had walked it together and last week they'd signed the adoption papers and become a family. She bit her wobbling lip and smiled. First Christmas nerves. She hoped she'd done it all right. 'Should we go and see?'

'Wait for me.' Alex shoved back the covers and bounded across the room, sweeping up the three-year-old into his arms and tickling his pot belly. As she watched them in cahoots and disappearing towards the stairs, Beth pinched the back of her hand just to check this was real. Because if it wasn't and it was just a dream, she didn't want to wake up.

Downstairs she was greeted by delighted squeals and a happy bark as Boy ran between their legs, not understanding what the fuss was about, but knowing it was something special. From behind, Alex wrapped his arms round her waist and hugged her hard. 'I told you that tree was too big. It's too tall for the ceiling and bent at the top.'

She turned in his arms and kissed him. And again. 'Alex Norton, hush your mouth. There is no such thing as a too-tall tree. Or too much Christmas pudding. Or being too happy.'

'And are you?' He tilted her chin so she could see his eyes. So blue. So true.

'More than you could ever imagine.' She leaned against his chest as the mayhem of torn paper and more coloured plastic than was healthy for a three-year-old littered the carpet. 'Are you?'

'Well, it is Christmas, so I have to be merry and jolly, right? That's the law.' Grinning, he pulled a little velvet box from his track-pant pocket and held it out. 'But I will be very happy if you say yes.'

'What?' Hands shaking, she took the box. *Another pinch me moment.* So many lately. And opened it. Inside was… A lump filled her throat. 'Oh, Alex. Is this…?'

'The ring I bought you all those years ago.'

It was still the most perfect, beautiful, stunning diamond ring she'd ever seen. And she loved it. Had always loved it. There weren't enough words. 'But I thought… I decluttered it.'

'You did, but apparently your mum salvaged it and let me know she had it. *Just in case…*' Smiling, but also a little uncharacteristically nervous, he took her hand. 'This is my just in case, Beth. This is my everything, my wish. My dream. Will you marry me?'

It was her dream too. Always had been. She just couldn't believe it was finally coming true. 'Oh, my goodness. Yes! Yes, I will marry you, my darling man. Oh, Alex, I love you, so much.'

He crushed her against him; she could feel his heart pounding. A jolly, merry kind of beat. 'Then I am the happiest man alive.'

* * * * *

MILLS & BOON

Coming next month

THE MIDWIFE'S SECRET CHILD
Fiona McArthur

'Let us see where this leads us, Faith. I will not let you down again.'

Her barriers quivered under the strain but held. 'As you say. We'll see.'

She watched his eyes narrow at her less than trusting response.

He held out his palm and reluctantly she took his strong fingers in hers and his warmth seeped into her like it had from the first moment they'd met years ago and did again – until their hands separated, slowly.

She tucked her fingers behind her back. Instead of stepping away he stepped closer. His bulk blocking out the light from the open door. His male scent coated with the salt of the sea. His strong jaw coming closer as he leaned in and she turned her head until he kissed her cheek. His breath warm on her face, his mouth even warmer, and despite herself her body softened even with that light touch. His hand came up and caressed the other side of her cheek. Cupping her face with more warmth and such tenderness that slowly she turned her head towards him. Towards his full, sensuous mouth, until their lips were a breath apart. Inhaling the life force between them as they hovered on the brink of the kiss that shouldn't.

Yet, it was she who leaned forward and offered her mouth, her first sign of trust, her first forgiveness.

But it was he who propelled them slowly but surely into a kiss that buckled her knees and sent her hands up between them to clutch his shirt. His arms came around her with a certainty and possession that jammed them together until her breasts were hard against his rock like chest. She wanted to be lost like this so much.

She pushed him away.

He stilled at once. Nodded, turned and left before she could make her feet move. Her breath eased out. She sagged against the door she moved to shut. Phew.

Continue reading
THE MIDWIFE'S SECRET CHILD
Fiona McArthur

Available next month
www.millsandboon.co.uk

MILLS & BOON
True Love
Romance from the Heart

Celebrate true love with tender stories of
heartfelt romance, from the rush of falling
in love to the joy a new baby can bring,
and a focus on the emotional
heart of a relationship.

MILLS & BOON

THE HEART OF ROMANCE

A ROMANCE FOR EVERY KIND OF READER

MODERN

Prepare to be swept off your feet by sophisticated, sexy and seductive heroes, in some of the world's most glamourous and romantic locations, where power and passion collide.
8 stories per month.

HISTORICAL

Escape with historical heroes from time gone by. Whether you passion is for wicked Regency Rakes, muscled Vikings or rugg Highlanders, awaken the romance of the past.
6 stories per month.

MEDICAL

Set your pulse racing with dedicated, delectable doctors in the high-pressure world of medicine, where emotions run high an passion, comfort and love are the best medicine.
6 stories per month.

True Love

Celebrate true love with tender stories of heartfelt romance, f the rush of falling in love to the joy a new baby can bring, and focus on the emotional heart of a relationship.
8 stories per month.

Desire

Indulge in secrets and scandal, intense drama and plenty of s hot action with powerful and passionate heroes who have it al wealth, status, good looks…everything but the right woman.
6 stories per month.

HEROES

Experience all the excitement of a gripping thriller, with an ir romance at its heart. Resourceful, true-to-life women and stro fearless men face danger and desire - a killer combination!
8 stories per month.

DARE

Sensual love stories featuring smart, sassy heroines you'd wan best friend, and compelling intense heroes who are worthy of
4 stories per month.

To see which titles are coming soon, please visit

millsandboon.co.uk/nextmonth